I0587160

BENEATH THE BEDROCK

JULIEN BRADLEY

ISBN 13: 978-1-63489-149-3
eISBN: 978-1-63489-150-9

Library of Congress Catalog Number: 2017930740
Printed in the United States of America
First Printing: 2018

22 21 20 19 18   5 4 3 2 1

Cover and interior design by Steven Meyer-Rassow

Wise Ink Creative Publishing
807 Broadway St. NE, Suite 46
Minneapolis, MN 55413
www.wiseinkpub.com

To my eldest daughter Kimberlee, who mirrors my passion for writing. Through her courage and determination, she has provided the clandestine inspiration for me to follow my own dream.

CHAPTER 1

NATE

Wisps of snow swirled upward like mini funnels out in the yard, while snowy fingers drifted over the driveway. Pulsing like the hand of an abominable creature, it seemed itching to grab anyone foolish enough to traverse across its path. A gust of cold air seeped around the windowpane of the old farmhouse, making him shiver. Nate Ferguson walked toward the coffee pot, welcoming the warmth of it around his hand. Against his better judgment, he'd driven home last night after the ten o'clock news just as the predicted storm front moved in. He should have stayed, but doing so wouldn't have changed the outcome. His friend Buddy had given him a lot of shit for having hitched up the snow blade to his truck so early in the season. They'd even wagered a case of beer predicting the first heavy snowfall. Nate won the bet, but neither of them had predicted the record cold that plagued December 2013.

The two first responders, brother and sister Shawn and Shannon McDonald, sat at the kitchen table drinking coffee. The three of them went way back and ran in the same circle of friends during their high school years, long before their quiet hometown earned the nickname *Boomtown*. Williston, North Dakota was in the heart of the Bakken basin, one of the largest, richest oil fields emerging on the North American continent. It had been through many booms and busts over the years, but even the current prosperity could not stop the grief that befell them now.

"Is it all right if we take him?" Shannon McDonald repeated her question.

A volunteer firefighter and first responder for the William County department, Nate knew the protocol. Only the doctor or coroner could officially pronounce someone dead before a body could be removed from a scene, even when it was blatantly obvious. But the coroner, snowbound and forty miles away, had made it clear he wasn't about to drive on unplowed roads, and told the two first responders to drive carefully when bringing the body in. Nate was no expert, but he guessed his friend must have passed sometime around dawn. He had immediately gone into the house when he'd finished plowing, and found him in his recliner, his body marginally tepid to his touch.

"I should have called her," he said, staring down at his coffee mug. Shawn and Shannon exchanged glances and Shannon walked to where Nate stood, placing a hand on his shoulder.

"She would have never made it through the storm," Shannon told him.

When he'd gotten up around four that morning, Nate had felt a profound emptiness inside as he contemplated the unwanted change that was about to occur. He'd regarded Buddy as family and could only imagine how Buddy's last living kin would feel hearing the news. Nate lifted the coffee pot. "Is there anything more I need to do around here?"

Shannon hesitated. She'd known Nate Ferguson all her life. Always a fun-loving guy, he'd been the prankster of their group of friends, which made his sadness even more difficult to bear. With his boyish grin, a full head of sandy brown hair, and a body he'd kept in shape, Nate was as handsome to her now as he'd been in his youth. Talented, charming, and smart, Nate would have graduated two years ahead of her if he hadn't run off halfway through his senior year, after the girl he'd been in love with broke his heart. Not an entirely bad situation in Shannon's estimation, for Nate had joined up with a rock and roll band out of Denver, and had truly made a name for himself, something far better than if he'd have stayed on the farm.

"Do you know what Buddy wanted to be buried in?"

The question made Nate look up from his task, cursing when his mug overflowed. He darted to the sink and Shannon snatched the paper towels off the counter.

"Sorry," she said, wiping up what had spilled onto the floor. "Doc asked if Shawn and I would bring in glasses, dentures, you know, for the mortician."

Nate ran his hand under the cold water. He felt oddly uncomfortable answering the question. Was it his place to divulge such information? Because the truth was, he knew a lot about Buddy. His father's business partner, Buddy had been more than a mentor in the repair of aeronautical engines, he'd been a good friend. They had a rhythm between them, helping one another on their respective farms with the spring wheat planting and harvest and raising honeybees. The two families would get together for their annual hunting trip to Montana, and Nate and Buddy could often be found at their favorite watering hole, watching a game on the flatscreen. Some nights when the bar was quiet, the owner would let Nate play the baby grand kept in the corner of the stage area. Nate could always stretch out Buddy's stay a while longer when he pulled out some of the old country songs by Charlie Rich or Ray Price. The pleasure it brought his friend had been Nate's small gift of gratitude for taking the measures to ensure he'd had proper lessons, recognizing his musical talent when he was nothing but a kid plunking around on the piano.

"Everything is earmarked in the closet," Nate told Shannon, tearing off a piece of paper towel to wipe his hands. "I'll go pack it up."

The door to Buddy's bedroom stood ajar, almost welcoming. Stepping around the corner, he peered inside, and was surprised to see that the bed was made. Nate imagined if he lifted the comforter, the sheets would be tucked in hospital corners pulled so tight he'd be able to bounce a quarter off them. Such were the habits of a former military man. It appeared as though Buddy hadn't slept in the room for days, perhaps weeks. The furniture was minimal: an old oak nightstand, a bureau, and a long dresser with a mirror. On the long dresser, he noticed several dusty pictures frames; curious, he went over for a closer look. It was an eclectic collection of milestone pictures: sports events, concerts, graduations, weddings, births, airplanes. All them filled with him, his brother Massey, and Buddy's *wildcat with wings* at various ages, smiling in each. For a moment, he lost himself in the photos, reveling in those happy times. The sound of the creaking floorboards by the doorway snapped him back to the present, and he looked up to see Shannon watching him. Her eyes went to the photo in his hand, then back to his face. Her expression was somewhere between pity and aversion. She cleared her throat.

"Nate, when you're ready, can you help us move Buddy?"

Nate held onto the photo. He knew Shannon's grievance toward the woman in the picture, and frankly, he'd never understood it. *Women.* Anyway, he didn't give a shit what Shannon thought. She didn't know her. No one really knew her. Nate had thought he'd known her, once, but that was a long time ago.

"I'll be right there," he said to Shannon, returning the picture to its place of prominence. "I just need to grab Buddy's uniform out of the closet."

Nate and the two first responders reverently lifted Buddy's body from the recliner where he'd fallen into eternal sleep and placed him on the gurney. Nate stood on the front porch watching the taillights on the rescue truck as it bumped its way back out the driveway. He was glad he'd plowed a path for them, thinking it had been a miracle they'd even made it out on the township road in the first place, let alone all the way up the drive without getting stuck.

The newfound quiet in the house was eerie. The lack of voices in this once happy place gave him heebie-jeebies. He already felt lonesome, and had to remind himself he had a life beyond the things he did with Buddy, though not much of one. With his days of rock and roll fame well behind him, he indulged in simple hobbies such as hockey, or played keyboard with a local cover band from time to time. But for the most part, he and Buddy had spent their evenings together playing a game of pinochle for pennies like the bachelors they were until the ten o'clock weather report came on. Then Nate would head back to his own house waiting for the next day to come. Mundane as it was, it was the simple life Nate had longed for after a career rocking out for the masses. Most likely because it reminded him of an early time, a time before she had gone.

Passing through the living room, his heart rate spiked a little when he caught sight of the brass lamp on the baby grand piano glowing bright. The Handel-Halvorsen Passacaglia rested against the easel like a silent sentinel protecting a sacred tomb. Closing his eyes, Nate recalled the countless hours he and she would spend playing "The Impossible Duet." At an age when most kids occupied long winters playing board games, building snow forts, or playing hockey, their battlefield had been made of ebony and ivory. They'd done their share of those other things, but instead of sinking their opponent's ships with plastic token torpedoes or hurling snowballs at one another, their weapons were those of wit and skill as they one-upped each other, outplaying the other's part until they knew the duet forward and backward. For Nate, this piece of music had been akin to riding a bike, and to this day he could play it by memory. *Could she still play it too, or had that been forgotten by her as well?* A sad smile crossed his face, and he stood for a long moment flexing his fingers, resisting the temptation to play. He was stalling, he knew, and his smile faded at the fond memory. He clicked off the music lamp.

Lost in the haze of a memory, Nate made his way back to the kitchen and reached for the cordless phone, hitting speed dial one. The female voice on the other end picked up before the second ring.

Moistening his lips, Nate swallowed hard, steeling his resolve. "Yeah, hey, it's Nate." There was no easy way to say it. He took a deep breath, forcing himself to say the words. "Buddy's dead."

CHAPTER 2

JOHN

*A*ye oh, let's go; Aye oh, let's go; Aye oh, let's— The ring tone jolted him, a persistent irritation that had interrupted his REM sleep. Just out of reach, John ignored it and flopped back onto the pillow. He'd just crawled into bed. Typically, he reserved such feral behavior for the weekends, but the tall, statuesque brunette with the fuck-me heels and button-down, tailored silk blouse had other plans. She'd just bank-rolled a couple million thanks to him. It wasn't his style to indulge in pleasure so soon after business, yet somehow the attentive, recently divorced client had managed to spin a simple business dinner into an all-nighter. She started out innocent enough, with an invitation to stay for "just one glass of wine"—a celebratory gesture finalizing her divorce. One glass turned into an expensive bottle of Chateau Mouton Rothschild Pauillac 1986, the year he started practicing law. Which led to, "You vacation in Cancun at Live Aqua? Me too!" That spilled into lime, salt, and tequila shots, followed by, "It's getting late, let's split the cab fare," as if saving money were an issue. That was followed by, "I'm drunk. Patron makes me soooo horny." Resulting in a trip to his place and a night of LARPing dom-sub sex complete with handcuffs and a riding crop, ending with an "I'll rock your world" blowjob. He looked over to the other side of the bed, found it void of its former occupant, and muttered, "Thank God."

Aye oh, let's go— John's hand shot out, fumbling across the nightstand and knocking over a bottle of ibuprofen and his wallet. Grabbing the cell, he grumbled, "Finch."

"John? Jesus Christ, where the hell are you? I've been trying to reach you for twenty minutes." Not waiting for a response, the familiar, panicked voice of his administrative assistant Franklin cracked across the receiver. "You have to be on the 2:15 train to Williston. There's urgent business with Monroe Oil Company. Big deal, big, big deal, with an exclamation point."

The theatrics reminded John of one of those wacky announcers for some cut-rate car commercial; he tried not to laugh. In direct contrast to his rant, Franklin followed up in a hushed tone. "They want you there before the corpse is in the ground," as though the corpse were able to hear and take offense.

John reached for the lemon-lime Gatorade on his nightstand and took a long swig, smacking his lips. The hydration loosened the dried saliva in his mouth. He drank, half-listening, before saying, "Sounds cryptic. Tell me what you mean by corpse, and where the hell is Williston?"

Franklin explained that a farmer near Williston, North

Dakota had just died, and apparently had no heir to the substantial parcel of land he had owned, which included two producing oil wells. He did a singsong of Jordan Sparks's "No Air" for a beat, then seemed to remember why he was calling.

"I've emailed you everything I could find about the owner. All you have to do is pack and get your little fanny perpendicular over to Union Station. You have less than two hours, thanks to ignoring my calls."

John frowned. He didn't appreciate the judgmental undertone.

"The ticket is on your company card, just use the quik-trak kiosk at the station," Franklin said, all business again. "I was able to reserve a sleeper car, so the ride shouldn't be too bad. The company transport will pick you up in front of your apartment in thirty-five minutes." He took a breath, and John leaped in.

"Wait, North Dakota? It's the middle of December. What's the fuckin' temperature up there? And why am I not flying?"

The question elicited an exasperated sigh. "No flights, everything's totally booked. The company jet had no flight-worthy pilot on short notice, and did I mention it's urgent? It's bad enough you'll lose an entire day traveling, but it was the best I could do given the time I had to work in. John it's already past noon," Franklin pled. "You're lucky there's not a game in town today or you'd never get out on time."

As irritating as Franklin could be, John had to admit: he loved messing with the guy. He teased, "I have to sit on a train for how long? Christ, how urgent could it be?" Oblivious to the taunt, Franklin urged, "Check your email attachments. I've been researching this place a little bit online and—" He paused. "I have a bad feeling about this one, John. It looks like you're headed into some cutthroat country, literally. You know, wildcat oil men and rough-rider cowboys. The kind who shoot first and ask questions later—that sort of stuff. I read some of the bigger oil companies fly call girls in from Las Vegas to keep the guys in the 'man camps' happy. Have you heard of such a thing, a man camp? I read that dancers at the local nightclub can get anywhere between one to three G's a night in tips."

John started humming an AC/DC tune, blocking his thoughts on what Franklin's perception of what a man camp might be.

"Do you own a gun?" Franklin retracted the question. "Forget I said that. Good luck, John, and keep me posted." With his last breath, Franklin ended in a staccato voice. "And make. That. Train."

More cryptic remarks, John grumbled inwardly, and tossed his phone on the bed. He attempted to stand, only to have gravity force him back to the mattress. Shit, he wasn't going anywhere if he couldn't get his sorry ass out of bed. He drank the rest of his Gatorade and took a few deep breaths. As the hydration seeped through his veins, he felt the fog begin to lift from his brain and cautiously stood. This time he made it without toppling over and took a step forward. He ventured out into the living room and paused in front of the floor-to-ceiling windows.

He hit the remote button to open the blinds. The view overlooking the Chicago River was solemn with the gray overcast. Down on the plaza, the wind cracked the flags like a cleaning lady shaking out a throw rug. The rent to his condo and all the amenities came at a ridiculous price, to say the least, but a top-floor unit had been well worth it. Besides, not only did he have a fantastic view of the city, he had one of Lake Michigan as well. As the blinds slid open, he saw whitecaps lap into the harbor. It wasn't called the windy city for nothing.

Staring out at the dreary weather, a familiar tedium oozed into his consciousness. The sobering truth of the business, drinking, and sex had left him feeling empty. A shiver ran through him. That's when John realized he was standing in front of the window naked. He stumbled back to the master bathroom and stood in front of the toilet, taking a long piss. He rolled his neck back and forth, working out the kinks, then turned to face the mirror over the vanity. His eyes fell on the two bruised areas over his right nipple and left pec.

"That bitch," he grumbled. "What the hell am I, seventeen?"

While he showered and packed, John began contemplating his assignment. The Monroe Oil Company, based out of Houston, Texas, had become the Chicago-based law firm's leading lucrative client after they found success drilling on the Bakken basin of North Dakota. Thomas Monroe, owner and current CEO, had amassed an impressive portfolio during his tenure at his former company. Armed with good fortune and some insider knowledge, he'd managed to scoop up a significant portion of the former company's assets during an embezzlement scandal for pennies on the dollar. Eager to sustain his current company's ongoing success, Monroe embarked on an ambitious campaign, buying up land and mineral rights from foreclosed North Dakota landowners who went bust drilling for oil. Built on the misfortune of others, Monroe's gamble paid off; he'd sunk his first well in 2008.

An oil company was not a typical client for Temple, Rice, and Goldman, who specialized more in private real estate and small business law, but Monroe Oil had been John's find. Through his association with Monroe's son Jason, John had used his legal finesse to pull Jason out of a tight spot back in their college days. Less of a friendship and more an annoying acquaintance, the long and short of it was that it meant Jason owed John big time. John had been invited to a big ole Texas barbeque on the family ranch south of Houston later that same year for an afternoon of schmoozing and networking. Already in the old man's good grace, Monroe introduced John to all the head mucky-mucks of the Texas oil business world. John had a shoe in at Temple, Rice, and Goldman through his internship with the company. In a stroke of pure dumb luck, Monroe's only daughter, Tiffany, was engaged to Ethan Rice, son of Randall Rice of Temple, Rice, and Goldman.

It was like shooting fish in a barrel. All John had to do was turn on his Chicago charm and the partnership was a done deal. The best part was, he didn't have to relocate to Texas. With Monroe's daughter married and living in Chicago, old man Monroe thought John would be *more efficient,* working in his hometown where he could keep an eye on *"Monroe's assets,"* which suited John just fine. Truth be told, the old man didn't trust Ethan Rice, the "Yankee son of a bitch," any further than he could throw him. Insightful, since he had been fooling around on Monroe's daughter every opportunity he got. Becoming Monroe's eyes and ears, John provided regular updates and was compensated above and beyond his paycheck from the law firm. It was like whipped cream on a decadent dessert.

The cherry was that John knew of Ethan's indiscretions and had told him so. John would have kept it quiet, but the money on the side was nice all the same. While John kept Ethan's secret, he offered a comforting shoulder for poor, sweet Tiffany to cry on whenever she needed him. Tia had always been grateful for John's support and showed her appreciation in the most provocative ways. *Hmm, another bonus.* John grinned as he washed his genitals.

He moved to the marble sink to shave, and it was hard not to notice the telltale signs of his indulgence catching up with him. No matter—his dedication to kickboxing and martial arts had staved off any extra weight accumulation associated with most men his age, and standing six-foot-three, he was lean and muscular. His jet-black hair showed little signs of gray, although he'd rather have had gray than the receding hairline. Coloring was an easy fix, hair loss not as much. His dark-brown eyes were still sharp and intelligent, and his perfect teeth, paired with a wide smile, had always charmed the pants off the ladies, anytime, anywhere. It was his best feature, second to his cock, which was equally as charming in the right situation. But even as he considered his assets, John couldn't deny the truth. He wasn't a kid anymore.

Finished packing, he bolted to the elevator, catching the transport waiting for him in the plaza. It would be nothing short of a miracle if he made it to the train station on time.

He just made it.

The train pulled out of the station a few minutes behind schedule as his westward journey began in the familiar, un-syncopated rhythm. John looked out at the cityscape of his hometown, and a sense of melancholy washed over him. *Williston, North Dakota.* Even thinking of the name conjured an image of desolation and made him shudder. Settling himself into a familiar routine, John diverted his negative energy, unpacked his tablet, and delved into his research.

CHAPTER 3

MONY

By far the most scenic portion of the journey, outside of Glacier National Park, was the Hiawatha River Valley, abounding with splendor regardless of the season. Even winter possessed its own quiet beauty along the bluffs, exposing hidden limestone caves shrouded with cascades of frozen water curtains in colors of blue, green, and ghost white, while eagles soared between river and bluffs, swooping down over the open water to catch fish near Reads Landing. It was disappointing that the westbound Amtrak arrived in the southeast corner of Minnesota so late in the day. By the time the train left the station, its passengers missed out on the grandeur that made up the driftless region.

Ramona Brady-Strong wrestled with an oversized suitcase and duffel, stowing it in the luggage rack on the first floor, then carried her overnight bag up to her sleeper car. She'd cut it close. Between securing someone to watch over the farm and cover for her patients—the four-legged variety—she'd barely made the final whistle.

It wasn't her first train ride back home, but it would likely be her last.

The news of her dad's death had been yet another blow in a year filled with losses. She owed so much to the man who'd called her daughter, more than he'd ever know. He'd rescued her from a miserable existence, one filled with loathing and contempt from a self-proclaimed Christian man who refused to legitimize her mother's only child. When Ramona closed her eyes, she could still hear the whispers from the last funeral she'd attended, that of her late husband. *It always comes in threes.* First it was cancer, then her husband's death, and now Dad. Ramona opened her eyes and stared out the window that faced the bluffs, noticing the large cross someone had illuminated in white lights. It was an odd sight during a holiday filled with Christmas-tree lights and inflatable Santas. She thought, *I can count the cancer, right? It's like death, isn't it?* Turning her attention to the interior of the train, she secured her things and settled into her seat. The porter stopped by, asking to scan her ticket, followed by an attendant. The attendant was a short, stocky woman with big arms, tired eyes, and a gravelly voice. She handed Ramona a piece of paper. "Your dining car reservation is for 8:45. I'll turn down your bed while you're out," the attendant said, and quickly left.

The train pulled out of the station a little after eight. Ramona reached for the complementary bottle of water, took a long drink, and rested her head against the seat back. It had been an exhausting twenty-four hours. Too much to do, and not enough time. These were the moments she'd missed her husband Bob the most. He'd always looked after her, and the details of travel, unless she was piloting her own plane. He was another man who'd rescued her, this time from self-degradation and despair, and had given her son a real dad, one who had been loving and kind.

The dining car hostess seated an African-American woman with salt-and-pepper gray hair and sparkling dark eyes, about Ramona's age, across from her. Dressed in a bright red coat lined with a leopard-fur lapel, she wore it draped over her shoulders as though she were cold. She carried an oversized canvas bag for a purse; it sported a decal of Woodstock and Snoopy on the front and the letters "MOA, Mall of America" across the back. The woman said in a friendly voice, "May I join you?"

Ramona looked up into her expectant eyes. She wasn't eager to share her table with anyone, but she knew the protocol. Passengers were always grouped together to make room in the dining car to give everyone an opportunity to eat. "Yes, of course," Ramona said, hoping to sound polite. She knew she'd probably sounded anything but, and felt a little sorry for the friendly woman who deserved a more cordial tablemate.

"Don't worry, honey," the woman said, wrestling with her bag and sliding into the seat across from Ramona. "You'll only have to put up with me for dinner. I'll be out of your hair after that."

"You're not—" Ramona began.

"I'm Juanita," the woman said, extending a hand. "I'm on my way from Chicago, going to meet my new grandbaby for the first time. He lives in St. Paul. I can't wait to see him and my two granddaughters. I had to wait until I could combine my holiday time off with what little PTO I had left, but here I am."

"Good for you, and congratulations," Ramona said, reaching to shake the outstretched hand. She was surprised when Juanita seized it, cupping her other hand over the top, and held on.

"I won't be a nuisance if you don't want to talk. It's just—" Juanita looked around and leaned closer to Ramona. "It's just I hate eating alone."

Ramona nodded, and forced a smile. "That's okay, I'm just not very good company right now, but you're most welcome to join me."

Juanita released Ramona's hand and nodded sagely. "I know, you have a sad look about you and seem very distracted. That's not safe for a pretty young woman such as yourself."

Young, Ramona thought with a laugh.

Juanita canted her head. "Something's eating at you, girl. If you want to talk about it, I'm all ears." Ramona felt somewhat taken aback by the assertive yet accurate observation and waved off the comment. "All right then," Juanita said, not offended, and began digging around in her bag.

Ramona mentally kicked herself for her poor manners. "You know, I don't think I introduced myself. I'm Ramona, but most people call me Romy."

The waiter came to the table. He was a small man of Middle-Eastern ethnicity. With a friendly smile, he gestured to the long sheets of paper left on the table by the hostess.

"Please indicate your car and room number and sign at the bottom. Are you ladies ready to order, or do you need a moment to look at the menu?"

Juanita spoke for both of them. "Why don't you bring us a couple of glasses of white wine and give us a minute." The waiter nodded and was off before Ramona could object.

"I hope you don't mind," Juanita said, reading her expression. "But I like to relax a bit before I eat, and wine helps me digest my food." Juanita stopped digging in her bag and reached on top of her head, where she'd stowed her reading glasses. She propped them on her nose and gazed at the menu. "What else are you called?"

Ramona looked up from her menu and gave Juanita a puzzled look, thought about it, then said, "Well in other parts, at least where I'm headed, they use to call me Mony. I'll answer to both. I don't know why I said my name is Ramona. Only my mother and Sir ever called me that."

"That's too bad, I rather like the name Ramona, but Romy or Mony suit you. Who's this Sir?" Juanita said with a raised brow.

Ramona's eyes skidded away. "The man who married my mother."

"Then your stepdad," Juanita clarified.

"No," Ramona replied, a bit brisker than she had intended. "He was no dad."

"I'm sorry," Juanita offered with sincerity. "Did you know your real dad?"

Ramona's eyes brightened a little. "Oh yes, and he was a wonderful man."

"Was?" Juanita clarified.

Ramona had to bite back the sudden rise of tears welling in her eyes, and was disappointed she hadn't had that random emotional outburst under control. Yet there was something about the warmth in Juanita's dark eyes that lured her into transparency; she said voluntarily, "Yes, he died early this morning. I'm on my way back home for his funeral."

"Well, no wonder you're sad," Juanita said, placing her glasses back on the top of her head. The waiter returned with two glasses of wine and took their order. When he'd left, Juanita said, "It sounds like you were very close to him. Why don't you tell me about him? People always tell me I'm a good listener, and it'll help pass the time on this train ride for both of us, hmm?"

Ramona rolled the stem of her wine glass between her fingers. She didn't share stories about her past with anyone who hadn't been a part of it with her. It was hard to know why, but the sincerity of the invitation melted Ramona's usual stony exterior and her tendency to shelter such personal matters. Then she thought, *What the heck. I'll never see this woman again anyway.* "It's hard to know where to start," she said.

"Start wherever you want," Juanita prompted, taking a sip of her wine.

Ramona considered. She wasn't ready to talk about her dad, not yet. She took a swallow of her wine. She decided to begin with an easier subject; her family. Juanita made it easy, sharing pictures of her own family from her cell phone. She was married to a man who worked on the Chicago police force in the narcotics K-9 division. She had only the one son, but had three grandchildren already. Ramona said, "My oldest daughter got picked up earlier this year by a publicist out in Portland, and is having some success with her children's series. She'd decided to take up residence in the Seattle bay area and found a cottage on Bainbridge Island where she continues her writing."

"What sort of children's stories?" Juanita asked. "Nothing with vampires or zombies, I hope."

Ramona laughed. "No. She's into pop culture, but her children's stories are about the adventures of two little foxes that get into all sorts of mischief."

"Like robbing the hen house?"

"No, people stuff, like going to a county fair, rafting down a river, flying an airplane, and such." Ramona pulled up a picture of a book cover on her cell phone—*The Adventures of Roman and Natty: A Lesson in Flying*—and handed it to Juanita.

Juanita examined the picture. "Very bright and colorful," she said. "Kiteri Katrelle, is that a pen name?"

Ramona smiled. "Actually, that's her real name, but we call her Kit Kat. It was the only good thing her mom had given Kiteri besides life."

Juanita looked bemused.

"Kit Kat is my husband's daughter from his first marriage."

"I see," Juanita said, and handed back the phone. "Do you have just the one child?"

"No, I have two other children. I have sort of a blended family. My husband brought Kit Kat, then there's Dane, and the youngest is Mindy."

"Three children. I imagine you were quite busy."

"That we were," Ramona said fondly. "My son and his wife are living out in So Cal working at what he calls his 'dream job' in aeronautical engine design, and we moved our youngest daughter Mindy out there just after Kit Kat left home to be closer to her siblings and finish her master's in marine biology."

Juanita made a low whistle. "Not bad. Your kids are successful, and you have some nice places to go and visit during the winter months. I'd love to see San Diego sometime and visit the Hotel del Coronado. It's where they filmed *Some Like It Hot*, you know."

"I know, and how about that Tony Curtis," Ramona chuckled. "He was hot as a woman as well as a man."

"You said it, girl."

Their food came, and they talked about the families they had raised. As fulfilling as that part of her life had been, Ramona confessed she and Bob had been looking forward to their kids moving away and having the house to themselves. She talked about the romantic plans they had made, of nights cuddling on the sofa by the fireplace, or long lazy afternoon naps and passionate love in the hot tub.

"Did you and your husband get out there often?" Juanita said. When Ramona didn't answer, she looked up from her plate.

"I wish I could say we had. We'd only gotten out there twice, first to move Mindy and the other right before my surgery."

"Surgery?"

Arrugh, what am I saying? That was definitely TMI, Ramona thought. But now that she had put it out there, she couldn't take it back. "Cancer, a complete hysterectomy," she said.

Juanita gasped, but Ramona shook her head. "I've been given a clean bill of health, but the experience threw a major monkey wrench in those romantic plans."

"I'll bet."

It had been a difficult time for Ramona and Bob. He'd been so stubborn and tried to do everything around the house himself. It was a recipe for disaster. Bob had been self-employed with ten employees to help him run his plumbing and heating business, and he needed to get back to it.

"I can't even get my husband to take out the garbage when it's falling out of the basket." Juanita chuckled. "Don't you like to be pampered?"

Ramona lifted her shoulder in an awkward shrug, "I just don't know how to handle attention. I've always been the sort of person who has spent most of my life concealing weakness, not acknowledging it."

"Need is not a weakness," Juanita chided.

"You're right," Ramona said ruefully. She understood that now, well in the aftermath, but at the time she had felt a failure, unable to pull her weight maintaining the household. Plus, she had her own business to run, a small rural veterinary clinic for both large and small animals. She thought about how Bob behaved like a caged animal, mulling around the house while she slept all day. He was the sort of man who needed to stay busy to feel useful. They were both like that. Ramona was certain he'd thought he'd done something wrong when she'd insisted he go back to work. Dear, sweet Bob, assuming fault or blame when it was unwarranted. It had been his most infuriating and most endearing character flaw. She shouldn't have been so broody, and it had been foolish, being upset over a uterus she'd never planned on using again. But before the surgery, bringing a new life into the world had always been a choice, until it wasn't, and Ramona had never been one who'd done well with ultimatums.

"I know the loss bothered my husband too, because we had a hard time, you know," Ramona leaned in closer to Juanita, "in bed." The waiter brought another glass of wine just then. Ramona blushed when she thought she'd been overheard, then shrugged it off.

She shared, unabashed, the real struggles between middle-aged couples who experienced life-changing events like cancer, and spoke candidly about her husband's obsession with her satisfaction, or rather her lack of satisfaction, which only perpetuated the situation. He'd taken special care in her comfort, but they struggled for months trying to regain some mutual level of satisfaction that hadn't, at the very least, left him feeling like a self-serving bastard.

"A friend of mine invited me to one of those Pure Romance parties, you know, sex toys and such," Ramona said with a slight flush to her cheeks that had nothing to do with the wine. "Anyway, the idea, when I first suggested, you know, to explore a new approach, took Bob way out of his comfort zone. He'd been raised a straitlaced Catholic, and had considered the matter closed."

"But you talked him into it, I bet," Juanita said with a knowing grin.

"Yeah, with a little coaxing, a new teddy, and a very large bottle of wine," Ramona said, holding up her glass.

"I don't think it takes much to talk a man into anything when it comes to sex," Juanita said.

They sat quiet, and Ramona's thoughts drifted to an early June when the sunrise had been tranquil and a gentle rain had fallen the night before. Bob had been particularly loving that morning. Even the cool morning breeze that blew through the bedroom window hadn't tempered their heated lust for one another. Sated in love, they lay naked together in the afterglow and pledged to one another to think on that moment in times of stress, when their love was perfect and the trials in life seemed inconsequential. She and Bob had both discovered something new and wonderful about each other in that respect. She would always love him for that.

It was nearing the end of dining hours, and the hostess allowed Ramona and Juanita to sit at their table enjoying another glass of wine and one another's company. With cloudy eyes, Ramona talked openly about her husband's passing, and the freak accident that had taken him from her just six months prior. The whole community had grieved the loss. Bob Strong had been a man who'd touched many lives through his business, his church involvement, and his civic interests. He'd been an outspoken opponent to frac mining, a process that stripped the limestone bluffs of the silt-like sand. A business that had been on the upswing with the oil boom going on in North Dakota, it was a controversial issue on both sides of the Mississippi River between Minnesota and Wisconsin.

"Your Bob sounds like he was a good man," Juanita said, dabbing her dinner napkin to the corner of her eyes. "How did the two of you meet?"

The hostess, who'd been sitting two tables away going over receipts, appeared at the table. She immediately picked up on the intimacy of the conversation and said kindly, "Excuse me, ladies—I'm going have to close the dining area in a few minutes, but you are welcome to take your wine glasses to the lounge car." Juanita and Ramona nodded and were about to take their leave when the hostess spoke to one of the wait staff wrapping plastic silverware in a napkin. "Josh, please see that each of these ladies has a full glass of wine."

The young man didn't hesitate. "Of course," he said, and walked to the serving station.

"Thank you," Ramona said, "that won't be necessary."

"Nonsense," Juanita piped in, "we will happily have another glass." She reached into her Snoopy bag for her wallet.

The hostess said, "That won't be necessary." The waiter returned with the wine bottle and capped off each of the women's glasses. Ramona left a tip on the table.

They sat in the observation area of the lounge car and stared out the window that faced out toward the river. There wasn't much to see over the expanse of Lake Pepin, a few yard lights that marked homes and cabins near the shore front. Ramona turned to face Juanita and began to recount her kid's favorite story.

She'd literally run into their dad when she'd blown past the *Closed for Maintenance* sign outside the women's bathroom on the university campus. Bob had been working as a custodian at the time, and she had been a student. Unable to make it to the toilet stall, she proceeded to vomit all over the floor after having attended an all-night kegger. Bob had offered his assistance and she'd been in no shape to decline. Ramona had no idea what Bob had ever seen in her, but in the few short weeks that followed, they'd been seeing one another every day. Bob had never hidden his little Kit Kat, an adorable four-year-old who loved *My Little Pony* and her pink teddy bear. Ramona had fallen in love with the little girl on sight, and date nights usually consisted of walks to the park, a stop at the corner ice cream stand, or studying at the kitchen table while Kit Kat colored. They'd blended into a family quickly and her dream of a career faded. It disappeared completely when she'd learned that the pesky nausea she'd associated with stress and nerves turned out to be morning sickness. Days passed, and as autumn gave way to early winter, the weight of her indiscretion had become more difficult to hide.

"We were walking along Minnehaha Creek when I decided to tell Bob. Kit Kat was feeding bread crumbs to the ducks gathered by the bank, when Bob suddenly reached around my waist, stopping me, and gently rubbed my belly."

"He knew?" Juanita asked.

Ramona nodded. "I thought, 'He surely wouldn't want me now.'" She'd remembered her experience living in the household of a man who wasn't her father. Then she thought of her dad.

"But he didn't leave you."

She'd worn a dress of satin, cream in color, with a billowing A-line skirt to hide her belly. She had a hooded cape of velour in deep purple, trimmed in creamy white, Kit Kat her miniature bride. They'd stood together in the park, where Bob had proposed overlooking Minnehaha Falls. A light snow fell that day, making everything clean and pure. A justice of the peace presided, her dad and Bob's grandparents witnesses to their union.

"In the spring, Dane was born. It had been a difficult labor and he was delivered by C-section. That fall, Bob sent me back to school. When I finished, we moved to southeastern Minnesota, where we bought the farm and started our businesses. Bob in plumbing and heating, and I had my veterinary practice. Just when we'd accepted we couldn't have any more children, Mindy Rose, *our baby,* was born in an emergency C-section, ensuring the finality of our family expansion and demise of my bikini figure."

Juanita sipped her wine and said thoughtfully, "A small price to pay for love."

The train emerged out from behind Barn's Bluff, the pale amber of a streetlight marking the upcoming town. As it slowed at the Red Wing depot, Juanita took advantage of the nonmoving train to use the restroom. It was a brief stop, and when the train resumed its westward journey Juanita hadn't returned to her seat. Ramona gazed out the window, the scenery dark until the train passed through the Prairie Island Mdewakanton community. She noted several *No Frac Mining* signs posted near the tracks.

"There's that look again," Juanita commented, startling Ramona. "Girl, I bet you make a terrible poker player."

The corner of Ramona's mouth lifted in a smirk. "True enough," she said, and pointed to one of the signs. "My Bob hadn't been in the ground a week, before I started getting harassing phone calls with offers to buy up the farm."

"Oh, why is that?"

Ramona and Bob had used every dime they'd saved to write the earnest check on the farmstead. Her dad had been skeptical when he looked over the property, a hobby farm tucked in a coulee with a rundown farmhouse and a couple of outbuildings. Primarily woodland, the only thing the land was good for was hunting and fishing, with a spring-fed trout stream that trickled through the pastureland. He'd even tried to talk them out of buying it. But like most young couples, Ramona and Bob had been blind to the blemishes, gleaning only its potential. Despite his reservations, her dad had given them the money for the down payment. They'd poured a ton of sweat equity into that little farmhouse and raised their three children, a motley crew in a home filled with mayhem and love.

"It's not the woodland or trout stream that runs along the bluff that's valued. There's a decommissioned quarry located on the property that everyone's after."

Juanita furrowed her brow. "Why would anyone want a quarry?"

"Frac sand mining. The county has a moratorium on opening new quarries, but ones existing on private property can extract the frac sand. Much of it is shipped to North Dakota for hydrofracing new oil wells."

"Interesting, and is that what your late husband been opposed to?"

"Yes. We'd taken out some of the run-off silt for cattle bedding, because it gets into the trout stream and blocks up the flow, but we hadn't actively mined for it. Bob wanted to protect the bluffs along the Mississippi River Valley, and it's worth protecting." Ramona sighed, staring at her wine glass. "It's just that it's too much for me alone, and the quarry has made the property very marketable. I'm torn over what to do."

She knew she'd have to make a decision about the farm sooner or later. The upkeep on the yard work and the garden alone was too much for her, not to mention the chores. The old farmhouse needed a new roof next summer, and the outbuildings needed a good paint job.

"People tell me I should do myself a favor and sell it. I'd get a terrific price, probably could retire." Ramona looked at Juanita. "Do you think they're right?"

Juanita's dark eyes shone with compassion and she shook her head. "I think yours is the only opinion that counts."

Ramona closed her eyes and squeezed back those pesky tears that seemed to keep showing up. "Bob and I were supposed to grow old together in that house." She pulled a tissue from her pocket and swiped at her nose. "I don't know what to do. I just don't know."

CHAPTER 4

JOHN

Four hours into the trip, and John had to avert his eyes from the tablet screen. Researching the general information regarding North Dakota was more like reading an advertisement. Tapping into the romanticism of Manifest Destiny, it was propaganda at its finest, with websites posting job ads enticing young, adventurous men to make their fortunes working in the oil fields. These men, more often than not, found themselves living in substandard conditions. Franklin hadn't been kidding about the man camps. There were actual camps, some upwards of 150 men living in FEMA-like trailers out in the middle of nowhere—some sites with no running water or sewer connections—just to work in the oil fields, and they'd been the lucky ones. Some men lived out of their vehicles parked in a warehouse store parking lot in frigid weather until they could find affordable housing. There were also the usual financial opportunities advertised, targeting middle-class Americans to invest in oil and gas businesses—get it while it lasts.

Alongside the propaganda were disturbing articles, reporting the sharp rise in the crime rate on the Bakken. Domestic abuse, spousal and family, had been increasing at an exponential rate. Women in the region were statistically outnumbered seven to one, and several articles spoke volumes about their questionable safety. John had come across one particularly gruesome headline reporting the story of a young nursing assistant who'd been out for a morning jog and had gone missing. Local authorities found her decayed remains in a ditch weeks later, forensics confirming she'd been beaten and raped before she was murdered. These stories were in direct contrast to an aggressive tourism industry, showcasing small town celebrations and reenactment events of pioneer days, church-sponsored quilting bees, and the grandeur of the Theodore Roosevelt National Park. All a last chance at the American dream, if you were rugged and lucky enough to survive. It was a myth. John was no economist, but the ravaging of the region by the oil companies impacted nearly every industry in the state particularly the service industry. In small rural communities, even physician salaries couldn't compete with oil company wages. It seemed North Dakota was reverting to the same wild, rugged frontier discovered by Teddy Roosevelt over a century past.

Rubbing his temples, John felt the throb of a headache coming on. Summarizing data was the sort of thing Franklin had been hired to do, not him. He stared out at the Midwest landscape and felt the motion sickness kick in. It was why he detested traveling for work. A creature of comfort, he was kept off his game by the disruption to his personal routine. He'd discovered that early on in his career at Temple, Rice, and Goldman, and it had been a source of contention between him and the senior partners until he'd learned how to manipulate his bosses and his clients into believing it was in their best interest to have his clients come to him. Pulling out all the stops, John had provided all-expenses paid trips to the Windy City, filled with shopping, touring shows, wining and dining at exclusive restaurants, and five-star hotel accommodations. For the more illustrious clients, he'd hit up the nightclubs or take them out on his sailboat, which always seemed to cinch any deal. Having control of the spending meant saving the company money, and as long as he brought in money for the firm, his disdain for business travel had been overlooked—but not this time. With a heavy sigh, John reached into the folder. "Well, let's see who the corpse is."

The first item was a newspaper clipping with a picture of the man. He had what looked like salt-and-pepper gray hair in the black-and-white photo, kept in a crew-cut style. John guessed him to be in his late twenties, early thirties. Clean-shaven, the man wore aviator glasses and had a thin line for a smile, with a big nose. Simply dressed, he wore a pair of dark work trousers, a bombardier jacket with a white T-shirt showing at the neck, and work boots. He stood in a casual pose next to a small-engine plane with the words *F&A Crop Dusting, Inc., Williston, ND* on the side door panel. The airfield in the background hadn't looked like much, and he checked the date stamp—June 1968.

John began tapping his toes and chuckled to himself, *F&A, sounded like fuck an ass.* He looked at the man in the photo and said "So, which one are you? The F or the A. And what do you have to do with oil?"

The article, it turned out, had been written about A. Buddy Altman, longtime resident of Williston, North Dakota. The airport in the background was merely an aircraft hangar that had just been built on his property when the picture was taken. The article revealed nothing extraordinary to warrant the two-and-a-half pages written about the man, but John learned long ago that things were rarely as they appeared.

Digging into the public birth records, John learned Altman had been born to a German immigrant farm family and was raised somewhere in south central Minnesota. He enlisted in the military in the early 1960s and had done two tours in Vietnam flying the defoliant missions. With a Medal of Honor, Air Force Cross Medal, and countless other ribbons and awards, he ended his service career stationed at the newly commissioned Air Force Base in Minot, North Dakota, training B-52 pilots. He was discharged from active service in early 1968.

During one of his tours in Vietnam, Altman's older brother had been killed in a car crash, rendering Buddy the sole surviving family member. With no one to return to, he sold off the farm in Minnesota and made a new life for himself in Williston, North Dakota, where he bought a small farm and started a crop-dusting business.

Eight years later, he struck oil. Even then, the Williston basin within the Bakken had been known to have oil reservoirs, yet little exploration had been done to exploit that potential. Altman had risked everything and gotten lucky. With a wildcat strike making local and national headlines, Altman's strike was counted among a rare number of drillings to have a blowout, most likely due to the gas fields also located in the region. Because he owned the land outright including mineral rights, having only invested his business share, he became an instant millionaire. Altman had given his business partner a generous portion of the profit, and together they formed their second company, the unimaginatively named F&A Oil Company.

Altman drilled a second time, sixteen years later, but by that time he needed no financial backing. Using a new horizontal method of drilling, he struck oil again without any exploration or mapping.

Knowing something about drilling, John rolled out the county plat map of Williams County with established sites for gas and oil and traced his finger between the two well locations. Both wells were edged up along Altman's property and bordered almost entirely by state or national protected land. The well sites were far enough apart to most likely avoid the same fracture lines, each pumping oil from its own source. Hobnobbing with Monroe's Texas oil barons, John had learned that fracture lines in the shale rock carried their own oil reservoirs, and it was desirable to drill a couple of wells along the same fracture line to pump out from the same reservoir at a faster rate. It also reduced the risk of someone else stealing it out from under you. Altman, however, had only one derrick pumping at each site. His wells were basically left unchecked, which afforded him the luxury of slow consumption. He could drill as close to the property lines as the law would allow and pull from the oil reservoirs under the protected land and never have any competition for it. It was a brilliant strategy.

There were no records of a marriage, and neither paternity suits nor heirs. *But here was something.* John pulled a news clipping from 2011. Altman had poured a significant amount of money back into the Williston community to build a new youth park and rec center with an enclosed hockey area—plus, he was a freaking tree hugger. With much of his land either in or around the state and national land preservation areas, Altman had invested in a massive environmental cleanup going above and beyond the EPA regulatory requirements to the land surrounding both his wells. It seemed in the final analysis that the biggest obstacle to Monroe's acquisition of the property would be Altman's business partner Ferguson, whose information made up the remainder and larger portion of the portfolio.

With a tired yawn, John stood and stretched his legs. His stomach began to growl and he checked his watch. Packing the Ferguson portfolio in his satchel, he decided to digest the Ferguson information over dinner.

He arrived in the dining car shortly before the dinner rush, and he had the luxury of being seated in a booth by himself. Unable to look at the passing landscape without feeling sick, John asked the server pouring water to draw the blinds. The server shot him an incredulous look.

"Motion sickness," he said.

The server closed the blinds and left. Ignoring the slight, John shifted his focus and took stock in his surroundings. The atmosphere of the dining car was casual, quiet, and relaxing. He tried to pull up the weather on his smartphone, then frowned. A no-travel advisory had been issued for parts east of Billings, Montana, through Powder country and the entire state of North Dakota due to frigid temperatures. A place called Beartooth Pass was closed. High wind with gusts up to thirty–fifty miles an hour was predicted. He remembered how hastily he'd packed. "Shit," John muttered. He hadn't planned for a blizzard.

"Don't worry," a young female said with an upbeat voice. "You'll reach your destination before the blizzard hits that area."

John glanced up at the perky, petite blonde with a streak of pink in her hair. She had bright blue eyes and pouty lips; she leaned in, looking over his shoulder.

"Can I get you started with something from the bar to take your mind off the weather, sir?"

John blinked out of his semi-daze. *Christ, the girl couldn't be more than twenty.* He decided to test his theory.

"I'll have an extra dirty martini," he said to the flirty waitress.

"Coming right up," she chirped, and strolled off with what he swore had been a little swagger in her hips.

Amused, John returned his eyes to the screen. It did look bleak. He made a mental note to purchase more robust gear as soon as he rolled into town. When his waitress returned, it seemed the joke was on him. She set his martini on the table in front of him and waited patiently, encouraging him to taste it.

She smiled at him prettily. "Is it to your liking, sir?"

Much to his surprise, it was perfect, and his satisfaction showed on his face.

"I made it myself," she said, and gave him a wink. "I'll give you a few minutes to look at the menu, so take your time and relax," she said, and fluttered off again.

John perused the menu. True to her word, the waitress returned to take his order two minutes later. He should have been flattered by what was clearly flirting, yet he felt oddly perverted, since he was fairly certain he was old enough to be her father. When she left, John snuck a peek out the window, lifting a panel on the blind. It was utterly dark now, and it irritated him how the dark outside mirrored his funk. His food arrived, delivered by the server without comment; the man set the plate down and left. A slave to habit, John pulled out the portfolio and began to read while he ate.

The cute little waitress appeared again. She asked, "How are the first few bites?"

John thought about the question. The food had been prepared exactly the way he'd ordered it, yet seemed bland and tasteless. Not wanting to make his waitress feel bad, John replied, "Fantastic." He then asked her to bring him some coffee. He'd decided to slow it down on the alcohol a bit, at least until he got through Ferguson's dossier.

"Of course, regular or decaf?" she asked in a sweet

voice.

"Regular," he said, "I'll be up for a while."

She beamed as if his statement held some secret meaning, then drifted away to tend to another table. Once fortified with coffee, John found reading Kip Ferguson a bit more interesting.

Ferguson, also a decorated Vietnam pilot, had embarked on a political career, becoming a county commissioner the same year of Altman's first oil strike. He ran for and won a state senate seat four years later and served multiple consecutive terms. In 1992, the same year Altman struck oil a second time, Ferguson vied for a seat in the US senate and won by a landslide over his opponent. He then served as a senator for two consecutive terms, and during his tenure had been a senior member of the Ways and Means Committee.

Ferguson retired from the political scene in 2008, but, he remained an active and outspoken member of the NRA and an advocate for the small business community, particularly for the independently owned family oil wells. *Shrewd man,* John thought. It made sense that Ferguson used his influence and position to protect the businesses he and Altman had built, which were speculated to be the last privately owned oil wells in the state.

Of his two sons, Matthew, the elder, seemed more inclined to follow his father's political ambitions. He attended the University of Minnesota on a full-ride hockey scholarship; then, following his undergrad, he studied two years of law at Columbia. For reasons unknown, he left Columbia and finished his degree at Stanford, and practiced law at a debt relief firm in Vancouver, Washington, in his early years. Gaining experience, Matthew moved on to a more prestigious law firm across the Columbia River in Portland. It was at or during that time that he met and married Michelle Evans, daughter of shipping mogul Lawrence Evan of Portland, and had two sons.

When the oil business began to boom back in the mid-2000s, he uprooted his family and returned to North Dakota, settling in Bismarck, where he worked as an associate legal consultant for one of the state's oldest law firms. They specialized in business financing and natural resources. In an unprecedented feat, he'd managed to become a full partner in less than two years, and in a reversal of fortune the board appointed him CEO after he acquired 51 percent of the stock holdings and controlling interest in 2009.

John made a mental note to gather more information on Matthew. The guy sounded very interesting, especially for the fact that he'd briefly attended Columbia, John's alma mater. John was also interested in how much Matthew was involved in the senator's business partnerships with Altman. It made sense. With Matthew's legal skill and power combined with his father's political clout and connections, they would be formidable opponents and pose a serious threat to Monroe Oil Company's quest in the acquisition for Altman's holdings. Matthew would also be the sort of person John would need to impress while investigating any under-the-table or unethical dealings F&A Company may or may not be involved in.

Younger brother Nathan, though, was less political and led a much more colorful life. Ditching his last year of high school, he ran off to Denver and ended up playing keyboard for a five-man rock-and-roll group called Mile High City, which had achieved modest success throughout the eighties and nineties.

John picked out of the folder a popular teen magazine still in its protective plastic wrapping, with a post-it note attached to it in Franklin's handwriting. *If you open this, I will kill you!* It was tempting. John examined the photo, and by God if it wasn't Nathan, aka the Fergmeister, on the cover, his arm banded around the waist of a bleached-blonde bimbo. Sporting significant cleavage, the woman wore a midriff-showing, off-the-shoulder T-shirt, Daisy Duke cut-off shorts, and stiletto heels. They both wore teased, mullet-like up-dos, posing for the camera with pouty lips and expressions of indifference while the rest of the band were featured off in the background.

"I know this band," John said, surprised, garnishing a perturbed look from the server passing his table. He'd recognized Nathan after seeing the magazine cover—he had liked their music back in the day. He may have even had a couple of their albums.

Greed, followed by bickering, broke out between the band members in the mid-1990s. Their final album, *Bombers from Hell*, made up of all heavy metal, had been their least popular, excluding the two love ballads, each written and performed by Ferguson. One, the critically acclaimed debut hit single "Come Back to Me," had earned the band a Grammy nod that year. They didn't win, but by that point what should have been a highlight for the band's career became its final demise. According to *Stage Door Axce$$,* much of the spotlight had been focused on Ferguson's talent, and became too much for the band's lead guitarist and singer-song writer. Fueled by drugs and alcohol, egos collided during an all-night party at an LA nightclub, where a highly publicized brawl drove the final wedge between the band members. By year's end, the band, as well as Ferguson's marriage to the woman in the photo, had split.

Ferguson had, however, remained in LA for a few years and achieved his greatest musical accomplishment, cowriting and performing the love theme for a popular indie film, *My Wildcat with Wings.* He earned his second Grammy nod for the title song. Then, just when his solo career seemed to be taking off, Ferguson dropped out of the music industry completely and returned to North Dakota. A divorcé with no children, the younger Ferguson took up a simpler life working the family farm near Williston and had been on the F&A payroll as a mechanic. The man apparently had skill with aeronautical engines. Being something of a celebrity, Nathan made the local papers often as a featured member for a popular local cover band, and captained an adult amateur hockey team. His only outward political ambition was advocating for the preservation of wildlife habitats at the local and state level.

Immersed in his reading, it took John a beat to register the change in the dining car atmosphere, and he hardly noticed when a gentleman with thick, silver hair took a seat at his table.

"All work and no play makes John a dull boy," the older man said with a warm smile.

Startled, John lifted his eyes from his work and tried to figure out where he'd seen the man before.

Acknowledging John's puzzled look, the elderly gentleman introduced himself. "Andrew James." He extended his hand. "We've never met."

John took his hand. "John Finch," he replied, and was surprised by the firm shake.

The sound of his name elicited a broad smile on the gentleman's face. "Your name, it was a lucky guess."

Putting his work aside, John focused on the present. "It would be a pleasure for you join me, Andrew James. I've already eaten, but your presence will give me an excuse to linger at the table a while longer."

"Thank you, and please, my friends call me Drew."

John collected his papers and stuffed them back into their folder. His motives were selfish, but he was a firm believer in karma, and right now, he needed all the good karma he could get.

The two men struck up a lively conversation over food and a few more martinis, neither one of them noticing they had crossed over the mighty Mississippi River.

CHAPTER 5

MONY

"Ladies and gentlemen," a soothing tenor voice announced, garnering Ramona and Juanita's attention. "We will be arriving shortly at the Midway Station in Minneapolis/St. Paul. This is a service point station, so passengers wishing to get out and stretch should do so. Be aware of the designated smoking areas and mindful of frigid temperature and wind chill, and dress accordingly. The recent snow has made the platform icy, so please use caution as you leave the train."

As the train passed through the outer suburbs and train yards, the illumination of the surrounding darkness and conversation with Juanita loosened the grip of Ramona's sullen mood. It was funny how the woman had made it so easy for Ramona to open up to her.

Juanita was sharing photos of her grandson when she said, "I'd like you to tell me about your dad."

And so Ramona did.

She'd stood on the tarmac between her mother and Sir, the small suitcase at her heels sustaining the proper distance between them. It had been a hot summer day, and difficult to stand still. Their eyes were trained skyward, watching, waiting. Hostility radiated off Sir like the waves of heat off the tarmac. His black, beady eyes racked the skies, always skeptical, always alert, shifting between the heavens and the horizon. Her mother, by contrast, had been a bundle of nerves, poised and stoic yet anxious, clutching Ramona's arm with a moist, tremulous hand every time a plane approached.

"People used to tell me I look a lot like my mom," Ramona said absently, "except for my eyes."

"Do you have a picture of her?" Juanita asked.

Ramona pulled up a photo on her cellphone and handed it to Juanita. It was a picture from Dane's wedding. He had been bending down to give his grandmother a hug. Ramona's mother's posture was rigid, with a look of surprise on her face even though it was a posed snapshot. It was the same stiff posture and expression Ramona remembered when she had looked up at her mother at the airport.

"How much longer?" she had asked her Mom quietly, but Sir had overheard. He grasped her shoulder with his talon-like fingers and shook her until her teeth rattled. "Do you have ants in your pants? For Christ sakes, stop fidgeting," he scolded. He'd have hit her if her mother hadn't been standing there. Her Mother gave him a pleading look, and his hand fell away.

"My grandpa used to tell me that I had reminded Sir of someone my mother once cared about, and he was angry because they couldn't have children. When I asked Grandpa if it had been my fault, he'd just pat me on the head and take me out for ice cream. His cure-all to life's injustices."

Juanita snorted. "I don't understand; if this Sir hadn't wanted you, why weren't you with your father in the first place?"

"Because my father was dead."

Juanita blinked, confused. "But you said you lived with your father."

Ramona smiled. "You're getting ahead of the story."

Juanita scrunched her nose and made a zipping motion across her lips.

It had all reached the breaking point when Sir announced at the dinner table one night that he'd made arrangements for Ramona to go live with her father. She'd almost choked on her mashed potatoes, and it was the first time she'd been blatantly defiant.

"I told him my *real* daddy died a war hero in Nam." She laughed. "That earned me a backhand across the mouth and I was sent to my room. After brushing my teeth, my mom came to tuck me in bed."

"Your mother had lied."

Ramona nodded. "My mother always maintained that my dad's plane had been shot down over the jungle and his body had never been recovered. She said he was MIA and was a true American hero. At least she'd gotten the hero part correct."

That night, Ramona had learned the truth about her dad. He was alive, and had been away for a long time. He'd wanted to meet his little girl, now that he was back, and wanted to take her flying with him the next day. Maybe she could try living with him for a while.

It was hard to know what to believe anymore. She remembered thinking how it would be nice to be away from Sir for a while and asking her mother if she was coming too. The poignant expression on her mother's face as she kissed her goodnight had been her reply.

Her vision followed to where her mother pointed in the sky: a small twin-engine plane, which seemed to float like a feather on a gentle breeze before descending from the heavens. In a fury, it landed with ease on the runway and idled a few hundred yards in front of them. Ramona watched, mesmerized, as her dad disembarked the aircraft.

He jumped nimbly from the cockpit and walked with purpose toward them. He wasn't a tall man, but he stood proud with his lean waist and his lanky shoulders pulled back. He wore a crisp, light-blue shirt with a perfectly knotted dark tie, dark trousers wrinkled from sitting, and a pressed cap on his head that he removed as he approached. Up close, Ramona had been taken aback by his funny haircut, pointy nose, and crooked teeth. But when he smiled, he seemed warm and kind and full of life. The caramel-brown color of his hair gave him a youthful appearance.

"When he stood in front of me, he seemed to radiate a sort of mischievous energy," Ramona said with affection. "Like someone who'd just gotten away with a prank."

It was his eyes that she remembered capturing her attention. When he lowered himself onto his knee and looked at her straight on, she could see he had happy eyes, brilliant, laughing, hazel eyes. Her daddy had her eyes.

Without warning, he grappled her into a big bear hug and hoisted her up into the air, catching her as she dropped. He extended a hand to Sir and gave it a hearty shake. Her dad spoke tenderly to her mom and kissed the side of her cheek. The gesture rendered Sir speechless, and he glared at her dad as if he were an insect to exterminate. Her dad seemed to ignore it. Sir stood almost a head taller than her dad but seemed to get shorter right before Ramona's eyes. It was fascinating how Sir's shoulders rolled into his chest and hunched together, as if his back bowed to the pressure of an unseen weight. Then he puffed out his chest and threw his chin in the air.

"The son of a—" Juanita paused and cleared her throat. "This Sir was intimidated by your dad." Ramona no longer responded, lost in the reverie of her thought.

Pressed against her father's chest, she'd noticed how he smelled of Old Spice and tobacco. He had a steady cadence in his mellow tenor voice, and she looked to her mother for clues on what her father might have said to upset Sir. She'd given a whimper when her dad had brushed his thumb over the cut on her swollen lip and cooed something apologetic. He continued talking in his controlled tone, and she'd understood Sir's abusive days toward her had come to an end.

She had felt a surge of panic right before leaving her mom and seen the painful truth between her parents. There had been a mix of sadness and relief behind her mother's eyes and regret in her dad's smile. She had wanted to be angry at both for what they had done, angry for their lies and deceit. But when the plane taxied down the runway, she had felt such a rush of excitement, the g-force pushing against her chest followed by the weightlessness of takeoff, and her anger fell away like the ground below her feet.

She peered out over the rim of the window and saw that her mother had stepped closer to Sir, closing the space between them.

The space where she had once stood. Sir wrapped his arm around her mom's waist, confirming the closure, and when her mom tilted her head onto Sir's shoulder, Ramona hoped she had been smiling. It was a comforting thought. Her dad shouted something over the sound of the roaring engine and smiled mischievously. In that moment of flight, Ramona had become conscious of what had been innate to her all along. She had never belonged there on the ground with those people, and she was finally going home.

They stepped off the train together into the brisk arctic air, two strangers who'd now become friends. They hugged one another and exchanged phone numbers.

"Anytime you need a weekend away," Ramona said. "Hop on the train and come visit me. I'm a fantastic cook, if I do say so myself, and I would love the company."

Their farewell was interrupted by shouting when Ramona heard, "Grandma!" Two young girls broke away from a man she assumed to be their dad and ran toward Juanita.

"I will, I promise," Juanita said as the two girls crashed into her with open arms.

Ramona held onto Juanita's hand a breath longer. She didn't have very many female friends and hoped Juanita would remain one of them. She watched the happy group exchange hugs and kisses, then walk inside the busy depot toward a young woman holding a baby. Juanita's hands lifted to her mouth in a gesture of awe as the mother handed over the bundle. Juanita cradled the child, blanket and all, close to her chest, rocking the baby in her arms. She looked out toward the platform with tear-streaked cheeks and smiled.

As they walked away, Ramona considered what it was in her own life that would bring her such joy. The answer came quickly. It was the hope and promise of new life.

She took advantage of the outdoors, deciding to stretch her legs one last time before calling it a night. Familiar with the upcoming stops, Ramona knew the cold and wind would only become worse.

Two inches of fresh snow covered the slick ice on the platform, making for a treacherous crossing. In preparation, the station safety crew had tossed down copious amounts of sand, salt, and deicing products between the train and the station's entrance, creating a pond composed of slushy ice, grit, and chemicals. Ramona shoved her hands deep into the pocket of her sweatshirt and strolled alongside the train, keeping away from the main stream of pedestrians and luggage traffic.

God, the air feels good, she thought on the fourth breath. But dressed for the comfort of a warm train ride, wearing a well-loved, long-sleeved fleece shirt under her college hoodie, paired with her favorite yoga pants, she knew it wouldn't feel good for long. Judging from the tingling around the tips of her ears, she had about two, maybe three minutes before running the risk of frostbite, which was just enough time to get back to her seat. As she neared the boarding entrance, she fished around in her pocket for a tissue when her lip balm fell out.

"Shit."

Crouching close to the ground, searching where she

thought she may have dropped it, Ramona spied the bright pink cap sticking up out of the snow right away. She was about to reach for the item when her whole body was shoved forward—she thrust out her arms in front of her. She almost face-planted into the ice, and sank past her wrists in the snow bracing for impact.

"Watch where you're going," a shadowy figure reeking of cigarette smoke scoffed as he continued his brisk pace toward the train.

"So much for Minnesota nice," Ramona muttered, performing a quick assessment of her hands and knees before moving. She felt the abrasion on her skin around both wrists. Other than that and the fact that it was cold, nothing else seemed injured, except perhaps a little of her dignity—and she hoped that no one saw her. But a man in a trench coat and leather shoes promptly extended a gloved hand.

"What an asshole," the deep tenor voice remarked, then asked, "Are you all right?"

Mortified, she reached awkwardly for the offered hand. It was a clumsy maneuver, but she had managed to balance on her knees before she dared a quick glance upward. Tipping her head back, she followed the length of his arm, arching her neck to accommodate the full view. *Wow.*

As she gazed through her snow-covered eyelashes, it took a beat before she could see his face illuminated by the glow of the yard light behind him. His raven-black hair hung to his chin, and the wind played merrily with the ends tussled with snow. He wore a brown fedora atop his head, a swatch of color in his argyle scarf matching dead-on. His shoulders were broad, and he had a lean, powerful build. He looked down at her from his imposing stance and frowned.

What was it with pissed-off males at this stop? She was beginning to regret her lip balm obsession. His eyes narrowed with a glimmer of amusement, and the corner of his mouth quivered into what might be construed as a smile. *How nice, I've amused Mr. Business.* Normally, she'd have been put off by a person delighting in someone else's embarrassment, but there was something about the way the flecks of snow crystals twinkled around the frame of his face that softened his intimidating posture, and she burst into laughter. That earned her a glimpse of his dazzling, megawatt smile. That chiseled chin, a dimple in the center and the fedora lent an old Hollywood look to his appearance—distinguished, debonair, and devilishly handsome. But it was the intensity of those dark brown eyes that drew her in.

Unabashed by her stare, he held her gaze, and there was something about him that kept her riveted—a polished machismo that exuded sex appeal. He was the kind of guy she imagined being highly adept at fucking—in the bedroom, in the backseat of a car, on the kitchen countertop, on the living room sofa, pretty much wherever he wanted, providing an orgasm that would leave a woman screaming incoherently and begging for more. Ramona felt the weight of his shrewd, assessing stare and cleaned up her deviant thoughts. She knew the offensive play; he was searching for a weakness.

Countering, Ramona launched an exploration of her own. There was the obvious—urbane poise, power, confidence—but that was the façade. Much deeper lay something more basic, more primal, and she gasped inwardly, recognizing the watchful gaze of a predator.

He shifted without warning, enforcing his grip on her hand and pulling her to her feet in one fluid move. The rapid change in position sent the blood rushing from her head, and her balance faltered. He pulled her close, banding an arm around her waist, and supported her standing weight. Legs like Jello and head spinning, she was off her knees at least, though she was no closer to assembling any level of dignity. The higher vantage point proved just as awkward, and she blushed as she felt the heat of his body radiate through the long coat. The humid mist of his breath pulsed against her cheek and she almost swooned. Christ, she couldn't help it. Those strong arms, his body heat, and the invasion of her personal space were messing with her senses. His pupils darkened, exposing an air of protectiveness, or perhaps possession. The arm he had bound around her torso tightened, making it difficult for her to breathe. Ramona sought for purchase against his chest and tried to push away, but the power in his arms and firm grip flexed what was certain to be a set of well-defined pectoral muscles under the surface of his coat, rendering escape futile. As Ramona stood there, wrapped in the intensity of the stranger's embrace, she felt an unexpected calm take hold, slowing her breathing, and her body relaxed of its own volition as she curved into him.

"That's it," he murmured with a seductive timbre. "Don't fight me. You'll only end up hurting yourself. Just relax, the dizziness will pass."

There was something about the firm yet gentle command that felt liberating in an odd sort of way. For the first time in what seemed like forever, Ramona felt a sense of complacency and peace. The moment was fleeting, however, when she realized that she'd just exposed such a rudimentary need to a stranger.

Christ, what am I doing? Ramona mused, trying to get a grip on herself. *He's just helping you up from the snow.* Though it had been a while since she'd felt the comfort and protection of a man's embrace, igniting the embers of a fire she had long since abandoned.

He relinquished his hold and narrowed his gaze, scanning the platform. "Should I go find the bastard and kick his ass?"

The ferocity of his threat caught her off guard, and she gasped instantly, wishing he hadn't said it. He had an invigorating smell, a heady combination of citrus and mint accentuated by the crisp, cold air. It wasn't one of those perfumy colognes, aftershaves, or body sprays advertised, but a clean fragrance. Whatever it was, he smelled divine, with a hint of tobacco on his lapel. She lost all semblance of common sense and practically salivated over his delicious scent.

Shaking herself out from her self-indulging stupor, Ramona managed to say, "No, then I wouldn't be Minnesota Nice." She crooked her head back to stare at him. "Besides, do you always volunteer to rescue fallen damsels and offer to beat up their assailants?"

"I'm not from Minnesota," he drawled in that seductive tenor, "and I'm not that nice."

The sexual undertone and laughter in his velvety voice made Ramona blush despite the cold. The comment brought sex to mind, unadulterated sex. The kind of sex men who command and conquer had a reputation for. Once again she found herself pulling her mind out of the proverbial gutter.

The conductor's voice came over the PA and broke her corrupt thought. Cognizant of his hold, the stranger released his grip and allowed her to step away. Unprotected by the warmth of his embrace, she felt the shock of the cold air lash against her clothing and shuddered.

"Thank you for your help," Ramona snapped, a bit harsher than she'd intended. Modifying her tone, she said, "I need to get back on the train." She shuffled away backwards and stumbled. He caught up to her in one swift motion.

"Me too, let me walk with you."

He locked her arm in his, leaving no room to argue. Ramona yielded to his assistance, hoping maybe if she'd let him walk her to the train that would be the end of her embarrassment. She didn't know what to make of this stranger. He had charm and looks in spades, but that seemed very superficial, and she felt somewhat vulnerable to his persistence.

The stranger stopped walking. "May I?" His tone was filled with amusement as he removed the scarf around his neck. With a smug expression, he began wrapping the scarf around her. "What the hell are you doing out here half naked in this cold anyway?"

With a flash of irritation, she defended herself. "I'm not half naked. I was seeing a friend off, and out for a quick breath of fresh air."

He looked up from his handiwork and placated her justification with an admonishing grin. Ramona rolled her eyes inwardly, recognizing that chauvinistic, "whatever you say dear" look, but she couldn't argue. Had it been one of her kids, she'd have done the same.

Safe onboard, Ramona hoped to avoid an awkward Minnesota Goodbye. "Thank you for your help." She began removing the scarf, hoping he'd go back to wherever he'd come from. Attractive as he was, she couldn't shake the feeling that she was being stalked and didn't want him assuming an invitation back to her sleeper car. "I'm on the observation deck," she half-lied.

The stranger stilled her hands. "How about that, so am I." Slipping off his gloves, he held out a hand and gestured for her to go first. Ramona huffed in resignation and led the way. He followed and placed the flat of his hand at the small of her back, guiding her through the walkway. She flinched, and not from the cold. Turning to face him, she was met by a heated stare from his dark hooded eyes. The corner of his mouth lifted, and all the while he maintained his proprietary contact with the small of her back.

Don't read into that, Ramona scolded herself, trying to squelch her coaxed arousal. *It's just his amusement at your dorky expression, that's all.* She resumed walking.

After what seemed like the longest surreptitious, sensual

tease of her life, Ramona finally reached the refuge of the observation car. She hustled into her seat by the window, desperate to ignore the man who turned her on with a simple touch. She busied herself with whatever she could get her hands on, flustered by his presence. Fussing with the wine glass, she set it off to the side, quite ready to be done with the whole experience. Then he sat, uninvited, in the open seat vacated by Juanita and placed his hands firmly on hers. Normally, she would have lashed out at the condescending gesture, yet somehow this stranger's imperious act had almost made her want to cry. His touch soothed her volatile emotions, and once again she felt herself relinquishing control.

He said in a flat voice. "I have to finish some business in the lounge."

The overhead lighting dimmed, signaling the train's departure from the station, the time a little past 10:30 p.m. Ramona watched him warily as his eyes darted around the observation car. From the moment he'd plucked her out of the snow he had projected an air of confidence and control, but he now seemed preoccupied and distant. Ramona's eyes canvassed the car, and she wondered if the asshole who'd pushed her was close by. Not that it would have mattered one way or the other. She never got a good look at the guy's face and wouldn't have recognized him if he sat down right next to her.

"My seat is there, just ahead of you," the stranger said. He stood, removing his hat and coat, and gave them a haphazard toss into the open seat. He turned to face her. The self-assured, cocky smile was back, and he had a mischievous glint in those dark eyes. Placing his hand on the back of her seat, he leaned in close and said, "I'll check on you when I get back."

Ramona met the intensity of his gaze inches away from her face and realized he was telling her, not asking. Reaching for the scarf around her neck she began, "Here's your—" He clasped her wrists and directed her hands to her lap. She felt the frenetic rush of energy as he took the seat next to her. At eye level, she saw his response to their contact. His face was etched into an expression of passivity, but his eyes gave him away. She was relieved she hadn't been the only one who'd felt the connection. The corner of his mouth twitched, suppressing a smile. He'd let her see it, knew she knew it too. Releasing her wrists, he played it off.

"Hang onto it for now and warm up," he said. "And if you're good, I'll bring you a drink when I get back."

This time he was waiting for a response. In the space it took Ramona to answer, she noticed his confident swagger waver. She gave up on the scarf and settled back into her window seat. When he seemed satisfied, he stood and started down the aisle toward the stairs. He was almost out of earshot when Ramona called out, "Thank you!" then paused, embarrassed yet again when she realized she didn't even know his name. "I'd like a hot chocolate, please."

"With or without alcohol?" he called back, a hint of mirth in his voice.

"Your call," she replied and huddled into the seat.

As soon as he was gone she would slip off to her sleeper

car and be done with it, Ramona decided. The chances of running into him again were next to nil, and the worst that would happen was he'd be stuck with a cup of hot chocolate he didn't want and she'd have to pull out her vibrator. Then she breathed in the rich masculine scent infused with citrus in his scarf and abandoned the thought.

Letting the rhythmic motion of the train lull her into a tranquil thought, she considered the handsome stranger with the bossy personality and electrifying touch and let her mind drift.

Juanita and I must have been absorbed in conversation to have missed someone like that sitting right in front of us.

CHAPTER 6

JOHN

John ambled through the train cars and corridors, returning with a hot chocolate in hand. He wondered if after all the monkey business, the woman would even be interested in him. Every fiber of his being screamed lawyer, which usually played in his favor when it came to superficial, egotistical-type women. Would it be the same for a woman with substance?

An unscheduled train stop had created an influx of congestion in the aisles, ramping up John's sense of urgency. Using the minimal civility as social convention allowed, he navigated around the boarding passengers, circumventing the human obstacle course. He'd reached his final ascent to the observation car's upper deck when he came to a halt. Making her way down the stairs was a young woman, holding the hand of a small boy as he painstakingly negotiated each step. The kid couldn't have been more than three, maybe four, and was clinging to an old, tattered blanket, while towing a dingy suitcase behind him. *Great, just what this train trip needed: a kid*, he thought as he brusquely stepped aside for them.

Reaching the top of the stairs, John froze mid-stride. Looking out over the seating, he found that every seat of the once near-empty car had been filled. His eyes darted in a frantic search over toward the window, but he couldn't see her, and a lump of disappointment caught in his throat. A perturbed, "Ahem," interrupted him.

"Do you mind? I'd like to sit down sometime before the sun rises."

John whirled around, prepared to tell the wiseass to fuck off, and found not one, but three possible perpetrators glaring up from further down the stairwell.

"He won't move," one of the hostiles relayed to someone further down the rung.

"Asshole." The disgruntled retort wafted upward.

Comprehending that he'd bottlenecked the flow of traffic, John slithered off into the row of seats beside him and murmured a sheepish apology to the person whose space he'd infringed upon. As the line of people passed, John ignored the dagger glares and used the opportunity to continue his search. When the last person passed, he took up the rear and moved with caution along the aisle. As he drew nearer to her seating section, a familiar object caught his eye and it occurred to him: *Shit, what if that had been her stop?*

It seemed his postulation was correct. He recognized the argyle scarf draped over the back headrest and prepared for the inevitable. Standing parallel to the seating section, he peered into the row and found, to his relief, the woman who'd fallen in the snow. She was sitting much the way he had left her, except someone had given her a small blanket. She wore an angelic expression as she slept, the light, tan skin of her face unmarred by the lines of worry and grief from earlier. Mesmerized, he stood there basking in the radiance of her tranquility, drinking in her unpretentious beauty.

"Excuse me." A desperate female voice interrupted his serene thoughts. "Are you going to sit there?"

Snapped back to reality, John tore his gaze from the snow angel and faced the woman with the child from the stairwell standing in front of him.

"Can we sit here?" she asked again, pointing to the open seat next to the argyle scarf.

The shy little boy peeked out from behind the woman with a pouty lip and tear-stained cheeks, clinging to her thigh. His eyes were red and tired, as were the woman's. She looked down at the little boy with a weary smile and cupped his head.

The moment of decision had been thrust upon him to commit to the plan or forget it. An internal battle raged between predator and intellect as John looked over again at the woman in peaceful repose. The blunt truth of the matter was he'd be better off returning to his room and drinking the goddamn hot chocolate himself. He didn't have time to cultivate the sort of connection he'd been conjuring in his whimsical thoughts with the woman and her beguiling hazel eyes.

Forcing the word past his lips, he said, "No," and the sound of finality hit him like a bucket of ice.

Dejected, the young mother took the child's hand and

turned to walk back the direction they'd come, when the little boy stopped and pointed toward the seats in front of them. His mother tried to coax him along, shaking her head, but instead, the little boy raised his gaze toward John and asked, "Mister, are those your seats?"

John followed the line to where the little boy's finger pointed. It was where he'd tossed his coat and hat. Shamed again by his self-indulgence, John crouched to the boy's level and lowered his voice. "Actually, I had just left my things there to go get a beverage." He held up the thermos mug as if to strengthen the validity in his remark. Unimpressed, the little boy frowned. "But," John added "I could move over here so you two can sit together." He glanced at the snow angel. "I don't think the sleeping lady will mind, do you?"

The young woman turned, her face bright with surprise, and blurted, "Oh would you, could we?" then cringed, embarrassed by her loud exuberance. "We would appreciate it so much," she said in a muted but no less grateful tone.

"Not a problem, glad to help," John said with forced nonchalance.

They switched positions and the woman wished him a safe journey before turning her attention to her son. She slid into the seat next to him. Rubbing his eyes, the little tyke looked up at his mother, and she leaned over and kissed him on the head.

As John watched the scene play out, it puzzled him, how such a little thing could make someone so happy. In his experience, it seemed happiness could only be derived when it involved a pint of blood and a pound of flesh at another human being's expense.

The train car resumed its previous slumbering quality, and John considered what it was that made him happy. He gazed at the woman beside him a long while, and it perplexed him how he found her tranquil repose so appealing. Whereas the young mother carried the weight of her worry on the outside for anyone to see, the woman by the window tried to conceal her feelings. He almost felt guilty for what he was about to do, and nudged her shoulder.

She murmured something, the corners of her mouth curving upward. *Was she dreaming,* he wondered, *or was that smile for him?* Opening the drinking spout on the thermos mug, he waved it back and forth, wafting the aromatic cocoa under her nose. The smile widened.

"You remembered the hot chocolate," she said, lifting one eyelid, then the other.

Her gaze hit him like a two-by-four alongside the head and he stuttered, "Yes," then stole the line from the bartender who'd made him the drink. "It's my own personal concoction. I hope you like it."

She blinked her eyes into a lazy focus. Stifling a yawn, she sat up straight and shimmied out from under her blanket. Lifting her arms up over her head, she did a long, slow stretch, taking one wrist in her hand and reaching to the opposite side, then repeating this on the other. Lacing her fingers behind her head, she threw out her chest and arched her back, moaning as her neck and spine crackled and popped. A mild scent of lavender wafted from her skin like a breeze of warm air from a summer garden. Watching her emerge from sleep reminded John of the way a cat stretched after a lazy nap, cute and playful. She seemed unaware of the allure she exuded with her quaint little ritual. It took all his willpower to keep from using his body to pin her back to the seat and kiss her senseless.

She pulled down the hood of her sweat shirt and revealed a sleep-tussled mess of wavy, auburn-brown hair, cut in a sort of pixie style. Short hair, not what he'd expected. But then, did he really know what to expect from this woman?

She self-consciously began fussing with the crop of unruly waves in a vain attempt to restore some semblance of style. While she fidgeted, John tried to gauge her age. He hadn't gotten a good look at her out on the platform, and was pleased to discover her to be more attractive then he'd first thought. She wore little makeup, if any, and her lids and lashes were a distinctive dark brown with soft, cherry-cola red lips. The natural look lent her a more youthful appearance, and except for the smile lines that bookended her twinkling eyes, she bore no wrinkles— she could have easily passed for late thirties, maybe early forties. Smitten by her simple beauty, he handed over the thermos mug to her waiting hands. She cradled her fingers around the tumbler's girth and let the heat from the steam rise, blowing on it a couple of times before wrapping her plush red lips around the lid. She took a cautious sip.

John found himself holding his breath, anticipating her approval, but she showed no expression one way or the other and he felt oddly disappointed. She took a bigger swallow. This time the ends of her lips curled into a sinful smile.

"Mmm." She took another sip. "This is no ordinary hot chocolate," she said, gazing up at him with a bright twinkle in her eyes. "This is an orgasm in a cup."

The audacious remark caught him off guard and he laughed. "What is it with women and chocolate?"

She took another sip, her toes tapping a happy dance on the floor. She asked, "How did you know I liked hazelnut?"

As she eased back in her seat, John felt her gaze study him while she sipped the cocoa. It was hard to know what she was thinking, with all her little *ums* and *ahs*. Then her cheeks flushed, betraying an inner thought.

"Are you okay?" John said with amusement.

"I'm—" she stammered. "I'm probably a bit overtired."

He shot her a dubious look. "Is that all? Tell me the truth."

"It's been a long day and . . ." A languidness suddenly took hold of her and she asked, "Should I be concerned about the special ingredient?"

John smiled wryly and leaned into her personal space. "I think I'm the one who should be concerned," he whispered. "If that is an orgasm in a cup, the next thing I know, you'll be writhing in your seat, moaning and crying out my name." He leaned back, gauging her response, then added, "Maybe I should have gotten one for myself, that way we could both have an orgasm together."

Her delayed response left him feeling he'd misjudged

his comeback until she threw her head back and sputtered an unbridled snort of laughter. She choked on her drink, and John patted her back. "I'm John, by the way, just so you know whose name you should be crying out."

"Ramona," she said, and pushed his hand away. When her coughing settled, she shook his hand, and John felt the tingle of awareness between them. She glanced at his hand, and smiled.

With introductions out of the way, they flirted for the next hour or so, chitchatting about superficial things, keeping the questions broad, using vague descriptions for more personal information. Her subtle enunciation of *O* divulged her Minnesota roots, a trait he found quite amusing.

When he asked her if she was traveling for business or pleasure, she canted her head to the side and said, "You know, I've never understood why people always combine business and pleasure in the same sentence," taking a sip of her drink. "To me it should be more like business and recreation or pleasure and pain, don't you think?"

The topic caught his attention.

"I love my work," she said with genuine conviction. "So, if we enjoy our work, wouldn't that be pleasure too?"

John formulated his response judiciously. "I suppose so."

She tapped her index finger to her lips, "So wouldn't business be more akin to work and recreation the same as play?"

John noted that her query seemed to be more introspective, yet she looked to him for affirmation.

"But if you're competitive in your recreational activities," she went on, "you know, like a sport, couldn't that almost be considered work sometimes? I trained for a 10K a couple of years ago, and I can tell you I worked my ass off getting ready. Plus, it was painful besides."

"I'm sure it was," John agreed.

"And don't get me started on pleasure and pain," she said with a laugh. "Those two sensations are practically inseparable." She flashed him a wicked grin.

John's eyes widened with intrigue. "And what do you mean by that?"

"John," Ramona admonished, "I can see you're—" She paused, considering. "I'll use the word, competitive? I think you go after what you want, and you are quite accustomed to acquiring what you go after. I like that sort of work ethic in a person."

John lifted his shoulder in a shrug, "No pain, no gain, that sort of thing."

"Exactly, and how can you experience pleasure without a little pain? After all, isn't pleasure the gain?" She gave him a flirty wink.

John leaned in close enough to smell the alcohol-infused chocolate on her breath. "Are you implying you could be"—he paused and twisted his lips—"shall I say, *interested* in experiencing this pain for pleasure?" She squirmed visibly. It was time to put her cards on the table or fold.

"What did you put in this chocolate? Are you trying to get me drunk?"

John recognized the stall tactic and wondered if

he'd read her wrong. "You didn't answer my question, Ramona." He was about to chalk up the chase as a lost cause when she finally answered with a devilish smile.

"Yes, John, I am interested. But the point is moot." Her eyes swept the car. "We're not exactly alone."

But John did have the answer. "As it happens, I have a sleeping car that may serve quite nicely for those ideas mulling around in that interesting head of yours."

Her eyes blinked with awareness, knowing he'd told a white lie about sitting across from her. Suspicion rose on her cheeks. He could tell she was still interested, she just needed a gentle nudge. Careful not to touch her, John leaned in and felt the response of her warmth to his intimate proximity. As she lifted her gaze to his, he felt the tantalizing magnetism of her visceral demand and heard her breath catch when he sealed his mouth around hers. She shut her eyes, succumbing to the kiss, while he savored the texture of her moist lips flavored with chocolate and hazelnut.

Whether fueled by alcohol or desire or both, he didn't care. She reached with a tremulous hand for the back of his neck and ran her fingers gently through his hair, caressing his nape with reverent strokes. She took her time cradling his neck, then opened her mouth, deepening the kiss, the succulent sound fanning his ravenous appetite for more. He felt rather than heard her soft moan of pleasure, so subtle John thought he'd imagined it, and delighted in her resonating fervor to his touch. In that moment, he knew she was his and eased away from the kiss. Shifting to his feet, John gathered up his coat and hat, then held out his hand: "Come with me, Ramona, please."

Looking up at him through those long eyelashes, she placed a tentative hand in his and couldn't have been more delectable if she had tried. His hand in hers, John led the way through the rocking corridors, grateful for the privacy of his sleeping car.

CHAPTER 7

MONY

They paused at the door of a sleeping compartment while John fished for something in his pocket. Ramona glanced down to where their hands were joined and resisted the urge to squeeze. John seemed reluctant to let go as well and made a fumbled attempt to open the door with one hand, but after a moment, he gave up and handed over his coat and hat.

She looked away, biting her lip to stifle a nervous giggle while she waited patiently. It took a second before she heard the gratifying slide of the door. John placed his hand at the small of her back, sending the now-familiar tingle racing up her spine, and ushered her inside. She stopped mid-step, causing John to bump into her.

"Excuse me, Madame," he said with a smirk.

Embarrassed, she muttered, "*Je suis désolée,*" and stepped out of his way.

John carried their things inside. Ramona stood in the corner of the room, recognizing that the dim lights and upturned bunk beds indicated the room had been readied for sleep. Her heart began to thrum against her chest. If she followed through with the carnal thoughts rolling around in her head, it would be the first time she'd be with a man other than her husband in over thirty years. She couldn't tell if the acute unease in her gut was from anticipation or fear. Was this really the best location? Ramona had traveled in a sleeper car many times before, alone, but not like this.

John was situated in a family-sized sleeper all to himself, which felt quite roomy compared to hers. She knew it hadn't come cheap either. It was why she'd considered flying her own plane for this trip, but she hadn't had the necessary time to log a flight plan.

John busied himself with the duties of a host seemingly eager to have everything in its proper place. Ramona eyed him with caution, and he smiled when he caught her staring. She noted how he hadn't exploited the space. Neither of them had shared their travel destinations, but John traveled light. With only a luggage bag and a briefcase tucked under the lower bunk, either he was that efficient at packing or he wasn't traveling far. His garment bag held little bulk, and the only coat he seemed to have was the one he was carrying. That ruled out North Dakota, Montana, and the mountains for a destination, unless he had more luggage stored down below.

Ramona ran her fingers along the fresh, crisp linen, reminding her how *un-fresh* she was; she wished she'd have had time to shower before leaving home, but she barely had enough time to make the train.

John caught sight of her by the bed. With a hint of

nervous enthusiasm, he spoke over his shoulder. "Make yourself comfortable."

She tried.

Slipping off her boots, she stretched her legs. She felt anything but comfortable, but tried to sound calm when she asked John to hand her bag. He did so, and she retrieved a pair of soft slipper socks. Clomping around in boots for the past six hours had made her feet hot and sweaty, and the cool air that tickled her feet felt good. She wiggled her toes with impetuous delight, swinging her legs onto the bed, and leaned back propped on her elbows. John padded over and sat next to her. Subtly, he unzipped her hoodie, pushing the sweatshirt off her shoulders, revealing the soft cotton V-neck tissue tee beneath. She continued her foot exercises, displaying an air of unconcern.

"Sweet Jesus, Ramona, are you wearing a bra?" John flexed his fingers before palming her breast through the cotton shirt. "It's pretty cold outside," he said, cupping it in his hand.

Ramona breathed a low sigh at the gentle caress. "Y-yes," she stuttered.

John crooked an eye brow at her. "Yes what?"

Her toes flexed involuntarily. Made of fine, delicate lace, the bra she wore was almost undetectable underneath her clothes. Because of the nature of her work, Ramona didn't own a lot of pretty clothes or professional outfits. That didn't mean she couldn't dress up fancy beneath her clothes. "Yes, I'm wearing a bra," she finally said. John ran the pad of his thumb over her nipple through the lacy cotton, smiling at the response.

She'd never considered herself a busty woman, but when John plumped her breast, feeling the weight of it in his hand, her pulse leapt, and she arched into his touch. *Oh, Christ, what the hell am I doing here?* But as John deftly fondled second base, she was damn well glad he knew what he was doing. It had to be the alcohol clouding her judgment, and she thought about leaving while there was still a chance. That was before John touched her with a particularly masterful stroke; the feeling was so exquisite that an unrestrained moan escaped from her lips. *Too late,* she conceded as her resolve crumbled under the dexterity of his fingers. *Besides, I'm already here, and if not now, when?* John's hands left her breast, and she glanced up, wondering why he'd stopped.

He took her chin in his hand. "Look at me." Ramona met his gaze, a startling mixture of lust and concern in his intense brown eyes. "You don't have to do anything you don't want to, Ramona."

Christ, had my inner conflict been that transparent? Ramona felt herself poised on the edge of a parapet. More than want, she needed him, here, now, but seemed paralyzed to move forward.

"But I really hope that you want to," John confided. "Don't worry, I know how this goes. I'll take care of you first." He pressed a kiss against her lips in a moist, supple tease. She opened her mouth, matching his fervor, and reached for the nape of his neck, pulling the strands of his soft, silky hair. She coaxed him deeper, his tongue serpentine in her greedy mouth, and she moaned her surrender against his lips.

"I want to."

She felt his smile on her lips as John acknowledged her consent and removed her hooded sweater. Undressing her slowly, he made a meal out of it, loosening her bra, before laying her back onto the bed.

Too fast—she was breathing way too fast. Ramona tried to relax, tried to savor the moment. John leaned over her naked chest, still penetrating her mouth with his tongue. She felt the surge of pleasure move all the way down to her toes, the stimulation pushing her to the verge of climax. His hand slid along the contour of her body, his seduction slow and deliberate. Unrestricted by the lace of her bra, he glided a hand over the swollen tissue of her breast and watched her face as he fastidiously worried her nipples. Ramona closed her eyes and muttered something incoherent.

"Eyes open, please," John commanded. He seemed to relish watching her lose control. Dipping his head, he placed his lips over her hardened nipple, wetting the tip with his tongue before latching onto it. She kneaded at his scalp, running her fingers through his hair while he sucked rhythmically until she cried out. The barrage of pleasure was both tantalizing and maddening. She wanted more, needed more, and grabbed at his shirt, clawing it loose from the waist band of his trousers. John slid his tongue leisurely to the other breast and paused, building the anticipation before taking it into his mouth. The sensation arrowed straight to her core, and she became painfully aware of the emptiness between her thighs.

"John, please," she whispered. This time she saw the smile cross his lips as he resumed his upward journey, suckling, nibbling before covering her mouth. Abruptly, John stood to pull his shirt over his head. Ramona slid over, making room on the bunk that was barely wide enough for one. As he towered over her next to the bunk, Ramona objectified his physique, raking her gaze over his body. He slowly unzipped his trousers, lowering his boxers over his hips, revealing his erection, and her pupils darkened with lust.

"Like what you see?" he asked in that seductive timbre. Her eyes fell on a faded bruise under his left rib, and she lifted off the bed for a closer examination. He took a step back.

"Kick boxing with a mix of martial arts," he explained and shimmied out of the rest of his clothes. As he leaned over her, she reached to touch him, and he seized both her wrists, lifting them over her head. Using his body, he pinned her against the bed and leaned his lips to her ear. "Nuh-uh, I've shown you mine; your turn."

She stiffened beneath him, felt the urgency of her lust falter. John lifted his head in bewilderment, and must have seen the panic in her eyes. He released her wrists immediately. *Shit, why hadn't I just had him turn out the lights so we could get on with it?* Ramona bemoaned inwardly, struggling to find the words to answer his silent query.

"I have—" Her voice wavered as the muscles seized tight in her throat. "Scars. I have scars." She averted her eyes. "They're not pretty." The sexual tension waned quickly between them, and she knew she'd made a huge mistake.

Certain he'd be repulsed by what he'd find on her less than flat tummy, she closed her eyes and felt the shame rise in her cheeks. "I'm sorry." A single tear trickled down her cheek, and she tried to lift off the bed. "I shouldn't have come."

John held firm. Using the pad of his thumb, he captured her rogue tear. "We all have scars, snow angel," he said, lifting the pad of his thumb to his mouth. He sucked the taste of her salty tear and stroked the back of his fingers tenderly across her cheek. "You don't get to where we are in life without having a few."

Something shifted between them just then, something more than waning lust or her insecurities of a less than perfect body. With Bob, sex had always been pretty straightforward, no surprise. It had been his way of building trust. Trust was everything for Ramona, who hadn't had much experience with this on a sexual level. She wanted him, ached with a need to feel him push inside her. John sidled next to her and combed his fingers through her short locks of hair. She closed her eyes at the soothing touch, and willed the tension to leave her body. *You can do this,* she told herself, struggling to slow her shallow breaths. *You can do this.* She knew he knew she wanted him; she just couldn't stop, not now.

"You can do this, Ramona," John said, echoing the words in her head. He stood and reached down for the waistband of her pants. "This is the hardest part, I promise. You'll know your way after this." Grasping her clothing at her hips, he carefully slid pant and panty past the curves of her butt and pelvis to her feet. There, he had her participate, lifting one leg and then the other, allowing her to pull free. He dropped the clothes onto the floor and gazed down at her nakedness, taking in her waist, her hips, the mound of delicate hair covering her sex, and reaching to touch it.

It had been a long time since she'd felt the heat of a man's touch there on her body, and the intense craving it provoked. Ramona understood then that her need for sexual intimacy hadn't died with her husband, and it had been long, far too long, to have gone without it. As he slid his hands to her inner thighs, she felt her muscle tense beneath the soft, padded flesh, and she tried to relax into his touch. John glided his hands to her outer thighs, working his way up along the sides of her hips. She relished the contact of his dexterous fingers as he felt along the crest of her pelvis. Then he lifted his gaze to her belly, recognition in his eyes when they fell on the faded line that crossed between the crest of her hips. Two small puckers of flesh marred each side of her navel, creating a dimpling in her skin. She splayed her hands instinctively across her stomach, a vain effort to cover the scar. John took her wrists, gripped them in one hand, and lifted them over her head, covering her body with his. When their gazes met, tears began to pool in the corner of her eyes, and she looked away, frustrated with her humility.

"It shreds me that you think yourself undesirable because of some little scar. You have nothing to hide, Ramona. You're beautiful, and I can tell you take care of yourself. Do you bike?"

The question caught her by surprise. "No," she said in

a hoarse voice, "jogging, hiking; some horseback riding."

"Horseback riding?"

His bemused expression made the corners of her lips curl into a slight smile. "You'd be surprised how much you use your inner thighs clinging to a horse and riding at an open gallop."

He gave a husky laugh. "Yes, I can see that."

With her thoughts in a better place, John turned his attention back to a more corporeal pursuit. "Be a good girl now," he commanded. "I'm going to let go of your wrists, but I want you to keep your hands above your head. Hold onto the pillow if you need to—I want to explore."

With a shaky breath, Ramona grasped onto the corners of the pillow and gave a consensual nod. John began his exploration, kissing away the tears from her eyes, then moved along to her chin and neck. He nibbled and suckled along her clavicle as his lips descended toward her chest. Lifting onto an elbow, he reached for her breasts, giving them a gentle squeeze. The stimulation was maddening, not being allowed to touch him. Ramona writhed, pulling the pillow closer to her head, clutching the corners, restraining the urge to touch his soft satin hair. He paused above her navel and dipped his tongue inside, gliding his fingers over her belly. Her skin quivered, the nerve endings fully alive, under his electrifying touch. With great care, John caressed over the scarred tissue.

"So beautiful," he murmured and pressed his lips against her belly. "You're doing very well." Sweat misted her flesh, the potent scent of pheromones blending with her lavender fragrance. "I have to taste you," John said in warning, and slid his shoulders between her thighs.

Ramona squeezed her knees tight against his body. "Don't." Her voice caught. "You don't have to do that. I—I haven't showered since very early this morning."

John retreated and stroked her inner thighs, massaging, kneading; working in from her knees to the apex of her thighs and said, "Just hold onto the pillow, Ramona. I told you, I want to explore." He worked his way outward again and continued the firm, gentle caress to her inner thighs, then settled between her parted legs.

Her hips began to churn, tantalized by the rhythmic glide of his hands. John propped on his elbow and cupped her sex, and with his free hand palmed the mound of soft hair. He fingered along her cleft, sliding leisurely back and forth, watched her hips strain upward, the lips of her sex clenching at his finger.

"You're soft and hot." He wet his fingers in his mouth, then slid one inside her. "Does that help?" John asked in a voice that conveyed neither abhorrence nor judgment.

An overwhelming sense of gratitude took hold of her. He understood. He didn't question, didn't ask her to explain, nor did he take it as a slight against his male prowess. He retracted his hand and used finger and thumb to part the sensual flesh, exposing the delicate tissue to the cool air.

The need for release was unbearable. She tilted her pelvis, rocking her hips against his touch. "John, please," Ramona whimpered, the unsated demand building a restless energy. "I need you inside me."

"You're not ready," he said with authority, and his

hands left her.

"What?" Her hips fell to the bed, and she began to writhe against the mattress. "You're tormenting me on purpose," she growled, lifting her head. Gazing down the length of her torso, she noticed how he seemed to enjoy watching her squirm, amused by her irritation, and scowled at him, all the while still clinging to the pillow.

He ran his tongue over his lips and flashed her a wicked grin, then lowered his head between her thighs, parting the lips of her sex. She gasped when his tongue slid into the crevice, rimming along its edges, and he dipped and worked his mouth against the sensitive, swollen tissue. She made wanton sounds of pleasure, clawing the pillow beneath her head.

John looked up from between her legs, his lips glistening, his eyes heated with lust. "Oh, Ramona, you're going to implode when you come, I can taste it."

Her thighs were already trembling, and she drew in a sharp breath at the carnal promise. As he ran his hand over her belly, the muscles quivered in anticipation; he palmed the mound of her sex and slid a finger over and in, pushing deeper until her eyes lost focus. Pressing against the sensitive notch inside, he rolled the pad of his finger over the spongy ridge, kneading, coaxing while he rocked the heel of his hand insolently over her clit. The smooth muscles inside her grasped at his finger, clutching desperately. Sweat poured from her heated body, the muscles of her buttocks flexing against the strong pull. Frantic, she thrust her pelvis forward to meet the shallow penetration of his touch just inside her, massaging that oh-so-sweet spot.

Maddened by her resilience, John commanded, "Breathe, Ramona. Let it happen."

Tears welled in her eyes. "It feels so good," she cried, her voice weak and tremulous. She felt her sex clenching, rhythmically rippling; building. "I ca—"

"You can, goddamn it. Give it to me now."

Her neck arched, her back bowing off the bed. She came with a raspy cry of pleasure stealing breath and control. The orgasmic release tore through her body, rippling until the throbbing pulse subsided. She fell back onto the mattress, her chest heaving. Ramona let go of the pillow and dropped an arm across her eyes, soaking up the tears running down her cheeks.

A triumphant smile arched across John's lips as he watched her struggle to recover. "Been a while, hasn't it?"

Panting, Ramona muttered, "Too long. A good vibrator might get a girl where she needs to go, but it can never replace this."

He chuckled at her candor, and fondled the mound of soft hair between her thighs. Her legs began to tremble. John slinked his way up alongside her body. "Hmm, I think you may be onto something." He lifted her arm away from her eyes. "I'm far from finished with you, Ms. Ramona." John leveled over her body and sealed his mouth over hers, her words of protection lost as the kiss, starting out soft and slow, turned rough with urgency.

"I can't," she whispered, gasping under his persistence. Releasing her mouth, John stared at her with single-minded focus. "You can, and you will," he said, keeping the roll of his hips slow and measured. "This time, it's my turn."

Ramona's eyes widened at the wanton promise, and she decided to let him have his way. Tonight was but a breath. The new day was already here. In the afterglow of tomorrow, she would be gone.

CHAPTER 8

MASSEY

The delay around Devil's Lake added about fifteen minutes to the schedule; otherwise the train rolled into the station close to on time. Massey Ferguson stood on the east side of the depot, out of the wind. Looking out at the train tracks, he waited as the Amtrak slowly came to a stop. He watched the passengers exit the train in Williston, North Dakota, population 14,716. It was certainly not the sleepy little town it had been a decade ago. With a projected population of 20,000 by the end of the current year thanks to the oil boom, Williston was about to become the sixth-largest city in the state. He saw her step off near the rear of the train, and she spotted him immediately.

"Massey," she shouted, and waved.

He waited in the shelter of the building as she made her way over the cobblestone platform.

"I knew you'd come." She threw her arms around him. "It's so good to see you."

He hugged her hard to his chest and kissed her forehead.

"It's good to see you too, Mony."

She looked up at him, smiling at the familiar sound of her nickname. Massey breathed in Mony's familiar lavender fragrance, then caught the scent of something else as well. "I wish it was under better circumstances," he told her, rubbing his hands up and down her back, and made a mental note he should talk about that later.

A station attendant walked past with a trolley and he waved him over. "Thank you for seeing to her things," Massey said, handing the man a bill. The attendant nodded and handed off her luggage.

Matthew Joseph Ferguson, Massey to everyone except for his dad and stepmom, was a tall man with intelligent, soft brown eyes and a warm, friendly smile. A year older than Mony, he was her father's business partner's eldest son. He managed to maintain his lean, athletic build, despite his desk job, by playing in a men's over-forty hockey team captained by his brother. Ambitious as a young man, Massey Ferguson had been an all-American athlete back in his high school days. Every college in the country had been clamoring for the boy from the Rough Rider state, but Massey chose to stay closer to home and attended the University of Minnesota. He finished his law degree at Stanford to be closer to his brother on the coast. Graduating with the highest honors, he stayed on the West Coast, establishing a successful practice. It was also where he met his much younger wife.

When the oil industry started booming back home, he packed up his family and moved back to his roots. A force to be reckoned with, it wasn't long before Massey owned majority stock at the law firm he'd worked for. Wheeling influence and power among the state lawmakers and oil companies, he had a down-to-earth, no-nonsense approach and an innate ability to connect with the local landowners and businessmen who were his clients. It didn't hurt that his father was just as successful politically, and together they were a powerhouse.

"Jesus, Mony, are you still losing weight?"

Mony blushed, shifting on her feet, but said nothing. Massey hadn't seen her since shortly after her late husband's funeral, of course he would notice.

"Christ, Mony, you look like shit," a deep voice interjected from behind, and Kip Ferguson strolled into view.

"Dad," Massey scolded without looking, though he knew it would do no good. "Give her a break." Massey was about the only person who had the audacity to speak to his father in that manner and get away with it.

Mony skirted around him and walked up to Kip. "Hi, Kip," she said, forcing a smile, and stood on tiptoe to kiss him on the cheek. "I hope you've been well."

"Do I look well?" Kip scoffed. "And where the hell is your coat?"

Joseph Kipton Ferguson, Kip to Mony and most of the world, had never been a man to mince words, even when Mony had been a little girl. A juggernaut of a fellow, Kip was the mighty oak Massey had sprouted from. But unlike Massey's lean, athletic build, Kip had the body of a linebacker with the barreled chest of a former two-pack-a-day smoker.

"Let's get you to the truck," Massey said. "We've got some business to discuss before you head home." Mony looked like she was about to protest but held her tongue. It didn't matter—what they had to talk about couldn't wait.

They said very little on the way over to Massey's office. Mony leaned against the door—he could tell she was already wiped out, causing him to question the wisdom of their pending discussion, but the point was moot. The mighty Kip Ferguson had insisted they get it over with as soon as possible, and despite his reservations, Massey tended to agree with his dad. As they rode, he considered how Kip had almost been as much a father to Mony as Buddy had been. He remembered how she'd stood up to Kip the first time she met him. Kip always seemed to hold an expression of disapproval, yet somehow Mony had seen right through his father's intimidating façade and wrapped him around her finger despite his best efforts.

Their fathers had first met in Vietnam and were later stationed together at Minot Air Force Base when it had first been established. After discharge, it had been his dad who'd urged Buddy to go into business with him as the fly boy for their crop dusting operation. It hadn't taken much convincing. Buddy Altman loved to fly and would have worked for peanuts if Kip had let him. Never much of a long-range planner, Buddy didn't stress over things like making money, saving for a house, investing, or planning for retirement. Laid-back to a fault, as long as Buddy had a place to lay his head at night, work that kept him busy but not too busy, and cold beer on the weekend, the man seemed content.

Massey's dad, on the other hand, was everything opposite. Ambitious and driven, he'd whipped the F&A crop dusting business into the financial success it was today, along with having a huge wheat farm and cattle operation, and a political career besides. It was Kip who had encouraged Buddy to collect his only child after he'd gotten wind of her existence. Which had been a good thing for both Mony and Buddy, having Kip looking out for them all these years. Massey knew Mony loved and respected Kip with her whole heart. That didn't change the fact that he could still scare the crap out of her from time to time.

They reached Massey's satellite office on Airport Drive and walked inside. Mony stifled a yawn, and Kip asked Massey's secretary to bring in some breakfast food and put on a pot of coffee.

"You don't have to fuss, water's fine," Mony said with another yawn.

"Are you all right, Mony? You look a little flushed." Massey reached to press the back of his hand to her forehead. She paled. *If she makes it through the next fifteen minutes, it would be nothing short of a miracle.* Massey could sense she was hiding something, and he wondered if it had anything to do with her just-fucked hair and matching body cologne.

"Overtired, I guess. I never sleep well on the train. I'll be fine after a good night's sleep."

Massey gave her a skeptical look, but kept his thoughts to himself. Now wasn't the time or place.

"Can we get down to it, please?" Kip interrupted. "I have a two o'clock meeting at the bank and no time to dawdle."

Mony crinkled her forehead. "So what's the big deal?"

"Did you bring the papers I asked for, Mony?"

She nodded and asked Massey to hand her the satchel. He did.

All eyes were trained on the manila envelope Mony set on the table. Massey recalled the story behind the contents, which were acquired during an impromptu visit shortly after Mony's husband had died. Between the venison steaks she'd grilled that night for dinner and dessert, Massey, Buddy, and Mony had gathered around the kitchen table, where Buddy had announced he needed to talk over *business*.

The news of his cancer had hit her hard, but when Mony learned that the entire Ferguson family had known about the diagnosis months before she knew, she'd been outright pissed. As Buddy rolled out his options, which were palliative at that point, Mony launched into a barrage of questions, insisting that he seek a second opinion and try experimental treatments. The severity of his prognosis shouldn't have surprised her. He'd ignored all the early warning signs and had been well past any sort of chance for treatment. So soon after her own cancer scare and losing her husband, Mony faced losing her dad. She had barely recovered from the shock when Buddy dropped the second bomb, which had brought her to her knees.

The document in the envelope was the first time Buddy Altman had ever planned anything. On the threshold of becoming the heir to her father's fortune, October 2013, fifty-three years after her birth, Mony became legally recognized for what she and everyone had known from the moment she came to live with Buddy. She became Ramona Louise Brady-Altman Strong.

"Mony, you're about to step into a shitstorm," Massey said in a solemn voice, "and Dad and I want you to be prepared for what you'll be up against."

Mony lifted her gaze from the envelope. "Jesus, Massey, is something wrong?"

"No," he said, too quickly. "It's just with this crazy oil boom, everyone is trying to seize up whatever they think might be considered unclaimed mineral rights."

"I don't know what you're talking about. Why would anyone think Dad's land is up for grabs?"

Massey shook his head. "Your dad's land isn't up for grabs. It's just that he's amassed a considerable amount of it, and things being what they are in North Dakota we want you to be prepared."

Mony pursed her lips. "Christ, Massey, I know I haven't lived here for a while, but I haven't been living under a rock either. I know goddamn well Dad and Kip have made several land purchases over the years, and I know the land isn't worth a plugged nickel if the mineral rights aren't attached to it." She got up from her chair.

"Sit down, Mony," Kip said. "We're not done talking."

Mony crossed her arms and remained standing. "So what's the shitstorm? I know it's not the farmland that's valued; it's what lies beneath the bedrock. I know Dad owns two producing oil wells. I remember Kip and Dad hooting and hollering in the farmyard covered in oil after his first strike. He has a burn scar on his left arm from the blast. Are you saying Dad doesn't have the mineral rights?"

Massey cleared his voice. "Mony, there are several oil companies that have been wanting to buy out your dad for years. With Buddy's passing, they're all thinking his land is up for grabs, because—"

Kip cut in. "They know I'm his business partner, but they don't know there is an heiress to his estate."

"There are a couple of companies that want to make a play for the mineral rights," Massey said, "lock, stock, and literal barrels."

"Wait, wait, what are you saying?" Mony turned her focus on Kip. "You're Dad's partner, how in the hell can they take anything?"

"I control what I own. I would have to buy out Buddy's shares the same as anyone else. Only an heir would be able to assume the property and mineral rights outright. Massey has been managing your father's affairs for twenty-five years now and knows all the details of your father's final will and testament."

Mony stared at Massey. "So how much land are we talking about, and are the mineral rights attached?"

"As you know, the original farmstead had been about 880 acres, give or take," Massey said. "Some of it tillable, but a lot of it bordered the wildlife management area and was considered wetland, unsuitable for agricultural use. That made it public domain. But after a series of droughts, a bunch of area farmers had gone bust trying to drill on it in the late Seventies, early Eighties. Buddy and Dad bought up the land in bits and parcels surrounding the management area. Since no one had found any oil beneath it, it was considered worthless, and let him have it for cheap, until Buddy struck oil a second time in the nineties. But by then, F&A Inc.—"

"You're stonewalling, Massey," Mony snapped. "How much land?"

"Now remember," Massey cautioned, "this is what—"

Mony rolled her eyes in exasperation. "How much?"

Massey exhaled. "Your dad's share equals around fifteen thousand acres in all, excluding the original 880-acre farmstead."

Mony lowered into the chair. "Holy hell, Massey, what did he need with all that land?" She threw up her hands. "And how is it that no one knows about me? I lived here for over a decade. Everybody knows I'm Buddy's daughter."

Kip didn't answer and kept his eyes trained on Massey.

"Mony, there's more."

"What do you mean, there's more?"

"Settle down," Kip cut in. "They're only looking for next of kin on paper. A paper that, up until two months ago, didn't even exist. You're still Ramona Louise Brady-Strong in the local public court records for right now. You have to file the papers in that envelope to legally prove you are the heir."

"But—" Mony stammered, her voice rising an octave beyond its alto range. "My God, wouldn't they have asked around? For crying out loud, I went to high school here.

Buddy's little blonde bomber, remember?"

Massey's jaw clenched. *Too soon.* The approach to this conversation was all wrong. He tried reaching for Mony's hand, but she jerked away.

"And I will not settle down." She ran her fingers through her hair. "You're telling me I have to prove Dad is my dad, that he owned over twenty square miles of land, yet you won't tell me if he owned the mineral rights. How is that supposed to make me calm?"

He was losing her. He'd seen it a million times before, the last gasp of adrenaline before a person overwhelmed folded in on themselves in self-preservation. "Mony," Massey said softly. "You know how people are around here. They don't let strangers in, and they don't give away information. No one wants to reveal you're Buddy's daughter unless absolutely necessary. Keeping you a secret, well, it's like giving a middle finger to the big oil companies." He paused to see if she was listening; she was. "Buddy and Dad are the last family-owned oil operation in the state, maybe the whole country. This is a point of pride for our community, as well as goddamn self-preservation."

Kip nodded in agreement.

"Buddy and Dad have reinvested a lot of money back into the town of Williston and William County, and people here don't forget a good deed. They don't turn their backs on their own, either. This is your land, our land. They understand, the minute those other conglomerates find out about you, they will be on you like stink on shit trying to force you to sell."

"I get it, Massey, really I do," Mony said in a weary voice. "I've been dealing with that myself, with the farm. It's just . . ." She lifted her shoulder in an awkward shrug. "It's just hard to believe that, you know, no one's let it slip."

Here, Kip cut in. "We need to get the paperwork filed before the reading of the will, making your claim part of the public record."

Massey watched Mony's head nod inattentively as Kip rambled on about legalities. Eventually he got to where Mony came in, needing to show "active use" of the land.

"Stop, just stop right there."

Kip stared at her, not used to having his authority challenged.

"Look, Kip, I trust you'll see to it that my rights are protected. But I can't think about drilling right now. I've come home to bury my dad." She seemed bolstered, saying this aloud. "Besides, I thought you just said if there was an heir, they didn't have any right to anything except to pressure me to sell. I have no idea what kind of cash flow is required to drill in the first place. Would we have the resources?"

A triumphant smile whispered across Kip's lips, and Mony cringed. *She walked right into that ambush,* Massey thought. Mony must have sensed it too, because her expression turned grim.

"You may as well tell her everything," Kip instructed. "Just get it all out on the table, Matthew."

Massey sighed. "Dad has done a geological search, and there is oil located on the back four-forty parcel, where the Ferguson and Altman properties are joined."

Mony nodded her head. "I know of it."

"During the search, I tried to track down the title and the deed, as well as whether or not the mineral rights are still intact. This is important, since this parcel of land had been acquired after your dad's original land purchase, and the true ownership seems to vacillate between the state wetland management area and Buddy. Originally, it may have been a piece of the wetland management, and up until a few years ago, your dad had always planted on that back forty. I'm still working on this information."

Mony placed an elbow on the table and rested her forehead in the palm of her hand. Absently, she began rubbing her scalp with her fingers.

"It's a deep vein, and could be very expensive to get at. But you hold the key, a potential economical solution. You are aware of hydrofracking."

Her body stiffened. "Excuse me." Mony stood and left abruptly.

Massey had seen it coming, and directed her to his private washroom. She'd just made it to the toilet when she bent over and began to vomit. When he was certain she'd finished, Massey handed her a washcloth for her face, then helped her back to his office. He sat her on the couch; within a few seconds she was out cold.

Massey and his dad sat quiet for a long while; the only sound between them was Mony's soft snores. Massey had grown accustomed to this form of communication with his father, but it was Kip who finally broke the silence.

"She needs to trust us, and to trust, she needs to know

the truth," he said, reaching for the cola bottle on the table. He took a swallow, then crinkled his nose and checked the label. He set it down. "Better she hears it from us than some son of a bitch as soon as she got off the train."

Massey didn't disagree; it was the approach that troubled him. "We don't even know for sure that her identity is still a secret," he said, disheartened. "She's been through too much already today, Dad. She doesn't even have Bob to talk—"

"Bob," Kip scoffed. "Bob was a good shot with a rifle, and knew his way around a furnace and a hot water heater, but he couldn't find his way out of a wet paper bag if you showed him the opening. If you ask me"—he jerked his chin toward Mony—"she was the brains of that operation."

"Dad, she's alone," Massey defended.

"She's not alone. She has family. We're that family. Mony understands this, and she's stronger than you're giving her credit for."

Massey didn't want an argument now. There had been way more to Robert Strong than his dad would ever give the man credit for, dead or alive, but it would serve no benefit trying to change Kip's opinion on that issue. "She's been gone for almost thirty years—has her own place, business, the kids, a life she's built far away from here."

"You'd rather she'd be fielding the harassing phone calls and intrusions by herself?" Kip retorted. "Shit, I'd no sooner received the call from your brother that Buddy had died when I got my first harassing call. Phone's been ringing nonstop ever since."

Massey pinched the bridge of his nose, tuning out his father. Why was he even bothering to explain? His old man had it all planned in his head, and was just getting started. He cut him off anyway. "She can't do anything until probate review is complete. Besides, what if she doesn't want this? Did you ever think of that? It was the fracking that did her in," Massey said, suppressing his anger. "You know that, don't you."

It wasn't a question.

Kip pointed a thick finger at Mony. "That woman sleeping right there is sitting on more wealth and resources than one person should be allowed in two lifetimes. A little fracking to get a couple of wells drilled won't destroy the entire Mississippi River Valley. We just need enough to get the job done."

"And just how much is enough, Dad?"

Kip finished the rest of the flat soda sitting on the table, scowled, and looked at his son. "When I say it is."

time in a long while had left John feeling satisfied lying beside the warmth of a woman's body. Making no long-term demands, she had taken nothing from him, except maybe a bit of his heart.

The depot was dead as a doornail. Aside from a TV mounted in a corner of the room streaming the Weather Channel and a clicking sound behind the closed service window, the lobby was void of travelers. Franklin had said there'd be a driver there to pick him up. So, where the hell was he? Then John remembered, *What a dumbass*. He'd been the last one off the train and headed out toward the parking lot. When no one was standing outside holding up a sign with his name on it, John considered hailing a cab, then noticed there were none. The parking lot was completely empty aside from a couple of trucks idling at the far end of the lot. He pulled out his smartphone and scrolled through the itinerary.

The link indicated he was staying at a hotel called the Prairie View Inn, wherever that was, and he reached into his other pocket to fish out a pack of cigarettes. John had never considered himself a nicotine addict, though he indulged in the habit in moments such as this. Lighting up, he took a long, satisfying drag and looked out toward the town of Williston, North Dakota. He despised the place instantly. Just up the rise from the station, he could see a cocktail lounge and an adjoining business called Homewreckers. It sounded like a strip joint. A gust of wind swept down the rise and it made him shiver. *You need to get a grip*, he scolded himself again. *She's gone, and there's not a damn thing you can do about it.* All that was left

CHAPTER 9

JOHN

The last one off the train, John disembarked feeling a heavy weight of disappointment. After an hour searching on his own, he still hadn't been able to find her. The attendant he'd slipped money to turned out to be a poor investment, choosing to assist a handicapped woman off the train instead of searching for Ramona. He couldn't blame the guy. He was only doing his job. Besides, it had to look scandalous when John wasn't even able to tell the attendant her last name. *Why did she have to leave like that?* He'd have considered it all a dream had it not been for the light scent of lavender still clinging to his scarf.

A nasty wind whipped at the bottom of his wool coat. Cold and tired, John reached down for the luggage at his feet and trudged toward the depot. *Get a grip, man, you don't even know her. For Christ sakes, she could have robbed you blind.* But that felt empty; it wasn't just a random sex partner this time, at least not for him. They'd connected on some level, an intimate connection that for the first

From that day forward, Jason proclaimed John his lucky charm and became his ward, so to speak. Jason's father retained John's providential talents by providing the necessary resources to keep his loyalty. He should have walked away long ago, but the money had been too good to pass up.

"What's the matter, Johnny boy?" Jason slurred through some spittle. "You homesick?"

Clenching his fists at his side, John knew he'd regret anything that came out of his mouth and chose not to respond.

"This will all be over in time to get back home for Christmas," Jason went on with a flick of his wrist. "Which, by the way, I'll be spending with my family in the Cayman Islands." He sloshed his beer can toward John. "You're invited of course." He gave a loud belch.

John edged closer to his door. "You're not going to be sick, are you?"

Jason banged his head against the side window. "No, no, I've got it all under control."

That was doubtful.

John was relieved when the sign for the Prairie View Inn came into view, but as they pulled into the driveway, his heart sank. It wasn't very impressive. Hell, it didn't even have a canopy for drop-offs and pickups despite being rated the best and newest accommodations in town. The driver parked out front, and John quickly exited the vehicle, anxious to distance himself from Jason. Collecting his bags before the driver had a chance to set them on the ground, he made a dash for the door. He searched for the automatic door opener to no avail and wrestled his luggage through the double set of doors, reminding him how much he hated business travel. He checked in and went straight to his room.

Kicking out of his shoes, John flopped onto the bed and stared up at the ceiling. *Babysitting.* So much for sucking it up, sticking to a plan, making an offer, winning the bid, and closing the deal. He was never going to get the fuck out of this frozen hellhole and back to the civilized world.

he been told? Old man Monroe would have been the one to send the little prick. The dumb son of a bitch. What was he thinking? John felt the making of a trainwreck coming on and took another swallow of whiskey when an image of Ramona drifted in his mind.

She was lying naked on the bed in front of him, her hand splayed across her belly. "We all have scars, angel," she said, echoing his words back to him. He felt the squeeze of her greedy sex engulfing his dick as she wrapped her legs around him and—

"Did you hear me?" Jason sputtered. "I've checked out this Ferguson's liquid assets. There's no way he'll be able to buy up the mineral rights."

John jerked away from the memory. "Yeah, man, it's a slam dunk."

Jason Monroe was not what most people envisioned when they thought about a Texas oilman. A sawed-off runt with a stocky build and shifty eyes, he stood first in line as heir to the Monroe Oil Company fortune based out of Houston, Texas. He had no neck to speak of, his melon just sitting there propped between his shoulders. With an impetuous personality and a cocky smile to match, you immediately distrusted the guy. He was a spoiled, rich little bastard, whose arrogance had an uncanny knack for trouble. John recalled the night they'd met, when he'd bailed Jason out of jail after a "mishap" with some underage girls. Jason had narrowly dodged the rape and molestation allegations, due in part to the mysterious gringo who fronted the money in order to satisfy the terms of the original financial transaction, plus a sizable amount of money to make the young sex slaves disappear.

"It's not even noon yet, man," he remarked, pointing to the beer; then he considered his options. "If it's going to be that kind of day, you'd better give me one too."

The driver jumped behind the wheel and pulled out of the parking lot. Jason reached into the cooler next to his feet and snatched a beer. Flashing a shit-eating grin, he shook the can and tossed it to John.

John held the can out at arm's length toward Jason, cracked the tab with a flourish, and reached over to clank their cans together. "Here's to heated vehicles, cold beer, land for the taking, and money for the making." He tossed back the beer, suds and all.

Not to be outdone, Jason said with arrogance, "I'll do you one better." He reached into his jacket pocket, retrieving an expensive bottle of whiskey. He held it up. "Here's to stupid hick bastards dying with no succession plan, leaving the richest motherfuckin' oil field in the world up for grabs." He sing-songed the last part and took a long pull from the bottle.

"To the highest bidder, of course," John muttered.

Jason leaned forward, oblivious to the remarks. "I'm going to put Monroe Oil Company right up there with Exxon and Chevron." He held the liquor bottle in salute. "This will be my legacy. You and me, Johnny boy, we'll never have to work another day for the rest of our lives." He took another gulp of liquor and handed it to John.

John took a drink from the offered bottle and stared out the tinted window. He needed to clear his head and focus. He needed to think. The first order of business was to find out what the hell Jason was doing here, and why hadn't

CHAPTER 10

NATE

Nate felt her gaze at his back and looked up at the second-story window to see Mony watching him. He imagined the sight he must have presented, wearing his old parka and bright snowmobile gloves emblazoned with Arctic Cat trademark colors. On his head, he wore a blaze-orange Mad Bomber hat with the fur-lined flaps pulled down over his ears. She laughed.

Ramona Louise Brady-Strong. There were no words in the English language, or any language for that matter, that could accuracy describe what she meant to him. In his mind's eye, he could still see the youthful girl whose long, blonde hair turned white in the summer sun as she stood on the raft in a polka-dot bikini down by the lake. Her hair was auburn now, short, with a touch of gray that accented the wisdom in her hazel eyes. Those eyes paired with a knowing smile had seen their share of hardship, and pain, and survived.

She'd always managed to stay healthy and fit, though she didn't look it at present. Her cancer scare along with the recent death of her husband had taken its toll. But he knew his Mony—knew that whatever life threw at her, she would withstand the fire and rise from the ashes, stronger, wiser. He knew the woman cold, but then, Mony Strong could say the same about him. It had been that way between them forever, preordained from the time they'd met.

She came up from behind and smacked him between his shoulder blades. "Lift with your legs, man, not with your back," Mony scolded as he struggled with a heavy bag. It made him cough.

"Bring half of your house with you in these bags? I know you're high maintenance, Mony, but jeez, there's a limit, even for you." He clutched his lower back to exemplify his injury and tried to straighten.

Mony rolled her eyes at the theatrics. "I brought you a special treat from Schell's, Leinenkugel's, and New Glarus."

"Schmaltz Alt?" he asked with a hopeful gleam. Nate loved trying the new beers Mony brought with her whenever she came back home. Sharing in Minnesota and Wisconsin's finest specialty beers was just one of the many simple pleasures they had in common.

"No, but I—"

"Christ, Mony, will you get a coat on?" Kip barked and thrust out her long wool coat, holding it open. Mony reached to take it, and he shoved a sleeve over her extended arm. "Here's my scarf. This will hold you until you get to the farm." Before she could protest, Kip had wrapped it around her neck and tucked the ends into the open V of her jacket. The gesture made her smile.

"I don't know what you're grinning at. People lose tips of ears and digits running around dressed like that." Kip glanced down at her feet. "At least you're wearing sensible boots." His lumbered off toward his candy-apple red Ford F-150 with Eco Boost and said over his shoulder, "I'm going to get this processed." He held up the envelope that contained the paperwork for Mony's name change. "I hope you don't mind."

They both knew darn well it didn't matter what she thought, Kip was going to do it anyway. She looked like she was about to be angry with him, then must have thought better of it. Mony could never stay angry at Kip long, assuming his old man had her best interest at heart. Nate had his doubts.

The two stood quiet as they watched Kip drive off. Nate suspected his old man was probably pissed Massey had asked him to drive Mony out to the farm. He tried not to read into it, but it was hard not to. His dad always seemed to find fault with the choices he'd made, as if his life were any of the old man's goddamn business. Kip's truck rounded the corner out of sight, and Nate felt the tension leave his shoulders. He looked at Mony. "Let's finish loading."

They set the bag down behind his two-tone jade colored 1978 Ford F-150. Mony heckled. "My God, man, you're still driving that old thing?"

Nate ignored the dig and unlatched the end gate, sending a trickle of rust floating toward the snowy ground. He pivoted to face her, his hand over his heart.

"You wound me with your scorn, woman. This old girl and I have seen a lot over the years. Am I supposed to just dump her because she's old?" He stroked his hand across the end gate. "There, there, my sweet, don't listen to her. She's just jealous."

"Oh for Christ sakes, Nate, if that old girl could talk—"

Nate interrupted. "If this old girl could talk, I'd be rotting in the county lock-up," he said, snorting. "But we don't have time to talk about that now." Sweeping his arm, he gestured toward the cab. "Come on. Let's get you home."

Backing out of the parking stall, Nate dropped the shift into low gear. He punched the throttle, setting the rear tires spinning. "Besides," he said as he cranked the steering wheel, "how am I supposed to spin donuts with all-wheel drive?" Nate sent the back end of the truck into a fish-tailing spin, flipping a couple of 180's before launching into a full 360 spin. He spun around twice before letting off the gas, then spun the truck in the opposite direction, sending Mony's luggage sliding all over the back of the truck bed.

"You better not have broken any beer bottles, bonehead," she shouted, shoving at his shoulder.

"Oops." Nate stopped messing around, and they both burst into laughter.

On the ride home, he filled Mony in on the latest gossip, taking care to avoid the biggest news in the area, her father's death. He told her about the newest oil strike north of Dickenson and a recent housing project that had gone up so fast, the city council was now questioning whether the building had met fire safety codes. Fast as the buildings were going up, they still weren't keeping up with the housing shortage, local investors remaining skeptical after being burned from the last boom and bust.

The recent snowstorm brought the US 85 four-lane highway project south of Williston to Watford City to a screeching halt, turning it into a frozen, muddy mess. Dwight Mitchell was off again with his on/off marriage to Mony's high school friend and college roommate Cindy Van Dyke. The Williston high school football team had a rough season and ranked last in the conference, but the hockey team was showing promise so far at two and zero early in the season. The city parks and rec men's over-forty league had begun its season as well. Nate's team, the Trouble Shooters, consisting of several of their high school friends, was seeded number one again, and expected to capture the title if everyone's knees and joints held out. Up until last week, they'd been practicing on the lake near the edge of Buddy's property. Nate broached the subject.

"If it's all right with you, me and the guys would like to get in a practice tomorrow." He turned off the main highway onto the township road, noticing his rearwheel drive faltering to gain traction. The increased traffic of the heavy oil-rigging trucks and tankers were beating the meager, low-maintenance roads to a pulp.

Mony stared pensively out the side window. "Of course, it will be fun to see everyone," she muttered. "The kids love hanging out with the gang."

Mony's kids, now there was a trio of trouble. Full of piss and vinegar much like their mother, Nate had liked them immensely. Mindy, the youngest, was a carbon copy of Mony, who'd also taken up flying. Dane, a bit quieter and contemplative, was a cracker-jack with a hockey stick. He and Grandpa Buddy had influenced Dane early on, dragging him out to the hangar while they worked on plane engines, and he had made a career out of it. Even Kit Kat, who wasn't Mony's daughter by blood, possessed tremendous creativity, and had Mony's sharp mind for business. Nate couldn't see their father's influence in any of them. But then, Nate had never really gotten to know the man either.

"We could do a bonfire," Nate said, filling the awkward silence between them. "When are the kids coming in?"

Mony turned from the window to face him. "Dane, Diana, and Mindy's flight will be in tonight. Kat's taking the red eye out of Vancouver and should be coming in sometime early tomorrow morning."

"Fantastic. I have an extra pair of skates if Dane's inclined to join us. You don't mind, do you?"

Mony shrugged. "He's a grown man; he can do what he wants. Just remember, I'm holding you responsible for any injuries."

Ah, there she is. Nate sighed inwardly. He wasn't sure what to make of this subdued version of the woman he knew. The Mony he knew was brash while being circumspect, a bit of a control freak. "It's hockey, for Christ sakes. It's not a game unless someone goes home with a bloody nose or a missing tooth."

"I have no problem with that, as long as Dane's not the one missing a tooth." She turned back toward the window.

With each mile marker closer to home, Nate felt an unwelcome anxiety radiating off Mony and tried not to read too much into it. He turned on the radio to fill the silence. She was only fooling herself if she thought she was hiding it by staring out the window.

"Would you mind picking them up, the kids I mean, from the airport?"

Her voice was so small Nate hardly recognized it. He'd expected sorrow at the loss of her dad, but not this pale, worn-down person sitting next to him. Though it had been a long while since he'd seen Mony really happy—too many losses. "Of course, what is family for?" He smiled and reached for her hand, tugging her toward him. She slid over.

"You know, you're not going to attract any women with this shaggy beard of yours," Mony teased, rubbing at the scruff on his chin. She hated it when he wore a beard. Nate draped his arm around her shoulder, and she settled in, like old times. It was hard to know how that made him feel—happy, sad, angry. Nate decided it was best not to label it for now. It felt too natural, too right to question.

Rounding the lake, her farmhouse came into view. The vista hadn't changed much. The old two-story house was the same, except the porch, which was now made of embellished composite wood and had an ornate railing spanning the front. The old wooden siding had been replaced years ago with aluminum steel. For the roof, Buddy had chosen a dazzling robin's-egg blue color, also made of steel, that looked like a big swimming pool from the air. One hundred yards from the house, a steel pole

barn had been built where the machine shed once stood
serving as a garage for Buddy's old Army jeep, his Olds
Bravada SUV, and the tractor plow. The old, rickety red
barn had long since been torn down to make room for
Buddy's beloved hangar, complete with a grass air strip
off to the west side. Mony lifted her head from his chest,
noticing the twinkling light in the kitchen window.

"Poppy's here," he said, picking up on her silent query.
He swung the truck around the circle drive and pulled up
close to the front door. Poppy stood on the porch, waiting
with outstretched arms.

"I'll take it from here," she said as they approached.

Nate knew better than to needle his stepmom in a
moment such as this. She had been stress-cooking for
the past two days and was liable to snap his head off.
He stood by the door as Poppy walked Mony over to a
waiting chair.

"There's my girl," Poppy murmured with affection and
kissed Mony on the cheek.

Patricia Marie Campbell-Ferguson, Poppy for short, cut
an imposing figure. She was a tall woman with soft, blue-
gray eyes, an aristocratic nose, and a diamond-shaped
face most women and some men had to look up to, in
more ways than one. She hadn't changed much over the
years, aside from a few gray strands in her long, dark hair,
which she maintained that Nate, Massey, and Mony had
put there. She was a handsome woman, with long legs,
broad shoulders, and curvy hips. She could have been a
model in her youth, and it was easy to see why half the
men in the county were attracted to her. But beauty was

the least remarkable thing about Poppy. Hardworking, generous, and kind, Poppy was one of the most caring people you'd ever want to know.

She'd been passing through town one hot summer day on her way to who knows where, shortly after Mony had come to live with Buddy. According to the gossip mill, she had been married to a rodeo cowboy who'd recently been killed while roping a bull. Others speculated she'd run away from an abusive drunkard and so on. Whatever her backstory, Poppy wound up staying in Williston and opened a diner on Main Street called Poppy's Place. It became an instant hit for both the cooking and the gossip. It was during that time she had also managed to attract the eye of a respectable business man with jet-black wavy hair and steel-gray eyes.

Kip Ferguson pursued Poppy for the better part of a year, dropping by the café often for lunch. They married that following summer. Even though she'd become stepmom to Massey and Nate, Poppy doted on Mony equally as much, if not more, treating her like the daughter she'd always wished she had.

"Sit down and eat, Nathan, before you go out again," Poppy instructed, and began ladling the chicken-and-dumpling soup from the big cook pot. "You don't have to worry about the guest rooms," she said to Mony, nodding at the chair across from her where she'd set Nate's bowl of soup on the table. "I've already made up the beds for the kids when they get here."

Mony paused mid-spoonful. "Thank you," she said for the benefit of both.

Poppy plunked down at the head of the table with a cup of coffee. "I can't wait to see the kids. We had so much fun when they were all home for Buddy's birthday party, didn't we?" She breathed a big sigh, remembering. She added, "Help yourselves to anything on the table. Oh, except for the pies." Poppy pointed to the corner of the table. "Those are for later."

Nate savored the aroma rising from the soup bowl, his own personal tactic to stop him from digging into the hot soup too soon. His stepmom was an amazing cook. Had it not been for Poppy, he and Buddy would have starved to death long ago. Nate didn't even possess the manly skills of the barbeque grill, nor did he care to learn.

Besides the soup, Poppy had baked goods in the oven and a fresh pot of egg coffee cooking on the stove. There were two Crockpots going, one filled with a three-bean casserole, the other containing country-style pork ribs with sauerkraut. At the far end of the counter, her famous frosted cinnamon rolls and a pan of caramel rolls with crushed pecans sat cooling, special for Mony. The corner of the table was covered with the makings for two apple pies, while a cherry and a blueberry cooled on the other side. There was her homemade plum butter setting out on the table, along with honey gathered from the bees Nate and Buddy kept. In all, it was a grand feast to be sure.

Poppy sipped her coffee. "I've called the funeral home. We decided to hold off the wake until Friday to make sure everyone's flight made it in on time."

Mony missed her cue; Nate nudged her foot under the

table. She jumped in with a delayed response. "That's fine, I'm sure everyone is grateful. I know I am," Mony said with a weary smile. "I had an awful time finding coverage at the clinic on such short notice."

Poppy's shoulders visibly relaxed. Nate knew his stepmom had been fretting over Mony's reaction to her involvement in Buddy's funeral planning.

"There wasn't much to plan," Poppy said, sounding relieved. "Buddy had everything arranged, right down to the songs for the service."

"There's a surprise," Mony said with an affectionate laugh. "Considering no one could get Dad to plan further out than Friday night, let alone his funeral. Go figure."

Nate and Poppy appreciated the irony. "Since Buddy was a veteran, Tad Jensen—you remember Tad, don't you?"

Mony nodded, grunting around a bit of her buttered bread.

"Yes, well, Tad will be heading the honor guard at the services. Buddy has been prepared for an open-casket viewing, but I think you already know he wanted to be cremated."

Nate noticed that Mony began lifting her spoon in a more robotic motion, eating out of necessity rather than pleasure.

Poppy noticed it too. "The only thing you have left to do is show up," she said in a rush. "The visitation starts at one o'clock, so you and the kids should be there around eleven-thirty for the family viewing."

"All of you will be there too, won't you?" The inflection

in Mony's voice sounded like more of a plea than a question.

Poppy got up from her chair and went to Mony. "Of course, sweetie—we're family, aren't we?" She stroked Mony's hair. "And since Buddy hadn't belonged to any church, the service will be held at the funeral home with a luncheon to follow at the VFW after the graveside service."

Mony wrapped her arms around Poppy's waist and leaned her head against her surrogate mother.

"You should know," Poppy went on, "there was quite a hubbub going on between the First Lutheran ladies' auxiliary and the Catholic council of women from Our Lady of Perpetual Sorrow over who would be providing the food for the luncheon. Leave it to Tad to settle the matter." She cleared her voice. "I've decided the Lutheran ladies will bring casseroles and bread, and the Catholic women will bring the relishes and desserts," Poppy mocked in Tad's inflections. "So problem solved. I suppose Buddy would have liked all of those women fussing over him."

"I don't know," Mony countered. "Dad didn't seem to care much about things like that."

Mony's comment had brought an unpleasant thought to mind, but the question had to be addressed. "Is your mother going to make it for the funeral service?" Poppy asked, struggling to keep his tone civil.

Mony shook her head. "I don't think so. Her husband just had a hip replacement, and I doubt he'd let Mom travel alone. She couldn't drive that far by herself anyway, neither one of them could. Plus, he's too cheap to let her fly, even though they have the money."

"I wouldn't pay those prices either," Poppy said with a hint of satisfaction in her voice. The Fergusons' strong dislike for Mony's mother wasn't any secret. They'd all considered her claims as a parent null and void the day the woman had let her husband barter Mony away like a commodity.

Finished with lunch, Nate got to his feet, eager to get the rest of Mony's things into the house. "Poppy, you're gonna have to help me with that brown bag," he said, clutching his lower back. "It's a beast."

By the time Nate and Poppy had brought in the rest of her things, Mony was gone from the kitchen. Nate carried her bags upstairs and found Mony standing in the middle of her bedroom wearing only a bathrobe. Not wanting to intrude, he stopped in the doorway. When she seemed to ignore his presence, he announced, "Got all the stuff in, your majesty," and waited for her banter. It didn't come. Nate was about to turn and walk away when he noticed her blank, catatonic expression and realized she hadn't heard him. She looked lost. Lost in a space so familiar that it hadn't changed since the day she'd left home. It killed him seeing her like that, but it wasn't his place anymore to do anything about it. That was the one thing that had changed.

Mony looked at him, then said in a lethargic response, "Thanks. You didn't happen to see my shampoo and bath wash?"

Nate rested his hands on top of the doorjamb, resisting the urge to enter. "As a matter of fact, I did," he said, leaning his body slightly past the doorframe. "I left it in the bathroom next to the tub. Oh, and I turned off the water. You were about to have a flood."

Mony tightened the sash around her waist. "I appreciate that," she said wearily, and walked toward him.

Her eyes were distant as she stepped under his arm. Nate clutched his hands on the doorframe, allowing her to pass. He wanted to take hold of her, tell her everything was going to be all right. Instead, he followed behind, watching again from doorway.

She sat down on the closed toilet seat and reached into the tub, testing the water temperature. She began loosening the sash on her bathrobe when an uncontrollable sob escaped her, and he couldn't bear it any longer. Nate entered the room and knelt on the floor in front of her.

She looked at him with tearstained eyes. "I can't believe he's gone," she murmured, and the words brought tears to his own eyes.

Nate was about to give her a hug when he felt the authoritative clutch of Poppy's hand on his shoulder, urging him aside. "I'll take it from here," she said quietly.

Nate walked from the room, stopping at the door to look one more time at the woman who'd always been so strong and defiant, sitting there broken and crying like a child. He walked away and latched the door behind him.

CHAPTER 11

MONY

She felt a weightlessness, and the troubles in her life faded away. The sensation wasn't like when she flew but more like lying on the raft out by the lake, bobbing lazily on the waves of the water's current. Transported to a billowy cloud, she lay upon its welcoming surface and felt a warmth at her back, cradled between two strong arms. Rough fingers, callused by hard work, caressed her face and combed gently through her hair. She gazed out over the sea of clouds and saw her father's plane. He flew closer, and she could see his crooked-teeth smile. He waved. She waved back, and her mind drifted to her first homecoming.

It hadn't turned out to be quite the fairytale Mony had envisioned when she'd left the airport in Minnesota. She'd known better, but still, it had been quite a shock seeing the old farmhouse for the first time. They'd landed in an airport smaller than the one she'd left. Her dad lifted her out of the plane with one arm, her worldly possessions tucked under the other. They walked over to a funny-looking vehicle with no roof or side windows that he called a Jeep. It was fun riding around at first in the warm summer sun, until they headed north out of town.

Her eyes began to dry and her lips became parched as they drove along an endless, flat road that stretched on for miles, filled with grassy prairies and huge wheat fields as far as the eye could see.

When they turned onto a gravel road, she spied the first body of water. The "lake" was nothing more than a sea of long, green weeds and looked more like a marsh back in Minnesota. They drove some more along the dirt road that seemed to lead to the middle of nowhere, then pulled onto a rutty driveway that looked like a field approach before finally reaching their destination.

There was no grove of trees, or even a shrub to distinguish it as a yard; her dad parked among a scattering of old buildings, a raggedy red barn with a roof caving in, and an empty machine shed. In the middle of all this was a broken-down windmill, missing part of its tail, which made a horrible squealing sound when it turned in the faint breeze. But it was the house that looked downright awful. It was a small, two-story structure, with whitewashed wood siding weatherbeaten by years of neglect.

As they approached the porch, she noticed the roof sagging in the middle, folding in on itself like a taco. Some of the windows were cracked or broken. When they climbed the rickety steps, an angry, buzzing sound came from the corner of the ceiling, where a huge hornet's nest protruded from one of the sconces. Her dad opened the screen door, which nearly fell onto his hand, the hinges were so rusted. He had to lift her over the threshold to get inside due to the cracks in the floorboard.

As he retrieved her suitcase, Mony studied the ominous space designated as a kitchen and noticed the cupboards were painted in the same whitewashed color as outside. Pieces of tile were either cracked or missing from the dingy, black-and-white–checkered floor. The only furnishing was a small Formica table in the corner and two mismatched, vinyl-covered chairs. She heard more angry buzzing and looked across the crimson-colored counter top, where a swarm of big black flies gathered around a greasy, cast-iron frying pan sitting on a gas-burning stove. But the worst thing was the horrible smell, which made Mony's eyes water and her nostrils burn. She'd started to sneeze and had still been sneezing when she turned to face her dad bringing in her things.

"Aw, baby." He closed the gap between them in two strides, gathering her up in his arms, and she began to cry. She curled her arms and legs around him, grateful for his protection. "I know it needs some work," he told her with an assuring smile, "but we'll make it into a home, you'll see." And they did.

Because summer was his peak busy season, her dad left with the rising sun and didn't come home until well after its shadow slipped below the horizon, leaving her alone to fend for herself. She wasn't accustomed to being on her own, but she adapted quickly and began to explore. She ventured into the attic one day, where she found a chest filled with treasures.

Her dad's steamer trunk held a plethora of memorabilia from his past, including ladies' clothing, along with a smart-looking blue uniform adorned with pretty ribbons and brass decorations. There was a Brownie camera and a box of pictures, and Tinker toys. She'd spent the day sorting the treasures, and had been wearing the hat with a satin ribbon and beaded necklace when her dad found her that evening.

Caught, she apologized and braced for the punishment that was sure to come. It never did. She told him, "I'm pretending to be Mommy." He smiled, but it didn't reach his eyes. He helped her put everything back into the trunk, telling a story behind each item. That evening during supper, he instructed her not to go into the steamer trunk anymore, saying it had been his little suitcase when he'd left home and he wasn't quite ready to share it just yet.

She had been down in the basement using the toilet one afternoon when a small salamander with pale yellow spots scurried out from under the bottom step. Screaming had no effect on the lizard, who stuck out its tongue, taunting her, then proceeded to settle on the floor space between the toilet and her route of escape. It was after dark before she heard the floorboard's creak above and the call of her dad. When he finally figured out where she was, he came bolting down the stairs, but he forgot about the low-hanging wall halfway down. He smacked square into it, falling on his back, knocking the air out of him. He cursed after catching his breath, and the lizard disappeared into a crack in the foundation. She wet the bed that night, too scared to go in the basement. Her dad ended up washing her bedding the next morning and stuffing a rock in the hole where the lizard had lived.

No longer curious to find what other creatures might be lurking in the house, Mony had turned away from exploring, tried to remember what her mother would have done all day at home, and started to clean. She must have done a good job, because her dad always rewarded her with great praise and an approving smile when he came home at night.

It went on like that, and one day she'd decided to make him dinner. Given strict orders not to use the stove, Mony could only make for him what she'd made for herself all week, a PB-and-J on white bread with a pickle, potato chips, and a Little Debbie treat on the side. It would have been a good plan, if all the food *weren't gone. Scrounging together what she could, Mony set the table and waited. It didn't take long before she was startled by the beep of a car horn. Peeking out the window, she saw a big blue car idling in the driveway.*

She had company.

Mony watched as a big, burly man stepped out of the car and started toward the porch. Her dad had warned her that it wouldn't be good for her to be found home alone, but she managed to muster enough courage to meet the man at the front door. She stepped out onto the porch, and the bees began buzzing. The man stopped at the foot of the stairs. He stared at her for a long moment before introducing himself. "My name is Kip Ferguson—where's your father?"

She was ready for that question and had concocted some weak story about how her dad was too busy to come to the door. The man named Kip didn't buy it and launched into a long, boring explanation about how he was her dad's business partner and needed to speak with him right away. Mony tuned him out, her eyes drifting over to the car, where she noticed two heads bobbing in the back seat. Ignoring the man, she went over for a closer look.

They were two boys, close to her age. One of the boys had sandy brown hair; his blue eyes were all red and swollen. He looked as though he'd been crying. The other boy had thick black hair like the man and sat with his arms crossed, staring out the opposite window. He looked as mad as Kip, and she wondered if they'd been picking on the little boy with the sandy brown hair to make him cry.

It took some finagling, but the clever man named Kip used her curiosity about the boys to make his way into the house. She was especially worried about the boy who'd been crying. Inside the kitchen, the big man looked around and frowned. When his eyes fell on the plate she'd made for her dad, he dumped the food in the trash. In a commanding voice, he announced that he would be making supper and sent the boys back out to the car to fetch a bag of groceries.

While Kip fried meat in a skillet, he gave them each a task: cleaning vegetables and setting the table. Because there were only two chairs, the black-haired boy and Kip let Mony and the sandy-haired boy eat first. Neither said a word while they ate, and they kept their eyes trained on their plates, but that was alright. By then, Mony was too hungry to talk and gobbled up everything on her plate, earning her an approving nod. The big man scowled at the sandy-haired boy, who hadn't eaten a bite.

After the kitchen chores were done, Kip had them wash while he retrieved two sleeping bags and flat pillows from the car. He sent Mony off to her room that night and had the boys sleep in a room down the hall, where he tossed the sleeping bags on the floor and closed the stairwell door without saying goodnight.

It was after sunset when the yelling began. Peering out her bedroom window, Mony spied two shadowy figures in the pale moonlight. She knew one to be her dad; the other was the big man named Kip. They were arguing. Kip shoved her dad, hard—then the fists began to fly. Terrified, Mony sprang from the floor and almost ran into the two boys who had quietly entered the room. They stood gawking at each other for a long while, before the black-haired boy took hold of her shoulder and the sandy-haired boy took her hand and held onto it tight. In mutual, silent agreement, the three sat down together on the floor in front of the window and watched the scene in the yard unfold.

Mony had never seen such violence before. Between the flashes of heat lightning, they watched as their fathers battled, as though it were a necessary thing. The whole time, the black-haired boy kept a firm grip on her shoulder and the sandy-haired boy squeezed her hand. The moon was high in the night sky before the two men's anger burned out. Then, they sat on the ground, drinking from a bottle they passed between them, behaving as if none of it had even happened.

Satisfied, the black-haired boy was the first to get up to leave— then, as if he'd just remembered something, he introduced himself. "I'm Matthew." He nodded his chin toward the other boy. "But Nate here calls me Massey. He's my little brother."

After they'd exchanged introductions, the children stood in an awkward silence for a long while. Then the boy named Massey did something very peculiar. He kissed her. Not a romantic kiss, but a quick kiss on the forehead. The kind her mother used to give her after Sir had punished her.

Mony called, "Goodnight," to him as he left the room, but the boy named Nate clung to her hand. Mony never forgot the haunted look on little Nate's face when he asked in a shy voice, "Can I sleep by you for a while?"

Mony held onto his hand and walked him over to her bed, where they crawled in together. In a tangle of arms and legs, Nate told her the story of how his mother had taken him and his brother on a trip, one his dad hadn't come with them on. They'd traveled through a place called Yellowstone, and he'd seen a great geyser called Old Faithful. His mother had been telling him they were on their way to visit her family when his dad had caught up with them. Nate began to cry when his dad wouldn't explain why he wouldn't let him or Massey go with her. His dad took him away from her, and his brother followed. They left her crying in that dusty little town. Through his sniffles, Nate told of how he'd begged his dad to go back for her, but he wouldn't listen. Massey had told him to keep quiet, and finally he did. In a hushed voice, Nate confessed he was afraid of his dad, but his brother told him he was just being silly. They drove night and day before coming to Mony's house, stopping only for groceries, gas, and bathroom breaks.

All this felt familiar to Mony—she held him tight, despite the heat, until they fell asleep. Sometime early the next morning, the rains finally came, and Mony and Nate woke to find Massey lying on the sleeping bags next to the bed, where they all watched the storm together.

A gentle breeze of warmth kissed Mony's temple and a whispered voice spoke softly next to her ear. "I love you, my sweet Mony. Don't you know? I will always love you." She felt a single raindrop fall upon her cheek. It was a dream, a sweet and wonderful dream.

CHAPTER 12

JOHN

The squeaking wheel of the utility cart roused him from his sleep, followed by a sharp rap at the door.

"Housekeeping."

John looked at his watch. "Shit." It was nearly seven o'clock. He never slept that late, even on a Sunday. Peeling out of his clothes, he quickly unpacked the luggage bag he'd tossed haphazardly in the corner, then stumbled around looking for his garment bag. Finding it halfway under the table, he picked it up, stowed it in the closet, then grabbed his shaving kit and headed toward the feeble-looking shower. Uncertain what the day had in store, John dressed for business in a solid black suit, with a white shirt and black tie. Sitting on the bed, he picked up the shoe closest to him lying the floor.

"Fuck my life."

The leather shoes he'd worn were cold and wet. John walked over to the radiator, cranking the fan on full heat, and set both shoes laces-down onto the vents. He'd padded in socks over to the desk and powered up his electronic tablet when his cellphone rang. He answered in a clipped voice, "Finch."

"John, is that you?" The deep Southern-gentleman voice resonated in the receiver. "This is Monroe, Thomas Monroe. Can you talk?"

Knowing damn well it didn't matter either way, John shifted from clipped to cordial. "Yes, Mr. Monroe, of course! How can I help you, sir?" He felt the palm of his hands begin to perspire. *This can't be good.*

"Tom, please," Monroe automatically corrected him. "Have you arrived in Williston yet? I haven't heard from Jason in almost forty-eight hours. I'm very concerned."

John noted the mild irritation in Monroe's voice and rubbed at the stubble on his face. He'd forgotten to shave. *Christ, already off my game.* Choosing his next words carefully, John hoped the boldfaced lie he was about to tell would land. "Yes, I'm here. As a matter of fact, Jason and I had a meeting yesterday afternoon to do some preliminary planning."

Monroe made a sound of relief. "Good, I'm glad to hear it, John. Take care of this deal. We're in a good position with the competing oil companies, and we want to get a decent price before the international companies find out about it. I sent Jason ahead to do some local PR. I hope you don't mind. Did he say if he'd met with Senator Ferguson yet?"

John failed to hide his contempt. "You sent Jason for that?"

Monroe heard it. "Why, is there a problem?"

For such a successful businessman, Monroe sure could be

a moron when it came to family matters. John replied with equally forced calm. "No problem, just trying to get a handle on things."

Thomas Monroe launched into his standard lecture. "We need to give Jason an opportunity to estab—" There was a sharp rap at the door, the sound like nails on a chalkboard. John clinched his teeth and crossed the small floor. He opened the door a crack, half expecting to see the housekeeper. Ready to launch into a rant, he stopped short when he saw Jason leaning insolently on the doorjamb.

Wearing the oversized Columbia parka and bright-colored ski cap from the day before, Jason hissed, "Let's go, man." He jabbed a finger at his watch. "I want breakfast." He noticed the phone next to John's ear. "Who's on the phone?"

Dropping the phone behind his back, John mouthed, "Your old man." Jason rolled his eyes.

"John, John, you still there?" the muffled voice demanded from behind John's back.

He stepped away from the door, letting it slide shut with a loud click.

"Yeah, Tom, must be a weak signal," John murmured, putting the phone back to his ear. "Jason and I are finishing breakfast now and on our way to the office." Jason began pounding his fist on the door. John moved further away and decided that when he got off the phone, he was going to strangle the little prick.

"Well why didn't you say so in the first place?" Monroe Senior chastised in a voice full of mixed relief and impatience.

"Yes, well, Jason's—" The room phone started ringing. John fumbled with his cell, gritting his teeth audibly. "Jason's on the phone with Senator Ferguson's secretary right now," he lied. "We didn't want to get your hopes up until—" John rubbed his thumb over the receiver. "Okay. Jason tells me we should know shortly what time the meeting is scheduled and we can begin informal negotiations."

He heard the tremulous clinking of crystal in the background and the familiar sound of liquid being poured into a glass. "Good. Not too unofficial," Monroe Senior cajoled with a humorless laugh. "I knew Jason would get the job done." He cleared his throat with a smoker's hack before he continued. "Ferguson is the key, John, and from what I hear, he's a tough nut to crack. Looks out for the welfare of his state and all that."

The pounding at the door resumed.

"Yes sir," John agreed.

They ended the call, and John exhaled in exasperation, having just had his suspicions confirmed. *Babysitting. Fuck.* The pounding persisted.

"Shit, I'm coming," John yelled. He grabbed his briefcase and reluctantly donned his soggy shoes before unbolting the door.

They made their way through the hallway into the narrow stairwell, where Jason barged in front of John like a ten-year-old bully. They were descending the stairs when Jason turned and said, "I know this great place that serves prime rib with their eggs for breakfast." John couldn't have cared less.

Once seated in the SUV, Jason looked down at John's shoes and laughed. "You're going to need warmer footwear for what I have planned today. Maybe we can stop at Walmart and buy you some boots or something."

John's feet were already freezing. "Yeah," he muttered, the *duh* implied, but his thoughts were preoccupied with more important matters. Old Man Monroe had made his expectations clear and was annoyed by the fact that he'd already lost two days. He needed to meet with Senator Ferguson, and it had to be today. Gathering a feel for what trouble Jason may have already started, John said with nonchalance, "I understand Senator Ferguson's office is not far from your satellite office."

Ignoring the question, Jason said, "Doesn't it snow in Chicago, John? Last time I looked, it was part of the Upper Midwest. You're likely to lose a toe or something before this is all over." He tisked as if he'd proven himself to be some sort of winter-wear expert.

"We need to make an appointment with Senator Ferguson. Today," John persisted. "The man holds the key to acquiring Altman's land. I've been going over the—"

"Yeah, yeah." Jason waved an impatient hand. "My old man's already given me the lecture. I have one set up for later this afternoon."

John's brows shot up in disbelief. "You've already scheduled an appointment with the Senator?"

"Of course," Jason retorted with an air of indignation. "You and the old man are both alike, always underestimating me."

Irritated, John said, "Why didn't you say something right away?"

"What, and miss the stupid expression on your face, Johnny boy?" Jason gave John a menacing glare. "I told you yesterday that I have it all under control."

It sounded like a load of crap, but John had no choice but to believe him for now.

They exited the SUV and shoved through the oak double doors. The Blarney Stone, it turned out, was a pub and grill. John and Jason walked through the vestibule, bombarded by hundreds of twinkling green Christmas lights. John was sure it was probably the norm, minus the balsam fir Christmas tree that stood festively decorated in the corner of a small performance stage next to a magnificent baby grand piano. There was a gas fireplace burning merrily in the center of the room, with a sitting area comprised of a grouping of old chairs and a sofa surrounding a low table and lending a sort of coffee-shop ambiance. Except for a couple of old farmers in bomber jackets at the end of the bar, the joint was empty.

A friendly female bartender with flaming red, bushy hair, emerald eyes, and a pale, freckled face sashayed to the counter with menus. She leaned her arms on the countertop, accentuating her voluptuous bosom. "What'll it be, gentlemen?"

Jason's gaze slid over her chest; he handed back the menu. "I already know what I want," he said suggestively. The bartender reached to retrieve the menu, but Jason held onto it and leaned his forearm against the counter as if to impart a secret. He lifted his gaze from her chest. "I'll have coffee, cream, and sugar if you have it."

"Of course," she responded without inflection.

Jason deliberated a bit more, then placed his order. "I'll have the breakfast special. Prime rib and eggs, meat well done." He gave her a wink.

The redhead all but rolled her eyes. "And your eggs?"

Jason made a slow circular motion with his finger on the bar top. "Why, sunny side up, of course. I love piercing those little yellow bulbs and smearing that yolk all over my meat."

One of the farmers choked on his coffee, and the redhead used the diversion to turn her attention to John. "And for you, sir?"

John had been so caught up in Jason's disturbing stupidity that he hadn't even looked at the menu. Jason leaned both elbows on the counter and rested his chin in his hands. The smug expression on his face was impossible to ignore. Aware that if he ordered anything but burnt for his steak in front of the Texan he'd never hear the end of it, he thought, *Screw it.* "I'd like a bowl of oatmeal, no sugar or milk, a piece of fruit if you have it, and coffee—black, please," John said.

"Okay, coming right up." The bartender reached behind to the back counter and grabbed two coffee mugs with one hand, then sauntered over to the coffee station. After pouring the steaming hot liquid from the metal pot, she reached below the counter and retrieved a glass silo sugar container with a handful of nondairy creamers. She set cream and sugar in front of Jason, then strolled back to the kitchen.

They drank their coffee in silence, which was fine by John. Except for the game show on the TV mounted in the corner behind the bar, the place was relatively quiet, and he relished the peaceful atmosphere. Sipping at his coffee, which was actually very good, he almost felt for the first time since he'd arrived that he hadn't just stepped into an ambush.

"Listen," Jason blurted, shattering John's tranquil mood. "I want to show you an aerial view of the property. I've scheduled a chopper to take us over around one o'clock."

John crooked an eyebrow. "I thought you said we had an appointment with the Senator this afternoon. Won't that be cutting it kind of close?"

Jason poured sugar into his coffee. "It'll be fine. He can wait a few goddamn minutes if were running late," he said flippantly. "It's just a formality anyway." Jason set the sugar down and rubbed his hands together. "This is going to be fantastic. There's a couple of buildings and an old farmhouse standing in our way, but it's nothing a bulldozer can't handle. Our surveyors tell us it's the perfect spot for drilling."

An awkward stillness fell on the little pub and an unsettled feeling began gnawing in John's gut. Out of the corner of his eye, he gave a quick glance at the two elderly gentlemen sitting at the end of the bar, their attention on the game show as they sat and drank their coffee. A sense of foreboding pricked at the back of his neck. This was neither the time nor the place to be having this discussion. John tried to steer the conversation away from the topic, but Jason kept on rambling.

"There's a swamp nearby, but I don't think it will be much of a problem. Maybe we can use the sand for hydrofracking."

John breathed a sigh of relief when the bartender approached, carrying their plates of food. Placing them on the counter, she set the overcooked steak with its ribbon of crispy animal fat to Jason's right and the platter of hash browns swimming in a pool of melted cheese and sour cream between them. Misinterpreting John's expression, the bartender said, "Just in case you wanted to share."

Jason scowled and slid the platter closer to him. "Not on your life." He dumped his eggs on top of the potato-and-onion concoction, then plunged his fork into the center, shoveling a heap into his mouth. The bartender set John's food down next. "Bon appetit, boys."

They remained silent for most of the meal. The bartender checked on them from time to time, topping off their coffees. When they finished, she set their separate tabs in front of them. Jason snatched up both slips and slapped down his credit card. "My treat, Johnny boy."

John let him pay. It didn't matter one way or the other, and if Jason thought his self-exalting tactics would impress the redhead, so be it.

The bartender returned with his credit card receipt, handed it to Jason, and looked at John. "There's a local cover band playing here tonight," she said casually. "They're pretty good and play a fun mix of '50s–'90s rock, pop, and some country, if you're interested. We'll have two-for-one beers and rail drinks all night. Check it out if you're around." She gave him a wink and started clearing the dishes.

Jason signed off on the receipt and threw a twenty on the counter. "That sounds great, sweetie, we'll check it out." He turned to John. "Come on, lover boy," he said with a hint of venom. "Let's get you some boots."

As the SUV pulled away from the curb, the bartender walked over to the two old men with a fresh pot of coffee. She canted her head, lifting the pot in silent inquiry.

"That's enough for me, Shannon, thanks," Kip said, placing his hand over the cup.

Turning to the other gentleman, she said, "Sheriff?" Sheriff Wagner shook his head, and Shannon McDonald reached into her pocket. She handed the receipt to Kip.

"Thanks, Shannon," he said and donned his reading glasses, examining the slip.

Propping her elbows on the counter, Shannon sipped at her coffee and asked, "Who is he?"

Kip scrubbed his fingers across his chin. "Jason Monroe. So, the old man sent his smartass son to do the job." He handed the receipt to the sheriff, who gave it a quick glance and returned it to Shannon.

"Who's the other fellow with him?" the sheriff asked.

"I got a good look at his driver's license," Shannon chimed in. "His name is John Finch. Address says he's from Chicago. Do you think he's going to be trouble?"

Kip's eyes narrowed. "Maybe. He seems to have more

sense, that's for certain. Not sure if he holds any power though. I'll have Matthew check him out."

"What do you want me to do about them flying out to the farm?" the sheriff asked.

"Let them," Kip said with an unconcerned air. "So long as they don't land. I seem to recall the Trouble Shooters hockey team has a scheduled practice on the lake this afternoon."

CHAPTER 13

MONY

Mony blinked at her surroundings. She remembered now—felt the feather mattress at her back and recognized her room. *How had she gotten into bed last night?* The last wakeful thing she recalled was taking a bath, then having the sweetest dream. She'd felt the sensation of two strong arms wrapping around her, making her feel wanted and protected. Thoughts of her dad had always made her feel that way: safe, warm, loved. And there was Nate. She hadn't thought about the day they'd met for a long, long while. He'd been so sweet as a boy, needy and vulnerable, but then so had she. Mony cleared her thoughts, stretched her arms over her head, and yawned. Judging from the light pouring in through the window, it had to be at least eight o'clock, which meant her kids were already there.

She slid her feet to the floor and was surprised at the feel of her moccasins waiting next to the bed. *Poppy.* Slipping into them, Mony walked to the cedar chest where her fleecy robe had also been laid out and slipped it on. Looking out the window off in the distance, she noticed a small group of people hard at work clearing snow down by the lake. Smoke spewed from the chimney of the warming house, which was more like a lake home, and a dozen or so snowmobiles along with a couple of trucks were parked by the shore. She recognized one of the snowmobiles: a beautiful black and green 2009 Arctic Cat XF 1100 Turbo LXR Crossover, one of the fastest machines in the world. Nate strolled over to it, decked out in his trademark racing jacket, a female figure bouncing alongside him.

He mounted the snowmobile as the female straddled the seat behind him. He turned to face her, and she gripped her arms around his waist. Mony could hear the roar of the machine through the closed window as they sped off toward the airstrip. When Nate reached the open runway, he let out the throttle and machine lurched forward like a runner out of a starting block. In her mind's eye, she could hear her daughter's squeal of delight. *Ah, boys showing off with their toys.* Mony made her way down the hall, passing the spare room, where she found her eldest daughter still dressed in sweats and sprawled across the bed. She crept in and pulled out a quilt off the closet shelf.

"Mom?" Kiteri purred as Mony placed the quilt over her.

"Get some sleep, hon. I'll wake you when it's time for lunch." Mony kissed her daughter's forehead.

Kiteri snuggled into the blankets. "Hmm, thanks, Mom," she murmured, and went back to sleep.

Closing the door behind her, Mony heard a roar of laughter wafting up the stairwell. When she opened the door at the bottom of the stairs, she was hit by a blast of warmth and a heavenly aroma. She took in the gathering. Dane; his wife, Diana; Massey's wife, Michelle; their two boys, Devon and Derrick; and the Virgil and Vernon the Sanquist twins, members of Nate's hockey team, were all seated around the table, enjoying coffee, juice, and Poppy's mammoth-sized cinnamon rolls. Poppy stood busy at the stove, multi-tasking, frying bacon and eggs, and flipping hash browns like a short-order cook. Mony drank in the scene, catching the tail end of one of Virgil's stories. The laughter rose to a fever pitch as Virgil delivered what sounded like a reenactment of a deer-camp prank at Nate's expense. Poppy stepped away from the stove and doubled over with her arms around her middle.

"I washed those clothes three times." She hooted through tears of laughter. "I finally gave up and burned the damn things with the rubbish."

Vergil and Vernon exchanged a look of concern. "You burned Nate's lucky hat."

No one seemed to notice, let alone care, that Mony was parading around in a bathrobe and slippers. That was one of the many wonderful things about being among family; you could be yourself without judgment. Mony poured coffee from the thirty-two–cup coffee pot brewing on the counter and thought, *Hmm. Apparently, it's going to be that kind of day.* After she took the open chair next to her nephew, Devon, Poppy set a huge caramel roll with pecans in front of her. Dane came up behind Mony and leaned over her shoulder.

"Morning, Mom, did we wake you?"

Mony turned to face her son and hugged him around his neck. "No. What time did you kids get in last night?"

Diana walked to her mother-in-law and gave her a hug. "Dane, Mindy, and I got into Williston a little before eight. We came in on the same hop Michelle and the boys did, so Uncle Massey gave us a ride to the farm."

Mony turned toward Michelle and mouthed a silent *Thank you*, then smiled at the boys' bookending their mother. It had always amazed her how Massey's sons mirrored him and his brother Nate when they were younger.

"And how was your flight?" she asked the boys. "Did you have a good time at Grandma and Grandpa Evans'?"

Derrick, in that awkward preteen stage, shrugged his shoulders and muttered "Good." Devon, his older brother, dispensed with the pleasantries and got straight to business.

"Uncle Nate said if you come out and play hockey this afternoon, he'll let me and Derrick play for a while too." He bubbled with enthusiasm. "Are you gonna, oh, please, please, please?" He flashed her his big puppy dog eyes and waited for a response.

Mony crooked her brow in amusement. "Oh, did he, now?" She wound up promising her nephew that she'd think about it, which wasn't the response the boy had wanted to hear. She was about to explain when Nate and Mindy burst through the kitchen door. Red-faced from the cold, they were laughing hysterically like two people in their own little world. Mindy immediately noticed Mony.

"Oh, Mom, you've got to let Uncle Nate give you a ride on the Cat. The powder's bitchin'." She tromped across the kitchen floor, and Poppy whirled away from the stove.

"Hey, hey, what did I say about tracking in snow?"

Mony could tell Poppy was trying her best to sound stern, but truth be told, on a day like today, with all her family around, she doubted there was anything that could ruffle Poppy's feathers.

After breakfast, the men headed out to the rink, leaving the women to clean up the kitchen. Mony and her daughter-in-law worked on the neverending pile of dishes, while Mindy and Dane scampered off rummaging through closets to find some dry winter clothing.

A little past noon, Kiteri stumbled into the kitchen, sleepy-eyed, hair a tousled mess. She plopped down on a kitchen chair next to Mony, who'd been peeling carrots. Poppy launched straight into motion, setting a bowl of chicken-and-dumpling soup, fresh bread with butter, crackers, and a glass of milk in front of her. Taking a break, Poppy grabbed a cup of coffee for herself and sat across from Kiteri.

"Now, I want to hear all about your book tour."

Kiteri began to recount a dining experience she'd had at a popular restaurant located in Seattle, but her story was interrupted by a sound like a herd of elephants coming down the stairs. Mindy emerged, waving two hockey jerseys in her hand.

"Kit, we've got to wear these out to the rink," she said, holding up the shirts for everyone to see.

Mony recognized her keepsake hockey jerseys: a Minnesota North Stars CCM vintage throwback NHL number seven jersey, circa 1981, and an official USA Olympic number nine jersey, circa 1980, from the Miracle on Ice US hockey team. Her gaze narrowed. "Where did you find those?"

Dane strolled into the kitchen wearing his own Golden Gophers jersey and held up Mony's vintage Gophers jersey with Massey's old number on it. "Mindy was digging around in your cedar chest again," he said in a tone of admonishment, and tossed the jersey over to Mony. She caught it deftly and held it up for size, amazed that the thing might fit her.

"What have I said about going into my stuff?"

"The only way this is going to work," Dane interjected, "is if we all wear them and Uncle Nate and Massey are out there wearing theirs too." He smirked at Mony. "Just in case a fight breaks out."

First Nate, and now my kids. Mony felt the manipulation prickle at the back of her neck, then gave an exasperated sigh of defeat. "It could be fun, I guess."

Tossing one another mischievous glances, Mony's kids shouted in unison, "We are so in."

Forty-five minutes had passed before Mony arrived at the rink in her dad's old Army jeep. Hauling the beer Nate had called and asked for, she was surprised to see how the small gathering had grown since earlier that morning. There were at least a couple dozen people on the ice, the group made up mostly of Nate and Massey's high school friends and their significant others, who were gathered around the bonfire talking and drinking. She opened the jeep door, and Nate began to sing into the crystal-clear afternoon a pitch-perfect rendition of a Billy Idol song. The choir of skaters harmonized in a not-so-pitch-perfect variation of a profanity-laced chant directed at Mony. This on-again, off-again key went on for a couple of stanzas until the choir got a look at her hockey jersey.

"Christ, not another one," someone groaned, which was promptly followed by a barrage of curses, jeers, and snowballs.

Mony ducked behind the jeep, shielding herself from the onslaught as Nate and Dane skated into the crossfire. Unconcerned, they each took a couple of snowballs in the back, slipped on a pair of blade protectors that had been sticking up in the snow bank, and trotted over toward her.

"You sure know how to kick a hornets' nest," Nate said, pretending to sound scandalized. "Devon says you plan to skate. Are you crazy, wearing that?" He lowered his voice. "Dwight's here you know. You step on the ice dressed like that, and he's going to smear you and that jersey all over the rink."

Mony glanced at her son. It was her first good look at him—she noticed his lip was bleeding, and he radiated hostility. Then she felt it, the unmistakable tension in the air. Something was definitely afoot. As lighthearted as everyone tried to appear, there was a solemnity to the friendly gathering, as if they were expecting an eviction notice. She should also have known Dwight Mitchell would have been a member of the men's over-forty team even though most of the guys despised him. *But hey, what else could they do?* There weren't a lot of men over forty willing to slap on a pair of skates.

"Well you're the one who set it up, genius," Mony hissed back. "Besides, Massey and Dane are wearing their Gophers jerseys, and the girls have theirs one too."

Nate turned to where his brother was skating on the opposite end of the ice, passing a puck back and forth between Devon and Derrick. "Yeah, well, you're not Dane or Massey, are you?"

Dane narrowed his gaze at the rink. "I'm going to kick that fucker's ass," he snarled, spitting a dark red wad of blood into the virgin white snow.

Mony blinked at her son. "Where the hell is that coming from?" She knew her kids were well-acquainted with Williston lore. One of their favorite pastimes during the family's annual hunting trip was sitting around the bonfire at night telling stories. Many of those stories, she suspected, involved Dwight Mitchell. The Mitchells had once been a prominent name around the Williston parts, tracing their roots back to the early fur traders who explored up the Missouri and Yellowstone Rivers. They had had little competition for their affluent status until the mid-'60s, when Kip Ferguson and Buddy Altman started up their business. Not only had Ferguson and Altman stolen the Mitchell family's thunder by having more wealth, power, and popularity, but they were just plain more. Dwight hated Massey for playing D1 hockey while he had been stuck playing intermural. He hated Mony for refusing to date him back in high school, and he hated Nate most of all for emasculating him his senior year.

The testosterone level rolled off the ice in waves. Mony scanned the ice—near the edge of the rink, a six-foot-three, 280-pound mass of bulk skated by himself around the goal net. Dane's eyes maliciously tracked the skater's movement. Dwight glanced up, catching Dane's stare, and glared back at him with a knowing smile.

"Well, now that you've set the stage so nicely, dumbass," Mony snapped at Nate, "what the hell am I here for?"

Massey skated over to join them, both his boys in tow. He, Nate, and Dane looked at each other, silently scheming. Dane's eyes flickered back to Mony.

"I've got an idea."

Nate skated to center ice. "Let's get this game started then, shall we, ladies?" he asked, then turned to Dwight. "Who should we pick for captains?"

Dwight snapped at the bait. "Oh, no you don't, Fergy. You and me, we're the captains."

Nate gave a casual shrug of his shoulders. "Fine by me," he said, then asked the team, "Any objections?" When no one responded, Nate continued. "Okay, now, Massey's boys here want to play a little, so until the first goal is made, no rough stuff. After all, we're just having a friendly practice. Does that work for everyone?"

Mony and the rest of the female cohort lined the perimeter of the ice rink. The team bobbed their heads— Mony could tell most of them weren't entirely comfortable with the teenagers on the ice, but no one protested. Devon and Derrick, on the other hand, had nearly leapt out of their skates.

"We're so in!" they exclaimed.

"Oh, and one more thing," Nate interjected. "Since it's home ice, Mony's going to ref while the boys play to make sure there's no funny stuff."

Mony stepped onto the ice and gave Devon a wink, letting him know that she'd kept her end of the bargain. He gifted her with a big grin.

Dwight waved his hand, unconcerned. "Yeah, yeah, whatever," he scoffed. "Just stay out of my way, Altman." He began skating toward the opposite end of the ice.

Mony watched Nate struggle to suppress a smirk. "Should we make the game more interesting? A little wager, perhaps?"

It took a moment before Dwight turned and faced him. "Okay, how about this? Whoever makes the first goal gets to decide what to do with the losers."

"I like where your head is at," Nate said, then pointed out, "But you have to state your condition before we start playing. That's how it works." He skated past Mony and rolled his eyes.

"Okay, how about the winning captain kicks the losing captain off the team," Dwight countered.

This suggestion was met with an uproar of shouts rippling among the other players. "No," "Oh, too harsh," "No way," and "I'm not going for that," were some of the more family-friendly remarks. Massey, who'd remained silent during the negotiation, skated over toward Dwight.

"How about this?" he said loud enough for all to hear. "Whoever wins becomes the official captain of the Trouble

Shooters indefinitely." It wasn't a secret that Dwight resented the team for having chosen Nate as captain. Nate had half the hockey experience as Dwight, but was far more likable. The team shuffled like a herd of nervous gazelles, and Mony could tell most of them didn't like it—still, no one contested.

Dwight pursed his lips. "Agreed." Then he huffed. "It doesn't matter, though, cuz Fergy's going down."

The two captains skated toward opposite ends of the ice to pick teams, but when Dwight turned around, he saw that Dane, Massey, Devon, and Derrick were already standing beside Nate.

Nate pivoted to face Dwight. "I guess that leaves breaking up the set. Virgil," he called. Virgil's twin brother Vernon made an audible groan.

Dwight gave a derisive snort. "Really, that's what you're going with? It's your funeral."

There was a collective gasp both on the ice and off. Everyone fell silent, and Nate and Massey had to snatch Dane by the shoulders to stop him from going after Dwight.

"Fucker," Dane muttered under his breath.

Dwight heard it. "Aw, too soon," he mocked and skated toward the center of the ice.

Nate motioned his team into a semicircle. "Virgil, you're—" But Virgil, who'd anticipated his position, was already skating toward the net. Nate smiled at his friend's retreating back and turned to the rest of his team. "On three."

Nose-to-nose, the two captains faced off. Mony

prepared to drop the puck when Dwight glanced at her. "I'm going to enjoy splitting your son's other lip," he taunted, and shifted his eyes to Nate.

Mony was used to trash talk on the ice, but the threat caught her off guard, and she failed to get out of the way, catching an elbow in the mouth. Dwight seized advantage, knocked Nate to the ice, and claimed possession of the puck. He made a quick pass to Vernon. Vernon's possession was brief, however, when Dane tapped the puck from behind for the steal and passed it off to Nate. Slipping into a familiar rhythm, Nate tipped the puck toward Massey. Mony watched Massey pass the puck off to Devon, then gasped when Dwight barreled toward the boy, intent on bodily harm. Right before impact, Dane slipped in between them, taking the brunt of the hit. More focused on causing injury, Dwight missed the puck, and it skipped merrily over the snow embankment. He cursed and skated around Dane, taunting, "Did that bitch of a mother teach you how to skate?" The air was filled with jeers and boos, disapproving of the unsportsmanlike conduct. Dwight merely scowled and shouted back, "What? If he can't skate, he can get the fuck off the ice."

Mony climbed over the embankment, retrieving the loose puck, while Nate helped Dane to his feet, holding onto his arm an extra beat. Massey kept his distance, skating backward in a circle with his son as they waited for the game to resume. Mony marveled at the way Massey had stayed so calm knowing Dwight had intended to hurt his son. *There was a reason why Massey was so good at his job.*

Returning to center ice, Nate and Dwight took their

position along with the rest of the team. Mony let the puck loose, this time managing to get out of the way. Dwight, hell-bent on making the score himself, closed in on the net. One of his teammates shouted something, but Dwight ignored it and slapped the puck. What the shot lacked in aim it made up in ferocity as it skidded wide of the goal and bounced over the embankment.

Mony rolled her eyes. "Nice shot, dumbass," she muttered, then remembered she was supposed to be impartial and hoped she hadn't said it too loudly. It didn't matter, since Dwight's teammates were shouting much worse.

"I don't see any of you other assholes trying to play here, so shut the fuck up," Dwight retorted back at his team, but that just made everyone laugh, which only antagonized him even more.

It was critical now. The testosterone level was so high it nearly melted the ice. Mony's hand shook a little when she released the puck. This time, Dwight threw a punch at Nate before taking possession. Nate tore after him. Laughing, Dwight skated toward the goal when young Devon snuck up alongside him and stole the puck. It would have been a perfect steal, if the boy would have missed the elbow jab before passing off the puck to Massey.

With Devon down, Dwight knew Massey would have to pass off the puck to his brother, and he set his sights on Nate. Tossing his stick, he took on the momentum of a speed skater before realizing, too late, that he'd forgotten about Mony's son. Dane skidded in front of him, dropping to the ice, and caught Dwight at the kneecaps. The speed combined with the abrupt stop sent Dwight airborne, like a boulder out of a catapult. Almost a foot off the ice, he traveled several feet before landing in the icy snowbank. He at least had the wherewithal to extend his arms, but not before face-planting in the snow.

Nate tipped the puck back to his nephew, Derrick, who did a double-deke play and slipped the puck past the goalie for the score. A roar of cheers erupted from the rink's edge as Derrick raised his hockey stick, pumping it in the air over his head.

Ten minutes went by before someone finally took pity on Dwight and hauled his sorry ass off to the ER. The rest of the team gathered around the bonfire, eating hot dogs, laughing, and drinking. Mony held a chunk of snow to her lip, Dane an ice pack to his ribs.

"I think it's only fitting," Nate said in a loud voice, "that we acknowledge the man who gave a bunch of rowdy boys a great place to hang out and stay out of trouble." He winked at Mony, "Well, for the most part. So raise your glasses to our good friend Buddy. May the tradition he began live on for generations to come."

"To Buddy," they all cheered.

Massey came up behind Dane and patted him on the shoulder. "I don't *ever* remember that play working so well," he said.

Nate sat down next to Mony and gave her a squeeze, then reached over to give Dane a high-five. "Way to take one for the team, man. Well played."

Mony leaned her head against Nate's shoulder, basking in the support from the family and friends around her, when a thrumming sound off in the distance captured the attention of the happy group as a helicopter approached.

CHAPTER 14

JOHN

"Sons of bitches, what are they doing there?" Jason shouted into his headpiece. "Take me over there right now. Right now."

It's a good thing Jason is buckled down in his seat, John thought. He'd been bouncing around the cabin like a super ball since they'd left the airfield and was pressed against his seat harness; it looked like he was about to snap the straps right off their hinges.

"Christ, man, take it easy," John said, trying to stay calm. "You're liable to fall out of this thing." John didn't mind flying in general, just in helicopters. He felt too exposed.

As the pilot circled the frozen body of water below, it was hard to tell where the water ended and the land began. A group of about thirty or so people looked up toward the sky, shielding their eyes against the snowy glare.

"See, it's just a bunch of high school kids having a bonfire," John said with relief. "Look, they've made themselves a hockey rink on the ice."

"I don't give a shit what they're doing," Jason snapped.

John noticed some of the onlookers waving up at the aircraft, a few others holding up a middle finger. The pilot snorted in amusement.

"What, you think that's funny?" Jason hissed.

"Yup." The pilot laughed.

Jason was acting like a twenty-two-year-old frat boy hopped up on energy drinks. "No one's supposed to be on that property," he shouted.

"Technically, they're on the lake," the pilot pointed out.

Jason lost it. "Get me down there now, right fucking now." Undaunted by the screaming in his ear, the pilot prepared their descent.

Ruminating in his mind, John thought of several reasons why setting the helicopter down was not a good idea, beginning with logistics. Had the lake been frozen enough to support the helicopter? How big was it? Would they be close to the shore? Was the homestead nearby even Altman's, or was it someone else's private property? He hadn't had time to grab his maps before they took off, so he was at mercy of Jason's word, which, so far, hadn't accounted for much. And high school or not, there were a lot of big guys down there, outnumbering John and Jason at least seven to one. Poor odds. In an attempt to defuse Jason's mania, John tried making light of the situation.

"Hey, we were kids once too," he said with a humorless laugh. "Just radio the sheriff to kick them off. They'll probably be gone anyway by—"

Jason wasn't having it. "No, no, no. I said put it down.

Put. It. Down."

John used a different approach. "Look, Jason, you have no authority here. You have no rights; you don't own it." He felt the pounding of his heart against his chest wall as the helicopter descended.

"You think I'm going to stand with my dick in my hand and let Ferguson take it out from under me? Dad sent me up here to do a job, Johnny boy, and that's just what I'm going to do."

"You're being irrational." *And paranoid*, but John kept that second thought to himself. "Let's just go back and meet with Ferguson and sort things out."

"I'm irrational? You've been here less than a day. I've been here close to a week. I've watched these people. You have no idea what they're capable of."

John rolled his eyes inwardly. "So, what are you going to do?"

Jason didn't answer and began fumbling with his safety buckles. John reached to grab his arm, but he wrenched free. The moment the helicopter's landing blades lit on the ground, Jason slid off his seat and was out the door, trudging through knee-deep snow.

John's breath hitched as three large men broke away from the crowd and formed a semicircle around a smaller guy wearing what looked like a Minnesota hockey jersey. *The delegation.* As they drew closer, John realized they weren't high school kids at all; they were grown men, all built like Paul Bunyan, except the short one in the middle. He watched in disbelief as Jason, outnumbered four to one, tore into an animated tirade.

The menacing three-man arc was clearly there to intimidate. One of the guys made a waving motion to the larger group to stay back. *That was a good sign. At least one of them showed some sense.* The shorter spokesman stood very calmly and seemed almost bored by Jason's antics. Through the fading whine of the propeller, John strained to hear but only caught bits and pieces. Suddenly, the tallest of the three men lurched forward, his hockey stick raised over his head.

"Christ, what did he say?" John asked the pilot, who lifted a shoulder in a lazy shrug. More yelling ensued; the spokesman in the center intercepted the lunatic with the hockey stick, who lowered it and stepped back in formation. Then the spokesman stepped out of his arc of safety and walked toward Jason. That's when John realized it wasn't a man at all. He cursed when she peeled off the stocking cap, letting loose pixie locks of hair.

"Ramona—my God, it's Ramona." Confused, John's ears buzzed with the roar of his own blood. *What the hell is she doing here? She's supposed to be on the train heading for the coast.*

Her posture was loose, relaxed, impassive. Jason seemed to have picked up on her indifference, which only ramped up his agitation, and exploded into a barrage of vulgar insults. Fumbling to release his safety straps, John announced to the pilot, "This has gone far enough," and jumped from the aircraft.

He immediately regretted the impetuous action, but it was too late to turn back. He trudged through the knee-deep snow, moving as quickly as he could toward the group. He decided to deal with Ramona later. Right now, he had to focus on how he was going to defuse the situation before Jason said or did something that would surely get the shit kicked out of them both, or worse.

It was worse.

As he drew closer, Jason reached for something inside of his jacket when the unmistakable reverberation of a rifle pierced the serene habitat. John hit the ice with a thud. The only sound was the raging beat of his heart and the disturbed waterfowl somewhere off in the distance. He assessed himself for injuries. When he'd ascertained that a bullet hadn't hit him, John slowly lifted his head and was relieved to see Jason still standing. He looked past the group and two identical men standing at the far edge of the rink, each holding a rifle in his hand. One aimed a 7mm Remington Magnum in his direction, while the other kept his .300 Winchester Magnum trained on Jason. He cursed. That shitstorm he'd been dreading had finally arrived.

Tapping into an unknown source of courage, John shouted, "Wait, please, wait." He thrust his arms over his head and awkwardly tried to get up off the ground, slinking like a snake onto his knees before standing. It would have been comical had it not been for the gun pointing at him. "I'm unarmed," he called to the gunmen off in the distance. Neither of them lowered their weapons.

John hadn't read up on the laws governing trespassing on private property, but felt damn certain it was still unlawful to shoot an unarmed person, even in North Dakota. "I'm coming in." He waited for the response. The silence dragged on for what seemed like an eternity before the levelheaded man waved him in. He trudged through the snow, making a conscious effort not to make a move or gesture that might be misconstrued for aggression. It was a struggle.

When he was close enough to see Ramona's face, his mouth lifted into a smile, but what flashed in her eyes was neither joy nor welcome. She locked her piercing gaze on him like he was the bullseye of a target, in a look that conveyed disdain, mistrust, and betrayal. John swallowed involuntarily. He had to decide quickly whether or not to acknowledge her, and it killed him inside not to be able to reach out and touch her, explain the whole stupid mess. But she'd made it clear, at least for now, that she had no intention of acknowledging him. Therefore, he held his tongue and, assuming she was still the spokesperson, said, "Listen, we don't want any trouble. Please, can we talk?"

The three men at her back closed ranks, surrounding her like a fortress, privy to all that was being said. John stepped beside Jason, noting that his hand was still in his jacket. He caught a whiff of something foul and glanced down at a pool of yellow snow near Jason's boot. Hiding his revulsion, John cleared his voice and said, "Mr. Monroe here and I were just taking an aerial survey of Mr. Altman's property. He represents Monroe Oil Company, perhaps you have heard of it?"

His comment elicited no reaction, and John couldn't decide if that was good, bad, or indifferent. "Anyway," he continued, "he's considering to bid on the property and until it's confirmed whether the bid has been accepted, we'd like to ask you to stay off."

The man who had raised the hockey stick shouted, "Are you fucking kidding me?"

Up close, John could see that he was much younger than the other two men but no less threatening. The kid was a hothead and itching for a reason, any reason, to use the weapon in his hand.

Eyes boring into the back of Ramona's head, the kid snapped, "How much longer are you going to listen to this bullshit?" He shifted his gaze toward Jason, glaring at him with unadulterated hatred. "And who the fuck are you, talking to her like that?" He clenched the hockey stick in his hand, preparing to strike.

Ramona ignored the remark. She hadn't so much as flinched. She just kept her eyes trained on John with an implacable expression. John studied the young man, then looked at Ramona. Their eyes were an undeniable match. He took a closer look at the other two men. *Similar features. Coincidental? Was she married after all?* It seemed the living proof was standing right in front of him, and his mind raced with the possibilities. Assimilating what this new information might have to offer, he asked. "I didn't catch your name, Miss?"

The sensible man who had waved off the larger group said, "And you are?"

Caught off guard by the gunshot and by Ramona's presence, John had failed to introduce himself. "Sorry." He extended a hand. "John, John Finch, attorney for Monroe Oil Company." The man gave no sign of cordial formalities, and he retracted his hand. "I'm here to assist Mr. Monroe with the legal formalities. I believe Mr. Monroe was about to hand some papers to you?" *God, he could only hope.* From where he stood, John had no idea what was in his jacket at this point, and it was all a crapshoot. Jason gave a small nod, and the levelheaded man stepped forward, relieving him of a white legal envelope. John watched the man's expression as he read through the contents, and the warning alarms started going off again. He hadn't seen the letter, and hated the disadvantage it lent to an already lopsided balance of power. The levelheaded man folded the paper, stepped closer to John, and reached to shake his hand.

"Mr. Finch, my name is Matthew Ferguson, attorney for Mr. Altman's estate. I don't understand what a restraining order against Senator Ferguson has to do with us. What's this all about?"

John's grip went flaccid. *Ferguson, naturally.* Frustrated that he'd been denied disclosure to Jason's activities, John begrudgingly asked, "May I see the papers?" Ferguson arched a brow and handed over the document.

John scanned the first few paragraphs, unable to suppress his look of surprise. It was indeed a restraining order, just as Ferguson had said, against Senator Kip Ferguson to keep him from trespassing on the property. It didn't make any sense. Why would Jason be carrying a restraining order around in his pocket, and what the hell was he up to? He became cognizant of the stinging sensation of pins piercing his toes as the wet and cold seeped into his cheap boots. He had to get someplace warm and dry, somewhere there wasn't a gun pointing at him.

"Mr. Ferguson, can we talk somewhere more appropriate? Mr. Monroe and I happen to have a meeting scheduled with Senator Ferguson in about—" John checked his watch. They were already twenty minutes late. If they left now, maybe they'd make it an even hour. "Thirty minutes," he lied. "Could you meet us in thirty minutes at our office?"

Jason's body started to shake as beads of perspiration trickled down the side of his forehead. It was the first sign of movement he'd shown since the rifle shot. From the corner of his mouth he whispered, "No appointment."

John didn't want to believe his ears and must have visibly deflated. The situation just kept getting worse and worse. It had to hit bottom at some point.

"I have nothing to discuss with you, Mr. Finch," Ferguson said. "Your business is with Senator Ferguson. I will inform you, however, that Mr. Altman's final will and testament, along with his estate settlement, won't be read for several days." He gave a quick glance toward Ramona.

John caught the discrete exchange. Had Ferguson just shaken his head *no* at her? Uncertain if he'd seen or just imagined the discord, John snagged the only lifeline left with both hands.

"Maybe I should be talking with someone else?" John directed his attention toward Ramona. It shredded him when she turned that implacable glare toward him as she stepped further from her circle of sanctuary.

She took everyone by surprise when she said in a voice

as arctic as the weather. "I'll go with you, Mr. Finch, and hear what you have to say."

Her announcement met with an immediate outcry from the young man, as well as the older man standing next to him, who said, "No, absolutely not."

"Over my dead body," the younger concurred, taking a step forward.

Ignoring their rebuttals, Ramona faced the attorney. "You need to deescalate this situation right now and get your dad on the horn. Let him know what's going on." With each word, she pounded a pointed finger into the palm of her hand. "Take care of this family first." She cast a glance toward the riflemen and back to Ferguson. "And for Christ sakes, tell those two boneheads to put those guns away before someone gets shot. I'll be fine." Her words were clipped, direct, final. Ferguson broached no argument and nodded, lending credence to John's earlier assumption. She was the spokesperson.

Ramona turned and marched toward the two other men. Because they were facing him, John could see their expressions fill with pain, anger, and fear. It made for a volatile combination. Standing in front of the younger male, her voice was maternal, and resolute. "Take care of the girls—I need to know they're safe," she said. "I'm counting on you to do this for me."

The young man's eyes blazed with anguish. Clearly, he wasn't on board with that idea, but he nodded his head obediently and remained silent. Then Ramona pivoted toward the other man, and John finally recognized him. He was the other Ferguson, the rock star, his face shrouded in a full beard that made him look much older than the pictures on his album cover. Ramona moved in closer, pressing her body against him. Ferguson closed his eyes, his posture so rigid John wasn't sure if he was about to push her away or tackle her. Bowing his head, he lowered his ear to her lips, and Ramona placed the palm of her hand on his chest in a gesture of familiarity. The transparency in Ferguson's expression exposed a torrent of emotion; he bracketed her in the shield of his arms as she imparted her instructions. The intimate exchange reminded John of the tenderness he and Ramona had shared just hours ago, and he had to look away. Abruptly, Ramona broke away from Ferguson and trudged past him, heading toward the helicopter. John glanced over at the two riflemen, then grabbed Jason by the shoulder. Jason gave a stunned look of comprehension and stumbled behind John back toward the helicopter.

Already strapped in with the radio headgear on, Ramona sat in the copilot's seat chatting with the pilot. She fell silent when John helped Jason into his seat straps before securing his own. Jason had become uncharacteristically quiet, much to John's relief. He hadn't a clue what was going on in Jason's head, but before the ice rink debacle he'd been hell-bent on action. The gunplay had mellowed him.

A familiar anxiety took hold as they prepared for takeoff. The enclosure of the cabin reeked of urine, making John feel queasy in the claustrophobic space. They were airborne in minutes, and John peered out the window, seeing the crowd already disbanding. Leaving in trucks or on snowmobiles, they all headed in the direction of the farmstead—all except one. The lone snowmobile had already cleared the lake and was nothing more than a streak of green and black several miles ahead on the horizon.

John glanced over to Ramona's profile as she stared pensively toward the moving object. The corner of her mouth twitched in a wry smile, and she tipped her head back, pointing to the green dot on the horizon. "You see that Cat out there? It will be in Williston before Mr. Johnson here can even land this bird. That's how long you've got to talk." She tapped her wrist. "Tick-tock."

CHAPTER 15

NATE

Nate sped along the familiar trail, oblivious to the cold pulverizing his face. It was of no consequence, and he pushed his machine to its maximum speed. He had a single thought in mind: *I'm going to hit that son of a bitch lawyer the first chance I get.*

He'd seen the look in Finch's eye when he confronted Mony. There was a predatory austerity under that business façade. The man was assessing for a weakness, and he thought he'd found it in the woman standing among the safety of men. *The jackass.* The lawyer was about to become the second victim for the trio of trouble today.

As he sped along the familiar trail, it surprised Nate how quickly his emotions had resurfaced toward Mony, his primal instincts kicking in in a proprietary sort of way. He should have been angry for what she was asking of him. After all, it wasn't his charge to see to her protection. Mony was a grown woman, and she knew how to take care of herself. Not that he hadn't wanted to once, but she'd made her choice long ago when she ran off and married the plumber. She'd shut him out of her life and left him picking up the pieces of a teenage boy's shattered heart. He wasn't a teenager anymore, yet Nate still found himself caught up in her drama after Mitchell had clocked her—then it had all escalated when that fuckhead Monroe verbally accosted her. Fire coursed through his veins, and Nate couldn't decide what had made him angrier, the idiocy of the two trespassers or his emerging feelings for Mony. He'd spent nearly three decades trying to forget his love for her and thought he'd had his feelings well secured in that matter. Then she touched him, and he crumbled like a dried-out piece of clay.

She'd asked him to come for her, and so he was doing just that. Her son had been angry too and had nearly taken Nate's snowmobile to fetch her from town himself. *Maybe he should have let him.* Mony's impetuous decision to go with Finch was reckless, yet Nate had seen it coming, and perhaps Dane had too. Mony had always had a warped sense of self-worth, and what she'd just done was one of her oldest strategies. Serve as decoy; move the threat away from family. Protect at all cost. It had been the same tactic they'd used to bait Dwight. Whether drawing danger away, or luring her foe into a trap, Mony would do whatever it took, fully confident that the consequences were always more severe toward the fool who threatened the ones she loved. It was why Dwight Mitchell was lying in an emergency room. He may have not liked it, but Nate understood. Mony's love had always been unconditional. It was why he couldn't stay angry at her, why he couldn't stay away. Her commitment to him had been for life, even after she left him and bore another man's children. Deep down, Nate understood that too. But could she love him as more than just her surrogate brother, more than a dear friend? In a blaze of emotion, his mind flashed back to a time he'd never forgotten.

His life had been perfect—then, before he knew it, she was gone, off on a new adventure without him, both she and Massey. Attending college a state away. It felt as though an appendage had been ripped from his body. His every waking thought had been filled with impatient longing, his nights filled with erotic dreams of a lover's passion, waiting for her return. When it came time for him to choose his college, Nate would follow his big brother to Minnesota, and the three of them would be together again, and he would feel invincible.

When Mony had returned the summer of Nate's senior year, he knew right away that things were different between them. Yet, what else could he have done? Tell her the truth? Out of the question. Mony was a college woman, and what could she have possibly wanted from a high school boy and his puppy love?

There came a day when he felt a glimmer of hope, the afternoon of the end-of-summer bonfire. He and Mony had planned to spend the afternoon together, just the two of them, on a raft by the lake—he could tell her how he felt. But the word had leaked out about their little rendezvous. Everyone showed up, including Dwight Mitchell. The gang spent the whole afternoon swimming and baking in the sun. Mony hung out mostly with the girls, teasing and flirting with the boys, and never once noticed Nate's sullen mood. Finally, they all headed back to the farmhouse to change when Nate got an idea. Mony would be the last one out of the house, so he took his time changing his clothes. He was going

to tell her how he felt, but as he walked up the stairs, he heard
Mony shouting and rushed to her room. What he saw made his
blood turn to ice. Dwight stood just inside the doorway, catching
Mony in the act of changing out of her swimsuit. Nate flew into
a rage, and it had been lucky for Dwight that he'd only seen
her partly naked, or he'd have been dead. Nate threw him onto
the floor and beat the shit out of him, a boy a whole head taller
than he. Mony let out a scream, and suddenly his brother Massey
appeared and had to pull him off.

As Dwight lay groaning on the floor, Mony stood there with
her arms across her chest, wearing nothing but her bikini bottom.
All Nate could do was stare. He couldn't help it. He'd seen her
that way long ago, but they had been small children then, still
innocent and naive. It was a woman who stood before him, so
beautiful in her anger. Instinctively he reached for her, and she
took a step backward. It was like a punch to the gut. He left her
in a rush, tearing out of the driveway in his truck. He glanced
into his rearview mirror and saw her stepping out onto the
porch. Immediately, he wanted to go back, but knew he couldn't,
not then. Something fragile had shifted between them when she
took that step away, something that would take decades to repair.
Yet they would find sanctuary in one another's arms one more
time, though it would take the loss of someone dear to bring them
both together.

As Nate neared the city limits, he felt the tears stinging
behind his goggles. He slowed his speed and focused on
the present, using caution as he took the service road
toward Airport Drive. In the periphery, he noticed the
red Ford F-150 paralleling him on the highway, closing in
from behind. His father planned to intercept. Beating the

truck to the intersection, Nate cut in front of it and drove along the airport road slowly, forcing his father to trail behind. Nate drove right up to the helipad and killed the engine as his father did the same.

A blind person could see that Nate still had deep feelings for Mony, and Kip Ferguson was not blind. But there was nothing for it, not when they were kids and certainly not now. Nate would go to Mony, protect her in any way he could, and no one was going to take that from him, least of all his old man. Buddy's death had left his life in a state of flux, and Nate hated change. He needed stability; he needed to feel a sense of purpose, and even though it brought with it a boatload of complexities, Mony was familiar. He'd have to accept that.

Kip climbed out of the truck and walked toward him as the whirling sound of propellers grew louder. Side by side, the two men stood in a familiar silence as they both focused their attention on the approaching helicopter.

CHAPTER 16

JOHN

Ramona's eyes seemed transfixed on the spot where the two men stood. John wondered why she'd even agreed to fly along; she'd barely spoken three words the entire flight. He leaned as far as his seat harness allowed and asked, "Would it be possible to speak to you privately after we land?"

She bristled. "There is nothing to say, Mr. Finch," Ramona responded in a flat voice. "I simply wanted to get your client away from my friends before someone wound up shot."

John fell back against his seat. She was right, of course. Jason's antics had clearly marked them both as a threat. What red-blooded American wouldn't have practiced their second amendment right? A white SUV with "William County Sheriff" on the side panel pulled up near the helipad and parked next to the red truck. The driver got out, approached the big man, and extended his hand before shaking Ferguson's.

John persisted with his question. "Maybe we could

have dinner later? I know a place in town that serves amazing cheesy hash browns. Come on, what do you say?"

Mony gritted her teeth audibly. "The Blarney Stone, I know it. It will hardly be quiet, Lonely Boot's playing there tonight."

John blinked in surprise. "That's right. I could pick you up, but I don't even know where you're staying." He paused, but she didn't answer. She didn't wait for him either, disembarking the helicopter. Ramona walked to where the burly man stood alongside the county sheriff. They exchanged handshakes, and the burly man draped an arm over her shoulder.

"I see you're still in your hockey gear. Did you play?"

Ramona shook her head. "No, just reffed, if you want to call it that. Derrick got the first goal."

"Is that right?" The burly man beamed. "Well, good for him."

Up close, John recognized him now. He'd been one of the two men sitting at the bar this morning, and sure as shit if the other hadn't been the County Sheriff, which would make the burly fellow Senator Ferguson. The senator was examining Ramona's lip—he shot John and Jason an angry look.

Ramona played it off. "Dwight got in a cheap shot before we pulled the old dip and trip on him."

The senator snorted a laugh and turned his attention back to John and Jason.

"Gentlemen, Ma'am, let's go inside. We have a room ready for us."

The F&A Conference Center exuded masculinity, with a surreal blend of a military command center, rustic pioneer spirit, and an exclusive gentlemen's club. The room had all state-of-the-art equipment. A large touch flatscreen with a mounted ceiling projector filled an entire wall space. The control center to all this technology was located on the entrance side of the room, sectioned off with a three-foot–high railing, access limited to authorized personnel only. Opposite the entrance doorway were floor-to-ceiling windows with a beautiful vista of the airport tarmac, topped with remote-controlled blinds. At the back of the room there was a wet bar made of rough, reclaimed wood. But the focal point of this shrine to male virility was the stunning boardroom table made of Peruvian mahogany wood. The colors were of rich red and consistent brown, with a soft semi-gloss finish to highlight the wood's deep, natural tone. It was a powerful place where men made important decisions affecting the domains which they mastered.

The senator assumed the foot of the table, gesturing for Ramona to sit to his right while the sheriff sat at the head, flanked by Monroe. John chose the seat next to Ramona, preferring her lavender scent to urine. The senator made introductions and offered refreshments. Ramona accepted a bottle of water and rolled the wet condensation across her forehead.

The sheriff had just begun speaking when Attorney Ferguson walked briskly into the room, apologizing for the interruption; he handed the sheriff an envelope and quickly took a seat to the left of the senator. The young bartender set a Pellegrino water next to the attorney's forearm as the sheriff donned a pair of reading glasses, reviewing the documents just handed him. His face was impassive as he scanned the paper, then set it on the table looking over the rim of his glasses. The sheriff addressed the senator first.

"Am I to understand, Senator Ferguson, that you were on the Altman property?"

The senator leaned slowly back in his seat. "No," he said evenly. "You had asked me to refrain from stepping foot onto my partner's property. And, even though the request prohibits me from conducting my business with F&A Crop Dusting Incorporated, as a courtesy, I have complied with your verbal request." The sheriff furrowed his brow then turned to John.

"Am I to understand you are the legal representation in this matter, Mr. Finch?"

John stood. "Mr. Monroe had invited me on an aerial tour of the Altman property, and when he saw people trespassing on the property he—"

The sheriff interrupted. "Sit down, Mr. Finch. This isn't a legal proceeding, I am just gathering information to ascertain the purpose for this meeting." John lowered into his chair and the sheriff continued. "It was my understanding that the document here in my hand was to be invoked only if Senator Ferguson had entered the Altman property. Can you explain how it is Matthew Ferguson has possession of this paper?"

John took in a calming breath. "As I was saying, Mr. Monroe and I had been on an aerial tour over the Altman property when we saw a large gathering of people. Mr.

Monroe requested that the pilot land so that he could ascertain if Senator Ferguson was among them. Mr. Monroe approached Mr. Ferguson, Ms. Strong, and two other men to determine if they were trespassing on the property. Two men from the larger group fired shots and pointed their rifles, one at Mr. Monroe and the other at myself. I had asked Mr. Ferguson," he pointed to the attorney, "if he would come to our office to discuss the matter, but he declined. That's when Ms. Strong agreed to discuss the problem at our office, but instead we were directed here."

"I was the one who requested to meet here," the sheriff replied in a matter-of-fact tone. "I thought a more convenient, neutral location would be more appropriate."

"Hardly," John muttered. "The room is named after Senator Ferguson."

"Would you have rather met in one of the interrogation rooms at the law enforcement center?" The sheriff turned to Attorney Ferguson. "Do you have anything to add, Matthew?"

Attorney Ferguson leaned forward. "As you know, the Trouble Shooters hockey team have had a standing weekly practice on the lake, located in the wildlife management area for the past twenty or so years. And while the lake is public domain, the only land access to the warming house is through Mr. Altman's property. The team had a scheduled practice this afternoon when Mr. Monroe and Mr. Finch landed on the lake. Mr. Monroe approached Ms. Strong, questioning her presence, then threatened her in front of witnesses."

"We landed to ascertain if Senator Ferguson was among the gathering on the lake—"

The sheriff lifted an eyebrow. "I didn't know you skated, Kip," he said with a sarcastic tone. The senator snorted.

Attorney Ferguson went on some more about not having been properly notified of the aerial inspection and air rights violations, while Ramona sat there looking bored. But her body said otherwise, radiating a sort of nervous energy. When the attorney finally stopped talking, John said, "I'd like to ask you, Mr. Ferguson. Do you always bring loaded weapons to a hockey practice? And why had two members of your cohort drawn their weapons on me and Mr. Monroe? I had said that I was unarmed."

The senator interjected, "You're not from around here, Mr. Finch, so let me enlighten you." He launched into a dissertation regarding hunting and gun carry laws. Everyone at the table let the senator have his say before the attorney cut in.

"In Mr. Finch's defense, he exited the aircraft well after Mr. Monroe, so he would not have heard the threatening remarks made toward Ms. Strong."

John cringed inwardly at the syrupy sincerity on his behalf. He didn't need Matthew Ferguson's so-called understanding of what he may or may not have known about the course of events. *Or did he?* They went back and forth for a while about who threatened whom, while Jason sat quietly in the background. *This is very weird.*

"Ms. Strong, tell me, were you, or did you feel threatened by Mr. Monroe in any way?" the sheriff asked.

Ramona flashed a demure smile. "Mr. Monroe did make verbal threats, just as Matthew had said, but please don't ask me to repeat his vile comments." Ramona's eyes clouded, and her voice began to quiver. "My family was standing there right next to me." John noticed a tear trickle down her cheek, and the senator handed her his handkerchief.

"Take your time, Ms. Strong, and gather your thoughts," the sheriff prompted.

Oh, she was gathering her thoughts, all right. John noticed the disdain burning in her retina as she twisted the knife a little further.

"His belligerent insults were heard by everyone. So, I suppose when Mr. Monroe reached into his pocket for his gun—"

There was a collective gasp around the room.

"Gun?" John exclaimed. "Sheriff, I rode with Mr. Monroe to the site. He did not take a gun with him. The only thing in his pocket were the papers in your hand."

"How would you know, Mr. Finch?" the attorney interjected. "You didn't even seem to know Mr. Monroe had a restraining order against the senator until I handed the papers to you."

It was true, of course, John conceded, but totally off topic.

Ramona jumped in. "Excuse me, Sheriff, but is Mr. Finch calling me a liar?" She turned and faced John. "You should know, I had a conversation with Jarvis."

John had no idea who she was talking about.

"Our pilot, Jarvis Johnson. I talked with him before

takeoff. I understand that Mr. Monroe is your friend and all, but Jarvis informed me that he suspected Mr. Monroe packed a handgun in his jacket before you left the airport."

John felt his mouth gape, but no sound came out. Realization smacked him alongside the head with the brutal force of a two-by-four. He'd been set up by everyone in the room, including his dumbass client.

Ramona muttered, "If I'm not mistaken, it looked to be a SIG P226."

A cop gun. John looked to Jason, whose face turned a deep red.

"That's ridiculous," Jason spewed, the brutal purple vein pulsating on his forehead. "She's fucking lying." He bolted up from his chair, and the entire room went into instant motion.

The attorney was halfway around the table and on top of Jason before the sheriff had a chance to clear his gun. The senator grabbed Ramona's chair and yanked it behind him. Even John found himself reacting by putting his body between Jason's line of sight and Ramona. *It's a mess, a big fucking mess.* She had them convinced that Jason was carrying a gun.

"Are you going to uphold the restraining order or not?" Jason screamed from the floor. "I want to press charges against those bastards who pointed a rifle at me and this son of a bitch on top of me."

With reckless abandon, Ramona moved out from behind her human shields and rose from her chair. "Sheriff, you won't find the gun on him now," she said passively. "He tossed it from the helicopter before takeoff."

The color drained from Jason's face, and he began muttering like a simpleton. "These bastards are crazy around here. A man has a right to protect himself. Well, doesn't he? It's my constitutional right."

The senator lost his composure. "Sheriff, this is outrageous. He open-carried a loaded handgun and I want the landing site thoroughly searched for that weapon—"

It was a three-ring circus. The sheriff patted down Jason and was about to cuff him when a sudden blast of cold air swept in from the corridor. Rockstar Ferguson burst into the room, moving swiftly toward Ramona, glowering at John as he passed behind him.

The senator spoke to his son. "Take her home. I'll let the sheriff know."

A hostility that hadn't been apparent at the landing pad crackled between father and son, but the younger stood down. Nathan Ferguson reached for Ramona's arm, and in an instant, they were out the door.

CHAPTER 17

MONY

They walked into the Blarney Stone arm-in-arm, laughing like a couple of schoolkids who'd just cut class. Mony had thanked Nate a half-dozen times for getting her out of the conference room and agreed to a quick one at the bar, Nate's asking price for her gratitude. She wasn't keen on the idea, but what could she say? She was riding shotgun, and what a ride. Nate tore up the open field surrounding the airport perimeter like a Tasmanian devil before taking to the side streets and heading into town. Covered in snow from head to foot, they stomped their boots in the entry, garnering a scowl from the bartender.

"Hey, keep it down, you two—this is a respectable establishment," she half-ass scolded with a broad smile.

Mony recognized the bartender, Shannon McDonald, a tall, well-built woman with bushy red hair and sharp wit. She was a few years younger than Mony, closer to Nate's age. Shannon and her brother Shawn had bought out Poppy's little café a few years back, converting it into a bar and grill. Mony's dad had even fronted them the money for the down payment. Nate and Mony made their way to the fireplace while Nate called to the bartender, "Hey, Shannon, set us up with a couple of beers and Jameson shots. Mony here has had an eventful day."

Shannon flicked back her bushy red mane. "Oh, really?" She grabbed a couple of pint glasses and began filling from the Grain Belt tap. "And do these events involve a former Trouble Shooter hockey mishap and two dumbass oilmen who crashed said hockey practice this afternoon?"

Nate stopped mid-step and his brows shot up. "Yeesh, word gets around fast in this town. I swear, I never get to be the first one to spread anything. Who the hell told you?"

Shannon set the pint glasses down, letting the foam settle, and reached for a couple of shot glasses. "You know Virgil and Vernon are worse than a couple of Polish wash women for gossip. They had that news spread on Twitter about two minutes after the helicopter lifted off the ground." The Blarney Stone was considered gossip central, aided by the fact that Shannon and her brother Shawn were also first responders. If anyone wanted to know anything about anything, all they had to do was stop in at the bar.

"Hold the Jameson," Mony said to Shannon. "Poppy is making dinner for everyone out at the farm tonight. I suspect she'll want us to be there on time."

Nate plopped down on the overstuffed sofa cushion next to Mony. The sudden shift in weight had nearly bounced her off the seat. Mony retaliated by slugging

Nate's shoulder, but all that did was make him laugh, and he grappled her in a bear hug. Shannon walked over with a tray full of drinks.

"Hey, hey, get a room or take it outside, you two."

Mony backed down. She didn't want to flirt in front of Shannon. She knew Shannon had had a crush on Nate ever since high school, and suspected they may have even hooked up in more recent years. Even though Mony was three years Nate's senior, it had always been assumed that she and Nate were a couple. They'd run in the same circles and hung out all the time. Such was life in a small, rural town. Mony also suspected Shannon had been somewhat jealous of that fact, making her own relationship with the redheaded woman tenuous at best.

Nate flicked a thumb back at Shannon. "She sounds like Poppy." He smirked and sprang to his feet, slapping Mony on the thigh before strolling away.

Mony tried to take a swipe at him and missed when she noted Shannon's eyes sliding over Nate as he stood by the popcorn machine. A pang of possessiveness stirred in her gut, and she began to make small talk. "The place looks great, Shannon," she said through a forced smile. "You and Shawn have really made it your own. It's hard to believe this was Poppy's café once."

"Thanks," Shannon muttered, offering no help in the conversation.

Nate turned just then to find them both looking at him. "See anything back there you like, ladies?" he teased in a low, sexy voice. Mony rolled her eyes but heard the shaky inhalation Shannon made as her childhood crush sauntered toward them carrying a basket of popcorn. Nate was still impossibly gorgeous in her mind; his heated blue eyes were fringed with thick black lashes that were such a cruel waste on a man. Mony felt her own heartbeat quicken as he sat down, draping his arm across the back of the sofa. He offered her a kernel of popcorn, dangling it above her so that she had to tilt her head back to look at him.

"Hey, Sis," Shannon's older brother Shawn called from the back entrance. "Could you hand me a fuse for the Christmas lights?"

A bruiser of a fellow, Shawn stood around six-foot-four and weighed in at over three hundred pounds. He had a bright red, bushy beard and would have had a mop of flaming red, wavy hair like his sister if he hadn't kept it shaved. The same age as Nate, he was yet another high school friend.

Waving the arm he had draped behind Mony's shoulder, Nate shouted, "Hey, man, we missed you at practice today."

Shawn forgot about the lights and stomped across the floor in his wet boots. He high-fived the hand Nate held up in the air and rounded the sofa. Seeing her struggle to get up off the soft cushions, Shawn offered Mony assistance by reaching down to snatch her into a big hug.

"I was hoping to see you," Shawn said, lifting Mony off her feet. "So sorry about Buddy. We're sure going to miss him around here." Left breathless by his constrictive arms, Mony could only manage a weak, "Thank you."

"You really missed a great match up at hockey practice

today," Nate said to Shawn, beaming like a proud papa. "You should have seen our boy Dane in action."

"Yeah, I heard you did the old dip and trip number on Mitchell." He slapped Mony on the back hard enough to make her cough and let loose a boisterous laugh. "God, I would have loved to be there to see that."

Mony quickly recovered. "Yeah, well, what can I say." She buffed her fingernails on her chest. "Acorn doesn't fall far from the tree."

Shawn eyed the cut on Mony's lip. "I can see that. Is it true that Mitchell has a broken nose and two broken wrists?"

The cook yelled out from the kitchen, and Shannon left the little huddle of friends, heading back behind the bar. A half-dozen people or more came up to Mony offering condolences and listened to Nate recount the details of Dwight Mitchell's ass-kicking. But that wasn't the story Shannon wanted to hear. She wanted to know what had happened at the airport meeting. Neither Nate nor Mony spoke a word about it, which didn't surprise her, considering Massey Ferguson's notorious reputation for keeping family affairs close to the vest.

Mony suddenly tossed her head back in a fit of laughter, and Nate reached around her waist to steady her balance. *A nostalgic scene.* One that would make anyone who'd known them in high school wonder what the hell happened that they had never ended up together. Shannon had been privy to part of the reason, but not the whole story. That was another secret big brother Massey kept locked down tight.

A shrill whistle shook Shannon from her introspection. "Hey Sis, bring another round, will ya?" Shawn hollered from the foosball table. "I'm going to school Nate here in the finer points of table soccer."

Shannon grabbed a couple of pint glasses and glanced over at Mony sitting on the sofa. One minute it had seemed Mony and Nate would be together forever, then Mony up and married some guy in Minnesota and Nate was off for Hollywood to become a rock star. It all seemed surreal. Everyone else said, "*C'est la vie,*" and left it at that, but not Shannon. Circumventing Massey's tight security, she'd learned the gist of the story from Mony's former college roommate and Massey's jilted high school flame, Cindy Van Dyke. There was a dark secret hidden under the Ferguson and Altman façade. Secrets that could be useful in the right hands for the right price. She carried the tray of beers over to where Mony was sitting and set the tray on the old coffee table.

Mony stood this time, not appreciating Shannon's towering over her. "I didn't get to finish telling you, I love what you and Shawn have done to the place," Mony said, "and the piano. It really adds something special."

Remembering the person who had donated it, Shannon muttered, "Thanks." Then, as if to mind her manners, she added, "I just want to say, I'm sorry about your dad, Mony. Shawn is right, we'll all miss him terribly around here. He really was a great guy." She offered a weak smile and, feeling she'd done her duty, walked back to the bar counter.

Mony sat back down and took advantage of the brief

solitude. With only a dozen or so patrons, the place was relatively quiet, but it wouldn't stay that way for long. The after-work crowd would be rolling in soon, and once the live band showed up, the place would go crazy. Lonely Boot was a local favorite.

She reflected on how less than an hour ago she'd felt anxious and afraid, but Mindy had been right about the snowmobile ride. It had been just the thing she'd needed, or maybe it was the company. Nate always had a way of distracting her from unpleasant thoughts, and she wondered if that was what he was now to her, nothing more than a distraction. She held that thought as Nate returned to the sofa.

"Better luck next time, man," Nate taunted, clearly full of himself for besting Shawn at his own game. He turned to Mony. "You know, Shannon kept Grain Belt on tap just for me and Buddy." Nate took a long drink. "Buddy always liked his beer."

"It's still one of my favorites too," Mony said wistfully. "But I think the beer is more for your benefit than Dad's. That girl still has a thing for you, you know." She tried to say it without inflection and failed.

"Shannon knows where I stand on that subject," Nate said flatly, and held up his pint to Mony's. "Here's to the best drinking Buddy in the world." He clicked his glass to hers, wiggling his eyebrows. "See what I did there, *Buddy, buddy*?"

Mony rolled her eyes.

Shannon appeared again, standing over them with some menus. "It's going to get pretty crazy around here in about twenty minutes," she said. "So, if you two wanted to order anything, you might want to do it now."

"Better not," Mony said holding up her hand. "No offense, but we won't be staying much longer. As I mentioned, Poppy has dinner waiting for us."

"Hey," Shannon ignored her and nudged Nate's arm. "Since you're not playing with Lonely Boot tonight, why don't you play a song before you go? It's been a while since you've tickled the ivories, and it's good for business."

Nate's lips cracked into a slow grin. "Um, I don't know," he said, shaking his head. "I'm not sure we have time for that."

Mony's eye's narrowed. "Don't think that I don't know what's going on here. I've just spent the better part of the day conniving and scamming myself. I know when I'm being hoodwinked." But she caved and said to Nate. "You're taking the heat when Poppy is pissed that we're late."

Nate gave an ostentatious wave of his hand. "Psh, I can handle Poppy." He winked at Shannon. "Now, if you ladies will excuse me?"

Nate strolled off; Shannon said, "I hope you don't mind."

Mony knew darn well Shannon wasn't sorry at all but said anyway, "Don't worry, I think he's been itching to do this all day. Besides, he could use a healthy outlet to blow off a little grief right now. It's better than drinking, right?" But Shannon wasn't listening. Mony watched the woman eye Nate as he situated himself on the stage.

"Thanks." Shannon said absently and excused herself.

The bar patrons bubbled with anticipation, taking notice of Nate at the baby grand. It was always a treat for anyone who happened to be in the bar when Nate took the stage. Anybody who knew him, which was everyone in town, had been aware of the stardom in their midst. Even though Nate's band's music had been very generation-specific, with a sex, drugs, and rock n' roll sort of vibe, Nate Ferguson was not. Nate had an innate ability to reach people's hearts through his music on a multigenerational level. Folks appreciated that about their hometown boy and regarded him with the same sense of pride they reserved for the senator and Nate's older brother. Those who loved Nate knew the depth of his genius and that his success had never been a question of if, but when. What had remained a mystery to most people was why Nate had left the music business. Mony was certain her dad had known. Buddy seemed to understand Nate better than anyone. He'd told her many times that Nate would return to Williston one day, not because of failure, but because the core of his inspiration had been rooted in the stark, open prairie land. Her father had been right, and for that, the locals could enjoy the first-class musician and native son in their midst.

Mony drank her beer while Nate got himself settled at the piano. She watched with amusement as he goofed around with some warmup drills, the kind a piano instructor made an eight-year-old do during lessons. What a clown. Her lips twisted wryly at the familiar exercise, recalling how she'd had hated that part of the lesson until Nate joined her practices and made the most menial task seem fun. Nate worked the silliness out of his system and settled into a more serious warmup. Playing through various chords, he found the key he wanted and locked his gaze on Mony. Her heartbeat quickened when she recognized the light, delicate chords of the semplice melody as Nate began to sing a Billy Joel tune.

The protective shell he displayed for the rest of the audience melted away for only Mony to see, revealing a confession cleverly hidden in the lyrics. Mony tried to look away, but couldn't, riveted by his transparency. In the presence of Nate's naked heart, she felt the near-tangible passion resonate in the space between them, stirring a restlessness deep inside her, a resurgence of hunger she'd forsaken long ago, awakening like the roar of a storm. It was too much. She felt too exposed and on the verge of tears. Music had always been Nate's way of expressing what lay deepest in his soul. As she was held rapt by his passion, a memory crept into Mony's conscious mind.

It was the summer she turned seventeen, a season of many firsts. After she'd begged for three years in a row, her dad had finally agreed to take his wildcat with wings to the air show in Oshkosh and promised to let her pilot the plane. It would be their first vacation together and the longest flight Mony had taken with Dad since he'd brought her to North Dakota. Nate wasn't excited about the news at all, and it marked their first fight. Mony shouldn't have been surprised by Nate's reaction, but his controlling nature and the depth of his fear at her leaving were overwhelming. Buddy picked up on the tension and offered to take Nate along, but Kip forbade it. Mony and Nate argued bitterly the night before she left, and he refused to see her off the next morning. She left in a sullen mood, but the flight to Wisconsin also gave her perspective. Mony and her dad never talked the way they did during the flight. They talked like two adults about things that truly mattered, reflecting on love, desire, and dreams in their many forms. Her dad explained that no matter how noble, love always came at a price, but if it was truly your heart's desire, it was always worth every penny.

When Mony returned late that Sunday evening, she found Nate at the house, waiting by the piano. She went to him and took her place by his side while he played for her. There were no words of apology exchanged, their anger forgotten and forgiveness assumed. But something changed between them from that moment forward. They never spoke of their disagreement again. It seemed each had been too frightened by the heartache they shared, unaware it was only the first of many.

Mony watched with admiration the practiced movement in Nate's arms, how his back and shoulders flexed with controlled restraint. The grace and fluidity of his actions were like that of a lover's caress, gentle yet powerful. Closing her eyes, she gave herself freely to Nate's soulful voice and dared to think on what their life might be together. They knew each other so well, reacting to every need like the other was an appendage of their own body. They only had to think it, and the other responded intuitively. To be separated was almost like being without one's own essence.

Mony had often wondered over the years if the anguish they'd endured had been worth the secret she kept from Nate. Had it not been for Bob and Kiteri, she would have given up long ago when life had been at its darkest. Yet, through it all, Mony and Nate had somehow managed to flourish separately, each leading full and successful lives. But were they so independent?

She opened her eyes and saw a lover's smile reflecting back at her. It was Nate who revealed Mony in every way: every corner of her heart; every inch of mind, body, and soul. Everywhere save one. But someday Nate would learn of that secret, the one that lay coiled like a viper ready to strike if disturbed. All the pain they'd been through over their years apart would be nothing compared to his knowing, and still, how could they ever be truly together if she withheld the truth?

As Nate finished the song, the mundane bar had become livelier. Patrons clapped and whistled with enthusiasm, shouting, "One more, Nate!" and "Sing another!" Each barked out their request. He ate it up with a spoon.

"Thank you, thank you, I'll be here all night," he teased, waving to the crowd as the whistles and cheers grew in intensity. Mony shot him an exasperated look.

"Oh, just kidding." He flashed her a sheepish grin.

Mony picked up the two shots sitting on the coffee table and walked to the piano, handing one to Nate. They clinked glasses and tossed them back, the gesture fueling a frenzied roar of approval from the crowd. Nate slid over to give Mony room on the bench and struck the piano keys with chords from a familiar Jerry Lee Lewis tune guaranteed to get any party started.

Shannon walked to the front door, where Shawn was checking IDs, and grinned. Looking over the crowd of patrons singing, dancing, and drinking, she shouted above the noise, "Leave it to Nate to bring down the house."

Shawn nodded. "You think it might have something to do with the company he is keeping tonight?"

Shannon stopped grinning. As much as she hated to admit it, she had to concur. Mony's presence did bring out a whole other level of exuberance to Nate's music. She thought about what Mony had said about music being Nate's cathartic outlet. She couldn't remember the last time she'd seen him so happy and carefree. It made her jealous, but it had also warmed her heart. By the end of the song Mony was playing piano alongside him. *Buddy would have approved.*

The customers kept the pint glasses full for Nate and Mony, hoping to keep the party rolling. Shannon was about to have her brother tap another keg when a half-dozen riggers from Monroe Oil strolled in. It wasn't unusual for the riggers to come into the bars, nor had their business been unwelcome. They were entitled to a good time of drinking and listening to the music same as anyone else, and a customer was a customer. But an unease fell between Shannon and Shawn. Vergil and Vernon, who'd just shown up for their shift, picked up on the vibe too. Shannon barely registered the person at the counter touching her forearm. Then the familiar voice shouted over the crowd, "I thought you said a band was playing tonight?"

Shannon looked up from her beer tap. *The lawyer.*

CHAPTER 18

JOHN

"They're playing a little bit later," the redhead said above the noise. "This is just the happy hour entertainment. Do you like?"

John nodded and turned his head in the direction of the stage. "So he won't be playing long?" From the corner of his eye, John sensed the shift in Monroe's posture when he spotted Ramona and Nathan Ferguson. Heat began to radiate from his body and his muscles tensed. The bartender had picked up on it too.

"No, they won't be here long," she said, and quickly changed the subject. "What can I get you boys this evening?"

"Double shot of JD and a beer," Jason said without turning to face her.

"It's two for one—"

"Yeah, yeah, whatever." Jason cut her off with a flippant wave of his hand.

John bristled, already regretting his decision to come to the bar. He knew Jason was jonesing for a fight. After the sheriff had handcuffed Jason at the meeting and threatened to fine him for a concealed weapon, he'd been hell-bent on a plan for retaliation. According to Senator Ferguson, the sheriff would have been well within the law to arrest Jason, and he only had himself to blame. Somehow John had managed to talk the sheriff down to a verbal warning—maybe because it would have required a search for the alleged gun, which no one seemed eager to pursue. It didn't hurt that Attorney Ferguson had negotiated that charges be dropped against the riflemen at the lake in exchange for the warning. It pissed John off to no end that he hadn't been able to make a better first impression. Yet here he sat with Jason, still playing it stupid. He knew Jason had made an impromptu call to some of the riggers, inviting them for free drinks. Since nothing came for free, John was sure it had been in exchange for the muscle Jason would need to inflict a serious ass-kicking if Ferguson or any of his cronies showed up at the bar. John hoped it wouldn't come to that. Of course, hope was a piss-poor plan and pointless when it came to Jason averting trouble.

The bartender moved from Jason to John. "What will it be for you, sir?"

"John, my name is John," John said with overt friendliness and extended his hand.

She shook it. "Okay, John, what can I get you?"

"I'll have a light, whatever beer you have on tap." He turned, pointing toward the stage. "Say, that fellow at the piano, isn't that the Fergmeister from the band Mile-High City?"

The bartender looked at him with surprise. "Why yes, do you know them?" she asked.

"Another fuckin' Ferguson," Jason bit out. "How many of those bastards are there?"

John clinched his jaw at Jason's lack of subtlety. Jason's so-called PR visit had failed miserably. The guy had a thirty-six-hour jump on John, and he was still clueless of who the big players were in town.

"You'd know if you had done your homework, jackass."

"Do you want to pay now or start a tab?" The bartender interjected.

Without looking, Jason flipped a fifty onto the bar counter and reached for his shot.

John took a sip of his beer. Everyone knew Altman and Ferguson. The two had money, power, and popularity, and had dutifully shared their wealth with the community. They were decorated veterans in an unpopular war, and Ferguson had raised two successful children. It all seemed so air-tight and squeaky clean it made him nauseous. *But does everyone like them?* John considered that a moment. A rich man had the potential to make just as many enemies as he had allies and friends. Had all their benevolence been used to buy votes? Purchased popularity was a shaky investment, John knew, and he decided to do some more sleuthing. The bartender returned with Jason's change.

"The woman sitting next to Ferguson's not half bad on the piano," John said in a pleasant voice. "Who is she?"

"That's Mony Strong," she blurted, a bit too cheery.

"Mony Strong, is she from around here?" John asked.

"Yes."

"They play pretty good together. Is she related to Ferguson?"

The question made the bartender laugh. "Family friend."

"So Strong is her maiden name?"

"No," the bartender said with disinterest.

"Then she's married?"

"Was."

For a bartender, the woman was sure being evasive. He pressed a little harder. "Was she married to Ferguson?"

The redhead gave a curt laugh. "No. I really have to get back to my customers. If you'll excuse me." She collected the empty pint glasses and moved to the opposite end of the bar.

That struck a chord. She was hiding something, he knew it. He just hadn't hit on the right question, yet.

A collective groan rose from the crowd. John turned to see Ferguson standing next to the piano, leaning over Ramona. She tilted her head back to look at him with her lips inches away from his. All she had to do was lean a little forward and they would be touching. Instead, she flicked her tongue along her bottom lip while Ferguson's eyes followed the movement. His body tensed and Ramona smiled. She slid her fingertips down along his arm to his wrist, then circled the neck of his beer bottle. Tugging the bottle loose, she wrapped her lips around the top and took a long pull of his beer, her throat working with each swallow.

John's mind fell straight into the gutter as he recalled those lips wrapped around him and wondered how

Ferguson refrained from nailing her on the piano right then and there. Ferguson smiled and headed down a hallway toward the bathrooms. Next to John, Jason eased off his stool and his movement caught the attention of a couple of riggers sitting around a table nearby. They stood, following Jason in the same direction where Ferguson had disappeared. For a split second, John was torn on what to do—keep Jason's sorry ass out of trouble, which he'd been paid to do, or use him as a diversion.

Several people had stopped Ramona as she passed through the crowd, offering her hugs. It seemed her appeal flowed outward toward everyone. She had a gift for connecting with people. He felt a sting of jealousy, and it occurred to John then that he and Ferguson weren't the only ones who were enamored by her charm.

Ramona reached the sitting area by the fireplace and picked up her hat, scarf, and gloves. Wrapping the scarf around her neck, she turned toward the bar and froze when she spotted him watching her. He flashed what he hoped was a winning smile, and she seemed startled by his presence. John thought that maybe it had worked when he felt something shift between them. It wasn't the steely cold she'd given him at the ice rink or the conference room. She became flustered and didn't seem to know what to do next.

Once again, John faced a now-or-never moment, and for a split second debated the wisdom of his impulsive action, then thought, *Screw it.* He took a deep breath and walked directly toward Ramona, watching her eyes widen as he approached.

"Walk with me. We need to talk, now," he said.

Ramona gave a glance toward the bathrooms and nodded.

He linked his arm in hers, and they walked briskly out the door. John steered down the sidewalk past a couple of storefronts before she rounded on him.

"What the hell do you want?" she snapped.

God, she sounded pissed. John fought back the urge to throw her onto the hood of a nearby car and kiss her senseless. "Ramona, I just wanted to talk to you alone for a minute," he said with forced calm. "But you seem to have an entourage wherever you go."

Ramona bristled at his proximity. "What do you want from me?" He noted her eyes darting up and down the sidewalk and toward the street. *She was planning an escape.*

"I— I just can't believe you're here, in this town of all places, that's all," John stammered. He felt confused and thought she had to have known there was a possibility she might run into him tonight. Had she talked Ferguson into bringing her to the bar? He had to know. "Why didn't you tell me you were coming tonight?"

Ramona crossed her arms across her chest and said nothing. She was so close, too close, and he could feel the heat emanating from her body. Even after being in the bar, she still smelled divine, with a hint of lavender and another delicious scent he couldn't place. Cutting off her escape route, John held his ground. He wanted to reach out and hold her, but kept his arms close to his sides, certain she would run, or worse. There were so many things he had wanted to ask her, but the question that burned most in his mind had nothing to do with North Dakota, the Fergusons, or oil fields. "Why did you sneak off like that?" he asked.

Ramona flinched as if John had pinched her, and she eyed him suspiciously. Her face was a mask to her emotions; then, as if she had made some weighted decision, she stepped into him. John had braced himself for a slap, and was caught off guard by the sudden change in disposition.

"I didn't sneak off on you," she said with a coy smile. "We both knew where things would end up. Can't you let it be a wonderful night of passion and leave it at that?"

But there lay the problem. He couldn't, John realized. He wanted more.

Ramona took his hand in hers. "It's okay, John, really it is," she said soothingly. "We're adults; you don't owe me an explanation."

"It was wonderful," he murmured, returning the squeeze, and felt the warmth radiate from where her fingers touched his hand and spread through his body.

She stepped in closer. "Please, just let it be." Ramona reached for his upper arm and gently stroked it up and down with her free hand.

It was difficult for John not to feel the growing disconnect between her words and their physical connection. Challenged by her elusive air, he grabbed hold of her outstretched arm and pulled her to him. Wrapping his arms around her, he kissed her with narrow-minded voracity. Her shocked reaction only fueled his determination as she tried to pull away. He backed her toward the building, bumping her back against the wall. The jolt did nothing to knock the fight out of her, and he pressed the advantage. He could taste the desire on her lips, and her tongue triggered a hunger deep inside his core. The wind whirled around them, mixed with soft powdery snow, and she shivered, yet her body grew hotter by the minute. John couldn't help but wonder if Ferguson had ever dared to kiss her that way. Her body gradually softened, succumbing to his persistence.

"That's it," John murmured gentling his kiss. "Don't fight me, Ramona." He took his leisure, using slow, plunging licks of his tongue, sucking along her bottom lip and sliding his mouth along her jaw.

She reached for the nape of his neck and whimpered a moan of pleasure, drawing into him, a much-needed sign of consent. Then suddenly she tucked her chin away from his mouth, and her body began to tremble. She seemed to lose strength in her knees, and her cheeks flushed. She crisscrossed her arms over her chest, closing her body off, but not before he'd found what he wanted to see. She wasn't indifferent to the attraction between them, and he felt her warm breath mist against his lips.

"John, please, just let me go."

John leaned his lips next to her ear. "You're driving me crazy, Ramona." He nuzzled her hair, breathing in the scent of her. "I'm drawn to you. Can't you see?" He ran his lips across her cheek, and her lips parted to accommodate her quick breaths. Lowering his voice, he said in a deep, seductive tone, "Tell me what I have to do to see you."

A ruckus near the front of the bar distracted John from his carnal pursuits. Rockstar Ferguson burst through the door, stumbling onto the sidewalk, looking frantically out into the street at the passing cars. He spun around, nearly tripping, then caught sight of them. It was all the diversion Ramona needed to pull away.

It happened so fast. In three strides Ferguson was on top of John, landing a well-executed right hook to his jaw, followed by an uppercut that was hard enough to snap his head back; then he drove a hard punch to his gut. John barely knew what hit him, and he buckled over, the last blow stealing his breath. Ferguson reared for a second assault.

"I'm just getting started," he snarled and reached for John's hair. But before he could do further damage, Ramona threw herself between them, blocking the next punch. She threw her arms around Ferguson.

"Take me home, Nate. I want to go home," Ramona implored, holding in the tension that coiled in Ferguson. He froze instantly, and she repeated her appeal. "Nate, take me home."

Ferguson pointed his finger at John. "If this motherfucker thinks that jackass and his posse were going to distract me, he's way dumber than I thought." He winced suddenly, staggering back a step. Ramona pulled him forward, shifting his weight against her shoulders. The man's eyes were wild with alcohol and fury, and it took all her strength to stay between Ferguson and John.

"It's okay, Natty; I'm okay. Will you take me home, please," Ramona beseeched. "We need to go home now."

John stepped back, distancing himself from the two of them. It was reckless of her to put herself between two men engaged in violence, and he considered pulling her away from the crazy son of a bitch, but he had neither the will nor the strength. As he contemplated his next move, John watched in astonishment as Ramona weaved her magic spell. She had completely enveloped Ferguson, keeping his head tucked close to her chest. Stroking and petting his arms and hair, she rocked him back and forth in her arms. She'd already defused the situation, John realized, and if he made a move now, he would only make things worse.

Without a backward glance, they walked away. It was almost comical, witnessing her smaller body bearing the weight of the much larger man. She helped Ferguson onto the snowmobile, taking her seat in the driving position, then donned a pair of gloves and snow goggles. She grabbed hold of Ferguson's arms, wrapping them around her waist like a seatbelt, and he tightened his hold as she brought the powerful machine to life with a deafening roar. She eased the snowmobile out into the street, where she drove to the end of the block, turned the corner, and was gone from sight. Dazed and confused, John felt a bizarre sense of déjà vu as he stood there with his mouth gaping, his feet cold, and his gut and jaw aching.

No sooner had the roar of the snowmobile dissipated than it was replaced by another burst of commotion. Jason Monroe came hurtling out onto the sidewalk. He tumbled into a snowbank. A brute of a man followed him out.

"Blarney Stone will not tolerate that sort of behavior, Mr. Monroe," the bouncer, named Shawn according to his shirt, said in a tone that invited no argument. "You need to leave now, and your patronage is no longer welcome." He turned on his heel and disappeared back into the bar.

John walked over to where Jason was lying in the snow and offered him a hand up. Jason hesitated at first, but there was something about being in the cold, wet snow that humbled a man. He grabbed onto John's outstretched arm and winced when his lawyer took hold of his hand. It was a bloody mess, with a gash next to his thumb and abrasions across his knuckles.

Standing under the streetlight, John could see the outline of a bruise forming under Jason's right eye, his cheek already red and swollen. He could only imagine what he looked like under those same lights. They were both a bloody, beaten mess, and his entire body started to ache. He felt a sudden onslaught of exhaustion. He was cold, and what he needed right now was a nice hot shower and a chance to regroup. Clapping a hand on Jason's shoulder, John implored, "We need to get the hell out of here, man. I don't know what you were doing in there, and I don't really give a shit about that now, but if this was your idea of a PR mission for Monroe Oil, it's officially fucked."

Jason shrugged John's hand from his shoulder and staggered back a step. Fed up with the bullshit, John got into Jason's face and stared into his wild, antagonistic eyes.

"You have to trust me. I am not your enemy. We're both out on a limb here and we have to plan a new strategy." John turned away and surveyed the empty sidewalk and street. "And we can't do that standing out here."

Vibrating with agitation, Jason heaved up air from his lungs like a locomotive, then gradually slowed his breath as the truth of John's words sank in. He reached into his pocket, pulled out his cellphone, punched a button, and slid it back into his pocket. He shot John an incredulous look. "Happy?"

John let out a breath. "Ecstatic." Though he knew he wasn't out of the woods. Yet. Jason's anger had receded into defeat, which made him dangerous and unpredictable. Fishing out his cigarettes, John lit one up, offered one to Jason, and began pacing up and down the sidewalk to keep himself warm. *Ramona must be the linchpin in all this, she just has to be.* She couldn't possibly be here without a reason, and was clearly more to the Fergusons than just some family friend. It wasn't coincidence that she'd shown up after the death of Ferguson's business partner—or was that a false pretense? And why were the Fergusons so damn protective of her? John took another drag off his cigarette. It didn't add up.

"We need a new plan, Jason. We've way underestimated this situation. You pissed off old man Ferguson and we got our asses handed to us." He held up two fingers. "Twice. We need to be smarter. They must have at least one enemy. We just need to find it."

The SUV pulled up—John was thankful to be out of the cold. Once they were rolling, Jason spoke like a man with a renewed sense of purpose. "I'm not only going to get Altman's land; I'm going to destroy that Ferguson and everyone associated with him."

Staring out the window, John said nothing. That had been just the response he'd feared.

CHAPTER 19

MONY

The grueling ride out to the Ferguson farm had nothing to do with distance or lack of speed. Nate was leaning so heavily against Mony's back, it was all she could do to maintain control of the snowmobile while keeping him from tumbling off the seat. Her body screamed in protest every time they hit a rut, and she felt an urgent need to pee. *Goddamn John.* He'd whisked her out of the bar so fast she hadn't had a chance to relieve her bladder, and she had half a mind to pop a squat right there in the middle of the trail.

Nate nestled his chin between her shoulders and remained quiet most of the ride. Mony tried to gauge how much he might have had to drink. He'd been singing almost the whole time they were at the bar, so it couldn't have been that much more than what she'd had. Three, maybe four more beers at best, but that wouldn't be kicking his ass. She began to worry if his stupor had something to do more with the ambush he'd accused John of orchestrating, rather than alcohol consumption.

Maybe it was a combination. Nate's lip had been bleeding when he'd approached her and John on the sidewalk, and there was evidence of a shiner blooming below his right eye, which was odd, since John hadn't gotten in a single punch. Still, a bloody lip and a black eye wouldn't have wiped him out, not like this. The man knew how to handle himself in a brawl as well as his liquor, and it was disconcerting that Nate had been incapacitated enough to prohibit him from driving the Cat. Mony practically had to drag him onto the snowmobile.

Was it all a conspiracy as Nate had asserted? It felt like paranoia, but the plan would be simple enough: split the two of them up, Monroe takes Nate out, and John slinks in. But for what gain? Mony thought about it, then rolled her eyes at her own naïveté. *Revenge, of course.* Yet, the idea seemed so absurd. It was their own stupidity, challenging two dozen North Dakota boys on their home turf. If it hadn't been for the fact that Nate was hurt, the notion would be so ridiculous it was laughable. But why target him? Until he'd punched John outside the bar, Nate hadn't been involved in any of the afternoon's events except to haul her out of the conference room. And what would be accomplished by ambushing Nate at the Blarney Stone? Shawn was his best friend, for Christ sakes, and had dealt with way worse troublemakers than that slimy son of a bitch from Texas and a couple of his punkass thugs. Maybe John and Monroe were as clueless as Nate suggested. If that were the case, neither of them would last long in North Dakota. They were making enemies far too fast.

Conspiracy. It left a bitter taste on her tongue, and Mony found admitting that to herself very disappointing. Yet how could it be any different? She didn't know John, not really. He simply might be that good a con artist, or perhaps she'd just been that gullible. When she thought about it, what man went out of his way to help a strange woman up out of the snow unless he had an ulterior motive? He'd used his male prowess to bait her, and his charm to conquer. Her anger at her own folly provided a useful source of energy the rest of the drive home.

The Ferguson house was dark when they arrived, which meant Massey, Michelle, and the boys were still at her place. Her shoulders sank in disappointment. She sure could have used Massey's help getting Nate inside. Driving the snowmobile had taken all the energy out of her. She drove alongside the house, where she parked near the kitchen entrance. They managed to stumble their way to the bottom of the steps when Nate suddenly leaned away from her, taking a couple of steps before he dropped to his hands and knees and began to vomit. It took all her strength to hold him up from pitching forward face first into the snow. When he finished, Nate took a handful of clean snow, swished it around in his mouth, and spit it out; then he rolled over. Lying on his side, he curled into a ball and closed his eyes. Mony felt a sudden rise of panic.

"Oh, no, you don't," she growled, and felt as though a spike had been driven through her spine. She knew she had to get Nate into the house, or they'd both end up succumbing to hypothermia. Taking off her gloves, she gently stroked his face. "Natty, Natty, honey, wake up. I need your help. I can't get you inside the house by myself."

Nate didn't respond.

Keep it together, Mony told herself. The frigid air bit at her ungloved hand, and she shook Nate by the shoulders. "Nathan Thomas Ferguson, you get your ass up, we need to get into the house. It's too cold to stay out here." He still didn't budge, and she was close to hyperventilating. She began running first-responder scenarios through her head. If she couldn't get Nate to respond, she'd have to leave him and get help. The mere thought of leaving him here, freezing to death, paralyzed her. Tears began to stream down her cheeks, and she considered the possibilities for his condition. If it wasn't alcohol, it had to be some other type of poison—or perhaps he'd been injured more than she could tell on the surface? Driven by desperation, Mony slapped him hard across the face and screamed next to his ear, "We need to get inside, buster, right now."

Nate made a soft moan and muttered, "Okay, Miss Bossy Pants, you don't have to yell." He rolled up into a sitting position. Overwhelmed with relief, Mony managed to get Nate to his feet and started up the steps. They might as well have been climbing Mount St. Helena. Mony practically pulled Nate along using the raw iron rail until they reached the landing in front of the kitchen door. She leaned his head against the railing while she fished through his pockets. "Nate, where's the house key?"

Oblivious to their dilemma, Nate gazed at her through

foggy blue eyes and smiled. "Hello, my wildcat with wings." Without another word, he reached his arm up for the door knob, and gave it a simple turn until she heard the *click*.

Mony navigated the familiar layout of the house in the dark, directing Nate through the kitchen and straight to the main floor bedroom. He flopped unceremoniously onto the bed, and she went to work pulling off his boots, undressing him. Nate mumbled quietly, his head bobbling like a dashboard ornament with each tug. She pulled off his hockey jersey; as Nate's head cleared the shirt, he gave her a silly grin.

"You're really good at this," he babbled, and tried to nuzzle in her hair.

Undaunted by the distraction, she told him, "One more time, babe," and took his hands, gripping them. With a jerk, she brought him to his feet. "I need to get you out of your snow pants. Now behave and stand, please."

Nate complied, his silly grin still on his face. Mony shimmied the pants down to his knees, then made him sit again. He seemed more responsive now, and she felt encouraged that he was participating a little. She left the clothes in a heap on the floor, and Nate flopped down onto the mattress edge like a ragdoll. Sitting in a slouch, he rested his chin on his chest and began to snore softly. *This isn't good.* Mony needed to get a wet washcloth, clean up his face, and check for other injuries.

She didn't take more than two steps when she heard Nate fall back onto the bed with a thud. *At least he didn't tumble forward.* She took him by the feet and swung the dead weight onto bed. He lay catawampus, but it was the best she could do for now, keeping him relatively safe.

Feeling along the inside wall, Mony flipped on the light switch. The harsh fluorescent bulb over the sink flickered to life, and she began running the hot water. The linen cupboard was sparse, with only a towel and a frayed washcloth, but it would have to do. As the water warmed, she looked into the mirror and hardly recognized the reflection staring back at her. Hollow-eyed, with sunken cheeks and deep stress lines crevicing her forehead, it startled her how drawn her face appeared. *Did I look this bad all day? God.* Her dad's wake was tomorrow, and the funeral the day after that.

"You better have brought some magic in your makeup kit, because you're not going out with that face tomorrow," she scolded her reflection. It irritated her how pathetic she looked, but what did she expect, given the events of the past forty-eight hours?

"What are you going to do?" It was a question that bore no simple answer. Being an only child, Mony had always known the day would come when she'd be standing alone to deal with her father's affairs. But drilling? That idea simply never occurred to her. Naive as a child, she'd assumed her dad would just turn the wells and his share of the oil business over to Kip and that would be the end of it. Maybe she should do the same. She hadn't concerned herself with the money, power, or control. It wasn't important. It sounded smug, especially considering the countless North Dakota families who'd have killed to have such a problem, but it had been easy to absolve herself of the responsibility since for most of her life her every need had been met.

After she'd come to live with her dad, Mony couldn't remember wanting anything, material or emotional, except maybe her mother for a time. That didn't mean she'd been spoiled, unless one considered the Piper Dakota her father had given her—not an ordinary, run-of-the-mill item a parent bought for a child. But she was a pilot, and what pilot didn't own a plane? It seemed an entirely normal necessity in her estimation. At the same time, if her dad had never bought it, she might have missed it but wouldn't have lamented the omission. She had her own home, a business, and a fulfilling life. Plus, in the back of her mind, she'd always known if she ever needed help financially, her dad or Kip would have provided.

But now she had her own children to consider and what sort of legacy she would leave for them. Mony loved the life she and Bob had built for their children, simple and uncomplicated, yet full of challenge. Now Kip wanted to muck it all up and seemed to have the next phase of her life all planned, from drilling a new oil well to frack-mining her property in Minnesota. Just the thought of mining the beautiful bluffs made her ill, not to mention the principle of the matter, which went against everything she and Bob had believed in and fought for. At some point, she'd have to confront Kip on the matter. That was an inevitable fact, but it would have to wait. Right now, she needed to focus on getting through the next couple of days.

Mony picked up the warm, wet cloth and started washing her face. Looking at her reflection, she wondered what the hell John could have possibly seen in her, or what he meant when he said he wanted to be with her. It had to be part of a bigger scheme, his seducing her just a calculated fragment of a plot to get to her father's estate. The idea alone pissed her off, though it was mostly at herself, participating as a willing victim. It hadn't taken much, since he'd used her unmet sexual needs against her. She would have to accept that as well as the consequences for her impulsive actions.

Brushing the warm washcloth across her lips, she felt the sore tenderness of the bruise left behind by Dwight's cheap shot, intensified by John's ravenous kiss. She despised the lingering pull of physical attraction she felt toward him. John was her adversary now, plain and simple, and the passion they'd shared on the train, whether staged or genuine, was all that would ever be.

The resurgent call of her bladder had Mony scrambling to remove her multiple layers of clothing, stripping down to her bra and panties just to sit on the toilet. She barely made it. Propping her elbows on her knees, she rested her chin in her hand and slipped deeper into thought.

"And what am I going to do about you?" she said to the wall between the bathroom and the bedroom. There was, again, no easy answer. Would Nate still want her, now that Bob was no longer in her life? Distance had made it easier for Mony to keep her feelings toward Nate in check. But with each subsequent visit home since Bob's passing, she'd felt the thin veil that protected her secret

unravel like the frayed cloth in her hand, especially when
Dane was around. It was a truth that could destroy them
all, the life she had built with Bob, and it wouldn't stop
there. Massey's family would suffer too, and she refused
to bring that kind of trouble into his life. The Ferguson
boys were not her brothers, at least not by blood, but she
loved them as such, with one exception. Mony reflected
on that indulgence, and the events it had triggered.

*She'd just returned to college, her heart filled with remorse.
She'd hurt Nate in the worst way possible, and sought Massey's
counsel. He took her to his apartment, cleaning her up after
she'd been at an all-night beer party. They went to his room
to avoid the scrutiny of his roommates. Massey tried to console
her, promising that everything would be alright. He held her in
his arms, kissed her hair, her forehead, her cheeks, her mouth.
They woke the next morning, both lying half-naked under the
sheets. Had they? Jesus. Her last memory was of Massey's lips
on her mouth. She quickly got dressed, already late for morning
class. When Massey woke, he seemed just as bewildered, unable
to recall if anything had happened either. They made the walk
of shame past his roommates. They promised to talk, but they
never did.*

*The timing was right, Dane might have been his, but Massey
never sought legitimacy. How could he, aware of what the
exposure would do to his little brother? Further, Mony had never
been willing to take the risk. Why dredge up an irrevocable
wound when Bob Strong had already accepted Dane as his own?
Through silent agreement, Massey and Mony had let that be the
truth.*

Finished with her business, Mony went to the sink to

wash her hands. Her whole body ached from all the abuse it had absorbed throughout the day, and she cringed at the idea of redressing in the sweat-drenched clothing lying on the cold floor. She felt like a wilted piece of lettuce. Draping her thermal clothing over the tub and shower rail, she settled on sponging off by the sink. Standing naked in front of the mirror, she was shocked by the other black-and-blue marks covering her body. An angry scab stretched the entire length of her forearm, and she wondered how she'd gotten it without tearing through any of the layers of clothing. Palpating her lip, Mony winced at the bruising under the surface, a cruel reminder that even though she acted like one sometimes, she wasn't a kid anymore. Still, the pain was worth it, demoralizing Mitchell, and she smiled despite the aches. It was gratifying that as bad as she felt, Dwight would be feeling a hundred times worse thanks to Dane. Somewhat refreshed, Mony's spirits lifted a little; she slipped into her semi-dried bra and lacy boy shorts when a panicked cry slapped her out of her introspection.

"Mony, where are you?"

The high-pitched screech nearly stopped her heart, but it was the sudden crash that had her bolting toward the bedroom. She found Nate propped on his elbow, his legs dangling partway out of the bed. The crashing sound had been the alarm clock, which lay blinking on the floor. She sat on the bed and used her body to block him from getting up.

"It's okay, Nate, honey," she said, stroking his hair. "I'm right here, I just had to go to the bathroom. Lie back on the bed and rest."

Nate flopped back onto the bed, but not before wrapping his arms around her waist. "I thought I'd lost you again."

Mony noticed his eyes were still shut tight and wondered if he was dreaming. Nate had been prone to nightmares when they were kids, mostly about his mom, and would wake up screaming much the way he had now. She shifted her weight, and his grip tightened around her waist.

"Why does everyone try to take you away from me, Mony?" Nate muttered, more a rhetorical than a direct question.

"No one can take me away from you," Mony soothed. "Now come, let me check you over. I want to see if you're hurt anywhere else." She tried to get Nate to sit up, to no avail. Using a different approach, she reached for his thermal long johns, but the unyielding lock around her waist had her trapped in a terribly uncomfortable position. She tried to divert his attention. "Your lip is bleeding, were you in a fight?"

Nate's eyes flew open wide, and he searched the ceiling as if looking for a clue. "I don't know. Some asshole snuck up behind me and hit me while I was taking a piss, I think." Then he snickered. "I think I might have pissed on his shoe." Nate lurched up on his elbow, remembering something. "That bastard Finch, he was trying to take you away, wasn't he?" Nate looked at her straight on; his eyes were still unfocused. "Did he hurt you, Mony?"

Mony used the change in position to press him back onto the bed. He was still trapped in a nightmare. "Nate, I'm all right, please, don't worry. Now let me check you.

Are you hurt anywhere?"

He stilled, as if assessing. "No, I don't think so, though my head hurts like a son of a bitch." Nate reached to the back of his skull and winced. "I must have been cold-cocked from behind."

Mony used the distraction to lift Nate's legs back onto the bed, sliding his thermal long johns off in the process. That proved to be a huge mistake—she discovered he'd been commando underneath. She quickly slung part of the sheet over his groin. *Christ.* She couldn't even begin to think about what lay beneath the sheet right now and returned her focus to Nate's injury. Leaning over him, she prompted him to lift his head off the pillow. He snaked his arms under hers, wrapping them around her body.

"Just lift your head, please, I'm trying to feel for bumps."

Nate sat up, extending his legs out in front of him. He lifted Mony's hips onto his lap and pressed her body tight against his, caressing the bare skin of her back. "You don't have a shirt on, Mony," he said with a surprised grin, running his finger along the length of her torso. The sensation sent a tingle of awareness all the way down her spine and she shivered. "Hmm, you feel so soft," he said with a purr, lightening his touch until it felt like a tickle.

The feather-soft sensation made goose bumps dance along her arms. Mony tried to wriggle free of the awkward position. This time he let her, and she straddled her knees across his lap to face him. Taking his head in the palm of her hands, she urged him forward onto her shoulder and ran her fingers carefully through his hair, assessing the back of his head. Nate nuzzled his face into the crook of her neck, breathing softly while she continued her inspection. He was cooperative at least, but the gentle touch of his fingers over her skin was maddening. She had to keep telling herself, *Don't go there.* But the innocuous tease stirred a sensuality deep inside her. She willed herself to ignore the temptation. Neither one of them were in any kind of shape to take further action on where her carnal thoughts were leading.

Her exam paid off when Nate took a sharp breath as her fingers uncovered a quarter-sized lump on the back of his head. "Oh, baby, sorry about that, but you have quite a goose egg back there." She moved her hand away from the injury. "Does it hurt?" Mony continued to comb her fingers through his hair, searching for further evidence of injury. Luckily, she only found the one bump, though that was bad enough. Placing her palms on either side of his ears, she pulled his face from her shoulders. Head injuries and concussions had always been her worst fear as a hockey mom, and given the crazy day they'd just had, Nate could have sustained the bump at any time on or off the ice. What she wanted to do was check his pupils to see if they reacted to light, but the only light available was coming in from the outside yard light and the washroom, neither of which provided the means for an accurate assessment.

Nate studied her as she stared into his eyes and tipped his head from one side to another. He seemed to be tracking well enough; his pupils naturally dilated in the dim lighting, his blue irises responded, focusing and refocusing. He gave her a sly smile and pressed his lips to hers in a gentle kiss. Mony had seen it coming but didn't try to stop him. She felt the jagged edge of the cut where his lip had been bleeding, tasted the salt and iron of his blood. With great care, she kissed over his injury. Nate's hands stroked restlessly up and down her back, and Mony moved her face away from his lip. "Does that hurt?" she whispered.

His hands splayed open against her bare flesh. "No," he murmured, his lips pressed against her chin. Sliding his mouth along her jaw, he sucked her neck with soft kisses.

His reverence was disarming. Mony reached for the nape of his neck, returning the gentle caress. Nate moved his focus from her neck to her chest and brushed his cheeks over the top of her breasts. She stifled a moan of pleasure, afraid of the hunger stirring deep inside and closed her eyes. Attuned to her arousal, Nate continued nipping gently at her flesh. Tipping her chin back, Mony arched into his embrace, offering access, and let the sensation of his kisses quicken her heartbeat. Nate slid his hands down her back and cupped around her buttocks, lifting and pulling her body closer to his. Cradled against him, Mony felt his length against her boy shorts. His arousal paired with the glimpse of what lay beneath the sheet made her smile. She widened the spread between her knees, desperate to feel every inch of him, and rocked her pelvis into his erection. He quivered against the rhythmic friction, sending an erotic sensation pulsing across her sex. Nate fumbled to unhook her bra, but in a fit of impatience, pushed it up over the top of her breast, gaining the access he sought. He latched onto her nipple, no longer gentle, and pulled with lustful ferocity.

Mony gasped, reveling in the feel of Nate's mouth on her flesh, and pulled the confinement of her bra off over her head. He seized the advantage and rolled her beneath him, pinning her to the bed. Straddling her hips, he sat up, reaching for the top of his shirt, and yanked it over his head, tossing it aside. Naked, he laid his bare chest against hers and nestled his mouth in the crook of her neck. The sensation sent an electric jolt through her system, with every fiber of her being coming alive with want.

"Oh, Mony, you feel so good, and I want you so bad."

Mony stroked her fingers up and down the rippled muscles in his back, boldly sliding her hands down to his buttocks, where he had no butt to speak of. With only flexing muscle and flesh to hold onto, she dug in her fingers, grasping for purchase. His ragged breathing began to slow suddenly against her neck, and she felt the energy of his passion fading.

"Please don't leave me," Nate murmured as his body molded onto hers. "Stay with me, *forever.* I love you so much." He grew heavy against her, then drifted into unconscious sleep.

Mony's heart cried out in anguish, deprived of the satisfaction to her hunger that left her pulse racing and her clit throbbing. It was hard to breathe with Nate lying heavy on top of her, and she tried to wriggle out from under him. Finally, she shoved at his shoulder, the universal gesture all men seemed to innately understand, and he wordlessly tumbled onto his side. Scrambling to sit up, she gasped for air and gazed at the naked man who curled next to her, snoring softly. She reached for the bedding to cover him, but not before lifting the sheet for a quick peek. Overwrought with exhaustion and sexual frustration, she could still smile appreciatively, lamenting the lost opportunity. Snuggling under the blankets, she lay facing him and draped her arm over his torso.

Nate wrapped his arms intuitively around her body like vines of ivy and nestled his lips against her forehead. Her lacy boy shorts remained the only barrier of clothing between them. She began to tremble, a silent purge of the carnal ache inside, and cried softly, the only outlet left for her raw emotions. Nate's confession, the one he'd always reserved to express in music, encircled them, coiling in and around their bodies like a living thing.

They'd both dodged a bullet, each in their own vulnerable state. If they'd made love tonight, there was no telling where their relationship might have ended up in the morning, and it would have ruined any chance of that relationship succeeding before it even began. Nate might never let her go, no matter what the cost, unwilling to let what had happened between them as teenagers occur again these many years later.

Mony stroked the thick tussle of Nate's sandy brown hair, and whispered next to his ear. "I love you too. Don't you know you are my heart, my soul?" For her to have claimed Nate as her soulmate implied that he was something separate from her or that they required some sort of connectivity to be complete. But Nate was her, and she was him, one and the same. They felt one another's joy and hurt. If one struggled or suffered, the other was right alongside, and if they couldn't heal themselves from within, how could they help each other? Her dad's passing was too fresh a wound for both right now to lend the other the support, though she knew they would each try. Perhaps they had learned how in their years of separation. She could hope.

But that was only part of what she had to consider now. Two terrible secrets hung between them: a poor decision from the past and John. They would need to work through those first if there was to be any future between them. And if they couldn't? If Mony broke Nate's heart again, it would be the demise of them both, because deep down inside, she would never survive hurting him, any more than he.

Caressing the back of Nate's head, Mony found the bump and frowned. Had he fallen asleep due to fatigue and drunkenness, or was his unconsciousness because of a concussion? Part of her wanted to haul his ass to the emergency room right there on the spot, but she'd never be able to get him out of the house by herself. Besides, Massey would be home soon to take over the watch. Until then, it was Mony's vigil to keep, and she settled back into the possessiveness of Nate's embrace.

CHAPTER 20

MASSEY

Massey sat alone at the kitchen table drinking a beer. It was eleven o'clock, and he could hear his wife arguing with the boys upstairs, trying to get them to settle for bed. Mony walked into the kitchen dressed in the clothing she'd worn that afternoon, carrying Nate's coat. *She looks guilty.* It shouldn't have surprised him to see them lying together, nor had it been the first time they'd shared a bed. It was just that it hadn't been for a very, very long time. Massey got up from the table, walked over to the fridge, and grabbed another beer. He popped the top with a church key dangling on a chain attached to the door handle and handed the beer to Mony. She draped Nate's coat over the back of the chair, took the beer, and then sat it down on the table and walked over to the sink for a glass of water. After taking a long drink, she filled the water glass again and sat down at the table across from him. They nursed their beverages until the uncomfortable silence prompted Massey to speak.

"Dad and I wondered where the two of you went after you left the airport. It wasn't until I got a call about an hour ago from Shannon that anyone really knew." He took a swig of his beer. "Poppy and the kids were all worried, especially after the way you'd left." Mony opened her mouth to speak, but Massey held up his hand. "Don't worry, I covered for you." He gave her a hard look. "I told them you were fine and that Nate had taken you to Blarney Stone to blow off some steam. I told them he played a couple of songs and that he stopped by the farm to get the truck before he brought you home." Massey paused and took another long drink. He was aware of the time Nate and Mony had left the bar, yet he asked, "How long have you two been here?"

Mony bristled and ignored the question. "Nate was hit in the back of the head. I'm worried he may have a concussion; someone needs to watch him during the night."

"I know he was in a fight," Massey said in a calm voice. "Shannon told me." He bore his gaze into her. "Tell me you had nothing to do with that."

Mony bit back a response, refusing to rise to the bait.

"She also told me she'd seen Finch and you leave the bar together, while Monroe and a couple of his boys worked him over in the bathroom. According to Shawn, I suspect he'll have more than a bump on the head."

"Do you want me to stay and watch him?" Mony offered. "He'd asked me to stay with him."

Massey tossed back the rest of his beer. "Absolutely not," he said with cool vehemence. "I am hoping he'll be too drunk to remember you even sleeping with him.

Shit Mony, if he woke up with you in his bed he'd—"
Massey shook his head in irritation. "Well who knows
what he'd do."

"We didn't have sex," Mony snapped. "Not that it's any
of your goddamn business."

Pinning her with his gaze, Massey said, "Oh, Mony,
that's where you're wrong. You're not the only one who
cares about Nate."

"He's a grown man. He can make his own decisions,"
she challenged.

Massey slammed his hand down on the table. "Not
where you're concerned, he's not. Just your presence
alone reduces him to a teenager. Surely you can see that?"

The bluntness of his remark registered in her eyes and
her defiance waned. "What am I supposed to do?" Mony
lamented. "I'm bad for him when I'm around, and it hurts
him when I'm away. It seems so hopeless."

"You're not bad for him, and don't be so melodramatic.
Nate comes alive every time you're near him. He's—"
Massey paused, bemused in his inept search for the right
words. "I don't know. You're fused together somehow."
He smiled with empathy. "Like the morning I found you
both tangled together. The night our dads had that big
fight. You're two unwinding layers of the same cord fused
together. We can't give up on Nate. I can't lo—" His voice
caught, choking down the fear he wouldn't share. *Now
who is being melodramatic?* "It's time for you to go home
now. Don't worry about Nate. I'll watch him over night.
You both need some rest. We have a long couple of days
ahead of us."

Massey had seen to it Mony was safe inside the farmhouse before he pulled out of the Altman driveway. Heading back to his family's farm, he turned off the radio and took his time driving the familiar township road. He needed time to clear his head. He needed to think, but was distracted by the lingering fragrance of lavender. Massey let out a long breath. *Do you even know what you do to a man?* He cracked the window open to ease the distraction. *Does she even realize what she does to me?*

The sight of Mony in his brother's bed had conjured up all sorts of consequences in his brain, all of which scared him shitless. But whether there had been sex involved tonight or not, there would be no turning back. Nate would reclaim the stake he'd made on Mony long ago. A fate that had been sealed the day Kip had brought him and his brother back to North Dakota after leaving their mother crying in that godforsaken town.

It still made him seethe with anger when he thought about that night and the seven long days it had taken his father to find him and Nate. They'd left unexpectedly, Massey, Nate, and their mother, under the pretense of a sort of mini-vacation that their father hadn't been able to join. Intuitively, Massey had known something wasn't right, but she drove them out to Yellowstone, traveling through Beartooth Pass, stopping at the geysers and hot springs along the way. But when his mother pointed her compass further south instead of north, even a nine-year-old boy knew something had gone terribly wrong. Especially when his mother avoided answering the ever-present question. *Where is Dad?* What had driven his mother to such desperation, he could only imagine. She'd run away and taken her sons with her. Massey was only a small boy, Nate even more so, yet they both knew their father would have never agreed to such a cross-country trip, and it was only a matter of time before he'd come looking for them.

The vision was as clear in his mind as Mony and Nate lying together in bed less than an hour ago. How his father had remained uncharacteristically calm declaring the simple ultimatum. *Come back now, or leave without them.* The memory burned forever in his mind. There were times when Massey closed his eyes at night and could still hear his little brother's scream; he saw vividly the image of Nate's arms outstretched for their mother. Nate's struggle had only made matters worse as he flailed and cried. Kip merely tossed him over his shoulder like a sack of feed and carried him back to the car. As she reached out toward them, they left their mother like a garbage can on the curb, and then they drove away. In the rearview mirror, he'd seen her sobbing in a cloud of exhaust, then burying her face in her hands. *What had she done to deserve such cruelty?* The question still haunted him to this very day. It was why he never became a divorce lawyer.

The years before that awful day were only fragments, bits and pieces of a picture puzzle in his mind. But the picture had always depicted a happy family against a backdrop of sandy beaches and bright, sun-filled skies. Then his father had been deployed, and when he returned from Vietnam, the night terrors began. Massey remembered how his mother's eyes were always red from crying. She tried to be a supportive wife. Sometimes his dad would yell at her, sometimes he broke things, but mostly, he could be found the next morning passed out at the kitchen table, an emptied bottle of liquor in his hand. Kip would apologize to her, sometimes to them both. Then he would work day and night just to avoid sleep, until he'd crash from exhaustion.

The night terrors had stopped briefly when Massey's mother had become pregnant with Nate. She'd seemed happier, his dad less volatile, but it didn't last. His mother never liked living in North Dakota, where the wind blew cold and rain turned to snow. She often talked of how she missed the warmth of the southern beaches and the support of her community and friends. But mostly, how she missed her family.

"Why did you have to run?" Massey asked into the darkness, but the night yielded no answer. His mother's fears were understandable, but not his father's cruelty. She had tried to love him. She hadn't forsaken her husband like so many others had done; her husband had left her. Massey had long since given up on wishing things could have been different. After all, what was the point? Wishing couldn't change reality, and his only option had been to move forward. It was either that or get left behind on some curb like his mother. But that hadn't been his destiny; his father had seen to that. The almighty Joseph Kipton Ferguson had no idea the chain of events he'd set into motion the day he'd abandoned his wife. If Massey's father had put his stubborn pride aside for one minute, just one fucking minute, the old man would have seen it was his own goddamn arrogance that had single-handedly sealed the fate of his youngest son to a little girl the moment he'd pulled into Buddy Altman's driveway. Both Nate and Mony had been unwillingly taken from their mothers, and their affinity for one another solidified.

Massey used to wonder why his father had driven out to Buddy's house that day. He'd heard the shouts of anger during the fight, his dad's accusations toward Buddy for having an affair with his mother. It was bullshit. Even after Kip had bloodied his business partner with his own fists, Buddy swore it wasn't true. So why hadn't his father gone looking for his mother afterward? Was it pride or shame that held him back? If he had only asked him, Massey would have told Kip where his Mother was going. He'd overheard her talking on a payphone to her brother stationed at the Air Force Base in Cheyenne. She said she needed to be closer to family. She wanted to *come home.*

Instead, his father fated a little girl into taking a small boy into her bed that night, giving the little boy what he had needed most: a safe refuge from his sorrow and a child's maternal love. Protecting him like a celestial being, Mony soothed his pain, driving back the specters into the darkness, binding them together forever. Massey had seen all of this, knew how they'd felt one another's pain, and still he had coveted her. Why did he have to care about her too?

Massey clenched his jaw and slammed the heel of his hand against the wheel. *I'm a big brother; I'm supposed to be the one to watch over them.* He was supposed to be strong—the brave one, the smart one. He had been everything his father expected: an obedient son, the star athlete, a successful lawyer, a dutiful husband and father. He was the responsible one, the Secret Keeper. He'd grown tired of it. Massey swiped bitterly at the salty tear biting in the corner of his eye as he realized that soon it would be his turn to set life-changing events in motion.

His dad was expecting to inherit the oil business, and he wanted to drill. The business was his, yes, but not the land. And Massey had seen Mony's response to the idea of drilling. *She won't do it.* Buddy had taught his daughter well the value of land, taught her to protect it at all costs. Nor would she sell. That jackass Monroe and his inept lawyer were wasting their time. Yet he'd seen that Finch had somehow managed to make a connection with Mony, seen the recognition register in Finch's eyes when he saw her at the lake. Or perhaps Finch had simply been enamored with Mony's charm? *A laugh.* There had been something off when Massey hugged her at the train station, and it wasn't impossible for Finch to have gotten to her first. He'd have to talk to Mony about that at his earliest opportunity. Either way, if Finch had gotten to her somehow, by accident or design, it was of no consequence and soon would be a dead issue, which left only Nate.

If Mony wouldn't drill, she wouldn't stay, and if she didn't stay—well, he didn't want to think about what that would do to his brother. Or what it would do to him if she stayed. Massey could manage his feelings for Mony when she was married, raising a family, living life far away. They went about their separate lives satisfied and content, Massey playing the dutiful uncle, she the adoring sister, undiluted by the events of that night. He could have assimilated that too, if it hadn't been for Dane. Hardly a day went by he hadn't thought about his failings, letting everyone he cared about down in the worst way. Back at college for his senior year, he'd promised to meet Mony at some brownstone for a house party one evening. She said she'd been worried about Nate and needed to talk. He arrived late, too late. It had been well into the morning before he'd found her. It looked as though she had passed out, lying in a heap on the ground, until he tried to help her up and she whimpered in pain. Her mouth had been bleeding, and she had scrapes and cuts on her hands and arms. She was cold, and he had no idea how long she'd been like that or what the extent of her injuries was. Somehow he'd managed to get Mony to her feet and back to his place. He'd cleaned up her wounds as best he could. Even with tear-stained eyes, she looked beautiful to him, standing there in her bra and panties, the way she had in her bikini out by the lake that summer. That's when he'd noticed bruising on her inner thighs and tried to get her to explain what had happened, but she cried inconsolably. He should have taken her to the emergency room, but she begged him not to. When Massey tried to call her roommate, Mony insisted she didn't anyone to know where she was. All she wanted was to talk about Nate and how she missed him. She kept saying that she'd hurt him in some way, but wouldn't elaborate on the details. Massey held her in his arms and tried to soothe her tattered emotions. She seemed so fragile, like petals on a flower, her skin smooth and silky soft. Her supple body molded into his embrace, seeking comfort and safety. His last memory had been of him taking her mouth, the awkwardness of their kiss. It felt unnatural, infused with neither lust nor passion. Then he passed out.

To any and all eldest siblings in the cosmos, it is a known fact that Massey had violated the oldest law of the universe, which dictates that the moment an eldest sibling indulges in any sort of whim, lets their guard down for even a single second, or ignores that one call, will occur without fail each and every time, even if it only happens once in your lifetime. Maybe, if you're lucky, when said disaster strikes, it will be caused by some random chaos, something out of your control, instead of by your own hands. Scream all you want— *It ain't fair,* or *I don't deserve this*—and try to justify your actions. Try to convince yourself, *I'm not responsible here. I am not my little brother or sister's keeper.* But the law of the universe will show no favoritism, show no mercy, and it will prevail, each time, every time, without fail, until the end of time, defining that moment when you as the eldest sibling failed.

Over the years, Massey had come to trust his instinct that he and Mony hadn't had sex, even though he may have wanted to at the time. But something had happened to Mony that night while waiting for him at that party. Something she refused to talk about. And it had been his fault. Bob Strong may have known, but he'd taken that secret to his grave. Still, even the darkest secrets had a way of finding daylight. As her son grew, it became increasingly impossible to deny that Dane bore a familial look. Even though Massey and his brother were as close as any two brothers could be, Nate had neither confirmed nor denied consummating his love for Mony, nor had Massey asked, which left an indelible shard of doubt of what may have really happened between them that night.

Deep in thought, Massey nearly passed his own driveway, and he pumped the breaks quickly to make the turn onto the lane. He pulled his vehicle up near the kitchen door next to Nate's snowmobile and put it in park. Before killing the engine, he rolled up the windows and sat in the warmth of the cab, contemplating his next course of action.

"We can't give up hope, for his sake," is what he had said to Mony, and he believed that. But it wasn't just for Nate's sake anymore; it would be for all their sakes not to give up. Massey desperately needed Mony's cooperation in making that happen. They each had to speak the truth of what had happened the night she lay in his bed before any of them could move forward with their lives, wherever that path might lead.

Exiting the vehicle, Massey looked up into the clear night sky, beseeching the heavens. *Don't leave me sitting alone on the curb in the dust like my mother. I can't bear to lose either one of them.* Closing the SUV door, a faint scent of lavender fused with the cold night air. *I love them both too much.*

CHAPTER 21

THE FUNERAL

The private funeral service for Dana Carver Altman was held at the Hagedorn and Lundstrom funeral home in Williston, North Dakota, December 21, 2013. Only a handful of people knew Buddy's real name, and they were mostly military personnel. Having such a feminine-sounding first name, was it any wonder he'd gone by a nickname?

Massey looked around the largest room the funeral home had to offer. It still made for very tight quarters, so much so that the funeral director had his associates remove all the flowers to create additional floor space. Every inch of the room was covered with folding chairs except for the narrow aisle, which was wide enough for the casket and pallbearers to process at the completion of the service. Kiteri, Dane, Diana, Mindy, Derrick, and Devon held that honor. Those who were there considered themselves fortunate to be counted among the select few who had a seat, since so many had to be turned away. Massey, for his part, was glad he and his family held that

distinction. Kip had been correct about the Fergusons—
they were Mony's family. As he and his family took their
seats in the row behind Mony and her children, Massey
immediately noticed his brother had shaved off his beard
for the funeral. He kept rubbing at his face sporadically,
as if the loss had created some sort of phantom pain.
It made him look younger, more vulnerable. Waiting
for the service to begin, the lot of them already looked
exhausted. The hockey game, drinking, and wake the day
before didn't help the situation. But that's what happens
when the body idles during times of stress. You want to
self-preserve and shut down; you want to take a nap.

The wake yesterday had been something akin to a
dog and pony show. Over a thousand people had filed
through the receiving line throughout the day with
sorrowful expressions, offering their condolences.
Everyone wanted a front row seat to the biggest event in
town. Naturally, Kip, Poppy, Nate, and Massey were there
for Mony and her family. It was expected. Many eyes kept
casting speculative glances between Nate and Mony, all
wondering if they were an item now.

There were tears and laughter, jokes and stories of
all the crazy things Buddy had done in his life—and of
course the legendary story of Mony stealing her dad's
plane surfaced, the one that inspired Kiteri to become
a writer. Kiteri kept his sons occupied throughout the
day, playing dummy rummy in the family lounge, while
Mindy, Diana, and his wife Michelle visited quietly.
Massey could tell Mony's kids were having a difficult time
staying in the parlor next to Buddy's corpse, especially

the girls. After having just buried their own father six months prior, it was understandable they'd be ill at ease. For his part, Massey spent much of his time finalizing the preparations for the gravesite service after the funeral. It would be an emotional farewell, with a twenty-one gun salute, "Taps," and a rare appearance from the Minot AFB flight squadron. Then there was Nate.

His brother hovered as close to Mony as was possible without being obvious, but it was obvious. Mony and Nate were often observed standing side by side over Buddy's casket, arms wrapped around one another, with Mony resting her head against Nate's shoulder and his chin settled on the crown of her head. The mere sight of it irked Kip so much he'd accidentally crushed a Styrofoam cup he'd been holding. What a mess. The old man simply couldn't grasp the simple idea that Nate was grieving too. He'd blinded himself to the fact that Buddy had been as much a father to Nate as he'd been to Mony.

Mony, for her part, remained dutifully near her dad's casket. Nate and Dane kept fretting over her, encouraging her to sit down and pace herself and bringing her something to drink. They'd seen what had happened from the last funeral she'd attended, and didn't want Mony to end up in the hospital again with dehydration and exhaustion.

No one had said a word about the night Mony and Nate went to the Blarney Stone—a good thing. Massey was certain his dad hadn't caught wind of it yet, though Poppy may have suspected. She was more willing to acknowledge that a relationship existed between Mony

and Nate, though he doubted she knew its depth. The
military chaplain arrived, signaling that the service was
about to get underway.

A small group of cadets, men and women from Minot Air
Force Base, were standing at attention behind a wooden
podium in the corner near the front of the room. They
looked so young and could have passed for a high school
show choir had it not been for their crisp, pressed military
uniforms and solemn expressions. They sang acappella like
angels from heaven in perfect four-part harmony. Songs
like "Nearer My God to Thee" and "How Great Thou Art"
were performed with soul-wrenching tenderness. The
military chaplain presiding over the service maintained
an air of poignant simplicity, keeping the music and
readings moving along in a tightly disciplined formation.
Kip gave an eloquent eulogy summarizing Buddy's career
in the Air Force, their service time together in Vietnam,
and their business relationship, as well as their friendship.
He spoke of what a wonderful father Buddy had been
to Mony and talked of the numerous contributions he
had made to the community. When Kip finished, it was
Mony's turn.

She rose with elegant grace, standing tall and proud.
Her face was absent of the weariness Massey had
seen a moment ago, replaced by an etched look of
determination. She was a woman on a mission, a child
who had something to say. Sliding with ease past her two
daughters, she moved with fluidity toward the front of
the room, but instead of stepping up to the podium mike,
she walked to the head of the casket. Mony placed her

palm on the surface. She spoke to it.

"I know it has always irritated you, my doing this, and you would be scolding me right now if you could. But I think you and I have come to understand each other over time, and how important it has been for me to exercise the relentless spirit that would brim to bursting if I didn't say my daily psalm. I hadn't had the chance to do so the morning you died, so I must recite it to you now, just one more time before you go. Thank you, Daddy, for coming for me. Thank you for being my dad. I love you. I will always love you." Mony's silhouette was statuesque, her hand resting on the casket as she waited in silence for Buddy's rebuke.

A sob escaped his brother, who had been with Mony's dad the morning he died. He had told Massey how he'd felt guilty for not calling Mony sooner when Buddy's condition began to decline. It would forever be a regret to him now, one of many Nate would have to live with in the cycle of life's precarious choices. The room was motionless, utterly quiet, as if straining, waiting with bated breath to hear the gentle parental reproach. Mony lifted her fingers to her lips, then pressed them to the casket before returning to her seat, dry-eyed. Her face appeared soft and relaxed, as if the weight of her gratitude had been absolved in her profession of love. Mony's children draped their arms around their mother, leaning together in solidarity and support. The only audible sound in the room came in the scattering of sniffling noses, soft sobs, and clearing of throats. Or had it been Massey, who, teary-eyed, reached for the handkerchief in his pocket?

The military chaplain concluded the service with a final benediction and cued the pallbearers to begin the recessional. Mony was smiling now; with her shoulders pulled back and her head held high, an unseen force seemed to propel her along, a motion of habit, perhaps— one of neverending change, indeterminate and always trudging forward. Massey noticed that the long woolen coat Mony wore hung on her like a tent, much like the black dress beneath it. It was the same dress she had worn to her husband's funeral less than six months prior.

The hearse that carried Buddy's casket to the cemetery was merely a formality. He wouldn't be laid to rest there. Buddy's plans were to be cremated, his final resting place an undisclosed location until the reading of his will. A canvas tent of burgundy red had been erected near the Altman headstone to block the northwest wind as family and friends gathered to pay their final respects. The chaplain said a blessing and a prayer, then read a passage from the Bible: Psalm 23, "The Lord Is My Shepherd." An eerie silence fell over the gathering at the unnatural sound of thunder rumbling off in distance. Massey had known it was coming. Still, it elicited a startled response when the rifle guard fired off the twenty-one-gun salute. The rifles discharged, sending out a shock wave and shattering the quiet winter air as the roar of thunder drew near. Two men dressed in military uniforms approached the casket to fold the US flag and presented it to Mony. With a snap salute, they solemnly offered their condolences, while a lone bugle played "Taps."

Cupping their hands over their ears, everyone's

attention turned skyward as the rolling thunder assaulted fragile bones in the inner ears. The time-honored "missing man formation" flew over the funeral in a roar of awe-inspiring glory. Mony's undoing.

Her body never touched the ground, however, with Nate standing nearby. He snatched her up discreetly, holding her upright until the crowd began to disperse. He then escorted her to his truck, maintaining her dignity as much as he could by allowing her to use what level of power she still had left in her legs to walk. Opening the door to the cab, Nate blocked the view of curious onlookers as he helped Mony inside. Exhaust already spewing from the tail pipe, Nate had left his truck running, as had many, prepared to offer sanctuary and warmth from the bitter cold. Through the front window, Massey could see Nate cradling Mony in his arms and burying his face in the crook of her neck. His brother had also needed the sanctuary, for Nate was grieving too.

Mony's departure signified that the show was over. From the warmth of his own vehicle, Massey glanced out over at the gravesite and noticed Poppy and Kip still talking to Mony's kids. Their worried expressions were unappeased as their eyes kept a vigilant watch on Nate's truck. Somehow Kip and Poppy had managed to convince the group to leave, or maybe it had been the cold that motivated them as they moved with hesitance toward their own vehicles. Leading the processional of cars, Kip drove his shiny red pickup, heading toward the VFW, where a luncheon had been prepared. Skirting around Nate's truck, Massey glanced in the rearview mirror at the steady stream of traffic when a

sudden wave of sadness washed over him. He pulled out
of the procession, letting the rest of the vehicles past, and
placed his arm and head on the steering wheel. Michelle
draped her arm over him, lending comfort. His relationship
with Buddy hadn't been as obvious as his brothers', but
Massey knew him well, knew the details of Buddy's will
and the final dreams that had lain deep in his heart. He had
been a good man. Massey would miss him.

They walked through the door of the VFW hand in
hand thirty minutes later. Some folks had already started
eating off the dessert trays sitting on the table, while
others waited, staking their claims to different tables, and
drank coffee or a rail drink from the bar. Massey stood
next to Poppy in the kitchen, drinking coffee. She was
plating another dessert tray.

"What is wrong with people? Don't they know they're
supposed to wait until the family arrives before they start
eating?" Poppy complained. She added a dab of whipped
cream to an already overloaded pudding dessert. "For
Christ sakes, this is the fifth dessert tray I've had to refill.
I think they just wanted a free lunch." She tossed the
empty whipped cream container into the sink with an air
of disgust.

"It's all right, Mom, I'm sure there'll be plenty of food."

Poppy turned to him and said, "Go sit down now. I
want us all to be at the table when Mony sits down."

Massey didn't argue and began to head out of the
kitchen, when the sound of quiet laughter rose from the
family table, garnering both Massey and Poppy's attention.

Looking out from behind the serving window, Poppy stared at Nate sitting next to Dane, their ties loosened, their postures casual and relaxed. Her mouth gaped, and she must have seen what Massey had suspected for a long time. Dane clearly had his mother's hazel eyes, but his facial features and body were strikingly familiar. Both men had well-built torsos and long legs that stretched on for miles. Mony's husband Bob had quite the opposite build, with a long torso, long arms, and shorter legs. Excluding Dane's eyes and Nate's sandy brown hair, the two men were a match, feature for feature. Massey saw the unwelcome revelation punch his stepmom's gut like a fist, and she took a staggered step back. She stared at him, wide-eyed, but said nothing; then she reached with a shaky hand for a coffee carafe and began filling it with coffee. Massey wasn't sure what to say in that moment, and patted her shoulder before taking a seat at the family table.

Mony took Poppy's hand when she finally came and sat down. "You've done such a wonderful job arranging all this, Poppy," she said. "Thank you for not making people wait for me. I know how ugly a mob of Norwegians can get when they're hungry."

Poppy chuckled, but Massey could tell it was forced. She began loading up everyone's plates with goulash, ham sandwiches, pickles, Jell-O with fruit, and scalped corn, as if to keep her mind occupied. It wasn't long before the family table roared with laughter, Nate entertaining the group with a story told at Buddy's expense.

"So I said, 'Hello, is this the police?'" Nate mimicked in

a panicked voice. Switching to a female octave, he voiced the dispatcher: "'Yes. What do you wish to report?'" In a tone of disgust, he said, "I told her, 'I'm calling to report about my neighbor Buddy Altman. He's hiding pot inside his firewood.'"

There was a collective gasp of amused shock around the table.

"So, the police dispatcher says to me"—Nate used a high, squeaky voice—"'Thank you very much sir, for the call.' That afternoon, the police descended on Buddy's farm and searched the shed where the firewood was kept." Looking at his nephews, Nate stood and began to pantomime. "Using axes" —he swung his arms in a chopping motion— "they busted," —he huffed— "open every piece of wood." His slashing motion just about clipped the top of Mony's head and he gave her an apologetic look. "But they didn't find anything," he continued with a look of shock. "No weed, pot, marijuana, what have you—nothing—and they cursed at Buddy when they left."

Unable to contain himself, Derrick blew a low whistle. "Wasn't Buddy pissed? Why would you say that, Uncle Nate, if it wasn't true?"

Nate's eyes glinted with mischief and he said, "Well, I called Buddy after the police left his house, and I asked, 'Hey, Buddy boy, did the police come?' And Buddy says, 'Yeah!' And I asked him, 'Did they chop your firewood?' And Buddy says 'Yup.'" Nate paused for dramatic effect before he delivered the punchline. "So I told him, 'Merry Christmas, Buddy!'"

A surge of groans and boos followed. It was a bad joke,

but it had everyone breaking into boisterous laughter nonetheless. Not to be out done by his little brother, Massey piped in with a revealing tale from one of Nate's misadventures and more laughter ensued. The deer camp stories had always captured Mony's kids' interest, as well as Massey's two boys'. There was usually a grain of truth buried beneath the pile of bullshit somewhere, and they loved hearing what sort of trouble Mony, Nate, and Massey had managed to get into during their youth. Soon, the dirt was flying across the table with tales of shenanigans and mischief by the trio of trouble.

When the lunch crowd began to disband, Poppy promptly returned to the kitchen to oversee the cleanup crew, while others folks drifted into the bar to reminisce about old times. Mony's kids had decided they'd had enough for the day and took the Bravada back out to the farm. Nate and Mony were getting ready to leave as well when Massey went up to Mony and pulled her off to the side.

"Would you be able to come in an hour earlier on Monday before I read the will?" he asked. "There are a couple of things I want to go over with you beforehand."

If Mony was taken aback by the request, her expression gave little away. "Sure, what time do you have in mind?"

"I was thinking around, say, one o'clock, after lunch, if that works for you."

Mony eyed him cautiously. "Will Kip be there?"

"No," he said quietly, "and I don't want Nate there either. Can you manage that?"

Mony nodded. "Yes, I can do that."

CHAPTER 22

MONY

The afternoon following the funeral, Mony decided to busy herself by cleaning out the attic while her kids went into town to get a tree. Christmas had crept up on them, and with it only a few days away they'd all decided to spend the holiday at their grandpa's house under the guise that it would be too expensive to arrange another flight to Minnesota so close to the holidays. It was partly true, but Mony suspected it had more to do with the fact that it would be their first Christmas without their own dad, and somehow avoiding going back to Minnesota had made it seem not so finite.

The absence of sound in the house was so foreign to Mony's ears, it sent goose bumps creeping across her skin. As she rummaged through the kitchen utility drawer looking for a flashlight, she considered how her dad had managed living alone all those years. She got home three, maybe four times a year at the most, and he hadn't come to visit her much in Minnesota. It made her wonder what her dad had done with all his free time. Grabbing a beer from the fridge, Mony set off for the attic to see what sort of Christmas lights she could find.

She pulled the cord to the trapdoor in the second-floor ceiling. A draft of air from the unheated space sent a shiver of cold through her body; she regretted wearing the simple T-shirt and yoga pants but decided to tough it out. There was no light source to speak of in the dismal space except for what seeped in through a small window facing the east. The first thing she looked for was the old steamer trunk. It was gone, and she figured Nate must have helped her dad move it downstairs at some point. Even though he hadn't died there, it was hard for Mony to go into her dad's bedroom. With a sense of determination, she started grabbing at random boxes and carried each one down the ladder to the second-floor hallway below. It was tedious work. None of the boxes were labeled, except for a few that bore her own scribbling from years ago, and she had to open each one to see what was inside. One box had been filled with a bunch of old, worn-out, small appliances: a percolator coffee pot, hand mixer, toaster oven, waffle iron, and the like. *Jeez, didn't Dad throw anything away?* she mused.

Designating one side of the hall for trash and the other side for keepsakes, the trash side of the hall mounted fast. It was a stroke of luck that she found a decent pair of woolen socks and one of her Dad's favorite thermal-lined plaid shirts that she'd given him for Christmas. She put them on; the old shirt still held a faint smell of spicy cologne, and it made her smile. Fortified with the extra layer of clothing, the search for treasures continued. She found a large box of Christmas lights that looked a bit dodgy. She plugged in the first strand, and after sparks started to fly she yanked the cord out of the wall socket and threw them away.

Thirty minutes into her task, Mony realized that the stuff stored in the attic was mostly junk, and was about to give up when she found a box marked "Special." It was. Nestled between pairs of jeans were two strands of old-fashioned bubble lights. *I can't believe Dad kept these.* The bubble lights had always been her favorite, and she carried them like a sacred object to her bedroom. Cautiously, she plugged a strand into the wall socket. To her delight, it neither sparked nor spattered and all the bulbs lit. She checked the other strand. Only one wouldn't bubble, and once she gave it the old jiggle test it winked to life. Grinning with satisfaction, she left them in the corner of her bedroom and went back to the attic.

As she climbed the ladder, a wash of exhaustion overcame her. The trash side of the hall was already stacked three boxes high, and she had a killer side ache as she rested the heavier boxes on her hip. Time for a break. She rummaged through the box of old LP records she'd stashed in her room. She found her *Eagles Greatest Hits, Vol. 1* album and an old K-tel album, *22 Explosive Hits Vol. 2,* stored in their original record jackets. Mony stacked them on the old Emerson record player she'd kept in the corner of her room with the pair of kick-ass speakers Nate had made for her in shop class and cranked up the tunes. It sounded awful, the speakers only amplifying the well-loved LP records, and it gave her a headache. No wonder her dad had only let Mony and Nate listen to records when he was away. It made her laugh. Even back then, Nate had dreamed of playing in a rock n' roll band like the Eagles, and he'd made that dream a reality. She had always dreamed of going into the Air Force and becoming a pilot like her dad. She hadn't had Nate's success, but she'd done all right for herself and had a wonderful family to show for it. That was success in her eyes, though she'd had to sacrifice Nate to achieve it.

An hour passed; Mony managed to clear all the boxes that were near or around the opening and sat on the bottom rung of the ladder, drinking a beer. *Why is it that the first beer always goes down so good?* She set the empty bottle down on the floor and tipped her chin upward at the attic door. With an exhausted sigh, she trudged one more time up the ladder. Only one box remained, but it was too far out of reach. Mony had to turn to face the back of the attic and elongate her reach by stretching her body across the filthy floor to reach it. She cursed at the elusive box just beyond her grasp and gave another lunge, hoping to reach it. Her footing slipped off the ladder, leaving her feet dangling in the air. She tried not to panic and flailed her legs, feeling for the lip of the steps, when she was surprised by the sudden feel of two hands grabbing firmly around her legs. She let out a scream.

"Don't worry, I've got you," a calm voice said from below. He pulled on her legs with a strong grip, first by the calves, then knees and hips. Mony painstakingly shimmied her torso off the attic floor and slinked back down through the hole. He snaked his arms around her waist.

"You scared the shit out of me, butthead," she scolded.

Nate jumped backwards off the bottom rung, still holding her, and landed on the floor with a thud. She smacked him in the shoulder, but it only made him laugh. His laughter was infectious, and made it hard to sound serious. Mony gave up and grumbled, "What are you doing here?"

"I knocked and yelled but no one answered," Nate said. "I heard the music blaring, so I figured someone had to be home and let myself in." There was a twinkle of mischief in his blue eyes, and he pulled on the waistband of her yoga pants. "Should I check your shorts for Hershey squirts?"

Mony began squirming, then realized it was useless. She was no match for his strength, plus Nate had the upper hand—her chances of being depantsed were pretty good. She resorted to the last line of defense and stilled. It took a beat, but Nate got the message and groaned in defeat, sliding her down the front of his body. Her feet firmly on the floor, Nate held onto her and gazed down through his hooded blue eyes. The playfulness was gone now, replaced by an ardent look of longing. He lowered his mouth to kiss her. Mony flushed with embarrassment, imagining how ridiculous she looked wearing a dirty tee, her father's flannel shirt, and oversized socks. She felt anything but desirable and turned her head away. Nate placed his fingers beneath her chin, tilting her head back as he brushed his lips against hers. Closing her eyes, Mony felt her heart leap and her breath quicken.

"Why, Ms. Strong, you've been drinking," Nate teased.

"Had I known, I'd have stopped by sooner and joined you." He touched his lips lightly against hers, stroking back and forth, withholding the kiss. His denial was both infuriating and arousing, setting off an edgy restlessness.

"What were you looking for?" Nate asked.

Her lips began to tremble. "W—what?"

He smiled. "In the attic, what were you looking for?"

Mony's brain stuttered back into action. "Christmas decorations," she said, and parted her lips to accommodate her rapid breathing.

Nate trailed little kisses across her jaw. "Silly woman, it's just junk up there. I helped Buddy move all the good stuff to his room months ago."

Mony took a deep breath, trying to slow her respirations while Nate pressed kisses along the thrumming vein in her neck. "Why couldn't you have told me that before I got started?" she murmured.

"Because you didn't ask."

Mony felt her body draw into him, as if a rope had bound them together. They were playing a familiar game of tug of war, and Nate was clearly winning. Unable to resist his inexorable pull, she felt the cold of his skin having just come in from outdoors. He smelled divine, with a hint of pine needles on his clothing—fresh and clean. She breathed in the scent and felt herself relax. Their bodies touching, Nate was the adhesive that bound her together, making her feel whole again, not the broken human mess she'd become over the past year. Molded so perfectly against him, Mony wrapped her arms around his waist and nestled into his chest.

Exhaling a contented sigh, Nate kissed the top of her head. "You feel so good," he said, mirroring her thoughts. "You fit just right," he said, and squeezed her between his arms. "Right here, where you belong."

His words brought a sense of peace to Mony's troubled heart as her body softened in love's tender embrace. She listened to the beating of his heart and felt the rise and fall of his chest against her cheek quicken. The coolness of his skin gave way to a searing heat and his posture shifted as he loosened his hold. AS he pulled away from her, the tormented expression in his eyes frightened her.

"What's wrong, Nate?" Mony said, and he closed his eyes. When she repeated the question, he squeezed his eyes tighter, as if holding in some grave secret. The gesture triggered a profound feeling of guilt, and Mony swallowed hard as her own eyes began to well with tears. *What could she do or say to make things right with this man she loved?*

"Don't cry," he said, wiping at a tear with the pad of his thumb. "I didn't mean to upset you."

"It's me, Nate, I've upset you." Mony sniffled and brushed at the corner of his eye. "Tell me what to do. I can't bear to see you hurting."

"Nor I you," Nate said, resting his forehead on hers. He'd refrained from kissing her, invoking the same restless energy as before. Her body ached for him, seared with desire to have his mouth on hers.

"This is all it will ever be between you and me—brother and sister, won't it, Mony? Best friends, and nothing more."

The sad resignation in his voice broke her heart. They were the words Nate never spoke, but feared most. It was a fear that echoed in her own heart. Because the truth was, Mony had always wanted more. Her heart cried out for it. *Couldn't he see?* How could they be brother and sister when she longed for his sensual touch? A touch that transcended the need for food, water, and air. In bitter anguish, she told him, "Nate, I'm such a mess right now. I don't know who or what I am anymore. I—" She let go of pretense and impulsively flung her arms around his shoulders, her body straining toward him, standing tiptoed to kiss his neck.

He seized her mouth, kissing her fiercely. Their teeth clashed like gladiators, his tongue plunging like a sword staking a claim, piercing her soul. Want spread like a wildfire throughout her veins, and she kissed him back, matching the fervor of his passion, savoring the sweetness of his lips. Shoving her hands in his hair, she pressed the back of his head, holding him deep inside her ravenous mouth. He knotted his fingers through the ducktail of hair at her nape and pulled down hard, exposing her neck. He lunged at the naked flesh, suckling along the length of her shoulder, stealing her breath. Mony gasped for air, the growing throb between her thighs demanding attention. Bowing her back, she pressed her hips to his, attempting to quench the ache inside.

Capturing her wandering hands, Nate pinned them tight against his chest. "Mony, can there ever be more between us?"

She saw the blaze of determination in his eyes, or

maybe it was what she had wanted to see. She didn't care anymore what her reply should have been. Their future at this point was uncertain, and she refused to dwell on what the unspeakable truth might be. "Nate," Mony whispered in a low voice, "I need you."

He closed his eyes as if savoring her words. "That's all I need to know." He took hold of the flannel shirt, pulling it from her shoulders, and let it drop to the floor. The thin veil of the V-neck tissue T-shirt she wore betrayed her small, hardening breasts. Nate smiled appreciatively at the instinctive response and closed his hands over them. He watched her eyes glaze over as he placed the pad of his thumb over her nipple and massaged the tender flesh in slow, small circles, first one, then the other, causing each to tighten against her shirt. Relishing his stimulating touch, she moaned softly.

Inspired by the sound of her pleasure, Nate reached for the hem of her shirt and ran his hands up along her ribcage, hitching up the shirt and the paper-thin camisole she wore beneath. He'd reached just below her ribs when her sound of pleasure turned to pain, and he stopped. Nate glanced at the discoloration on her skin.

"Oh, baby, did I hurt you?" Without waiting for a response, he continued lifting her shirt, exposing the large black-and-blue mark. "That bastard," he cursed. "If Dane hadn't already broken his bones, I'd pummel another pound of flesh out of him." He was speaking of Dwight, but she didn't want to think about him right now. Nate stroked his fingers across her torso and she eased them away.

"My fierce protector." Mony lifted her arms, allowing Nate to remove her clothing. Wrapping his arms around her waist, Nate pulled her body against his, caressing her naked back.

"Your skin is so soft, Mony," he said and lowered his hold. Cupping her buttock, he yanked her feet off the floor, and she wrapped her legs around his hips while Nate carried her to the bedroom. He tumbled her onto the bed and held himself over her as Mony tugged Nate's shirt from his jeans. He stood, pulling off his shirt, and opened his jeans, shimmying out of them. Wearing only boxer briefs, he covered her body with his and teased her mouth with slow, shallow licks of his tongue. She rose to meet him, and they wrestled in an impassioned tangle, her hands groping between them, as she stroked up and down his length in seductive measure. She felt his body strain to maintain control, and she squirmed beneath him, struggling to get out of the rest of her clothing. Nate brushed the pad of his thumb over the hardened nipple, eliciting a shuddered "ah," and she stopped her movement.

"That's it, Mony," Nate said. "What's your hurry? I want to enjoy you awhile." He pressed his erection against the notch between her legs, making her moan. "A long while."

The boom of Mindy's voice echoing up the stairwell ended the foreplay. "Mom, you upstairs? Uncle Nate? We're back."

Half dismayed, half amused, Nate whispered, "Oh shit."

Mony's heart leaped into her throat, rendering her speechless, and she struggled to find her voice. Nate's mouth quirked into a grin, and she punched him on the shoulder. "It's not funny," she said with a hiss and tried to gather her wits. "Don't come up here, honey, it's a mess." And it was, in more ways than one, but she didn't say it. "Nate and I will be down in a minute." Nate suppressed a laugh, and Mony slapped him again, amusing him even more.

"Well, hurry up, wait until you see the tree we got," Mindy replied, and they heard the click of the stairwell door.

Mony tried to lift off the bed, but Nate held her pinned. "What are you doing?" she snapped. "Are you trying to get us caught?"

Nate propped himself on his elbow and gazed down at Mony with a silly grin.

Realizing the idiocy of her remark, she began to laugh to the point of tears, uncertain if they were from humor or pent-up sexual tension. Either way, they'd both carried on like that for several minutes before Mony could say, "We'd better get down there before Mindy comes charging up the stairs with the rest of the brigade. I know my kids, and they don't have a lot of patience."

Nate brushed the back of his fingers across Mony's cheeks. "Hmm, sounds like someone else I know." He pressed his hips to her pelvis, and she hissed a mixed sound of pleasure and frustration.

"Hmm, yourself," Mony chided, "and don't get me started again. Thanks to you, I need to use the bathroom and make myself presentable before I go downstairs."

Nate jerked back his head. "Me? What about what *you* did to me?" He lifted his body away from her, gazing down the length of his torso. "What am I supposed to do with that?"

Mony glanced down at Nate's unflagging erection and lifted her hips up to meet his. She gave him a sympathetic smile. "Maybe you should use the bathroom first."

A flash of chaos streaked across the kitchen floor, followed by a burst of laughter. Watching the two of them goofing around like kids, Kiteri tried to recall the last time she'd seen her mom so spunky. But being around Uncle Nate had always brought out the kid in her, especially at Grandpa Buddy's house.

Finished with dishes, Kiteri reached for a towel when Nate nearly crashed into her. He shot her an apologetic look, then danced off on tip-toe, skirting around the table. Kiteri shook her head and moved to a safer spot. With one ankle crossed over the other, she crooked her hip against the counter and watched the two of them go at each other in a full-out, no-holds-barred, wet-dish-towel fight. Nate let out a yelp when her mom found what she called *the sweet spot,* using a well-executed flick of the wrist as the towel snapped against Nate's bare skin. Grimacing, Nate covered the wounded site. The defensive reaction was ill timed, allowing the opening needed for a second attack, catching him on the thigh. Kiteri winced; even through denim jeans, that still had to sting.

The Strong siblings were well acquainted with the game

they were playing. No one was a match for their mom, not even Dane, who had most shots on goal. With the skills of a mad ninja their mom could roll away, dodging every snap of the towel, then sneak up on her prey when they became too cocky. Mony Strong was the master, and the rest of them were all just a bunch of little grasshoppers picked off one by one with a flick of the towel. Kiteri's dad had refused to participate in the challenge when he was alive, never liking the pain. He had been the smart one.

When Nate and Mony's flirting became unbearable, Kiteri left the kitchen, joining her siblings in the living room. She plopped into a recliner next to Mindy, who'd been sitting on the floor rummaging through a box of old clothes.

"I was wondering when you'd get your fill," Mindy said, glancing toward the kitchen.

The unceremonial thud of a box hitting the floor interrupted Mindy and Diana's tug of war over a pair of old jeans. "I hope you don't plan to take any of this with you," Dane said to his wife. "We're flying back, remember?"

The familiar family banter came to a halt when Nate and Mony emerged from the kitchen. Hands clasped right to left, they promenaded through the arch doorway. Their mom did an underarm turn into the living room. With his hand on her left shoulder blade and her arm over his right shoulder, they swept across the room, lifting on their toes, swinging, swaying to a three-quarter rhythm that only they could hear. There was a synergy to their motion, playful and light. Twirling in little circles, they did a double reverse spin as Nate whisked her across the floor and they made their way toward the baby grand piano, where they sat on the bench. Looking a bit dumbfounded at one another, the siblings sat back and watched the scene unfold.

Their mother began playing simple, staccato notes that transitioned into a melody. Nate joined in with intermittent chords of harmony; then she harmonized her own chords while Nate played a countermelody. As the duet unfolded, she maintained the simple base melody and Nate's countermelody grew more complex.

Spellbound, they recognized the familiar tune taught to them at a young age, yet they had never heard their mom play "The Impossible Duet" with such passion or skill. As the music built in complexity and tempo, one could almost feel the sense of urgency between the musicians in a crescendo of profound yearning. The two blended into one as Nate reached across his partner, playing his musical part, intermingling the original arrangement into a myriad of constructs, fashioning it into a masterpiece of their own design. There was a fervor enveloping the piece, the precision of their performance worthy of Carnegie Hall. But this concert wasn't intended for public display. This was something very private and personal.

When they finished, Nate turned to face his music partner, basking in the afterglow of musical bliss. Their music had transformed the quiet living room into a sanctuary, eradicating the obscurity of death, replacing it with serenity and peace.

"Wow, that was so beautiful," Diana told her mother-in-law. "I didn't know you could play like that."

Mony replied, "Only with my equal I can."

The air crackled with love's energy. They all knew they'd have to leave their reverent space and return to reality, but none of them knew how. As if awakened from a trance, Nate pressed a quick kiss to Mony's forehead and began to play a spirited rendition of "Jingle Bells." By the chorus, they were all singing along and ended the evening with Christmas carols around the piano.

The second snowstorm of the season had grown into a full-blown blizzard. And even though their farms were only a mile or so apart, their mom was not on board with Nate's plan to drive home. Anticipating the argument that was sure to ensue, Kiteri and her siblings scurried upstairs to bed. As much as they all liked him, Nate was on his own with that one.

CHAPTER 23

NATE

Years of traveling the familiar route in his old truck without incident had made him cocky, perhaps a bit *too* cocky. Nate cursed as he struggled to see his way in the near-whiteout conditions. The county plow had cleared a single lane, but it had been several hours ago, and had done nothing to smooth out the ruts left by the freezing ice. It made for slow going with the rear-wheel drive, even with the extra weight Nate had thrown in the truck bed. With the windshield wipers going full blast, they still couldn't keep up with the snowy assault. Nate began to seriously regret not taking Mony up on her offer to stay. It was bad enough that she was pissed he'd decided to go. Now, with the drive having already taken almost twice the normal travel time, he was certain Mony would have a trench beaten into the kitchen floor from pacing. Fulfilling his promise to call her as soon as he got home wasn't going to appease her, or save his sorry ass from a massive chewing out. *If I got home.*

It wasn't as though he hadn't wanted to stay, but

overextending his welcome at the risk of alienating Mony's kids this early in the scheme of things was a sure recipe for disaster. After all, hadn't he just showed up unannounced and invited himself in? But there lay his first dilemma. Buddy's house had always been as much a home to him as his own, perhaps more so. Mony understood that—her kids, not as much. Anyway, the whole evening had gone too perfectly to risk messing it up, and Nate had to shake himself a couple of times to believe it was all real. Trimming the Christmas tree, having dinner together, and singing around the piano had been just plain wonderful. They'd blended into an instant family, like the one he'd always dreamed of having with Mony, and he couldn't help but wonder if, even hope that, they might feel the same way about him. There lay the second dilemma. It wasn't his house, or his family, and he'd already pushed his luck with that little waltz and the piano duet. *Stupid.* After all, Bob Strong hadn't been dead a year. Her children might not have appreciated him making the moves on their mom so soon.

On his drive, Nate thought about the night before, when Mony drove the Cat home from the bar. He'd been pretty out of it, but his body still registered the warmth of her skin and the way her body melded into his. She hadn't forsaken their attraction; she had wanted him too. He would have rolled her beneath him and made her cry out his name if he hadn't been knocked over the head. She hadn't done so the night of their shared lost innocence. His first time, their only time, yet Nate's body and mind remembered it as though it had happened that very afternoon.

He'd just torn down the driveway, Mony standing on the porch in his rearview mirror. He wanted to go back to her, wanted to blacken Dwight's eyes for seeing her naked. His chest tightened with anger and made it hard to breathe. He wanted to scream, wanted to hit something. More than anything, he wanted to touch her, press his mouth to her lips, feel her breasts in his hands. Even more than that, he wanted Mony to feel the same way toward him.

He drove straight home and started his chores. Kip and Poppy were gone at a political fundraiser that evening, and he could get his work done in relative peace. When he finished, he took a shower, then checked the fridge for something to eat. That's where he found Massey's beer stash and decided to help himself. It tasted good, the carbonated beverage on that hot summer day. It went down fast and he drank another. Snagging the case, he skipped dinner and headed out to the party.

Everyone expected him to be the keymeister that night, his usual roll, but Nate had other plans. Let someone else have the responsibility. It was his turn to get drunk and have fun like everyone else. He lost count of the number of beers he drank and was swinging off the old tree rope into the creek when Massey arrived. Pissed as hell, Massey grabbed him by the back of the neck and dragged him off kicking and swearing. It wasn't so much about taking the beer, although he was plenty mad about that too, but for beating the shit out of Dwight and for tearing out of Mony's driveway. But Nate was mad too, though what about, he no longer recalled. He and his brother were about to come to blows when, from out of nowhere, Mony showed up and stepped in between them. She shoved at his chest, breaking them apart, and refused to yield her position.

Her touch burned like fire. Nate had spent the entire day fighting the urges his feelings conjured. He tried looking away, yet all he could see was her. Unable to be near her, though it had been exactly where he wanted to be, Nate shouted hurtful, angry things. He told her to stay out of his life, and said she was holding him back. When she just stood there, unyielding as stone, emotionless to his barbs, he told her to go to hell, then the image of her naked body flashed his head. Fueled by alcohol and rage, he stormed off. She didn't follow. The rest of the night was a blur. By midnight he was behind his truck, puking his guts out. Someone fetched Massey, who'd managed to haul his sorry ass back to their tent, where he blubbered for an hour before passing out.

A blinding gust of wind interrupted Nate's reverie. He glanced at the odometer, noting that he should be near the approach to his driveway. The driveway was barely detectable except for the nearly buried, four-foot-high reflective posts on either side. Drifting snow obscured the lane with a two-foot bank, blocking the entrance. Spitballing, Nate made a run and gunned at it. He managed to get about fifty feet up the drive before the rear wheels caught on a patch of ice and the truck slipped off the gravel, landing in the ditch alongside the driveway. With the truck buried past its exhaust pipe, Nate killed the engine and cursed.

Staring out into the storm, he contemplated what to do. He knew the warmth wouldn't last long in the cab, but it would be foolhardy to try the half-mile walk to the house on foot. From where he sat, he couldn't even see the yard light. But he could also count on the fact that as soon as he failed to call Mony in the allotted time, she'd panic, then call the farm, alerting his brother, and no doubt come out looking for him. He decided to sit tight a bit and leaned his head against the seat, slipping back into his thoughts.

Nate had always regretted the cruel words he'd said to Mony. Unlike his own bad behavior, Mony had never uttered a single unkind word to him, then or ever. It wasn't as though she didn't have a temper, but ever since their fight when she'd flown with Buddy to Oshkosh, she'd kept a tight rein on her anger, mindful of the things she said around him. Watching out for him the way she'd always done, Mony had been his utmost supporter in everything he'd ever done in his life. Hell, she'd even gone toe to toe with Kip a few times when he spoke negatively about Nate's music—not an easy thing to do. He should have felt grateful, but being treated like a little brother had been about the worst hurt of all. Her first year away at college had nearly killed him, or so it felt. Moody and depressed, Nate was either angry or volatile all the time. His grades began to slip, and he didn't care about hockey anymore. He'd started drinking, much to his high school pals' delight—they said he'd finally come in to his own, now that Mony and big brother Massey weren't around to hold him back. To his teachers and Poppy, he was a young man in trouble. To his father, he was acting like a child. Thank God for his music. Pouring his emotion into Buddy's baby grand piano, Nate had found solace, until his thoughts circled back to Mony. Living for each college break, he counted the seconds until she came home. He'd turned seventeen the summer of her sophomore year in college, and like a foolish boy believed having her home would set his world right again. He was wrong.

He'd awoken sometime the next day after the party, disoriented and confused. The campsite was quiet and Nate noted the cast of pale pink and yellow light filtering the eastern sky, signifying the approaching dawn. He was surprised he didn't feel more hungover and looked around for Massey to rub it in, but his brother wasn't there. He thought he was alone until Mony stirred beside him. Curled around him like a vine of ivy, she held him in the way she had the first night they'd met. All the anger and pain he felt earlier melted away in a single breath. He could hardly believe it. Massey had been right—Mony would forgive him.

Nate brushed back the hair across her cheek and whispered to her as she slept, professing his love. But fear tightened his throat when he spoke the words out loud, the fear he'd kept hidden deep in his heart that refused to be silent. "That's all it will ever be between you and I—brother and sister, best friends forever. Isn't it, Mony, and nothing more?" Hot tears stained his cheek when Mony stirred from her slumber. She was his pain, and he tried to put on a stoic smile. But she saw through his façade, the way she always did, clairvoyant to the deepest sorrow that lay in his soul. Unabashed, Mony crawled onto his chest to comfort him. "No, Nate, please don't cry," she said to him softly. Whether she had read his mind or had been motivated by her own culpability no longer mattered. They were in each other's arms again as it was meant to be—Nate's world righted itself again, and he savored her closeness. Wordless, she pressed her mouth to his and kissed him.

Her lips were feather light as she brushed them over his cheeks and eyes. Nate would have sworn he was dreaming if he hadn't savored the strawberry flavor of her lip gloss. She deepened their kiss, unleashing in him a torrent of emotion as a lustful hunger overpowered him. Without warning, Mony slipped away from his grasp, and a spasm of panic hammered in his chest. He lifted onto his elbow to reach for her, then froze at the sight of what she was about to do. Holding his breath, he watched as she undressed in front of him, first pulling off her T-shirt, then reaching behind to unhook her bra. The sight of her exposed skin awakened a want so deep in his groin he felt himself quiver. He wanted to feel the firmness of her breasts in his hand and reached with trembling fingers to touch her. Mony took his hand and guided it over her body, pressing the pads of his fingers onto her flesh, allowing his caress to glide over the swollen tissue of her silky, soft skin. Lured by the dark circles of her breasts, he rolled the tender tips between his fingers, fascinated by the tingling charge rippling between her flesh and his touch. His light tease made them harden, and she moaned softly.

The sound of her pleasure ignited a fire deep within him, and Nate felt his cock stiffen. Clutching his shirt at the waist, Mony ran her fingers along the bottom hem, hitching it up, and helped him pull it over his head. Goosebumps peppered his torso as the cool morning air collided with his overheated flesh. He moved closer. She drew his head to her chest, cradling him in her bosom, the fragrant scent of lavender so sensual, clinging in the mist of her perspiration. The magnetic pull of her bare flesh on his cheek beckoned his lips, and he put his mouth over each nipple, claiming them as his own. He suckled until she cried out, a sound that resonated deep in her chest. An edgy restlessness

built between them, and it was no longer enough to sit beside
her. He had to be closer, he had to be inside her.

Fumbling to unbutton his jeans, Mony knelt beside him,
placing her hands over his, and helped him out of his clothes,
then shook out of the rest of hers. All Nate could do was stare,
delighting in the wonder of her body. As they gazed at one
another's vulnerability, in that moment she was everything
he'd ever wanted, ever dreamed. She crept toward him, rolling
him onto his back, then sprawled him out naked on the ground.
She brought her leg over his hips, holding herself over him,
and rocked herself against him. The feel of her moist hot flesh
against his cock was so incredible, he moaned a ragged sound.
Mony closed her eyes, arching her neck while she rubbed against
him with the soft mound of hair between her thighs. Boldly, he
reached out to squeeze her breasts, kneading to the rhythm of her
movement, the motion coaxing a bead of something warm and
thick seeping from the tip of his penis.

He nearly came when she took his erection in her hands,
guiding him as he sank deeper through the soft passageway,
penetrating, as muscle resisted, contracted, softened, then yielded
in surrender. Sheathing him, she rocked her pelvis, gasping a
soft sound of pleasured pain as he thrust his hips upward until
an inarticulate sound escaped him. Calling out her name, he
released into her the urgency of his need, and when his possession
was complete, Mony lowered onto his chest and lay naked with
him, holding him tight. They didn't speak, each knowing they
would never experience that moment ever again, and in that
knowledge, they cried softly into the light of the new dawn.

A sound other than the howling wind caught Nate's
attention, and he strained his eyes to see out into the

storm. A light seemed to be moving off in the distance, though he couldn't be certain. The cab had grown cold now, the wind making a mournful buzzing sound as it blew through the power lines, mimicking the sorrow of the memory that came next.

He'd woken sometime around midday to find her gone. Frantic, Nate rushed over to Buddy's house, where she sat in her bedroom packing for her trip back to college. He stood frozen in the doorway with an agonizing pain in his chest. Why had she left him? The mere thought of it cleaved his heart in two, and he rushed to hold her. Mony fell into his arms, sobbing into his chest, saying words about wanting to leave with pleasant memories, not the sadness of her pending departure. As they clung to one another, he couldn't stop the words spewing out of his mouth, words like "abandon" and "promise."

They talked very little on the long trip to Minnesota that Labor Day weekend. When the moment of separation had been thrust upon them, it was as if they were saying goodbye forever. Then, the unimaginable happened. As Nate awaited her return for Christmas break, she never came. He'd hounded Buddy for an explanation, and was told someone had asked Mony to marry him—she'd said yes. When Mony finally did return that summer, it was with a husband at her side and a baby in her arms. By then, Nate was already gone. After months of arguing with his father, he'd finally had enough and ran away. But no matter where he went, there was no place he could hide, no bottle he could drown himself in, no woman who could ever love him enough to erase the memory of Mony in his heart. He was trapped, trapped between the sunset of a child's sweet memory and the lust-filled dawn of becoming a man.

The light flickering off in the distance drew closer, accompanied by the sound of a roaring engine. Nate hadn't been seeing things. It was the headlight of a snowmobile. He waited as Massey pulled along the driver's side of the truck, the engine roaring with a flourish. Nate rolled down the window a crack.

"Jesus H. Christ, Nate, are you trying to freeze to death?" Massey shouted above the howling wind.

Nate gave him a half smirk and yelled back, "I'd rather not today, thank you."

"Well then, you'd better get on this thing, before neither of our miserable frozen carcasses are found till spring." He revved the engine with a deafening roar.

Nate rolled up the window and tried for the driver's side door. It wouldn't budge, and he crawled to the passenger side to exit the cab. Sinking hip deep, Nate dredged through the snow-filled ditch climbing up the bank. The wind whipped at his face with a smack, and he pulled the bomber hat down tight over his ears. Massey had brought the Cat onto the driveway waiting, where Nate mounted the seat behind his brother.

Massey yelled back at him, "You are in deep shit, man; Mony is pissed as hell at you."

They headed up the driveway, and Nate couldn't help smiling at the thought.

CHAPTER 24

JOHN

The lazy, dense snowflakes from the afternoon had turned light and airy. Early that evening, the wind picked up too, making it difficult to see objects across the street. The darkness outside illuminated John's reflection in the window. He could make out the black-and-blue marks spreading along his jaw where Ferguson had jacked it a couple of days prior. Feeling like a caged animal, John began pacing the confines of his hotel room. He'd scrutinized the Altman and Ferguson portfolios at least a dozen times, looking for any new clue. The Wi-Fi service had been terrible since he'd arrived, and the hotspot on his phone hadn't been much better. He'd heard the sobering echo of the gun salute at Altman's funeral and the roar of the jets overhead. He didn't know Buddy Altman from Joe Schmoe, but found the reverberation of the accolades quite poignant.

It was clear Altman's death had been the biggest story around; still, the local newspaper offered very little, and John was eager to see what the Sunday edition held for information. He had better luck at the courthouse. The electronic records confirmed that Altman had no family left to inherit his amassed wealth, yet something wasn't adding up. John hoped he'd learn more going through the hard copy of land titles and deeds Monday morning. A fist pounded at the door. Answering, he found Jason Monroe leaning against the doorjamb.

"Let's grab something to eat," Jason said without preamble. "It's already seven o'clock and I'm starving." They left the room and found the SUV waiting outside.

"I still say we should have taken our chances and crashed the funeral," Jason grumbled once they were rolling. He'd been in a sullen mood ever since the Blarney Stone, and although it was easier to deal with the more subdued version of Jason, it had been no less annoying. "Long-lost relatives always come out of the woodwork where there's money involved," Jason persisted.

Normally, John would have been inclined to agree, but Jason's little stunt at the lake had nixed any possibility of that. After the debacle at the airport meeting, the county sheriff had prohibited either of them from showing their faces within 150 yards of the service and promised that if they did show, he wouldn't hold Ferguson responsible for any retaliation.

The two men shook off the cold as they entered the restaurant. The place was warm and inviting, and it had a rhythm-and-blues vibe with a robust hickory aroma that greeted people in the parking lot. Along the outside walls hung three large flatscreen TVs, with two more mounted at the bar—all televising NFL football, a TV reality show, and professional hockey. The female hostess, a woman of middle age, was decked out to the nines, wearing stiletto heels and enough hairspray to make her up-do spontaneously combust. Greeting them in a smoker's raspy voice, she said "Welcome, are you here for dinner?"

They walked to the counter and took two stools in the middle of the crescent-shaped bar. John surveyed the clientele and noted that only four tables were occupied. At one table sat three well-nourished young women, drinking colorful fruity drinks and sharing ribs served on a garbage can lid between them. In a booth sat a family of four, the father and son immersed in the hockey game while mother and daughter busied themselves on their cellphones. There were two tables pushed together holding several pitchers of beer as a group of guys watched the hockey game and eyed the women eating ribs. The lone occupant at the bar was a sullen fellow nursing a beer in the corner. He had one wrist in a splint and the other in a cast. John cringed. *Poor bastard.*

The bartender, a lean young man with a chiseled chin in his mid-thirties and struck up a friendly conversation. "The William County Snowmobiling Association will be crashing later this evening," he said with a cheery smile. "Then the place will really liven up."

A roar of cheers erupted in the quiet eatery. John glanced around and noticed that several patrons had their eyes glued to the hockey game. He caught the replay. A player in a Maroon uniform with the letter "A" swirled in white had just scored on a buzzer shot. The man sulking at end of the bar cursed.

"That's what you get for betting against Colorado," the bartender said to him with a smug smile. "Looks like you owe me." He walked over to where the man with the bandaged wrists was sitting. When the injured man turned to face the bar, John got his first good look at him. *Yikes.* The man's nose was swollen to twice the normal size, and his eyes were rimmed in black and blue. Jason let out a low whistle, and John grimaced as the man fumbled in his pocket with his injured wrists. The pained expression on his face was indicative of more than the lost bet.

The bartender showed no sign of pity and said with a smirk, "You'd better stay away from hockey for a while, Dwight. You're apt to be in a full-body cast with no way to pay for your hospital bill at this rate."

"Fuck off," Dwight snapped and managed to flip a fifty dollar bill onto the bar.

The bartender snatched the bill off the counter. "You know, you still haven't told me what happened."

"I did tell you," Dwight muttered in irritation. "It happened during practice out at Altman's. They did a piss-poor job cleaning off the ice. I fell."

Both John and Jason's ears perked up as they turned in unison toward the conversation.

"That must have been some fall," the bartender taunted. "Either you're a piss-poor skater or someone checked you but damn good."

"Alright, I was tripped," Dwight shouted. "It was a cheap shot."

The bartender laughed. "Is there any other kind?" He glanced over at John and Jason with an expression as if to say, *Am I right?* "Besides," the bartender continued, "since when do the Trouble Shooters trip one of their own guys in a practice?"

Dwight grumbled to himself as if deliberating, then said, "Me and Ferguson had a bet for the captain spot when that fucker put his bitch on the ice."

"Mony?" the bartender chuckled, flabbergasted. "You went after Mony on the ice? No wonder the Ferguson boys worked you over."

Dwight's raccoon eyes morphed into pure hatred. "Yeah, well, that fucker will get what's coming to him one of these days, and that fuckin' cunt of his too, and you can be sure I will be there to see it."

All levity left the bartender's face, and he tried to change the subject. "Hey, I heard some oil man came in a helicopter. Is it true she took off with them?"

Jason was about to say something—John kicked him in the shin, silencing the remark.

"I wished they would have pushed the bitch out of the helicopter, see how well she can really fly," Dwight muttered. "I'd have paid to see that."

The bartender rolled his eyes, no longer interested in the conversation, and laid Dwight's tab on the counter. Dwight scratched at the paper, trying to pick it up with his bandaged hands, then gave up and reached for his wallet instead.

John tossed a hundred-dollar bill on the counter. "Here, let me pay for that."

Both the bartender and Dwight gawked at the money, then each other, then John. John moved closer to Dwight.

Puzzled by the sudden interest, the bartender said,

"That's okay, mister, his credit is good."

"You heard the man," Dwight snapped. "Take care of it." He turned to face John and said with phony sincerity, "Ah, thanks, mister."

John introduced himself and Jason by first name only. The bartender returned with his change, and he held up his hand. "Hang onto it. I'll have another beer." He pointed to Dwight. "And whatever he's drinking."

A malevolent smile spread across Dwight's face as he glared at the bartender. "I'll have a Grey Goose martini, extra dirty, extra olives." He faced Jason and John. "Name's Dwight Mitchell. I'd shake your hand but—" He gave a sheepish grin and held up his bandages.

"Good to know you, Dwight," John said. "Do you have a few minutes to talk?" He gestured to a booth away from the bar.

Dwight eyed him skeptically. "What about?"

Defensive and paranoid, John mused. He asked, "What do you know about Ramona Strong?" Dwight's eyes lit up, as if he'd never been asked the question but had plenty to say about the topic. They had found the enemy.

The bartender interrupted with their drinks and cautioned Dwight, "Remember, the snowmobile club will be coming in around nine o'clock. That includes Nate."

Good to know. John sure as shit didn't want another run in with Nathan Ferguson, any more than the bartender wanted a brawl in his bar, which didn't leave a lot of time. Turning to Dwight, he said, "Let's talk."

Dwight Mitchell had to be the biggest lush John had

ever encountered, including his college days, and he was an obnoxious son of a bitch besides. John and Jason had been talking to him for nearly half an hour and they still didn't know much of anything.

"So what's it to you," Dwight slurred as he took another gulp of his martini.

John sipped his beer. "As I said, I'm new in town and just curious about her, that's all. I heard the story of her flying off in a helicopter with that Monroe fellow. Is it true?" Mitchell stared at him with a dumfounded expression. John clarified. "You know, from Monroe Oil Company. They've got a drill site west of town." John could feel Jason ready to slap the guy upside the head, and he couldn't blame him. The man was either dumber than a box of rocks or drunk past the point of useful information.

Resting both his elbows on the table, Dwight propped himself up for balance and gibbered. "She's a fuckin' whore."

Irritated Jason blurted. "Yeah, yeah, we got that. What's she got to do with those fuckin' Fergusons?"

Dwight reared his head back. "Are you stupid? They've been sniffing around that bitch like a couple of hounds in heat for years," Mitchell stammered, "especially Fergy. They were always together until she got knocked up and moved away." Dwight flittered his hand and seemed amused by his own pantomime.

"So she grew up around here, went to school here and all?" John prodded. "Who's her family? What's her name?"

Dwight began to weave where he sat, then closed

his eyes as if the answer were scribbled on the inside of eyelids. "She's Mony Brady. I guess that was her mother's name," he said, leaving spittle in his chin. "Heard her mother's husband didn't want her; gave her the boot." He made a hitchhiker thumb and thrust it behind him.

"Now we're getting somewhere," Jason said to John, not bothering to hide his enthusiasm. "Who's her old man?"

Dwight's head fell back, and he began muttering, knocking the back of his head on the wall behind the booth. He looked like a man whose last brain cell was about to piss out. John felt Jason's body tense.

"Oh, no, you don't, you son of a bitch. Not when I'm this close." Jason reached across the table and smacked Dwight across the face.

Dwight's eyes blinked open. "You're both the dumbest fucks I've ever met," he slurred, and began pounding his head again. "She's Altman's little bastard."

Stunned, John verified what he'd just heard. "Ramona is Altman's daughter?"

Dwight stopped banging his head. "Who's Ramona?" There was a momentary glint of lucidity, and Dwight looked John straight in the eye. "Hey, ever wonder why Altman never bothered to give her his name?" Then, without warning, he fell face forward, slamming his head onto the table with a crash, and passed out cold. The bar patrons turned in the direction of the noise, saw who it was, and resumed their meals and conversations. Some seconds later another ruckus disrupted the quiet milieu as the expected snowmobile club members clamored into the restaurant. The bartender shot John and Jason a scowling glance, and John thought miserably, *Perfect.*

Once they returned to the hotel, John took his leave for the night and trotted off to his room. He stared at the papers strewn about the desk and pondered—how had he missed it? If what Mitchell said was true, Ramona would surely inherit everything from her father, and even though she hadn't been married to either of the Ferguson brothers, John felt certain Altman and Ferguson would have taken appropriate measures to ensure the property's security. Further, Ramona Strong had made it crystal clear where her loyalties lay.

Flopping onto the bed, John gazed over at the desk chair, noticing his scarf, and reached for it, draping it across his face. He took a deep breath and could still smell the hint of her lavender fragrance, sending his mind adrift to their time on the train. That pursuit was pointless now too, knowing the history between Ramona and Ferguson. A strong gust of winter wind howled against the windowpane and seemed to punctuate his despair.

Their interaction at the lake; the way they'd moved together when they left the conference room; how Ferguson orbited around her, close when he needed to be, but not too close. It all pointed to a deeply intimate relationship. It could be felt in the small space between them as they sat at the piano playing music together. It was undeniable. There was symmetry to their movement—a balance. John had been so engaged in asking the redheaded bartender questions, he hadn't paid attention to the answer sitting right in front of his face.

But if they'd been so in love, why hadn't they married? To hear Dwight tell it, she'd unexpectedly up and married someone else, but why? Had Ramona and Ferguson had some sort of falling out? If so, what was it? Again, it didn't add up.

John thought about the three-man semicircle around her at the lake. Two John knew, but who was the younger one with the hockey stick? The young man's eyes resembled Ramona's, but his build seemed all Ferguson. Though John had to admit, he hadn't met her husband, and if he was cut from the same Norwegian stock that stood around her, it would have been difficult to tell either way. Then a random thought occurred to him.

What if the boy did belong to Ramona and Ferguson? Ramona would never have been able to claim it was, since Ferguson had been a minor. Dwight said Ferguson was still in high school when she'd gone off to college, and that she'd gotten pregnant while quite young. Yet what would it matter? A bit unorthodox, perhaps, but it wouldn't be the first or worst thing that ever happened to a couple of high school kids. But dwelling on this was nothing more than a distraction, and it was irrelevant when Ramona stood to inherit her father's land, rendering this entire trip a massive waste of time. John got up and began to pace when his cell phone rang. He answered with a curt, "Finch."

"John, did you get over to the courthouse and check the deeds to Altman's property like I told you?" Franklin said without preamble.

John rolled his eyes. "Not yet. We're in the middle of a

snowstorm out here."

There was a long silence. "John, you have to make that your highest priority. I'm resending you everything that has been electronically uploaded and made accessible by computer on Altman's property holdings, and I think I may have found that loophole you've been looking for."

"If you're going to tell me Altman has an heir, we already know that," John said with a note of irritation. "Her name is Ramona Stro—"

"Never mind about heirs," Franklin said impatiently. "Listen, there's a plot of land within the borders of Altman's property that doesn't have an electronic title or deed, and there may be a chance he doesn't own it."

John stopped pacing. "What do you mean?"

Franklin's voice morphed into a high-pitched trill. "If there is no hard copy of a deed or title at the courthouse, it may mean the property is still wildlife management, and therefore public domain. That would mean it could still be up for grabs, for the right price."

John flopped back down on the bed. "Jesus Christ, Franklin, that's got to be the best news I've heard since arriving in this frozen wasteland."

CHAPTER 25

MASSEY

His brother's boneheaded stunt landing him in the ditch the night before, mixed with the additional seven inches of newly fallen snow, had everyone scrambling that morning. Thank God said bonehead brother had buried his old truck and not his brand-new one, which sat in the heated garage. Bowing out of plow duty, Massey snagged Nate's keys off the counter. "I'll see the rest of you when you get into town," he shouted over his shoulder and headed out the door.

The county snowplow hadn't even bothered to tackle their little township road, leaving just enough time, if the main highway was clear, for Massey to prep before the reading of Buddy's will. Thank God his secretary had stayed in town overnight and would have everything set up in the F&A conference room before Mony, her children, and Nate arrived. He was sure his dad was already at the office, soaking up coffee like a sponge, restless and irritable. *Probably harassing the shit out of my secretary right now,* Massey mused, *insisting she call out to the farm every ten minutes for a progress report.* As Massey pulled onto the airport drive, he almost forgot that he'd asked Mony to come in before the reading. Now, he'd have to come up with a plausible excuse for having her stay later without blipping on Nate and Kip's radar. He needed to talk to Mony in private about her possible involvement with Finch, among other things. There was no way Massey wanted either his dad or Nate within earshot for that conversation.

Excluding Kip, the families arrived about forty minutes late. Mony's kids stayed huddled close together at one end of the table, somber and worn-out from shoveling. Massey speculated that their mood might also have to do with sitting through another will, an experience all too fresh in their minds. But Bob Strong's will had been straightforward, leaving everything to Mony. It would be different this time.

When everyone was seated, Massey said, "Shall we get started?" When there were no objections, he began. "I, Dana Carver (Buddy) Altman of Williston, North Dakota, revoke my former wills and codicils and declare this my last will and testament." It went like this: "To my wildcat with wings."

Massey read through article one, outlining Mony's name change to Ramona Louise Brady Altman Strong, garnering a soft gasp from her children who'd been unaware of Buddy's decision to legally give Mony his name. Article two outlined debit and expense payments, which were minimal. Buddy had even gone so far as to pay the gas and electric bills plus the property taxes a year in advance.

Buddy had Mony named as beneficiary of all his life insurance plans, 401K, 403B, military pension, retirement plans, cash savings, and stocks and bonds, all for which Massey withheld the dollar amounts to justify his meeting with her after the formal meeting. The amount would be staggering. Vehicles and cash assets were assigned to Mony's children. He'd left to Mony and Nate equal joint ownership of the original homestead along with the farmland in the original acres, including air and mineral rights. Nate was taken aback by the announcement, and Mony took his hand in a show of approval.

Before digging into the biggest concern, that being the oil business and mineral rights, Massey suggested they all take a break and reconvene in thirty. His secretary brought the light lunch prepared by his stepmom in on a stainless steel cart.

"How are you holding up?" Poppy asked Massey on his way to the bathroom, her face etched with concern.

"Dad's already flipping out that Buddy left Nate and Mony the original farmstead—he's going to have a cow by the time I'm finished with the oil company."

Poppy lifted her brows. "Really?"

Massey nodded.

"Well, good for Nate," she said with approval. "He deserves it."

When everyone was settled back in their seats after the break, Massey picked up where he'd left off, reiterating his father's acquisition of the crop-dusting business in its entirety. He felt the ripple of tension when he announced the final asset—the F&A Oil Company—and decided to skip the legal mumbo jumbo, keeping it simple and direct.

"Joseph Kipton Ferguson will retain all holdings of said business and all of its subsequent profits, divided between the newly assigned owners Ramona Louise Brady Altman Strong and Nathan Thomas Ferguson, who will retain all additional properties beyond the original property holdings and mineral rights associated with the oil business divided equally between them."

He could have heard a feather hit the floor.

It was four o'clock by the time everyone left except for Mony. She sat on the sofa in front of the floor-to-ceiling windows, drinking a lemon-flavored mineral water and stared out at the jet on the tarmac preparing for takeoff. Holding a bottle of beer in his hand, Massey joined her. They sat quiet for a long while, each deep in thought, nursing their beverage of choice. He finally said, "We need to talk."

"That's what I'm here for. Shoot."

Massey got straight to the point. "Is there something between you and Finch?"

Mony took a drink of her mineral water and stared out the window a long while, contemplating, before she finally met his gaze. "Yes, but it was only sex. I had no idea who he was at the time."

Massey let her words sink in before responding, "Good. I'm thinking he kept quiet at the lake to see if he could uncover more information, which he didn't. So, it's over, plain and simple." He took a long pull from his beer. "Are you going to tell Nate?"

Mony shot him an incredulous look. "And what, pray tell, would be the purpose of that?"

"Well for one, he wouldn't have to hear it from someone else."

"You're not going to—"

It was Massey's turn to cut her off with a look. "You would ask me that?"

Mony shook her head and her shoulders relaxed. "How could I have been so gullible? It could have been anyone on that train. Why did it have to be him?" She got up and walked over to the bar where the decanter of Irish whiskey sat. She reached behind the bar for two tumbler glasses and, pouring three fingers into each, returned to the sitting area and handed one to Massey. Mony held up the tumbler in a mock toast and tossed it back. Massey followed suit, grateful for the shot of courage for what he was about to say.

"Mony, if you think back on when you married Bob, you know it doesn't matter who you had sex with. It all hurts Nate. What I'm asking is, are you going to tell him about the night you stayed with me?"

Mony's stared out at the tarmac. *The night.* It was like saying the Wheat Field to a Civil War buff, or when her kids said, "Mom, make the Ice Cream Dessert." She knew immediately what they meant.

"God, I have no idea where to begin that conversation with him, or if I even should," she said, wiping her nose on the corner of her sleeve. "It was so long ago, and I'd have to talk to my son first. It would concern him more than anyone. I'd have to explain my actions, tell him things he won't want to hear, life-changing things." She shook her head, stood up, and began pacing. "Talking about it doesn't change what happened," she continued. "It's not worth all the lives it would ruin, and I'm not talking about mine. I'm talking about Dane's, and yours, maybe even my girls', not to mention what it would do to Nate. My kids just lost their dad; Nate no longer has Buddy to talk to. Best-case scenario is that Nate would hate me for the rest of his life. The worst: Nate would hate me and I would alienate my family. I can't live with that. Bob is gone and—"

He had to say it. "Am I hearing excuses, Mony? You haven't talked about that night to anyone, have you?" It wasn't a question. Massey knew Mony held a dark secret inside. *How I get her to open up?* "It weighs on you, I know it does, and has for almost three decades. You don't deserve that." He made her sit with him on the sofa. "I'm in large part to blame for what had happened. I should have been there. I could have—"

"Stop it," Mony said, hissing. "I don't want to talk about it, and I won't let you assume responsibility for events that were out of your control." She turned to face him. "Listen to me. If it hadn't been for you and Bob, I wouldn't even be here." Massey was about to rebuke her statement, but Mony silenced him. "I am glad for the life I've stuck around long enough to live. Burying what happened is a small price to prevent it from affecting the ones I love. It began and ended with me, simple."

A victim's logic, Massey thought bitterly, *and a survivor's.* "But, Mony, your suffering hasn't ended with you. How can you move forward having a life with Nate while denying the truth?"

Mony glanced away. "Maybe I'm not meant to have a life with Nate."

Massey thought about the two broken children he'd seen huddled in bed together that hot July night so many years ago. "I don't believe that. And I never will."

CHAPTER 26

JOHN

John noticed Ramona at the door of the private entrance, fishing for her gloves in her pocket, when Jason Monroe pushed her back inside. Fumbling with his briefcase, John was about five steps behind and hadn't anticipated the aggressive action. Rushing to catch the door, he barely made it before getting locked outside. Jason shoved Ramona again, sending her back a couple more steps, and John grabbed him by the arm. It was all the opening she needed—she kicked Jason square in the groin, sending him crashing to his knees. The elevator doors near the exit opened, and Attorney Ferguson stepped out in the middle of the chaos. In a blink, he was standing in front of Ramona.

"What the fuck is going on here? I'm calling security." Before Ferguson could act on his threat, Ramona sidestepped around him and was about to let Jason have it again when the attorney caught her by both arms, restraining them behind her back. Mony's legs flailed as the attorney lifted her feet off the floor, prohibiting her from further attack.

"Jesus Christ, you got her?" John shouted.

"I doubt it," the attorney fired back.

John bent down to check on Jason, whose face was white as a sheet. "That bitch," Jason squealed in a voice two octaves higher than his normal range. Ramona pushed back on Ferguson's hold, using him as a brace, and kicked at Jason, barely missing his nose. Jason fell back on his ass to avoid the blow and screeched, "When I get up I'm going to—"

"Will you shut that fucker up?" Ferguson yelled, glaring at John. "Agree right now that son of a bitch keeps his mouth shut the entire time, and I'll give you ten minutes in the conference room."

"What?" Ramona cried, and wrenched out of Ferguson's hold. She whirled around to face him, and he whispered something in her ear, then looked over her head at John.

"Your time starts when you enter the conference room. We'll be waiting."

It took nearly fifteen minutes before Jason could stand or walk. Entering the room, John noted a spread of food along with a variety of beverages sitting in a pan of melting ice on a stainless-steel cart. A woman was gathering up the used plates and silverware. She glanced up and said politely, "Would you gentlemen care for anything before I clear this away?"

John considered, and said, "Could you bag up some of that ice in a zip-lock bag, please?"

The woman gave him a puzzled look, then flicked her shoulders in a shrug. "Sure, give me a couple minutes."

He thanked her and directed Jason toward a seat at the head of the table, then walked to where Ferguson and Ramona stood at the other end. "I'll make this brief."

Jason sat quietly with an icepack on his balls as John pulled documents from his briefcase. "Since all the parties involved are not present, I'll forward the information to Senator Ferguson as well." The peculiar smile twitching at the corner of the Attorney Ferguson's mouth had gotten his back up, but he had to let that go for now. "I've made copies of Monroe Oil Company's bid for any properties available and mineral rights for sale from Altman's estate, for each of you. Having had the opportunity to perform only an aerial survey of the property, CEO Thomas Monroe is still willing to pay top dollar for the property and mineral rights without a full geological and mineral survey as-is." He slid two envelopes across the table. Both Ramona and Ferguson accepted their respective folders, but left them closed while they listened.

"We acknowledge that our business relationship has gotten off to a rocky start," John said and looked at Jason, cuing his acknowledgment. He gave a nod and John continued. "We sincerely apologize for any misunderstanding. Mr. Monroe's actions were inexcusable and a gross misrepresentation of how the Monroe Oil Company manages its business dealings. Know that his actions have been reported to the CEO as well as the board of directors, and his continued participation on this project has been suspended, pending a thorough investigation by our internal ethics committee. Once the investigation is completed, you will be notified in writing of that determination. Regardless of their decision, we will accept your verbal request to deny Mr. Jason Monroe's participation in any business dealings should you choose to move forward. Do you have any questions?"

Ferguson and Ramona deliberated. John noted a rush of color flush Jason's cheeks. He knew it had to be taking every ounce of Jason's willpower to keep his mouth shut, and he almost wished Ramona had kicked him in the teeth instead. What was unbeknownst to either Ramona or Ferguson was that Jason had already been given strict instructions to keep his mouth shut—a directive that came from the old man himself. The situation had gotten dire, so John had decided he needed to grow a pair.

In the biggest career risk of his life, John had informed Monroe Senior that he was terminating his involvement representing Monroe Oil Company in the Altman deal and all legal issues effective immediately. That got the old man's attention. He'd gone on further to say he was done being Jason's legal babysitter and was no longer willing to turn a blind eye toward his irresponsibility or the lack of consequences for his actions. And since his cohones had become large enough that he needed a Radio Flyer to haul them around, he'd even worked up the guts to call the old man out on for his inept decision to send Jason in the first place. He'd be goddamned if he'd was going to let Monroe's gross misjudgment or his son's stupidity ruin his reputation.

John had an ace in his pocket, of course, for salvaging the entire situation, thanks to Franklin. Once Monroe had humbly agreed to his demands, John had shared with him the information regarding the parcel of land within Altman's holdings. The one that was missing a title and deed, about twenty acres in all, and that by all known accounts might likely still be public domain. Before learning this, John had assumed that pursuing acquisition of the Altman property had been a waste of time, especially after meeting Senator Ferguson in person. John knew a man with a plan when he saw one. But something had changed. After intense discussion, Monroe had pledged to John his full support spearheading the expansion project in North Dakota. Jason's silence during the meeting had been just one of the many concessions. John knew he would have to deal with Jason's wrath at some point, but he'd worry about that later.

"As we move forward, my client and the governing board of Monroe Oil sincerely hope you will be able to put this unfortunate matter behind us. We are prepared to exceed any offer other buyers may be offering." Satisfied with his appeal, John reached into the inside pocket of his jacket and retrieved an envelope. "Because of the pending holiday, we'd like to give you time to consider the offer, and in good faith ask that you accept this earnest check." He handed the attorney the envelope. Ferguson accepted it without remark.

John gathered his things and looked around the room. He thought it ironic that the county sheriff had considered the F&A conference room neutral ground. *Bullshit.* It was a goddamn command center, fortified with all the clout of a political leader's forum chamber and the technology of a military stronghold. It was a place where the owners of the mighty F&A Company, Altman and Ferguson, could exert power and control over the regional resources. All because Altman, four decades ahead of the boom, had been lucky, and Ferguson had the wherewithal on how to invest his wealth. *Well, screw it.* John was no longer interested in beating the senator on his own turf or brokering a deal for Monroe. He didn't give a rat's ass how much money there was to be extorted from a bunch of North Dakota farmers, nor did he give a flying fuck who owned what property or mineral rights in that godforsaken land. In fact, if a massive earthquake swallowed up the entire state tomorrow, he could give a shit less if Ramona wasn't in it. His entire perspective had changed after seeing her again. He wasn't going to be sated by their brief interlude on the train. He wanted to get to know her, he wanted to win her over. He wanted her. It had become a challenge for him now, awakening the competitor inside, and something else too, but he wasn't quite ready to acknowledge that feeling, not even to himself.

They tersely shook hands. "Until the New Year, then, happy holidays to you and your family," he said, then faced Ramona. Shaking her hand had been like taking hold of a bare 220 electrical wire.

"Merry Christmas and happy New Year, Mr. Finch," Ramona said.

"And to you as well, Ms. Strong." For a split second John considered addressing her as Ms. Altman and wanted to offer her condolences for her loss. He thought better of it. She wouldn't have believed him anyway.

He turned to Jason. "We're done here." And they left the room.

CHAPTER 27

MONY

Christmas passed in a blur of holiday lights, gift giving, lavish meals, and lively board games. Then, in a blink, Mony was whisking her kids off two by two to their respective destinations. Mindy had decided to join Kiteri for the rest of her holiday break, and they caught the train earlier that day. Departing in a fanfare of hugs, tears, and kisses, they'd all waved goodbye at the Williston Depot as both the girls boarded the train heading west. That afternoon it was Dane and Diana's turn. Waiting for their flight in the F&A conference room, Mony, her son, and his wife skipped the farewell hubbub and relaxed, having a beer before they boarded.

Now, in the unnatural quiet of her dad's home, a pervasive eeriness followed Mony from room to room. Not easily spooked, generally speaking, she tried to brush it off. Yet the silence made her sanctuary feel something more akin to a horror flick, and her mind conjured up an image of some evildoer wearing a hockey mask lurking in the shadows. She looked over her shoulder at the living room window. *You're being ridiculous.* Refocusing on the task at hand, Mony sat among the boxes strewn across the living room floor, packing the Christmas decorations. The loud, energetic voices that had filled the house for the past week were now well on their way back to their own lives. On one hand, Mony felt a sense of pride that her little chicks were thriving outside the nest, but on the other, she wasn't looking forward to being alone. It would take some getting used to, all over again.

Her old hi-fi speakers hadn't sounded half bad when she played the radio, but the continuous Christmas music was not helping her mood. Still, some noise in the house, even Christmas music, was better than nothing. Being alone in her father's house was starting to freak her out, and she tried to recall if the place had ever been so quiet. In her memory, there had rarely been a time when someone wasn't visiting, and boisterous conversations had boomed through the rooms and hallways when her dad was still alive. His home had been a refuge for a lot of people over the years, particularly Nate. Whether they were playing cards with her dad, doing homework, playing piano, or hanging out down at the lake, Mony imagined Nate had spent more time at her house than he ever did at his own, even after she'd left for college.

Nate had turned sixteen her freshman year of college, and he'd already begun to see her as something more than an older sister. His feelings of brotherly love began morphing into something deeper, more intimate and powerful. It overwhelmed her at times. He'd become frightfully possessive, and like a cornered animal, like her dad, she had sought her own means of escape. While she empathized with Nate's fears of abandonment and maternal loss, his perception of her as surrogate savior versus an object of desire had tipped the scales beyond rationality, placing Mony on a precarious pedestal with only one direction to go. All she'd wanted was a little adventure, maybe to join the Air Force and see a bit of the world like her dad; but Nate would have none of it. If only he'd given her a little space to explore. If only he'd had a little more patience, but that wasn't his nature. He couldn't believe she'd have come back in time. But she would always come back for Nate.

That first year of college had been quite liberating. With Massey there looking out for her, Mony had begun to see new things and meet other people. She had caught a glimpse of what life could be like beyond her small county borders, and life had been exciting. Massey assured her often that Nate would be waiting when she returned home, and it was true. But then, what other choice did he have? They tried to pick up where they'd left off, which had worked for a little while. Until Dwight caught her naked, until—*the night.* She'd known then she would have no future beyond North Dakota without causing him pain, and Nate would have no future at all if she stayed. Unable to bear his suffering, Mony had resolved to leave Nate with one last gift and thought she'd gone in with eyes open when they'd made love. Stupid girl, still too ignorant to see how the act would link them together forever.

Mony looked down at the ornament she held in her hand, a clay print of Dane's hand from around age five or six. She smiled. It had been a Christmas gift for Dad. "I swear you never threw anything away," Mony murmured aloud. The attic had been clear evidence of that. From the old flannel shirt and wool socks she wore to the homemade ornament in her hand, they were all pieces of how her dad had held onto her, long after she'd left home.

She'd felt his presence before looking up from the precious memento. Lifting her gaze to where he stood, she wondered how long he'd been standing there watching her. Her eyes slid over his statuesque pose, noticing his entire posture was wrought with tension. His expression was filled with restrained longing and impossibly gorgeous. He came to her and gazed at the object in her hands.

"Buddy loved those little hands," Nate said as he ran his fingers over the fingers imprinted in clay. "I caught him more than once doing what you're doing right now before he'd pack it away." Taking the cherished gift from her, Nate laid it reverently in the storage box. "Come," he said, coaxing Mony to her feet. "You've had a long day."

Hands joined, they walked up the stairs in silence. Nate led Mony to the bathroom and had her sit on the toilet seat while he ran water into the old clawfoot tub. He poured a packet of fragrant bath salts into the water and dampened a wash cloth to wipe her face. With each tender stroke, he brought calm to her troubled heart, his attentiveness conveying comfort. It brought to mind all the more the sadness and pain she could bring to him, and she stilled his hands.

"Nate, I don't want to be alone. I'm afraid, I don't know ho—" She leaned forward, straining toward him. He lowered his lips to meet her, and he kissed her sweetly. She felt a low sound deep in her chest as his mouth and tongue pleasured her senses in a sensual tease, driving away her fears, until all she was cognizant of was how much she wanted him. He knelt in front of her, turning his attention to something he'd wanted to do the day she got off the train, and began undoing the buttons on her shirt.

"Are you hungry? I can get you something while you soak in the tub," Nate said, peeling the worn flannel from her shoulders.

Mony raised her arms as he drew up her shirt. "No thank you," she said. Her head cleared the shirt, and she wrapped her arms around her midsection, a self-conscious response that had nothing to do with the scars of childbirth. Nate clasped her wrists and unwrapped her arms placing them around his waist instead.

"Don't," he whispered, holding her arms in place. "Don't hide from me." Nate pressed his lips to a wisp of hair on the crown of her head. "I will always see you, and you will always be beautiful to me." Mony felt the moisture collecting on her cheek dampen his shirt and snuggled next to his chest, feeling him breathe. He asked, "What do you want, Mony?"

Mony lifted her chin, peering up at him with tears glittering in her eyes. She didn't care anymore what the future held for them, or if he saw the fear and vulnerability in her eyes. All she wanted was to feel him closer, be blanketed by his body and wrapped in his arms. "You," she murmured. "I just want you."

He hitched the hem of his loose-fitting T-shirt, drawing it up his arms. He bent forward, letting her pull the shirt from him, a welcome sign of consent. The bathroom billowed hot steam, yet gooseflesh coursed across his exposed skin. Mony wrapped her arms around him, bringing warmth back to his body, and nuzzled her cheek against his heart, a steady beat eliciting both comfort and contentment. Reaching behind her, Nate unhooked her bra, and she shook it loose from her shoulders, letting it drop to the floor.

"Join me," she said with tantalizing seduction, and rose to her feet, stepping away from him.

From his knees, Nate watched as Mony began unbuttoning her jeans and shimmied them over her hips, offering a little strip tease. But her balance was off, and there was more distance between them than she'd expected. She had to take a couple of shuffling steps toward him, and her awkward gait had Nate fending off a laugh. Reaching for his shoulder, Mony gazed down, trying to hold onto the playful seduction, but her lips broke into a wide smile and he tossed his head back with a lazy laugh. The rich sound pealed through the small confines of the steam-filled room and through the chambers of her heart. Holding onto his shoulder, she stepped on the hem of her jeans with one foot, then the other. Nate's arms banded around her thighs, hugging her pelvis to his cheek and nuzzling against the soft mound of flesh beneath her panties. She combed through his hair, weaving her fingers between the strands while he hummed, and smoothed the tousled mess only to begin again. Her hands stilled when Nate reached for the waistline of her underclothing. He peeled pant and panty over her hips and thighs, gliding his hands down the rest of her legs to her feet, where she stepped out of them. Running his hands along the insides of her legs, he reached the apex of her thigh and eased his thumbs between the soft, warm folds of her cleft, spreading them open and dipping his tongue inside.

She stuttered a sound of pleasure as her fingers resumed kneading against his scalp in rhythm with his mouth and tongue. The carnal bliss Mony felt as he savored her deepened her response and his voracity. Unable to manage the sensual onslaught, she felt her knees weaken as the orgasm built. He grabbed her by the thighs, offsetting her balance and forcing her to clutch both hands onto his shoulders. As her knees started to bend, Nate held her aligned to the position he wanted and fluttered his tongue over her clit. Her cry of ecstasy resounded like the crescendo of a song while Nate held her body upright until the last of her orgasm subsided.

"I won't be able to walk for a week if I don't get off my knees," Nate chuckled, lowering them both to the floor. Mony took advantage, crawling onto him, leaning her naked body against his, and pushing him to the floor. Nate flinched as his bare back touched the cold tile but pulled her to him, letting her soft flesh blanket him. He gazed over her shoulder and his eyes widened as water lapped to the edge of the tub.

"Babe, we gotta get up, or we're going to have a flood."

Nate lifted her from his chest, and Mony used the toilet seat to hoist herself off the floor. Legs still shaky, she sat with her hip on the edge of the tub and shut off the faucets. Reaching into the tub, she let out some of the water and adjusted the water faucets to her liking. Nate rose stiffly to his feet, and she felt the heat of his gaze at her back. She bent at the hips, reaching deep into the tub to reinsert the rubber stopper, and purposefully pointed her round derrière in his direction. When she straightened, she glanced over her shoulder and was greeted with a pair of lust-filled eyes. She crooked a finger at him in a come hither motion, and Nate stepped closer. The heat of his desire radiated from where she touched him as she grasped onto Nate's outstretched arm to steady herself and took a shaky step into the steaming bath. She hissed in satisfaction as she lowered into the water. Seated, Mony scooted her butt toward the spout and rested her back against the tub. She peered up at Nate. "Hmm, it's nice," she said with a dreamy smile. "Join me?"

Nate stood a long moment while he took in the sight of her floating languid just below the water's surface. Mony passed her splayed fingers over her navel and glided lower to the apex of her thighs. She paused and drifted her fingers over the hair dancing wispily in the water. She imagined Nate's hands touching her and moved her hand lower between her thighs, moaning with pleasure before reversing the direction. Brushing her hands over her breasts, she beckoned again. "Join me."

His eyes locked on hers while she watched him undress.

He tried not to appear self-conscious, yet the transparency in his heated gaze said otherwise. When his boxer briefs fell to the floor, she smiled with approval at the sight of his nakedness. As he stepped into the tub, Mony slid forward, letting Nate sit behind her. It felt like a dream. A wonderful, erotic dream. The slow cadence of his hands over her breasts—alternating, gentle squeezes—made her arch in response to his seductive powers. Reaching back, she ran her fingers through his damp hair, thrusting her breasts into his hands, and rested her head against his shoulder. Water sloshed onto the floor, but she didn't care, and she turned her body to lie against his chest. She felt the rumble of satisfaction surge from his core as the hollow of her belly pressed against his groin, his erection hardening against her skin.

"Oh Mony, you feel so good," he said.

Her pulse leaped at the swell of his erection, and she pressed harder against him. His breath caught, responding to the thrum of her heart. Nate pressed his lips to her temple. "What are you doing to me?"

His throaty growl impelled an overwhelming need to please him. "Come for me," she urged.

Nate banded his arms around her, stilling her movements. "No."

Her breasts were hard and heavy. Lying against his body did nothing to alleviate the ache. Her sex clinched with hunger, the throbbing pulse below her ribs intensifying. A quickening stirred in her core. Countering the pressure, she begged, "Come for me."

He tightened his grip, stealing the air from her lungs,

and took control of her body, pinning her in place as he flexed his hips. He thrust his engorged erection against her. Once, twice, groaning a pleasured sound of pain as his body stiffened.

"That's it," she praised, "now come for me, Nate. I need to feel you."

Bewitched by her siren call, Nate rubbed her body against him, increasing in intensity. "I want to feel your heat against my skin," she demanded, and felt his involuntary release beneath her. An impassioned moan rang from her lips, and she found herself chasing his climax, the rigid column of flesh between them subjugated to her bidding. Nate's neck arched with a ragged sound of pleasure as his seed spilled against her belly. The deliverance of his surrender edged her into a second climax, quenching the ache of desire between them.

They lay in bliss together in the bath, until the soothing water grew tepid. Mony thought about the first time they'd made love, the only time, and the naive notion of a young woman who'd thought that leaving a part of herself with him would make all things right between them. She realized now that she hadn't left anything—she'd found it. There was a history between them, an undeniable chemistry, a connectedness, validating in her mind once and for all that they had always been meant to be.

CHAPTER 28

NATE

It was the best night of sleep he'd had in ages. Bound together in a tangle of limbs and blankets, Nate awoke to Mony's movements as she struggled to extricate herself from her bonds. She tried to sit up and gave a low, exasperated growl. Nate shut his eyes, pretending to be asleep, but the more Mony attempted to wriggle from his grasp, the more it felt like foreplay. He reciprocated by tightening his hold, and when her buttock pressed against his groin, they both felt the quiver of his semi-erection come to life. She stilled, and he knew the jig was up.

"Don't know why you thought that was going to work." Nate chuckled and snuggled against her back.

"Nate, I have to go to the bathroom, right now," Mony said with urgency. He yawned into the back of her head and loosened his grip, then let her slip her feet to the floor before he tightened his grasp again.

"If you don't let me go, I'm going to wet the bed," Mony whined.

Nate released his hold and watched Mony scamper her

naked behind across the bedroom floor. He closed his eyes, reflecting on how he loved her ass—her breasts too, for that matter—her waist, her arms, her lips. He'd always believed Mony had been made for him, a creation just as beautiful to him now as she had been that early morning when they'd made love. He reflected on the weeks that had followed that life-changing day—how he'd gone from a boy to a man in the breath of a kiss and had paid a handsome price for that journey.

Mony bolted into bed and slipped under the warmth of their blankets, distracting him from his depressing introspection. She curled up beside him and pressed her toes against the warmth of his legs. He let out a yelp. "Jesus Christ, woman."

"Sorry," she said, not meaning it.

His eyes flung open with realization. "Mony, you're naked."

She wiggled out of his grasp, reaching her arms over her head to emphasize the point, and arched her back, elongating her legs in a slow, lazy stretch.

"Tease."

Mony looked at him with a coy smile, blinked, and said, "What?"

Before she could react, Nate rolled her beneath him, pinning her arms above her head. He planted his hips between her thighs and leaned forward, nuzzling his nose into her neck. On a deep breath, he savored her cool, fresh scent. They had chosen not to make love last night after their erotic bath, settling instead on holding one another until they'd fallen asleep. It felt so good to have Mony in his arms and to be in hers once more without interruptions. It was as if his whole crazy world had righted itself again, her presence chasing away the specters his mind. He'd been free to dream of the future that had been robbed from him so long ago. Yet now that the night had passed and sunrise sat poised on the horizon, his dreams gave way to doubt and confusion. They'd made love at dawn, that first time. Morning had always been their time. Dawn brought hope, held promise; it felt eerily familiar. Mony sensed his hesitation and flexed against his grip.

"Nate, I—" Her words caught in her throat, swallowed whole by his ravenous mouth. The semi-erection she'd woken lay thick and heavy between them, and he rocked his hips against her. He felt her pulse leap with a sense of urgency, stirring an erotic groan of delight. He kissed her long and hard, then banded both her wrists in his hand, holding them suspended above her head. His other hand roamed along the inside of her arm to her breast and cupped it in his hand. He teased the hardening nipple and she moaned with pleasure. Sliding his lips along her jaw, he left a trail of kisses along her neck. He knew just where and how to touch as her body bowed at the onslaught, succumbing to his fingers, mouth, and hands. Her surrender was intoxicating, and he tossed his own inhibitions to the wind. His brother had told him once to proceed with caution where his pursuit of Mony was concerned, that moving too fast, or too soon, could be their undoing. But Massey had been wrong, and the unbridled sounds that were escaping her mouth confirmed it. Nate didn't care anymore who might be taking advantage of who, or whether it had been wrong or right, so long as they were touching one another. Aroused by the sensation of his virility pressed against her, Nate saw in Mony's eyes the mirrored look of determined passion reflected back at him, kindling his desire. They made love that morning— slow and lazy at first, gentle and tender, as if the world belonged to them and time were irrelevant. But need gave way to urgency and overpowered control. Soon their love melded into desperation as they realized that this moment wouldn't last. Grasping, clinging, pushing, pulling, Nate thrust himself into her, and Mony opened to him greedily as he emptied inside her.

Languid in the afterglow of their lovemaking, they lay naked, woven into one. He thought about the security of her arms and how it had always brought him comfort. He wondered if their time had passed, or had it finally arrived? They had been brought together again through sadness and death, grief that cleaved them both open, leaving a gaping wound. Could it be possible for them to heal one another and be made whole again, or would the gift of the joint property they now shared become a curse? The inescapable truth was that their fathers had sealed their fate long ago. Would destiny be enough? Could they overcome the pressures that lurked in the fabric of their love, or would they crumble to the forces determined to keep them apart? Mony lifted onto one elbow and gazed into his eyes.

"Nate, we have to talk," she said. He gave her his full attention.

"Not now," she added quickly, "but tonight, perhaps. I'd like to make us dinner."

It felt to Nate as if she wanted to delay the inevitable as well. *It sounded like goodbye.*

"I have to go back home soon. I have—"

"You are home," Nate objected.

She smiled wistfully. "I've only made arrangements for my animals until the first of the year. I'm due back at my practice the day after that. If you and I are to move forward, we need to plan. But first, we need to talk. I need to tell you things, things you won't want to hear. Things that will impact how you and I move forward, if you even want—"

Nate pressed a finger to her lips. Her eyes were fearful and unnerving. "All right, Mony, we'll talk then. Tonight." He replaced his fingers with his lips. He didn't want to hear about the past or things he couldn't change. He'd been powerless then, a mere boy unaware of the precarious adult choices Mony had to make carrying a child. Now it would be their choice in planning a future together.

He hated leaving her that morning, but an unseen force seemed to be pulling him forward. Mony stood in the kitchen doorway wearing a sweatshirt and pants, a coffee cup in hand. He kissed her before starting down the porch steps.

She called to him. "Promise me, Nate. Promise me you'll come back so we can talk and you will listen to what I have to say."

Turning, Nate bounded back up the steps, taking her in

his arms and holding her tight. She spilled her coffee and began to tremble. It was the cold, Nate told himself, but it felt like something more. She was afraid of the unspoken words she kept inside, and he refused to let his mind race with the possibilities. He kissed her once more with all the reassurance his mouth and heart could convey. Only time would convince her he didn't care about the past. It was the future he held onto. He'd have to show her, that was all. It was as plain and as complicated as that.

When Nate entered the kitchen of his farmhouse, he was surprised to see Massey sitting at the table playing cards with his nephews on a workday. His sister-in-law Michelle was standing over by the sink and had plastered herself against the countertop as he darted past. Nate shouted over his shoulder. "Aren't you going into work today?" He didn't wait for a reply.

His nephews Derrick and Devon sprang out of their chairs and followed him in hot pursuit. Massey snatched his boys by the shirt collars as Nate took the stairs two steps at a time, and he could hear his nephews giggling behind him like a pair of monkeys.

"In a bit," Massey shouted up the stairs. If he said more, Nate didn't hear it.

He scurried around his room like a crazed animal. *Should have never slept in,* Nate scolded himself while looking under his bed; then he remembered. Heading back out into the hall, he rummaged through a closet and spied what he'd been looking for sticking out from a pile of wadded-up clothes on the floor.

"Ah ha."

Nate snatched the duffel bag buried beneath, leaving the mess where it lay. He hurried back to his room, digging through his drawers, and picked out a couple pairs of his favorite jeans, some tees, some socks, some boxers, and a couple of shirts, then bolted to the bathroom to grab a few toiletries. He took one last look around his bedroom, making sure he hadn't missed anything, when his eyes fell on a white, sealed envelope sitting on his dresser. With everything else going on, he'd forgotten that Massey had handed it to him on the day he read Buddy's will. Nate's mind was spinning as he considered what he had left to do before heading back to Mony's. Somehow he had to convince her to come with him, or at the very least to agree to plan B and travel with her to Minnesota. He wasn't crazy about plan B, but they needed more time together, and he couldn't stay here, not with Buddy gone, not without her. He'd known that since the day of the wake, maybe since the morning Buddy had died.

It had been Buddy who'd made life bearable for him in Williston. Buddy was the buffer that kept his old man at bay. With him gone, Kip would surely try to pressure Nate into spearheading his grand plans to drill for oil. Nate had neither the ambition nor desire to delve into the oil business. He just couldn't deal with it right now. For that, he'd need Mony.

Standing next to the dresser, Nate looked down at the envelope in his hand and considered opening it. He stuffed it in his duffle instead. Rushing down the stairs, he almost crashed into Massey. His brother began to laugh as his hands came up defensively, catching Nate in the chest.

"Whoa, big guy, where the hell is the fire?" Massey asked, chuckling. His amusement quickly faded when he caught sight of the duffel.

"Gotta get to town and run some errands," Nate offered and tried to skirt past his brother, hoping to avoid the cross-examination. Massey grabbed onto his forearm.

"Got a minute?"

There was something in the tone of his brother's query that got his back up, and Nate glanced down at where Massey held onto him. He loosened his hold.

"Two minutes, promise."

Nate nodded. "Sure."

The cards lay strewn across the kitchen table, void of their previous players. Massey took a chair across from Nate, looking him straight on. He dropped his eyes to where Nate held the duffel, then looked back at him. His face was grim.

"Have you thought it through, Nate? Do you know what you want?"

"I've never been surer of anything in all my life," Nate replied in earnest. Massey had opened his mouth to speak, but Nate interrupted. "Can't you see?" he said in a tone laced with mild exasperation. "I've been given a second chance here, and I just can't throw it away now, not without trying."

Massey stared at the duffel again. "Nate, I just don't want to see you hurt, that's all."

A tremor rippled through the flexed bicep of his arm. *This conversation was going nowhere.*

"No one wants to see you to be happy more than me,"

Massey continued. "I just don't see how that can be with Mony, not right now. Give things a little more—"

Nate stood abruptly, tipping over the chair. "You don't get to—"

Massey jumped to his feet and stood between Nate and door. "Just listen to me for a moment, please. Stop and think, Nate. Have you forgiven Mony for marrying Bob? Can you live with her past?"

Nate's head snapped back as if his brother had punched him. *He knows something.* Secret-Keeper Massey always knew things nobody else did. It was how he made a living, and Massey lived very well. "Why? Does this have something to do with what Mony wants to talk to me about?" he bit out.

Massey's eyes flickered. "How could I possibly know what Mony wants to talk to you about," he said with a deflated breath, then stepped out of his way. Nate paused for a beat, hoping his brother had something more to say, something useful, but when he remained quiet, Nate continued toward the door.

Calling to his back, Massey uttered in a hollow voice, "Good luck, Nate."

The "goodbye" Nate offered before he closed the door sounded equally empty.

Nate drove his new truck into town. It would be fine, he thought. They'd talk, and after Mony spilled about whatever she thought was so terrible for him to hear, he'd give her a hug, tell her that he loved her, and that would be the end of it. But that wasn't what bothered him. What bothered him was the fact that she'd be heading back to Minnesota in a couple of days. If they loved one another and wanted to be together, what were they waiting for? Nate could accept Mony needing time to work out living arrangements. After all, she had a farm and a business to settle. That was fine, he'd make concessions. But Nate also needed something. He needed it to be official. He needed to marry her.

Having just withdrawn enough money to make the teller suspicious, Nate was driving out of the bank parking lot with no particular direction in mind when the frightened look in Mony's eyes came to mind. She'd made him *promise,* and that niggled at him. *Why would she do that, especially after they'd just made love? Didn't she trust him?* Nate shook his head. He needed some perspective. He glanced at the clock on his dashboard. It was well past lunchtime and his stomach gave a low grumble, emphasizing the fact. *Maybe that's why his thoughts were so screwy—low blood sugar.* Nate made a right turn at the lights and stopped at the first food joint that came to mind. He immediately regretted the impulsive decision.

He stood in the entryway stomping off his boots when he caught sight of Shannon McDonald standing behind the bar, picking at a plate of chili fries. She was engrossed in a book she was reading and didn't see him come in. He hesitated. He and Shannon had been dabbling in a friends-with-benefits relationship on and off for the better part of two years. The benefits part of the relationship had diminished greatly after Buddy died, in part because Shannon thought he might need a little space. But mostly,

Nate suspected it had more to do with her disapproval of his pursuit in rekindling a relationship with Mony.

She looked up just then and smiled. "Well hey, stranger, long time no see and all that." Shannon put down the romance novel and reached behind to the back counter, pouring new grounds into the coffee maker. "I was just about to make a fresh pot," she said over her shoulder. "I'm glad I don't have to drink the whole thing alone."

It seemed that now was as good a time as any to say what needed to say to his favorite bartender. Nate took a seat at the counter. "Hey, Shannon." He shrugged out of his coat and draped it over the back of his bar stool. "Been a little busy, how have you been?"

Shannon set a ceramic coffee mug on the coffee burner and tossed out the spit's worth of the old coffee into the sink. When the mug was nearly full, she slid the pot beneath the brewing spout, replaced the mug, and brought the freshly brewed cup of coffee over to Nate. She rested her elbows on the bar counter. "Can't complain," she said pleasantly. "Santa got me an airline ticket to Cozumel later in January. Got a destination wedding I must attend. It will be nice to get away from the cold for a week."

Nate took a sip of the concentrated coffee and smiled. Shannon knew how much he loved freshly brewed coffee. He finally said, "Well, good for you," and he meant it.

Shannon placed his food order. While he sipped the coffee, Nate considered her as she busied herself with a business owner's duties. Shannon was a headstrong woman, and her driven personality could come off a bit brash at times. But at her center, she was a goodhearted person, and all he wanted was for her to be happy.

A few minutes later, Shannon returned her attention to Nate. "I'm looking forward to you singing with Lonely Boot for the New Year's Eve bash," she said, and gave him a coy grin. "We had a blast at last year's, didn't we?"

Nate averted his eyes and glanced around the bar. The place was relatively quiet with most of the afternoon lunch crowd gone back to work. There was a small crew of oil workers who sat around a table near the far end of the bar, immersed in a heaping plate of the house specialty. Nate drew in a deep breath. "I might be out of town that night," he said, looking back to her.

Shannon studied him as if deliberating, then pursed her lips. "That wouldn't have anything to do with Mony, would it?"

There was no getting around it. Nate conceded. "I hope so. In either case, I will be leaving the day after tomorrow same as Mony."

Shannon blinked in surprise. "Nate, you can't be seriously considering moving to Minnesota," she said with a tone of irritation. "Your life is here in Williston, and so are your friends and family." The timer dinged on the coffeemaker, and Shannon snatched the pot along with a cup, pouring herself one and offering Nate a refill. He let her top it off and waited as she took a swallow of the hot coffee. Then she snapped, "She'll only complicate your life, you know. Is that what you want?"

He knew what she was alluding to. His relationship with Shannon had been simple and easy, the way Nate liked to live his life. But that was gone to him now, gone in a way he could never reclaim. "I'm sorry, Shannon," Nate said with sincerity. "But I can't stay here without her. I just can't." He wanted to tell her more and explain how his heart had changed, but he knew it wasn't what she wanted to hear.

Shannon avoided his gaze. "Well, Nate, I hope it all works out for you but—"

"Order's up," the cook announced. Shannon broke off from her thought and walked over to the serving window.

Nate ate out of necessity, tasting none of his food while Shannon stood sulking on the other side of the counter. She stared pensively into her coffee cup, mulling something over, then said, "Well, I guess you've put Mony's past behind her then." She glanced up over the rim of her coffee cup to gauge his reaction. "You're a much bigger person than I would have ever been."

Nate pushed away his half-eaten food and said, "Why does everyone think I'm so hung up on Mony's past?" He was tired of the same old bullshit. First Massey, and now Shannon, as if she even had a say in the matter. "Another man beat me to the punch, asked Mony to marry him, and she said yes. At least the guy did the decent thing. I didn't like it at the time, couldn't do anything about it then, but I can now." He reached behind him for the wallet in his back pocket, fished out a twenty-dollar bill, and flipped it onto the counter. Shannon reached for his hand and stared at him in bemusement.

"Is that what she told you, Nate?"

Nate jerked his hand away as if she'd burned him. "No, why would Mony tell me that? Or are you assuming she has that low of an opinion of me?" He stuffed his wallet back in his pocket and reached for his jacket.

"Is that what Massey told you, then?" Shannon retorted.

Nate stopped. "Why would Massey say that? She was pregnant, she got married. It happens all the time." He thrust an arm in the sleeve of his jacket and reached for the other side. Shannon scurried out from behind the bar and grabbed at his arm.

"Then you know what happened, do you?" she said, her voice sickly sweet.

Nate blew out an exasperated breath. "And I suppose you're going to tell me."

Shannon frowned. "You're right, Nate, they both have a low opinion of you. I just assumed you knew. I guess keeping family secrets is what your brother does best."

"You're starting to piss me off," Nate warned. "Just spit it out, Shannon, so I can be the hell on my way."

Her face flushed with anger, and her hand dropped away from his arm. "I'm just surprised you'd be okay with Mony and Massey being together in that way. Cindy Mitchell said Mony had left Massey's apartment the morning after—"

Nate hit his fist on the counter, garnering the attention of the oil workers at the table. "What kind of filthy gossip are you trying to spread?" he snarled. His eyes were red with fury, and he was both interested and afraid of what Shannon *thought* she knew. "Isn't it enough for you that Mony has to deal with Buddy's death? I'd expect this sort of bullshit from Mitchell's ex, but you, Shannon? I thought you had more class than that." Reaching past her, he snatched his gloves off the counter.

Shannon stood a moment, stunned, as Nate made his way toward the door before sprinting after him. "Look, I'm sorry. I thought Massey would—"

Nate whirled around to face her, his fists clenched at his side. Not for the first time today, Nate wondered if anyone knew him besides Buddy. People always said, "Oh, you're such an easygoing guy, nothing gets to you. Oh, Nate, you're like the salt of the earth." And there was a thread of truth in that. He was a simple man and liked his orderly world, with his daily routine and spending time with Buddy. But that was all gone now, and he was desperate to restore some balance in his life. He'd hoped he could find it with Mony. Now here in front of him stood yet another person he'd counted among his closer friends who questioned his motives as if they didn't know him at all.

"You better think real hard of what you're about to say," Nate threatened with cool vehemence.

Shannon closed her mouth. There were tears now. Nate held his ground, refusing to be dissuaded. "I'm going to talk to my brother, and so help me God, Shannon—" but he couldn't finish the threat. If she had been lying, perhaps in time, Nate might forgive her petty jealousy. But if she had been telling the truth, and Massey had known something all along, his heart quaked at the mere thought of it. He stormed out of the bar to go look for his brother.

CHAPTER 29

JOHN

"We knew this was going to happen," John said for what felt like the hundredth time. He averted his eyes from the screen, rubbing his fingers over them. They'd been rehashing the same information for going on thirty minutes, and it had become increasingly difficult to hide his frustration. Old man Monroe had his face so close to the camera, John could see the hairs in his nostrils.

"Yes, yes, I know, you said that, but what's our next move, John, what do they want?" Monroe Senior persisted. "You said they wouldn't get back to us until after the first of the year, and they've already sent us a rejection on the offer? Did you disclose everything?"

John struggled to maintain an outward appearance of professionalism. Monroe senior's obstinacy was wearing him down. "There's nothing you have that they want, sir," he repeated.

Despite the tight camera zoom, Monroe hadn't managed to block out the shadowy figure pacing behind him from view. "That miserable little cunt played us right from the start," Jason's voice came from somewhere in the background.

Monroe Senior swiveled his chair away from the camera. "Jesus Christ, boy, what have I said about how you talk about people?"

Jason cut him off. "Yeah, yeah, I know. How you talk behind closed doors is how you project, blah, blah, blah."

Leaning back in his desk chair, John let father and son have at it, giving him a much-needed reprieve. He let his mind drift back. Ramona had played her part like a pro. The whole deception was well executed, and it made him wonder if she'd known who he was from the start. She had let him think he'd seduce her, had gone so far as to hop in the helicopter with them when Jason and John trespassed on her own property. He smirked. *She sure as shit played me.*

"What the hell are you grinning at?"

John snapped back to the present. "I was thinking about chinks in the armor."

The old man rocked back in his chair, looking perplexed. "In English, please. I'm in no mood for your medieval metaphors."

"Like it or not sir, the F&A Company owns their land free and clear; they wield a tremendous amount of political power on the federal, state, and local level; and they have an incredible amount of resources, plus liquid assets, and that's just what we've seen on paper. And," he threw in as an afterthought, "the whole damn community loves them so much they were willing partners in hiding Altman's daughter right under our noses."

"Not everyone loves them," Jason piped in, standing closer to the speaker.

John held his annoyance. "The only way we could dig up anything on these people was to get down in the mud, and—"

"Exploit it," Jason cut in. "We've got to exploit it. But you missed your shot, Johnny boy, when you failed to bring up the fact that Altman hadn't given his so-called daughter and only child his name until a month before he died. And there are credible sources that claim she isn't even his kid. Make your point already, John, before my old man kicks the bucket."

"Watch it," Monroe Senior growled.

John leaned toward his speaker. "So you're asserting that the drunken, bitter SOB we found sitting in a bar, who'd just gotten his ass handed to him by his own hockey team, is a credible source?" John focused his attention back on Monroe Senior. "We happened to be in the right place at the right time to find someone who was willing to give us some inside information. That doesn't mean it's credible. The community hates this Mitchell guy, not the Altmans or the Fergusons. Look, everyone has a backstory, a crazy ex-girlfriend, a jilted lover, a bad haircut, an illegitimate kid, a bully who stole their lunch money, a missed buzzer shot—their most embarrassing moment of their life that they don't talk about but everyone knows about."

Monroe Senior leaned into the camera. "Even tall tales have a shred of truth in them," he persisted.

True, but clearly, he's still missing the point, John mused. "Dwight Mitchell, the guy we talked to, hates the Fergusons and the Altmans because they made him look bad in his mind. Stole something from him—his status, a spot on the hockey team, his girlfriend, whatever—and there's generally a thread of truth buried somewhere in all that. But it has been my experience that people like Dwight Mitchell, nine times out of ten, have created their own misery through their stupidity. Rockstar Ferguson got the daughter of the wealthiest man in the region, and Mitchell's jealous. They are like feuding families, no more, no less."

"But he didn't get the girl. She'd married someone else, and what about the legitimacy angle?" Jason interjected.

"There is no angle," John shot back. "So what if Altman waited to give Ramona Strong his name? She lived with the man over ten years. Ask anyone. He raised her for the most part, and now she's got the documents to show she's legit. The approach we want to take is—"

Jason's voice boomed over the speaker. "I still think we should hit the legitimacy angle. It would make her life a living hell, and it would pull the legs out from under old man Ferguson's master plan."

"It's a waste of time and resources," John retorted. "Sir, the best chance you have of acquiring any of Altman's holdings lies in the parcel of land that hasn't got a clear title and deed. Once the will goes through probate and this is made clear, you have a chance to work with state, obtain drilling rights, and then negotiate an easement agreement to access the parcel. It'll just take time, that's all. You'll destroy any working relationship you might have with these people if you piss them off by questioning Ramona Strong's legitimacy."

Monroe glanced away from the camera at Jason, who was grumbling in the background. He looked back at John. "What do you have in mind?"

John decided to exercise some of his newfound authority and nurture that pair of balls he'd been growing. "I want Jason to leave the room."

"What?" both the Monroes shouted in unison.

John remained silent and stared into the camera, waiting for compliance. More shouting ensued, followed by the sound of a glass object breaking. Thomas Monroe moved away from the camera, and John seized the opportunity to get up and walk over to his mini fridge to grab a bottled water. The shouting continued, along with verbal threats and curses, concluding with the slam of a heavy wooden door. John was back in his chair when Monroe senior returned to the camera, his face red as a beet and covered in sweat. Reaching outside of the camera's angle, Monroe brought a crystal tumbler into focus and raised it to his lips. He took a long swallow.

"I hope you know what you're doing, Finch."

So did he.

"We have to sit tight, Tom. We need to know if Altman possesses both a clear title and the deed to the property holdings that are claimed to be his. The mineral rights are an entirely separate issue." He tried to put Monroe at ease. "I understand Jason is eager to get things moving, but let Ferguson and Ms. Altman's attorney do the work. There's confusion at the courthouse. Altman has the title, allegedly, but the property deed is missing. Not that they need both, but someone has screwed up. And where there's one screw up, there may be more. There has been a lot of back and forth with the land surrounding the wildlife management area as I understand it. It would be easy to confuse the public on who has ownership and mineral rights. You get my meaning?"

Monroe Senior leaned back in his chair. "I see where you're going."

"Antagonizing these people isn't the answer. If you do acquire the land and mineral rights, we'll still need some sort of easement agreement to access the land. We want them amiable to the idea. The process alone might wear them down enough to make them want to sell."

Monroe nodded. "I have about five more minutes until my next meeting, John, let's wrap it up."

"Sir, I just want to add an observation. The first time I saw the Fergusons and Ramona Strong at the airport conference room together, I noticed some interesting family dynamics. Nathan Ferguson came busting into the conference room like goddamn John Wayne with guns a-blazing, except that Ramona Strong wasn't in any danger. Shit, she had plenty of protection with Senator Ferguson, Attorney Ferguson, and the sheriff all in the same room if Jason or I had intended to harm her in any way. Hell, the room was named after her old man, for crying out loud. She was on her own turf. So why had the rockstar assumed she'd needed rescuing from his own brother, or his old man, perhaps? Why hadn't he come in for her right away? Further, there were some hostile vibes going on between father and son. It makes me wonder what's going on there. And when Jason and I crashed into the attorney's office, Ms. Strong was there with the attorney, but no Nathan Ferguson, and as I understand it, his name was on the homestead property title for a while. I'm telling you there is something odd about this family's dynamics, and that's where we'll find the chink in the armor."

It took a while before the lightbulb finally pinged. "Their strength is in a united front," Monroe said with a knowing smile. "So we need to divide to conquer." The man almost seemed to purr, as if he were savoring an expensive caviar. John decided maybe father and son weren't so different after all.

"That's right, sir. You don't have anything they want; they've made that clear. But what if we can make them not want what they already have? From what I can tell in the ownership agreements they must be united, or they have nothing. So, how do we do that?"

The old man's head bobbled like a dashboard ornament. "Do you have any suggestions?"

"We have to find the weakest link first. It's not the senator or the lawyer, they're solid, but what about the rockstar brother? What about Ramona Strong?"

"She doesn't live in Williston, as I understand it, which makes her low-hanging fruit." Thomas Monroe drew his face into the camera. "I understand she's recently widowed, and now that her daddy has just passed away . . ." He paused, considering. "You know someone who could, you know, give a lonely girl some comfort?"

John cringed inwardly at the implication, but he needed to take control of the plan spinning in the old man's mind. "I suggest I do a bit more research before we send anyone random," John suggested evenly. "I don't know how much Jason has shared with you about our meeting with her, but she's a shrewd adversary. She knows how to handle business, and men."

Monroe nodded sagely. "Check out that younger Ferguson, find out what he wants, or more precisely, what he doesn't want. Do your research, John. Get that Mitchell guy to cough up anything he thinks might be shady, no matter how small, and get back to me." He cut the video feed.

John sighed and leaned back in his chair. *I've bought you some time, Ramona, but you'd better come around soon. Things are about to get ugly.*

CHAPTER 30

MASSEY

"**M**atthew," Poppy said with a start, finding him unexpectedly standing in the mudroom. "I thought you'd be on your way back to Bismarck by now." She made her way over toward her stepson, carrying the basket of towels on her hip, and gave him a quick peck on the cheek. Looking behind him, she asked in a winded voice, "Where's Kip?"

Massey strolled in his stockinged feet over to the table, where he joined Poppy folding towels. "Dad has a meeting in Dickenson with a drilling company. I thought I'd stop by quick before me and the family head back to Bismarck." Poppy continued folding towels as if she hadn't caught his meaning. Massey knew better. She had been dropping hints since Christmas day that she wanted to talk. If she had something to say that she hadn't wanted Kip to hear, now was the time to say it.

An awkward silence built between them before Poppy finally cleared her throat and said, "Matthew, I need to ask you something, and I need you to be honest."

Massey kept folding towels. "Alright, what's on your mind?"

"Have you and Mony—" She paused and her face flushed. Massey stopped folding and gave his stepmom his full attention. He'd been waiting for her to confront him on what she'd seen the day of Buddy's funeral luncheon. "Go ahead, Mom, just spit it out."

Poppy took a deep breath, weighed her words in her mind, and then blurted. "Have you and Mony slept together?"

The direct question coming from Poppy would have almost been laughable if the situation hadn't been so serious. He told himself to be patient, find out what Poppy thought she knew. Massey replied in a modulated tone, "I think you have me mixed up with my brother. I seem to recall Nate was the one who used to sleep with Mony when they were kids. Besides, you wouldn't be asking me a question like that if you didn't think you already knew the answer."

Poppy threw her towel on the floor. "Don't use your lawyer crap on me, Matthew," she bit out, and reached with a tremulous hand to retrieve the towel. "Show me a little respect."

Standing at six-foot-four, Massey Ferguson cut an imposing figure, and rarely used his height to intimidate unless it was warranted. He hated using the tactic on his stepmom right now. "Then show me a little respect, Poppy," he warned in a dangerous voice, "and Mony some respect too."

The tactic worked. Poppy's anger faltered immediately,

and her hands trembled a little more as she folded the towel. She was on a fishing expedition, it seemed, and had just cast out her best bait. It broke his heart to see her eyes wet and shining like that, but it was time to get things out in the open.

"What do you know, Poppy?" Massey coaxed. "Whatever it is, you can say it."

Poppy struggled to formulate her words. Again, he waited and felt his own heart pound with a sort of panic.

"Dane is not Bob's biological son, is he?" It wasn't a question. She knew the answer; so did he. Massey had long suspected as much; what he needed was confirmation.

"Is that what you think, or what you know?"

"Massey, I saw Dane sitting next to your brother at the funeral luncheon. He's a Ferguson, there is no amount of denial that can change that fact. My question is, which of you is the father?"

Massey had wondered that himself many times over the years, and had dismissed the notion when he remembered their kiss. And as Dane grew into manhood looking so much like his brother, at least in his eyes, he'd felt certain of the answer. Yet as different as Massey and Nate were in personality, they were still similar in appearance, and he could understand why Poppy would suspect him. He too had felt that pang of doubt. A part of him wanted to come clean, right then and there, but he held his tongue. There were still too many important pieces missing to Poppy's claim, and he needed to be sure.

"Is that what Mony told you?"

The fire in her eyes returned. Poppy slapped her hand

against the table. "I know what my own eyes are telling me, and you two were off at college together, so I know it's possible that the two of you—" She broke off and flopped down in the chair beside her. "Oh, Matthew," she cried. "Is it you?"

Massey closed his eyes, trying to reconstruct in his mind the night he'd found Mony lying on the ground. She'd been assaulted, of that much he'd been certain. He'd taken her to his place. He'd undressed her, cleaned her up, tried to comfort her. They'd kissed, and he'd taken her into his bed—that was all true. But it came back to the kiss, that awkward brother-sister kiss that had convinced him Dane couldn't possibly be his son. Drunk as he was, instinct would have kicked in. He would never have gone through with it. Poppy's speculation held nothing new, nor did it clarify the events that had transpired, which left the possibility that Dane's biological father may have also been his mother's assailant. Someone of European heritage, Norwegian or German descent, built like him and Nate, big and burly, like a hockey player. Someone Mony may have known, perhaps.

He sat down at the table across from Poppy when a sudden awareness prickled beneath his skin. They weren't alone. Massey caught movement out of the corner of his eye as the shadowy figure looming near the mudroom entryway came into view. His back was leaned against the door frame with his hands shoved in his pockets. Nate's legs were crossed casually at the ankles. Only an idiot would fail to sense the icy fury seething just beneath the surface.

"Yes, I'd be curious to know the answer to that myself," Nate said.

Massey watched his brother uncoil like a viper as he moved from the darkened doorway into the kitchen's fluorescent light. The tension radiated across the room, betraying his deceptive calm.

"So, big brother, are you going to answer Poppy's question?"

Poppy's eyes widened with fear as she watched her two stepsons square off, both matched in strength and anger. Arms at his sides and his jaw clenched, the younger son's face was an implacable mask as he glared at the elder, who wore the same despicable expression. She stepped between them. Nate's eyes dropped to where she stood.

"You need to step out of the way, Poppy," he ordered in a cold and impassive voice.

Poppy thrust out her hands. "You stay right there, Nathan," her shrill voice commanded, an octave higher than her smoker's alto supported. "There will be no fighting in my house."

Nate halted in his tracks and directed his question toward Massey. "Fight? Why would we fight?"

An eerie quiet fell on the room. With each second that passed, the two brothers moved closer toward an inescapable fate neither seemed to want to evade. The abrupt ring of the phone shattered the silence. Poppy gasped, but made no move to answer it.

"Out with it, Massey," Nate snapped. "Is this what Mony is waiting to tell me out at the farm?"

"Jesus Christ, I told you before. I have no idea what

Mony wants to tell you," Massey lashed back. Then it was as if it was all the fight he had left his body. He was tired of the whole charade and decided to let the evolution toward the inevitable commence. If Dane had been his son, he wouldn't deny it. He loved both the young man and his mother, and he'd be goddamned if he'd degrade either one of them by forsaking his responsibility. But he knew it wasn't the truth. Dane's paternity remained a mystery; either he was the product of Mony's assault or he truly was Nate's son. In either case, it wasn't his story to tell. Massey heard the vibrating of his cellphone from his coat pocket draped across the kitchen chair. He ignored it and addressed both Nate and Poppy's question.

"The answer is yes, we were together, once."

Nate's head jerked back as if he'd been slapped, and his chest started to heave. Now his cellphone went off, but he didn't seem to notice. "Define together," Nate demanded.

Answering that question would betray Mony's secret, and she wasn't in the room right now to speak her truth. *How could he tell his little brother answers that only she knew?*

The landline began ringing again and Poppy screamed. "What's wrong with people? Don't they know they are making things worse?" Her body tensed with rage, but she remained poised between her two sons.

Undeterred by the persistent annoyance, Nate's gaze remained fixed on Massey. "Did. You. Fuck. Her?"

Poppy gasped in horror, but still Massey said nothing. He hadn't taken advantage of Mony, but someone had, and he'd failed to protect her, a regret for which he would never find absolution.

Nate choked past the unshed tears in his throat, and his voice rasped. "Massey, you owe me an answer."

This was his moment of atonement, and maybe now he could find peace, though keeping a secret as great as this one from his brother would take a long time to heal. Massey closed his eyes and surrendered to his fate. "I found her lying on the ground passed out at some house party. I took her to my apartment, tried to take care of her. She spent the night with me and left the next morning."

He'd barely spoken the words before Nate was on him. A second later he was bleeding. He heard the crunch as bright red blood gushed freely from his nose, and he thought Poppy may have screamed, but he couldn't tell. With silent precision, Nate pummeled his fists into his ribs, knocking him off balance, and the two stumbled backwards into the kitchen counter, sending a ceramic coffee mug crashing to the floor.

"Stop it," Poppy screeched, but the plea was lost in Nate's thunderous fury.

"You motherfuckin' son of a bitch," he roared, delivering another punch to the gut.

Wedging himself against the corner of the counter, Massey managed to stay upright as his brother reaped his vengeance. Blow after blow, it was the moment Massey had dreaded most of his adult life made manifest. He felt the sharp pain of another rib cracking, yet there came with it an inexplicable sense of profound relief in an odd sort of way. The physical pain was just a ruse. *Oh, destiny and her clever irony.* He took another hit to the jaw, hard enough to turn his head, and from the corner of his swollen eye he noticed Poppy's attempt to intervene. He held out his arm to fend her off, but his response was too slow, and she stepped into the trajectory of another swing. Nate knocked her to the floor, where she landed with a thud.

"What the fuck is going on?" a female voice shout from the doorway. Someone lurched at Nate from behind, grabbing his arms and pinning them to his back. Shannon McDonald appeared from out of nowhere. She'd done her share of breaking up brawls, and Massey was fairly certain she could hold her own. But as strong and proficient a fighter as Shannon was, she was no match for Nate's adrenaline-fueled anger and he easily broke her hold.

"Are you insane?" Shannon shouted and boldly reached out toward Nate.

Like a cornered animal, Nate whirled around and looked at her with murderous eyes. "Isn't this what you wanted?" He snarled, "Sending me after my brother? Now stay the fuck out of it."

Shannon recoiled and Nate turned his back to her. He blinked as though he'd remembered something, and with a guttural wail he sobbed. "Why? Why did you do it?"

Massey had used Shannon's distraction to regain his footing and leaned into the counter supporting his body weight. His breathing was quick and shallow, and he had to splint his rib cage with his arm, wincing when he rested it against his side. He braced himself before speaking. "Why?" he gasped, in a steadfast voice. "Why do you think you are the only one who cares for her?"

There was a collective gasp of horror at the wounded sound of Nate's agony. Grabbing him by the shoulders, Nate tossed Massey to the floor like a ragdoll and towered over him. Closing his eyes, Massey readied himself for the demoralizing smash of Nate's boot. It never came. Wheezing for air, he opened his least swollen eye, but he couldn't see Nate. He heard scuffling off in the corner of the room, and with painstaking effort rolled onto his side, straining his vision in the direction of the mudroom door. Nate's feet dangled off the floor as two massive biceps held him aloft, his arms pinned behind his shoulder. Writhing in place, Nate couldn't break the hold, and his feet flailed uselessly in the air. Shawn McDonald's broad shoulders loomed behind Nate as he dragged him backward out of the house kicking and swearing. Poppy crawled on hands and knees to where he lay on the floor, and Shannon rushed beside her.

"Don't move, Matthew," Poppy cried as her hands hovered over his body, not knowing where to touch.

Massey coughed up a spout of blood and a sharp pain tore at his side. "Don't," he rasped.

"For Christ sakes, Massey, lie still," Shannon scolded, retrieving her phone and penlight from her pocket. She gestured the cell toward Poppy. "Hit speed dial three, it's the non-emergency number."

"Don't let him get to Mon—" They were the last words Massey remembered before his body went lax against the floor.

His sense of smell had been the first to awaken as his

nostrils flared at the pungent odor of plastic. He tried to clear his nasal passages, but the breath caught when a sharp pain seized his rib cage. Someone was there beside him, and he felt a cool sensation trickling along his arm. His mind drifted.

He saw the three of them sitting on the floor in front of her bedroom window, Nate holding onto Mony's hand while he rested his hand on her shoulder. She didn't comprehend the violence happening in her own yard as the heat lightning illuminated the two men fighting below, one her father, the other his best friend. Nate had fallen asleep in her bed that night, the two of them a tangle of arms and legs in the summer humidity while Massey watched over them.

Then he saw the three of them together, floating lazily on the raft by the lake in the warm summer air, best friends forever without a worry or care in the world. Then, they were gone, faded, into the abyss.

CHAPTER 31

MONY

She waited a beat in front of the doorway of room 204, peering inside. A nurse stood over the lone occupant in the room, hanging a small IV bag of fluid and piggybacking it into the main line. The task completed, the nurse turned her attention toward the monitors at the head of the bed. Mony stood frozen, staring at where her dear friend lay, fragile, attached to tubes and wires.

The nurse touched his arm. "Remember, Mr. Ferguson, you can push the button on the IV pump every thirty minutes. Don't worry about pressing it too often; it's pre-programmed, so you're not at risk for overdosing. I'll be back shortly to check on you." She turned, and her eyes meet Mony's. Approaching, she offered a kind smile.

"Don't worry, he's awake. You can visit a while. He's been asking for you." She gave Mony's shoulder a gentle pat and stepped past, leaving the room. Speechless, Mony wondered how the nurse had known who she was.

He'd sensed her presence and turned his face to the door. Mony clutched her hand on the doorjamb, felt her

knees buckle at the initial shock of seeing him. His cheeks
and jaw were a mass of purple and blue, his blackened eyes
mere slits on his swollen face. His nose was so enlarged
that Mony wondered how he could even breathe, then
noticed the oxygen cannula resting above his torn lip.

"That bad, huh?" Massey croaked, a meager attempt
at humor, and offered a misshapen smile. Lifting his IV
hand, he crooked his stiff finger. "Come here, you."

Mony entered the room, walking over to the bedside on
trembling legs. Up close, she could see Massey's shirtless
chest wrapped in a binder. The parts of his torso that
weren't covered had bruising everywhere. "Oh, Massey,"
she said, not bothering to put up a false bravado. "What
happened?"

Massey said with a rough, raspy voice, "Shitstorm. I'd
say you ought to see the other guy, but all of his wounds
are on the inside." He tried to laugh at his own dark
humor, but it only made him wince, and he sobered.
"Besides, I think Nate pulled a few punches after he broke
my ribs."

Mony had only seen Nate in a fight once, and it was
equally as brutal. "Shit, Massey, I think you'd be in a
coma if he hadn't," she agreed grimly.

A long silence fell between them before Massey asked,
"Can you give me a drink of water?"

Relieved to have something to do, Mony held the glass
of water for him as he sipped through a straw. When
finished, he waved her off and coughed a little. She
withdrew the glass.

"Mony?"

Mony set the glass back on the table. "Hmm?"

"No one will tell me where Nate is. Did he try to . . . ?"

Mony bobbled the water glass in her hand. It killed her to hear Massey speak his brother's name with such sorrow. "I don't know where he is, Massey. He never came back to the farm."

"He didn't try to hurt you?" Massey asked pitifully, and she knew what he meant.

"I suppose no more than I had hurt him," Mony confided. "His bruises are on the inside, remember?"

The alarm went off on the IV pump, startling her. In less than a blink, Massey's nurse returned to switch over the IV piggyback to the main bag. Mony stepped out of the way, allowing the nurse unrestricted access to do her task. She observed the nurse intently, pleased by her bedside manner and the economic efficiency of her movements. It was a relief to know Massey was being well cared for.

"It's time for another dose of your morphine," the nurse informed him, and before Massey had a chance to protest, she pressed the plunger on the PCA pump. Turning to Mony, she cautioned, "He'll get sleepy rather quickly—you may want to say your goodbyes for now, and come back a little later." Gathering the water pitcher, the nurse left the room.

Mony felt the weight of grief crushing her to the floor. "Oh, Massey, this is all my fault." She knelt beside the bed, resting her head against the mattress. "I'm so sorry."

Massey slid his fingers along the mattress edge and rested them on the back of her head. "Shush, baby," he murmured. "It's not."

Mony was glad Massey couldn't see her and began to sob. All he'd ever done was try to protect her. "If only I hadn't gone to that party. None if this—"

"Mony," Massey chided in a raspy voice. "This is not your fault. What happened between me and Nate was bound to happen sooner or later. I'd withheld the truth from him. And the truth is, we both love you, just not in the same way. Nate doesn't understand my love for you. Hell, I barely understand it myself sometimes. Our only way past this is to face it head on, and Nate will never be able to do that until he hears the truth, in its entirety, from you."

Mony felt the light touch of his trembling fingers against her hair, and she reached for his hand. Muffling the sound of guilt and grief, she buried her face against the bed and held onto the man no word could accurately describe, except *brother*. Her love for Massey was so different than it was for Nate. There was an incredible force that had drawn both Nate and her together, interlocking like puzzle pieces that fit perfectly into the hollow spaces of one another's soul. Massey understood this about them and had borne the brunt of his brother's pent-up torment by keeping her secret. The brave façade and that suppression of what had happened to her long ago hadn't spared any of them of the pain that they shared now. Perhaps Massey was right about the truth; it was their only catalyst for healing and moving forward. Still, she felt afraid. Yet having Massey touch her, and being close by his side, had given her the courage and the strength to do what she needed to do. She stood.

"Is Nate Dane's father?" Massey asked. He was weary now, the medication doing its job, though he fought to stay awake. "Please Mony, I need to hear you say it."

Watching over him, she could see his consciousness fading, and wondered how much of what he'd just said he would remember. She leaned over and pressed her lips gently to his forehead. She whispered softly next to his ear, "Yes, my big brother, you are, and always will be, Uncle Massey."

A small frown line marred his forehead under the bruising, then faded as Massey drifted into a deep, sedated sleep.

Mony had somehow managed to stumble her way back to the elevator bank, entering reflexively when the doors slid open. Absorbed in thought, it startled her when she heard her name. Almost colliding into Shannon McDonald, she said, "Excuse me," then felt Shannon's arm hook with hers.

"We need to talk," Shannon snapped, letting the elevator doors close behind them.

The two women rode in silence among the other passengers, but the space between them crackled with animosity. When the doors parted on the main floor, Mony lurched forward as Shannon half-walked, half-dragged her out of the elevator and moved briskly through the lobby, the vestibule, and another set of doors. They were headed toward the visitor parking lot when Mony yanked her arm free of Shannon's grip.

"We can talk right here."

Shannon halted two steps ahead and whirled around. Stepping in front of Mony, she blocked any potential retreat and stared at her with laser focus. "You need to stay away from Nate."

Mony was neither intimidated nor threatened by Shannon's remark; given her current dark mood, she might have found the situation comical, except there hadn't been anything humorous about what had just happened to Massey. Mony had always liked Shannon and had to give her props for defending Nate, even ifshe was misguided. But if Shannon thought for one minute she was in a position to dictate to Mony what she could or couldn't do, the woman was seriously delusional. Still, eager to avoid a confrontation, Mony drew in a deep breath and nodded. "Of course. I'll do whatever Nate wants. Let's go ask him."

Shannon shot Mony a contemptuous glare. "What he wants? This is me telling you, whore." She poked a pointed finger at Mony's chest. "Stay the fuck away."

Forcing herself to remain calm, Mony neither rose to the bait nor indulged Shannon's absurd foolishness. "Shannon, Nate's not in love with you, he—"

Shannon closed the gap between them. "You don't get to tell me how Nate feels about me, bitch. He can do that just fine all by himself." She shook her head in disgust. "You couldn't be satisfied with one, could you? You had to have both."

Mony's spine stiffened at Shannon's physical proximity, but she kept her cool. *Let her think whatever she wants,* she told herself. *It doesn't matter.* Turning away, Mony circumvented Shannon and headed toward the visitor parking lot. As she made her way to her truck, she half expected Shannon to come charging after her and could feel the daggers of anger thumping her in the back. She went a few steps before Shannon spiked the killer blow.

"You are a lying, deceitful, manipulative bitch," Shannon shouted at Mony's retreating back. "You deserve to be alone."

Steps faltering mid-stride, Mony considered turning around and punching the redhead square in the jaw, but what would have been the point? Shannon neither required nor deserved an explanation. She kept walking.

"He was going to ask you to marry him." Shannon sobbed pitifully. "Marry you."

Mony closed her eyes. *A jilted woman's speculation.* That wouldn't help either of her brothers now. She turned around and made a beeline straight to Shannon. *This stupidity has to stop,* she decided, *once and for all.* There were more important things at stake, plus the woman needed to get a grip. Shannon gasped when Mony audaciously stopped in front of her, nose to nose, hands fisting at her sides.

"Tell me, Shannon, were you the one who told Nate the vicious lie that Massey and I slept together?" Mony said with unnatural calm. "Were you hoping to drive a wedge between us, is that it?"

"I never said that," Shannon retorted, but her response had been too quick, betraying the lie.

"Then what did you tell him? Because whatever you said is probably the reason why Massey is lying in a hospital bed and Nate is on the run."

Shannon's mouth opened, ready to speak, but no words came forth.

"What did you tell him?"

A strong breeze from the north blew across the half-full parking lot. Winded, but not without arrogance, Shannon huffed. "I told him what Cindy Mitchell told me, that you had spent the night with Massey, that's all."

Mony stood her ground and eyed Shannon with skepticism.

"That's all I told him, I swear," Shannon defended.

"When did you see him?" Mony asked.

"Around one today, I think—we'd just finished the lunch rush," Shannon said in haste. "I asked him if he was looking forward to playing with Lonely Boot on New Year's Eve, and he said he was leaving town, the same day as you."

"Why would Nate leave town?"

"How the hell would I know?" Shannon said an incredulous laugh. "I assumed he was planning to leave with you. Mavis at the bank told me Nate made a huge cash withdrawal this morning and he was driving his new truck. He never drives his new truck into town. The only time he drives it is when he goes to see Massey in Bismarck. He doesn't even take it over to Dickenson."

"You blindsided him," Mony said flatly. "How could you set Massey up like that?"

All haughtiness left her, and Shannon's shoulders slumped in defeat. "I had no idea Nate would react like that."

"Are you kidding? You were counting on it."

Shannon began to blubber. "I just wanted Nate to stop and think about what he was doing before planning on running off with you. His home is here, Mony. He doesn't belong with you in Minnesota. You've only brought him misery and sorrow. You didn't see him when he ran away the first time, and—"

"No," Mony said, exasperated. "Buddy was his home, and now Buddy's gone. And it is thanks to you he's on the run again."

"He was planning to leave anyway, he said—"

"Leave, not run," Mony snapped. "You shouldn't have told him about my staying at Massey's. That was mine and Massey's story to tell. You had no right, and you don't know the circumstances. Massey took care of me after—"

"After you were shit-face drunk at some party," Shannon accused.

Mony could no longer contain her anger. "You're an ignorant fool. I hadn't had a drink all night. I drank pop. I was sick, and I wanted to go home. Cindy wouldn't leave the party with me, and she left me to walk alone."

Shannon interrupted. "But Cindy said you were passed out on the lawn of some frat house party and—"

Mony was no longer listening, as the recollection of that night came rushing back to the forefront of her mind. "They offered a ride," she continued, her voice choked with tears at the bitter memory. "I never made it back to my apartment."

They'd been acquaintances, people Mony hung out with at various parties, and had seemed friendly enough.

She'd been desperate to get home, her stomach sick with the pain she had caused Nate. Her heart had felt as though it were a piece of shrapnel in her chest, tearing her insides apart. It had been a mistake to accept that ride, a terrible, terrible mistake. She should have waited at the party like Massey had told her. She should have trusted he'd come. Instead, she'd wandered off by herself like the naive country bumpkin she had been, as if she were walking down a familiar dirt road where everyone was your neighbor and looked out for you.

"They left me on the ground when they were done with me," Mony said, refusing to cry in front of Shannon. "I suppose they thought that was where Massey would find me, like a calling card or something." She lifted her icy gaze to Shannon. "You jealous, stupid woman. They used me to get back at Massey, blamed him for having been kicked off the hockey team instead of accepting responsibility for their own failures. They left me there a bloody, broken mess. Massey took care of me the best way that he knew how."

Wide-eyed, Shannon stood in utter shock, unable to speak. It was clear that this part of the story had never been revealed to her. Mony had often wondered if Cindy had known the truth all along, or if she'd been equally as clueless. Perhaps she'd been in on the ambush all along. What did it matter anymore? It was all in the past. A past that had come back to haunt her once again.

"Poor Nate," Mony murmured, her gaze focused off in the distance. "He'd barely turned seventeen. It would have eaten him alive knowing what had happened, and that there hadn't been a damn thing he could have done to stop it. Naturally, he would have looked somewhere to place the blame. And now you've made certain that burden has fallen to Massey. Nate believes his brother has betrayed him, when all Massey had ever done was try and protect me. Our Nate is on a long, lonely drive to nowhere, with a heart filled with pain and his head filled with lies."

Shannon stood silent as Mony turned and walked away. It took every last ounce of energy to make it back to her truck. Before she even closed the door, Mony Altman-Strong leaned her head on the steering wheel and began to cry.

CHAPTER 32

MASSEY

His dad arrived at the hospital a little past seven. He'd been in meetings all day with a new drilling company out of Dickenson, and hadn't heard about the incident until almost five o'clock. Massey could feel the suppressed rage billowing off his dad like a mushroom cloud, his breath shallow, quick bursts as he entered the room and took command.

"Poppy, you need to take Michelle over to the house and get dinner started. I swung by the farm and picked up the boys, dropped them off at our place. A good thing too, since Derrick was about to take Nathan's old truck and drive into town with Devon looking for you."

Poppy was about to say something. Massey's eyes were swollen closed, but he sensed his stepmom's irritation at being bossed around. Still, she didn't challenge him. Poppy and Michelle each said their goodnights. Massey squeezed his wife's hand before she left and said, "Remember what we talked about." She squeezed his hand back. For better or worse, they'd decided not to tell the boys *who* had assaulted their father, at least for now. The truth, that their Uncle Nate was capable of such violence, was likely to be incomprehensible to his young sons. Yet hadn't he, Mony, and Nate witnessed their own fathers' brutal fight as kids? Perhaps the boys would understand the circumstance better than either he or his wife had anticipated. It was a disquieting thought.

Massey sat with the head of the bed elevated while his dad took the vacated armchair next to the bed. He was drinking a Pepsi. Massey couldn't see, but he knew his dad was drinking a Pepsi. It was his go-to beverage whenever he was stressed. They sat a long while in a familiar silence as the commentator boomed an exciting recap of a brilliant save made by the Colorado goalie. Massey felt himself dozing on and off as thoughts from an earlier conversation slipped in and out his mind. Mony had called him *uncle* and said *yes* to his question when he'd asked if Nate was Dane's father. It was a relief having the words validated out loud, but it didn't change the situation. Nate was on the run again from the same thing that drove him away the last time, withholding the truth.

"Did you know drinking from an aluminum can is linked to early Alzheimer's disease?" Massey said to his dad without preamble.

Kip scoffed at the remark.

Massey asked, "Dad, where is Nate? No one will tell me where he is."

Kip took a noisy sip of his pop. "I don't know where he is, son," he replied. "No one does at present. Now you're going to tell me something. What the hell happened?"

"Shitstorm," Massey said, trying to piece together the sequence of events to the best his foggy brain's ability. Poppy had just asked the sixty-four-thousand-dollar question when Nate walked in on the conversation and had assumed that Poppy's implication that Massey was Dane's real father was true. He had just confessed to having spent the night with Mony when his brother proceeded to beat the shit out of him. As he told Kip the story, it still angered him how Nate had ignored the real tragedy of how Massey found Mony lying outside on the ground battered and bruised. Both Nate and Poppy had bypassed that point completely and went straight to Massey and Mony having sex. Neither had bothered to ask what had happened to her, and were oblivious to the possibility that Dane may have been a result of Mony's rape. It was infuriating.

"Why did you antagonize him?" Kip asked in mild exasperation. "Why didn't you just tell him you weren't Dane's father?"

Massey had wanted to say that he thought he was, which was better than acknowledging what he'd really thought. "I hadn't meant to antagonize him, I—"

"Yes, you did," Kip accused. "You wanted him to hit you, thought you *deserved* it for not having protected Mony back in college."

Massey stilled. "You knew?"

"Don't act so surprised," Kip said. "You're not the only one who can keep a secret. I don't know the details, and believe me, I don't want to know. God knows Mony has been through her share of abuse. But I understand why you can't accept that it hadn't been your fault, son. I do. Though I'm sure by now, you can see you've only made it worse letting Nathan believe you and Mony—" Kip broke off. Apparently saying the words "had sex" out loud was a bit much, even for a straight talker like himself.

"But I did love her, Dad, I still do. I'd kissed—"

"Christ, am I your confessor?" Kip retorted. "She's your sister, Matthew, in every way but blood, of course you love her." A nurse passed by Massey's room door, peered in at Kip, and scowled. He softened his tone. "I should have never taken you boys with me that night me and Buddy settled our differences."

Another revelation.

It was maddening not to be able to see his father's expression. It seemed Kip was full of surprises tonight. Not once had his dad ever referred to the night he and Buddy Altman fought, nor said what it was about. Massey wanted to hear more, wanted to ask questions. He didn't have to.

"I blamed Buddy for something that wasn't his fault. I couldn't just accept my own failure. Your mother told me she couldn't stay in Williston, so far away from her family and friends. She'd been isolated, out there on the farm with only Buddy a mile down the road to talk to. No wonder she confided in him, taking solace in their friendship where she couldn't find understanding from me. I was jealous, Matthew, horribly so. There was something between them, a bond of understanding that always made me feel on the outside of a window looking in. I should have listened to her. Instead I'd conjured an affair between my best friend and my wife. I needed someone to blame when she ran off with you boys, and Buddy became the perfect scapegoat."

He felt the weight of his father's guilt heavy in his chest and wondered, *Now who's confessing to who?* But Massey didn't mind. His father was talking, and he wasn't going to shut him out. "Did you still love her, Dad, even when she ran?"

Kip Ferguson closed his eyes, grateful his son couldn't see him. His mind flooded with images of the former Miss Congeniality on his arm and the night he escorted her in the beauty pageant. He'd fallen in love on sight with her beautiful dark auburn hair and otherworldly dark blue eyes, so unusual for a woman of her heritage. He'd taken her away from her family when he was stationed in Georgia, then abandoned her when he was shipped off to Vietnam.

"You both hated me when I came home from 'Nam," Kip said in a tone filled with remorse. "You were afraid of me, and with good reason. I was out of control, the nightmares, the drinking. I couldn't get a handle on my fears. I couldn't block the horrors of what I'd seen from my mind. But when Nathan came along, it was like a fresh beginning for me, for us as a family. I finally had the son I could build a relationship with, the one I hadn't been able to with you. You had always been your mother's son, bonded by the circumstances of war. Nathan was my chance."

"Why did you have to be so cruel to her, Dad?" Massey said in quiet anger. "You left her there sitting on the curb as if she were nothing but garbage."

"I felt betrayed," Kip said with brutal honesty. "She tried to have you both, and I just couldn't allow that. I wasn't going through life alone, not after what I'd seen it do to Buddy. He had given up on his love and his child until I pounded it into him to go fetch Mony. I wasn't about to do that with you boys. I couldn't stop your mother from leaving, but I could stop her from taking you away with her."

"You didn't even try," Massey said, unable to mask his bitterness.

"I'm sorry, Matthew. I'm sorry for making you choose between us, but I had to take him. I had to take Nathan."

Kip's confession had been one of many firsts between father and son that evening. It was the first time he'd talked about his fight with Buddy, and why. Massey had even learned that Buddy, like himself, hadn't thrown a single punch at Kip except to defend. Not only had Buddy forgiven Kip for his false accusation, but they'd built two successful businesses together, retaliating with the most powerful weapon of all—brotherly love.

"Buddy did get in a sucker punch once." Kip chortled. "It was right before Poppy had come into town. He punched me in the nose, broke it too. My eyes looked as bad as yours the first time I met Poppy, and she married me anyway."

Massey chuckled. "I remember that."

His father went on to tell how Buddy, much like Massey, had blamed himself for messing up Kip's stormy marriage, even though Massey's mother had decided to leave long before Buddy left to collect Mony. It was the first time his dad had talked about his mother and spoke tenderly of how they'd met and fallen in love, and how she'd tried to support him after his return from Vietnam. It was the first time his dad had ever said he was sorry for anything, but especially for how he'd left Massey and Nate's mother.

"I didn't choose between the two of you," Massey told his father quietly. Kip gave him a curious glance. "You'd said you were sorry you'd made me choose between you and Mom, but that had never been in question, Dad. I went where Nate went, and you had Nate."

In a sad voice, Kip replied, "Somehow, I must have always known that."

"You and Mom taught me well. You always told me, look out after my little brother, and that's what I did."

He'd already hit the call light when Mony stopped by after visiting hours. His nurse responded promptly with a Dixie cup of pills; he tossed them back with a glass of water, then gave a nod in Mony's direction. "My sister and I have a few things to talk about," he told the nurse, "and I would like her to stay a while longer."

The nurse offered no objection and left the room, shutting the door behind her. Mony stood quiet at the foot the bed. He understood the silent query.

"What? How else can I explain what you are to me? You're not my girlfriend, wife, significant other, or mistress. You're more than a friend or a business partner. You're not my sister-in-law, though I wish you to be, and you're definitely family, even though not by blood or law, so sister is about as close a definition the Webster dictionary allows."

"I have the same problem explaining you, too," Mony said, and walked over to his side.

Massey tried his best to smile, but the swelling in his jaw prohibited much for facial movement.

Mony took his hand. "I realized yesterday I'd never thanked you for rescuing me that night, after you'd found me lying on the ground. I was pretty messed up, you know, and you took care of me, just as you've always done. I forgot to say so before I left that morning, and I'm sorry."

Massey's fingers clenched down around Mony's hands. "God, Mony, you don't have to thank me or say you're sorry."

Mony gave a tiny whimper, and it took him a beat to realize how hard he was holding onto her. He loosened his fingers and tugged at her wrist. "Come here, you."

He slid over in the bed, making room. Mony sat on the edge, but Massey tugged her closer, and she lay down next to him, careful not to bump up against his battered body. As she rolled to face him, he draped an arm over her shoulder and felt her study him as she traced her fingers over his swollen features.

"We're going to be okay, Mony," Massey said, "though I think your journey will be much more difficult than mine. Your wounds are on the inside, just like Nate's. You'll both need time to heal, but I'm here for you, if you want me to be."

"And Nate?" Mony asked.

Massey took a slow, uneasy breath. "I'm always here for Nate. I don't know how not to be."

"I know," she whispered. "I'm so ready to move forward, the three of us, together."

As he closed the slits of his eyes, the tears flowed freely down his cheeks. "I want to, Mony, truly I do. Just tell me how."

"Help me find Dane's father, help me find a way to bring him peace—whatever you can, is all I ask."

"I can do that, if Nate wants to be found. Though I think peace is something he will have to find on his own. I think it has always been up to him. I just couldn't see it until he punched my lights out."

They remained side by side a long while, lying in his hospital bed, their physical closeness bringing healing beyond the traumas either of their bodies bore outwardly or within. Pledging their commitment to the treasure of each one's heart, Massey and Mony found sanctuary in their self-imposed absolution and blissful reprieve from the past that haunted them—together.

EPILOGUE

The rippling sound of jack brakes from the highway startled him from his fitful sleep. Blinking his heavy eyelids, Nate glanced out through the fogged-up windows of his truck and noticed a light dusting of snow covering the hood. Starting the engine, he thought again how the blowers on his new truck hadn't seemed to kick out the heat quite the way his old truck used to, and he felt a shiver. He checked the digital readout on the thermostat and saw that it had dipped down to a cold twenty-three degrees during the night. Though he wore his Carhartt jacket, boots, gloves, and cap, and had covered himself in the wool blanket he kept in the truck, there was no warmth strong enough to drive out the chill he felt deep in his bones.

Parked in an overnight campground off US Highway 26, he'd made it as far as Idaho Falls when overwhelming fatigue forced him to pull over. Gassing in Bozeman, he blew through the entire state of Montana, oblivious to his surroundings until he reached the mountain range where winding roads made him slow his speed. He skirted the western edge of Yellowstone and the Tetons, and it began to snow again as he crossed over into Idaho. Normally, it was no big deal in his four by four, but he'd hit that patch of black ice and had barely managed to keep the truck from going off the road. That's when he'd come to his senses. His entire drive had been fueled with rage and indignation. Now he was as tapped out and empty as the duel fuel tanks on his truck.

The whole trek across Montana, his mind had kept replaying the fight between him and Massey, as Massey's words reverberated between his ears. *"We were together once. Why do you think you are the only one who cares about her?"* It rolled like a thunderstorm in his head, like dice tumbling out of a cup—the toss always coming out the same. Massey never said he'd made love to Mony, thought the expression on his face had been filled with such agony and guilt it had looked like a confession. It wasn't until he hit the Wyoming/Montana line that Nate realized his brother hadn't thrown a single punch. To make matters worse, if that were possible, Nate had blocked out the real reason he'd sought out his brother. He'd wanted to learn the truth and hadn't even asked what had happened to Mony when Massey found her lying on the ground. *Why couldn't he have latched onto that?* He'd thought about going to Mony's after the fight and making her explain the whole story, until Shawn threatened to call the cops if he did. With nowhere left to go, he got in his truck and kept driving west.

An image of Mony's limp body lying on the ground crept into his brain sometime during the night, and he couldn't shake it. He felt the shame swell in his aching, tired joints; regret clenched around his heart like a fist. *Could it be true that Dane hadn't been the plumber's son? If so, how many people had known about it?* It was a bitter thought. Nate had been surprised at how quickly he'd jumped to believing Massey and Mony had slept together. He knew deep down that his brother would have never done that, and still he'd appointed himself judge, jury, and executioner. How had he turned so violent, so mistrusting of the two people he trusted most? Two people who had done nothing but give him unconditional love? What the fuck was wrong with him?

Just turn around, his heart urged, *right now, and go back to them.*

As he lifted his gaze toward the eastern horizon, the radiant eye of the morning sun emitted a soft yellow light, giving him hope; then disappeared as quickly as it came, unveiling a bitter truth. The window for reconciliation had passed. In one shot, Nate had killed the love they had for him, burning any possible bridge for return. The finality of it, the loss of hope and forgiveness, brought a sting of hot tears against his cold cheeks.

Aware that he only had himself to blame for his exile, Nate turned his eyes from the eastern sky and looked toward the west where a weighted dreariness loomed in wait. Nate eased the shift on the steering column into drive and headed toward it, facing the vast emptiness alone.

ACKNOWLEDGMENTS

First and foremost, I would like to thank my husband, Doug, and my family, Kimberlee, Andy, Michelle, Mary, and Drew, for their unlimited patience, emotional support, and moral support in my endless endeavor to find my voice and to make it heard.

To the team at Wise Ink, especially Laura Zats, for taking a chance on a novice writer; to Erik Hane for his magical work in editing, and to Steven Meyer-Rassow for his beautiful, creative work in making a lifelong dream a reality.

Finally, I wish to recognize my mother Darlene, a woman who, despite the hardships of her youth, rose above the perplexities of trying to meet the expectations of others and maintained her individuality. Thank you for passing on your passion for storytelling and the core belief that life is what you make of it. You are everything opposite the mother in this heroine's story. Without you, this story would never have been told.

Julien Bradley's debut novel, *Beneath the Bedrock*, is the first of the Bakken Series, which takes place in North Dakota's Williston Basin. Bradley lives with her family in the driftless region of southeastern Minnesota, where frac sand mining is a subject of passionate debate.